Margaret Lee

Dr. Wilmer's love; or, a question of conscience

A Novel

Margaret Lee

Dr. Wilmer's love; or, a question of conscience
A Novel

ISBN/EAN: 9783337030711

Printed in Europe, USA, Canada, Australia, Japan

Cover: Foto ©Andreas Hilbeck / pixelio.de

More available books at **www.hansebooks.com**

DR. WILMER'S LOVE;

OR,

A QUESTION OF CONSCIENCE.

A NOVEL.

BY

MARGARET LEE,
AUTHOR OF "ARNOLD'S CHOICE."

NEW YORK:
D. APPLETON AND COMPANY,
443 & 445 BROADWAY.
1868.

CONTENTS.

———

DR. WILMER'S LOVE;

OR,

A QUESTION OF CONSCIENCE.

———————

CHAPTER I.

IN WHICH MY SUSPICIONS ARE AWAKENED.

ONE cold evening in winter, I was sitting in my
little office, idly pondering over my life, weighing its
prospects, and wondering how I should support its
necessities. Considering my present position, the question was growing rather serious. Here was I, John
Wilmer, tall, strong, and twenty-eight years of age,
with my doctor's diploma framed, and hanging over
the fireplace, just where my eyes could rest on it, with
the least upward movement of my head. I had studied
and toiled hard for that diploma, dreamed of it at night,
thought of it by day; and now that it was mine, honestly
won, it somehow had not the power of raising my
spirits, or nerving me with fresh courage.

In fact, I had not a cent in my pocket or out of it.
I owed the landlady and the washerwoman, and my

tailor had long ceased dunning me, finding of how little use it was. For the first time, since starting in my career as a doctor, I thought of writing to my mother, and asking her to advance me a small loan. Pride, and the knowledge that the loss of even a trifling sum would deprive her of many little comforts, had, so far, prevented me from doing it. Thus, I was sitting, gloomily meditating over ways and means, when a loud peal at my bell made me start from my chair, with a slight hope that this might be a case where I could conscientiously ask a fee, in proportion to the skill and care expended. Hitherto my patients had not been of the paying class; poor and miserable in the majority, their cases had drawn heavily on my skill, and added materially to my practical medical education; but proportionate charges were out of the question.

While this wild hope was passing through my brain, I was making my way to the door. I opened it, and a man sprang in hastily, calling out—

"Are you the doctor?"

"Yes, I am Doctor Wilmer."

"The master is dying, and Doctor —— (naming a celebrated physician of the day) is out of town. The mistress told me to bring the first I came to."

While he was speaking, I put on my overcoat and hat, and we started together for the place. It was a fine house, situated in one of the most aristocratic streets in New York. The hall-door was opened noiselessly by a servant, who had been evidently on the watch for us, and she showed me, at once, into a hand-some room on the second floor.

The door leading into the adjoining apartment was open, and I heard a sound of heavy and labored breathing, coming from it. The servant went in to announce my arrival, and returned in a moment, followed by a magnificent-looking woman, of perhaps twenty-six years.

"You are a physician?" she inquired.

"I am," I answered.

"My husband is very low. He is suffering from disease of the heart, and our regular physician has been unexpectedly called away from the city. Have you confidence enough in yourself to undertake the responsibility of such a case?"

"I have had many such cases in my practice," I replied, "and have been in most of them very successful."

"You are so young-looking," she remarked, glancing at me from head to foot.

"I have practised seven years, part of the time with the gentleman whom your servant named as being your family physician." She stood for a moment or two, thinking, and then motioned me to follow her into the sick man's room.

I was surprised to find in the invalid a man approaching sixty years. He was propped up in bed with pillows; and in spite of the suffering he was undergoing, his eyes were clear and bright, giving evidence that the intellect was not yet weakened. He threw me a searching glance as I entered, smiled faintly, and put out his hand, which I took in mine. He was apparently conscious that his time was short, and was collecting all his remaining strength for the performance of one last object.

I took a seat beside the bed, to which he pointed, and prepared a medicine calculated to relieve him a little. It was very successful in its effect; when he spoke, his voice was full and distinct.

"Matilda, send for Masters and Mr. Parker, I must see them now, while I have strength spared to me."

His wife left the room. While she was gone, I raised the dying man, placed him in a more comfortable position, and gave him some of the soothing medicine. There was that in his whole manner and appearance that attracted me irresistibly, although I had never before seen him, and was ignorant of even his name.

His wife returned after a little while, and took her accustomed seat by his side. She had called him her husband, but for that I should have supposed him to be her father. While we awaited the arrival of the two men whom he had asked to see, I sat weaving in my brain odd fancies connected with this strangely contrasted husband and wife.

He was dark, and decidedly old for his years, with a likable face and gentle expression, in spite of his sickness. There was something in the eyes that denoted truth and goodness, something open and fearless, as if his conscience was clear and easy, as if he had nothing to dread, nothing to regret, now that his last hour was drawing near.

She was a blonde, with a profusion of light hair, most becomingly arranged, with handsome features, and a bright color in her cheeks. Her figure was elegant and most graceful, with the heavy folds of her dress, a rich dark-blue silk falling from the rounded waist, and sweeping the floor at my feet. Her neck and arms were shaded with costly lace, and the hand, which the dying man held in his, was like wax, soft and white, and covered with rings, the lights from whose diamond centres flashed in my eyes where I sat.

The room was in keeping with her appearance, from the carpet that felt like moss under my feet, to the elaborate toilet set, shining on the distant bureau. Luxury and refinement, blended in harmony, spoke from every thing surrounding her.

In spite of all her fascinations I took a dislike to her, while I sat, watching with her, the last hours of her dying husband. I caught a look that she fixed on him, while he lay with closed eyes, breathing heavily. There was something almost indescribable in that glance. There were mingled in it coldness, calculation, and dislike. While apparently performing the part of a devoted, loving wife, this woman's heart had nothing whatever to do with her outward actions. A moment after, she turned her eyes on me, and the aversion was increased. They were large, full, and calculating; in

1*

color, a bright blue; without real softness, and possessing very little depth.

I have a queer liking for examining eyes; I always look at them first, and I judge from them a great deal what the true character may be. To me they are the most expressive feature of the face.

We sat for nearly an hour, watching without speaking, and the old man lay with a patient expression in his face, waiting and collecting his strength. At last came a slight rustle, and the servant ushered in two gentlemen. They advanced toward the bed, and pressed the invalid's hands in theirs, while asking how he felt in subdued, earnest tones. One of these men was probably fifty years of age, with keen, bright gray eyes, white hair, and a kindly look in his face. The other was a dark, powerful-looking man, in the prime of life, with brilliant black eyes, and heavy beard and mustache.

For the few minutes that they stood quiet near their dying friend, waiting to hear his wishes, I noticed that the younger one kept his eyes on the wife's face, as if determined on reading her thoughts. She had merely acknowledged their bows on entering, and was sitting as before, her hand within reach of her husband's. He was looking from one to another of the group now, and breathing with great difficulty. I raised him again, and he thanked me with his patient smile.

"Shall I leave the room?" I asked.

"No, no," he answered. "Stay near me; you relieve me very much."

I resumed my seat. He turned to his wife.

"Matilda, my will—I want to hear it read over again."

His wife rose, and, taking some keys from under his pillow, walked toward a small safe placed at one end of the room. She unlocked it, and returned, with the paper in her hand.

"Read it to me, Joe," said the invalid in a faint voice.

The older man of the two opened the paper, and read it aloud, in a distinct, slow tone, as if wishing all the hearers to weigh well the meaning of it. I could recall the words, as they fell on my ears, in whole sentences, for months after. It was short and decisive; I understood the whole substance of it, though not very well versed, at that time, in legal terms. The first sentence, "I, Arthur Ferris," revealed to me the name of my patient. The property, which involved a large amount of real estate and stocks, was to be disposed of in this way: After some very liberal donations to charitable institutions, and some trifling legacies to old friends and servants, the bulk of it was to be equally divided between his wife Matilda and his daughter Arabella Ferris. Should his wife die before his daughter, the wife's share would revert to the daughter. On the other hand, should the daughter die first, unmarried, her half would go to the wife. The child was to remain under the guardianship of her step-mother, Matilda Ferris, who **was** also appointed co-trustee of her property with Joseph Masters and William Parker. In case of the death of Mrs. Ferris, the daughter was to reside with an aunt, her dead mother's **eldest sister. At** twenty, she would be of age, with full power over the interest of her money, and at liberty to marry whom she pleased.

The principal was to remain under the control of the **trustees** chosen by her father (they having, in turn, the **right to appoint** successors to their trust), to be invested for her benefit, and that of her heirs, until she should reach the age of thirty-five, at which time she would take complete possession of it all. The executors were Joseph Masters and William Parker.

The will being read, Mr. Ferris expressed himself satisfied with it, and, after a few minutes, asked to see his child.

"She is asleep," answered Mrs. Ferris.

"**Then waken her,** Matilda; **she** will not have her old father very long."

Mrs. Ferris left the room, and Mr. Parker walked after her. A short time passed, and then a woman-servant appeared at the door, holding by the hand a slight, pretty child, about eleven years of age. She quickly unclasped the detaining hand as she caught sight of her father's face, and with a low cry of joy she sprang into his extended arms, and laid her head softly on his breast.

"Oh, papa! I have not seen you for so very long. May I stay with you now?"

"Yes, little one, for a short time. Papa is very sick."

The child raised her head, looked in her father's face, and kissed him passionately, then she hid her own again, only murmuring, "Papa, papa," as if conscious of what was coming so very fast.

Mrs. Ferris returned.

"Belle, you will hurt papa, lying in that way on his breast. It prevents him breathing freely."

She spoke sharply, and stretched out her hand to remove the child from her place.

The little girl shuddered, and only clasped her arms still tighter around her father's neck.

"Let her alone, Matilda, it is for the last time," Mr. Ferris said with increasing difficulty. Then he turned his eyes, growing dim so fast, on the bright little face raised to his in awe-struck silence. "Kiss papa, darling, kiss me good-night. Perhaps I shall be better in the morning."

The little creature obeyed him, and, seeing how weak he was becoming, I lifted her in my arms and carried her into the adjoining room, where I placed her in the nurse's care, and then hurried back to my patient.

He was sinking rapidly. Mr. Masters held one of his hands, and watched his struggles with a womanly tenderness of look and manner, while restraining with difficulty his own sorrowful emotions. Mr. Parker was supporting him on the other side. His wife had thrown herself into a low chair, and covered her face with her handkerchief. In a few moments all was over; and having performed the few duties remaining to me, I left the house, and returned to my desolate room. The fire had gone out in my absence, it was cold and gloomy, and the furniture looked older and shabbier than ever. The contrast between it and the one I had just quitted struck me forcibly.

Though accustomed to look on death, under circumstances much more saddening than in this case, the impression left on my mind was of such a nature, that I could not sleep for hours after lying down; but instead, my busy brain wove long imaginary romances, founded on the strange will, and the people it affected. Even in my dreams the scenes of the night before repeated themselves, until at last I was glad to rise and go out in the cool morning air, to shake off their gloomy effect.

I attended the funeral some day after, and met there my old friend, the family physician. He told me a few things about Mr. Ferris that greatly interested me. He had married, rather late in life, a very beautiful woman, to whom he was passionately attached. She lived only a few years, and died, leaving him with one child, the little girl Arabella. Afterward, he married the half-sister of his first wife, the lady whom I had met on the night of his death.

"She is certainly very beautiful," remarked my friend. "But the first Mrs. Ferris was a far superior woman."

I also renewed my acquaintance with little Miss Ferris on that day. She came over to me of her own accord, from a distant part of the room, and held out her hand timidly, as if half afraid of a disapproving glance for her temerity. I was surprised at her remembering me, but she told me that she knew my eyes; a remark that made me look at hers, and they were well worth the trouble—large, soft, deep-brown ones, with a sad expression in them already. When I went home, I had to examine my own in the glass, to see if there was any thing very remarkable about them, but I could not discover it.

I received a check for my medical services rendered to Mr. Ferris, that surprised me by its amount, and not only paid all my debts, but left me a little balance to go on with again.

Two weeks after, I heard of an opening in Buffalo, that promised well to an energetic young man, and I secured it. I sold my practice in New York to a fellow-student, and having packed my trunk, and left it to be sent after me, I started, valise in hand, to walk to the Albany boat, in order to take a farewell glance at Broadway.

While about to cross a side-street, I came face to face with Mrs. Ferris and her little step-daughter, seated in a low carriage. The horses were going at a slow pace, and I had time to take a long look at them. Mrs. Ferris was quite bewitching, in her becoming widow's cap and strings, and heavy crape veil. Miss Ferris had a subdued, mournful look about her, and her black clothes served to make still paler her small, colorless face. I was nearly past her, when she looked up and recognized me with a bright smile. That smile danced before my eyes and lightened my cares for many days after, coming as it did from the warm heart and artless face of an innocent child.

I was a lonely sort of fellow anyhow. My dear mother, and my only sister, lived together in a quiet little village near Albany. They had just enough to support themselves comfortably. When I felt fagged out, I would run up to them for a few days, to be petted, and made much of; after which, I could return with fresh courage, to my old, dull routine of city work. My sister was some years older than I, and very fond of me. So it happened, that I never knew what it was to need a woman's love and care until I was alone in New York, struggling with others on the road to fame and fortune. If I ever had indulged in day-dreams, of a little home of my own, and a bright face watching for me at its window, reflection taught me that for some years at least, such a piece of happiness was quite impossible. So I courageously refused all offers of introduction to nice young girls, with or without rich papas. If a girl were good and pretty, and without money, what right would I have to gain her love, and then bind her to a long engagement, while I should earn the means necessary for her support? If she were rich, the stronger reason why I should keep my distance. I had heard too much of poor young doctors hunting for rich wives.

The result was, that when I quitted New York, to seek for wealth and fame in a new field of action, the only friends I left behind me were my old fellow-students, several of whom promised to keep me informed of matters in the city, how they progressed and how they retrograded.

As I jumped on board the boat, I came near knocking into the water an old gentleman, who was standing on the plank, exchanging some words with a lady on the pier.   Turning to apologize, I recognized Mr. Masters. He was on his way to the western part of the State, to transact some business connected with the affairs of the late Mr. Ferris.   After supper, we sat for a long time on deck, discussing various subjects, among the rest Mrs. Ferris.   It struck me that my companion had not a very high opinion of her.

"She is remarkably handsome," I observed.

"Yes, and confoundedly smart," was the answer.

My companion was smoking, a recreation I did not join him in, for two very good reasons: the first being, that I disliked tobacco in every form; and the second, that if I had cared for it, I had not the money to indulge the taste.

"Did you notice the wording of the will?" asked my companion, after puffing away for some time in a moody, meditative manner.

"Yes, I think I understood it, although I am not what you call up in law."

"Oh! it's plain enough; she would have it so.   It is

all her composition, though she has no idea that I see through her so clearly. She chose Parker for one of the executors. It was very foolish of poor Ferris to give in to her as he did. She has the child completely in her power, and Parker is her adviser. I only wonder now that my poor friend had firmness enough to hold out for me. She strongly opposed my being named as either executor or co-trustee."

"You think that she don't like you?" I remarked.

"I don't think any thing about it, I know it. Her acting deceived poor Ferris, it never did me for one moment. He died in the firm belief that she loved his child, and was devotedly fond of him. I know that she married him for his money and position, and that she dislikes the little girl heartily. You see, she was his first wife's half-sister, and considerably younger. She was always spending weeks and months at their house, and managed to understand the old man's disposition exactly. Then, when poor Mrs. Ferris (who really was a fine woman) died, she played a very good game. She nursed and petted the child, called it the most endearing names, sympathized with the father, and never ceased till she married him, and got possession of a handsome house and unlimited money."

"Did she make him happy?" I inquired.

"Yes, she certainly did. She played her cards well. I have to thank her for making the last years of his life pleasant to him. Still, I know the motive. She takes half his money—the child is delicate, and I believe very sensitive. There is a chance of the other half too."

"Perhaps you are hard on her. She is almost too young to be so very cunning."

"Dr. Wilmer, did you look well at her eyes?" The old gentleman turned as he spoke, and looked me straight in the face.

"I certainly did not admire them, though they are beautiful in shape and color."

"Exactly. Think of the expression of them. I tell you, Wilmer, that woman is capable of any thing. She would sell her soul for money."

"You will have to watch her closely."

"Yes, but you see my hands are tied. Parker is her friend, and I grow older every day. It will be two young heads and two unscrupulous minds against one old man. I can't match them in cunning, whatever I might do as regards honesty."

"Right and truth generally succeed in the end," I said. "You must hope for the best."

"And expect the worst," was the old gentleman's answer.

We travelled together as far as Syracuse, where we parted, with warm feelings on both sides, and I pursued my way alone to Buffalo.

CHAPTER II.

For some years I labored steadily at my profession in Buffalo. I found the opening, if any thing, better than it had been represented to me. I became attached to the place, its people, and my fellow-workers there. My health was good, my practice rapidly increasing and remunerative. My only vacations had been of two or three weeks in length, at long intervals. Then, confiding my patients to skilful hands, and leaving all cares behind me, I had gone East, for a visit to my mother and sister.

Once I had extended my trip to New York, but my old friends were scattered; some had gone South, others West; the old associations were weakened, and my pleasant recollections soon dispelled. I met crowds of people at every turn, but the faces were all strange ones; I had no interest nor concern in any of the things that engrossed their thought and time, and I found myself wondering what I ever had seen to admire or care for in the noisy, crowded metropolis.

I inquired for the celebrated physician under whom I had studied. He was dead some years. I walked past the house where Mr. Ferris died, recalling as I did so the scenes of that night, and the curious speculations to which they had given rise. Passing down Broadway, the sight of an old sign on the corner of a street brought back vividly to my mind the remembrance of a low carriage, with two figures in it, and a bright smile on a childish face. I asked myself what had become of that child. Most probably she was at some fashionable school, preparing to create a sensation in society with her beauty and knowledge. I thought of calling on Mr. Masters but gave up the idea the next moment. What were Mrs. Ferris and her affairs to me?

Thus six years rolled away. One sultry afternoon in September I drew up my horse at my own door, gave the reins to my servant, sought my comfortable arm-chair in the office, and threw myself back in it with a long-drawn sigh of relief. It had been a sickly summer, and I was worn out, not having taken a day's rest all through the warm, unhealthy months just passed. Latterly I had been making up my mind to urge my mother and sister to give up their own old house, and take charge of mine. For some reasons I hesitated about making the request. Buffalo was not, on the whole, as healthy a place as the one in which they were settled. Breaking up the old home and its associations might injure my mother's health and spirits; so I still debated the point with myself, not arriving at any conclusion.

Every little while my sister would ask me the same question in her letters. "John, why don't you marry?" and whenever we met, I always heard a discourse from both mother and sister on the same subject of interest. My answer was invariably the same—"The older I grow the harder I am to please," which answer only brought down on my devoted head another lecture, the chief point in which was, the self-conceit of men, and their growing indifference to the charms of married life. I had arrived at the dignity of a neat little house of my own, well furnished, and all paid for. Lying back in my easy-chair, I threw a glance of satisfaction around me, not unmixed with some pride, for I had worked hard for the comforts that I enjoyed so much.

My housekeeper, coming in with a long broom and duster, gave me a searching glance from under the border of her cap, leaned her hands on the table, and thus addressed me:

"Dr. Wilmer, you're as white as a sheet. There's three names on the slate; every one of them wants you first; and if you don't get some one to attend to your business, and leave the city for a month, it's my opinion that you'll soon be sending after a doctor for yourself." She then put the slate before me with a loud bang, and catching up her house-cleaning implements went into the next room, where I heard her, a moment after, expending her disgust with me, by ploughing up the dust from the carpet.

Having refreshed myself with some sandwiches and

wine, I left the house again, to attend to my duties; but coming home, I determined to follow Mrs. Marks' advice, and therefore stopped in at the house of one of my medical brethren, to make the necessary arrangements for an absence of a month. That done, I went home and informed the worthy woman that I was going to Niagara for some time, that I would start the next morning, and that I wanted my valise packed. Having astonished her by this address, I went to bed without waiting for her approval of it, feeling better already for my determination. I dreamt all night of catching fish so enormous that I could not pull them in, and of bringing down birds as large as turkeys. Remembering my visions, I supplied myself next day with apparatus for fishing and hunting, and took my departure for Niagara in fine spirits.

On arriving there, I engaged a room at the Cataract House, deposited my extra luggage in it, and with a light heart and easy mind started out to explore the curiosities around me. I was returning late in the afternoon, having penetrated to the cave of Æolus, with the sound of the rushing waters still in my ears, when my attention was attracted by two persons on the road some yards in front of me.

They were both females, one tall and strong in appearance, the other slight and frail-looking. As I neared them, I found that the larger one of the two was talking in a loud angry voice, and that the other was sobbing as if frightened.

Just at the moment that I passed them, the tall woman caught the other by the shoulders and shook her
most violently, stopping her in the path as she did so.
I glanced at them in turn. Something in both faces
struck me as being familiar. The tall woman was decidedly a servant of the better class, well dressed and self-
sufficient; the other a delicate girl, a lady in birth and
appearance, beyond a doubt. The older woman never
noticed me; the younger threw me a look sorrowful and
supplicating as I hurried past. Where had I seen those
two faces before? Where had I met those soft eyes, so
mournful in their expression, so lovely in their depth?
All at once I stood still in the path, and uttered a cry
of surprise. It had all flashed upon me in a second.
The eyes were those of Arabella Ferris, and the woman
was the servant who had brought her into the room the
night of her father's death. Shocked at my discovery,
I sat down on a piece of rock in the path, and awaited
their reappearance.

I had no fear of their recognizing me; in the six
years that had gone by I had grown stouter, and my
heavy beard and mustache completely hid the lower
part of my face. I had passed intimate friends without
being known; there was little danger of it here.

In a few minutes they came up the road toward me,
and I noted all I could in the short time given me.
Miss Ferris was plainly, but well dressed. Alas! it
was not her dress that struck me; but her face, that sent
a cold chill to my heart. There was a look in it which

conveyed the impression that the mind was unsound; a curious, inexplicable expression, a mixture of vacancy and wildness.

"Great Heaven!" I exclaimed to myself. "What have they done to her?" With the thought came the determination to find out the mystery, and, grasping my walking-stick firmly, I rose and followed the retreating figures.

What was my surprise, as I walked along, to find them bound for the same destination as myself! They entered the house before me, and disappeared through the door of a room on the second floor, the one next to my own. The gong was sounding for dinner, and I don't think I ever made a more rapid toilet in my life. I succeeded admirably, and having learned from a waiter where Miss Ferris usually sat at her meals, I obtained a place from which I could observe all that passed at the table.

I was just seated when the party entered the room. Mrs. Ferris was dressed in the deepest and costliest mourning, and looked, if any thing, handsomer than ever. I should have known her anywhere, but though she caught my eye observing her, there was no answering recognition in the careless glance that she bestowed on me. She had only seen me that one night six years before; we did not meet at the funeral; and she had probably forgotten my name, too, which was all the better for my plan.

She swept with a stately step down the long dining-

2

room, followed by glances of admiration from all sides. Miss Ferris, also in black, walked in a slow, hesitating way, beside the stout servant whom I had seen with her before that day. The woman took her place near her, as soon as she was seated, and waited on her with a show of attention and fond care that never deceived me for one instant. That this was a scene, necessary to be acted out, in the deep game that this woman was playing, I did not doubt.

It was with difficulty, and only in view of the after consequences, that I controlled myself from breaking out on them, then and there. Such a sight for a room full of eager watchers to gaze upon!

The girl, or rather child, for she was one in manners, seemed totally ignorant of any thing that could be called table etiquette. She pulled the meat apart with her fingers, and ate with them, regardless of knife and fork. Any thing that did not suit her was pushed away, half across the table, with a gesture of contempt rather than anger. If asked, I should have said that she was under the influence of some drug or stimulant. She seemed almost unconscious of what she was doing, and there was something unearthly in her decided beauty. Her cheeks were flushed to deep crimson, and there was an unnatural, fearful brilliancy in her large dark eyes, once so soft and serene in their expression. Her delicate features were sharp and attenuated, as if by much suffering; her form possessed none of the usual roundness of youth; it was thin and bent, and so weak, that her little hands trembled visibly, owing to her painful nervousness.

"What a wreck of physical beauty!" I heard a gentleman observe to a lady beside him.

As the meal progressed, the nurse appeared to be endeavoring to restrain her, while Mrs. Ferris wore a look of sad sympathy and despairing love. I noticed, however, that her grief did not prevent her from enjoying a hearty dinner. Now and then, a glance toward Mrs. Ferris from the dark, wild eyes, rather indicated that there was method in all this madness—such a look of despair, mingled with a restless gaze at the doors and windows, as if she were meditating an escape from this fond mother, and her loving care. At last the strange dinner-scene came to an end, and the party rose and left the table as they had entered the room. As I walked out, the waiter remarked to me, looking after the trio, and tapping his forehead, "She is totally gone, a perfect idiot."

I shivered at the look and the words. Mrs. Ferris was accomplishing her object. The present performance was to make the world believe that the girl was insane. What would be the next move? The child did not look as if this struggle could last very long. Her constitution, naturally frail, was undermined. The physical and mental forces were being slowly and surely sapped. "What will be the end?" I asked myself, as I slowly walked up and down my room. Should I write to Mr. Masters? Reason told me it would be to no purpose. He was powerless under the provisions of the will. What could be done? What could we prove? Nothing. There was no proof of ill-treatment on the part of Mrs. Ferris, and there was no legal way of taking the girl out of her custody. The servant was, no doubt a well-paid sharer of her mistress's confidence.

The debating of these points in my mind made me unconscious of the time slipping away; and when, at last, I looked at my watch, I saw that it was too late to carry out the plan that I had laid for my afternoon's amusement. I opened my valise, and was busy with my flies and hooks, when voices, rising in anger, reached me from the adjoining room. Two were loud and threatening, the third low and deprecating. At last there came a smothered cry, followed by a sound of heavy blows, falling rapidly. I started to my feet and ran to the door of the next room. The handle of it was in my hand, when again strong reason came to my aid. To make a scene at that time would do no permanent good, and might prevent its possibility forever.

The rooms were situated at the end of a long corridor; no one had been attracted by the noise, so I went back to my own, and listened with a swelling heart to the low moans caused by bodily and mental suffering. A short time after a firm heavy step came along the hall, and a gentleman opened my door, and put in his head.

"Excuse me," said he. "I mistook the room; it is the next one, I think."

"All right," I exclaimed, looking up hastily. The moment after, I heard him at the other door, asking for Mrs. Ferris.

I often feel thankful for my strong recollection of names and faces. This gentleman was no less a personage than Mr. William Parker, co-trustee of Miss Ferris, and one of the executors of her father's will.

"The plot thickens," I said to myself, and, taking my hat in my hand, I sauntered out of my room and down the corridor. Sure enough, there they stood together, in the window at the far end of it, so closely engaged in conversation, that I passed them unobserved, though not so indifferent myself to them. He had his arm around her waist, half supporting her, while together they no doubt planned the next move on the board. At supper he attended her to the table. Miss Ferris did not appear; but Mrs. Ferris called for a tray, and prepared with her own hands, and to the admiration of the lookers-on, a sumptuous supper for her afflicted child, which was carried to her room by one of the waiters. As the nurse was up there in charge, I could guess who ate it.

Afterward, passing through the parlor, I saw the pair seated on a sofa. She was fanning herself, and talking to him gayly.

"Whatever share of heart she possesses," I thought, "is his decidedly. She loves him as much as she is capable of loving any one."

"What a splendid-looking couple!" I heard some

one remark, in reference to them, as I passed up the stairs.

The next morning Mr. Parker escorted Mrs. Ferris to the breakfast-table. She looked still more beautiful in her elaborate white dress. The young lady did not appear. The same farce of sending her a nice meal was acted over again. I swallowed mine, hardly conscious of what I was eating, and, leaving them still at the table, went to my own room. I listened for a while, but could hear nothing going on in the next apartment; probably the poor girl was asleep, free for a short time from her troubles and misery.

At last I took my guide-book and a stout stick, and left my room, on the way to explore further the beauties of the surrounding country. I passed Mr. Parker and Mrs. Ferris, strolling together up and down the long corridor. What would I have given to know the plans they were discussing so eagerly! I caught one sentence, as I passed, that fell from Mrs. Ferris's lips:

"We can stay in Europe two years."

I repeated this over and over to myself, as I ran down the stairs and out into the road. There was a meaning in that sentence, what was it? Pondering this question in my mind, I reached Goat Island, and spent an hour there, the only person on it, as far as I could see.

Stretched on the grass, my face to the vast sheet of foaming, rushing water, and hidden by a rock from the notice of any one who might cross the bridge, I lay,

enjoying to the fullest extent the sublime works of Nature surrounding me on every side. A delicious sense
of rest came over me, caused by the sweet fresh air, the
singing and chirping of the birds, the perfume of the
wild flowers bending around me in rich profusion, and
the exquisite September coloring of the scenery. From
this state of repose I was suddenly aroused by hearing
a voice exclaiming in a wild, shrieking tone—

"I wish I were dead!"

"I wish you were, with all my heart; you're nothing
but a torment to yourself, and every one around you!"
answered a coarse, rude voice.

A scream and a struggle made me spring to my feet,
only to see a slight, agile form, with outstretched arms,
flying toward the rushing rapids. The woman stood
as if petrified. I sprang to intercept the desperate girl.
She had reached to within a few feet of the edge of the
bank, when her foot caught in an old root standing up
from the ground, and she fell heavily, striking her head
against a stone that lay in the water. I raised her with
some difficulty, for she was partly in the water, and I
was afraid of hurting her. She was insensible from the
contusion on her head, and I feared that she was otherwise injured. I laid the pale, worn face against my
breast, and, dipping my handkerchief in the cool water,
placed it on her head, trying to restore her to consciousness.

The woman stood by, looking at me, but not attempting to offer any assistance. There was a satisfied

expression on her face, which changed to one of vexation as the poor child opened her eyes and stared wildly around her.

"Where am I?" she asked, gazing at me wearily.

Before I could answer, the woman replied roughly: "Just wait till I tell your mother what you've been up to."

The young girl shivered from head to foot.

"You have had a bad fall," I said gently, "but you will soon recover."

She shivered again and looked about her, as if meditating another attempt on her own life.

"Come, Miss Ferris, get up; you'd better come home and put on dry clothes before your mother sees you," said the servant in a soothing tone. She was recollecting herself.

I lifted the young lady to her feet, but she tottered, and would have fallen, had I not put my arm around her.

"I am afraid she has hurt herself very badly," I said to the nurse. "We must carry her to the hotel."

"I am sure you are very kind, sir," she answered in a smooth, servile tone. "Mrs. Ferris will be obliged to you, for she dotes on the child, though indeed she is nothing but a trouble to her. She is out of her mind, sir, entirely."

Miss Ferris seemed quite indifferent to this speech. She was leaning heavily on my arm, her eyes closed as if in pain.

"Try and walk a little," the woman went on, turning to her and taking her by the arm as she spoke.

"I can't, Susan, my side hurts me so much," was the answer in a low weak voice. The wild fit was over; Miss Ferris was suffering terribly from the effects of her fall. I lifted her in my arms, and after frequent rests we reached the hotel. Miss Ferris did not speak on the way; now and then a low moan would escape her, and several times I observed her looking fixedly at my face, a troubled eager expression in her eyes.

The servant walked along by my side, not volunteering any remark, and I shrank from exhibiting any curiosity by asking questions. She looked gloomy and cross, and I was afraid of exciting her anger against the helpless creature that I was carrying. On arriving at the house, we found that Mrs. Ferris was out riding, and so I carried her daughter up-stairs and laid her on the sofa in her own room.

"I am a doctor," I said to the nurse, "and if you should require me, I am in the next room; at present you had better put her in bed, and keep wet linen on her forehead."

Going into my own apartment, I made up my mind that the servant would not have been very sorry if Miss Ferris had succeeded in her design. I began to think that I was fated to be in some way connected with the strange family so curiously met six years before. If they should need my further services, I thought it would never do to tell them my real name;

2*

it might bring me to their recollection; then, again, I
determined to risk it—they might never have heard it.
I was roused from this reverie by the sound of horses'
feet, and a light laugh floating in through the open
window. Mr. Parker and Mrs. Ferris had been taking
a ride that fine morning, and were just returned.

Soon after she passed my door, her habit gathered
up in one hand and her whip in the other. In her
room I heard a low hum of voices—a history, no doubt,
of the morning's adventure. I was dressed for dinner,
when a waiter brought me up a note.

"Mrs. Ferris will be happy to meet in the parlor,
before dinner, the gentleman who so kindly rescued her
daughter this morning."

On going down, she was standing waiting for me,
in a very pretty attitude, which displayed to much advantage her fine figure. I bowed, and announced myself, "Dr. Wilmer, of Buffalo." She took no notice of
the name, but asked me my opinion of her daughter's
state of health. If I had not been prepared for her, she
would have won me over in ten minutes, a firm believer
in her statement; as it was, I had to admire the hy-
pocrisy and cunning she exhibited. I felt like applaud-
ing, as we do when we see some fine piece of acting
on the stage.

Her poor little Belle had lost her reason partially,
owing to a terrible attack of scarlet fever.

"What age was she at that time?" I asked.

"She was not quite six," was the answer, so ready,

that it was evident her whole story was one well studied for strangers' ears. She thanked me over and over again for what I had done that morning, saying, with tears in her eyes, that her heart was bound up in her child, weak-minded as she was. Then she sounded me on another point. "Would you advise me to place her in a private asylum?"

"Not at all," I answered, "as long as she is quiet and harmless."

"I have been urged to do it by a number of my friends, and so far I have shrunk from it as being a last resource. But you see, doctor, when what occurred this morning may be repeated" (here she shuddered) "any time, what am I to do? She never made an attempt to destroy herself before, but this has terrified me. There are so many ways by which she could accomplish it, and then I am obliged to be in constant communication with our family physician about her treatment. He insists on country air, and I have been travelling with her all summer."

"Does he consider her incurable?" I asked.

"Yes," she sighed, raising her handkerchief to her eyes.

"Have you every confidence in his skill?" I inquired, determined to sound her in turn.

"Most entire confidence," was the answer. "Putting aside his long experience in such cases, he has attended her all her life, and is quite interested in her; besides, he understands her constitution perfectly."

I was not prepared for this last falsehood; of course the wonderful family physician was a myth, a creature of the imagination, an organ very largely developed in Mrs. Ferris's head.

"Of course," I said, rising, "in that case I would not interfere; if you were without medical advice, I should gladly undertake the charge, but—"

"But, doctor," she interposed, "you forget that the circumstance of this morning makes it necessary for me to have some one here to advise with, and of course I could not expect him to leave his duties for her sake. If you will undertake to attend her, in case any thing dangerous should result from this fall, until I am able to hear from our regular physician, I shall be satisfied."

"It is a responsibility, but I am willing to remain at your service, if necessary," I answered.

"You will remember, however," she remarked, with a curious expression in her face, "that it is only her physical health you will have to do with; her mental condition must remain under the charge of the gentleman whom I have already mentioned."

She bowed gracefully, and left the room. I took my accustomed seat at dinner, and watched her and her friend Mr. Parker as narrowly as good-breeding would permit; perhaps I did overstep the bounds, but my suspicions must excuse me. Afterward I was introduced to him in the parlor, and then, satisfied that there had been no recognition on his part, I went up to my room to await events. I read for some hours, trying with all

my strength to concentrate my thoughts on the subject
before me, a work which was at first very difficult to
succeed in, for my ideas would wander off in the direction of Miss Ferris and her guardian, and I would discover my book before me, at an angle of forty-five degrees, and my eyes gazing upward, seeing nothing. At
last, just as I had succeeded in comprehending one page
of the book, a tap came on the door, and opening it, I
saw Susan, the nurse, standing before me with a frightened face.

"She has a dreadful fever, sir, and we can't quiet
her; won't you come and see her?"

"Has she been asleep at all?" I asked.

"Yes, ever since," was the prompt reply.

I found my patient burning with fever, and talking
incoherently; her cheeks crimson, and her eyes brilliant. She was suffering from the bruise on her head
principally, although her side, the nurse informed me,
was dreadfully hurt. She was quite unable to move
without help, and, while I held her hand in mine, her
ravings became worse and worse, until at last, Mrs.
Ferris, who all this time had sat near her, rose with a
frightened expression of face and withdrew to a part of
the room some distance from the bed. Strange to say,
my patient became gradually more calm, and at last
sank into an uneasy sleep, out of which I charged them on
no account to disturb her. Mrs. Ferris took up a book;
and, leaving word to call me when she wakened, I withdrew to my own room. In half an hour I was sent for

again; she was worse than ever, and as I entered the room I felt sure that I detected a faint odor of brandy; still there was no sign of it whatever about the place.

"Did she waken in this condition?" I asked.

"Yes, sir," was the ready answer.

"You have given her brandy," I said, looking full in the nurse's face. "What was that for?"

"She always takes it," answered Mrs. Ferris. "It was ordered for her, and I thought, in her weak state, that it would be wrong to omit giving it to her."

"She was in no condition to take a stimulant," I answered; "you should not have given it without consulting me. That accounts for the state she is in now."

"I am very sorry," Mrs. Ferris said, "but we have become so used to treating her according to the rules given us, that I never thought of it doing her any harm."

"It must not occur again," I said sternly; "her condition is a very critical one, and if I assume the responsibility of it, my directions must be followed without any deviation whatever."

"Of course they shall be: the mistake was a careless one; but you know, we don't understand just what to do," Mrs. Ferris answered, looking very sorrowful and anxious.

"Will you want this?" asked the servant, putting a large vial of laudanum before me.

"Is she accustomed to using it?" I asked, very quietly.

"Oh, yes, sir, she takes it constantly; she would never rest only for it," was the answer.

"The opiate I have given her," I said, "is quite sufficient for the present, and remember on no account must you give her any thing without my advice."

Again I left the girl asleep and comparatively easy. At supper-time she still slept, and Mrs. Ferris appeared at the table, and afterward went out for a short walk with Mr. Parker, according to my advice, leaving her daughter under the care of the nurse and myself. I managed it very well altogether, for I sent the servant to a distant part of the room, telling her that she had been too much confined that day, attending on her charge; and then sat down quietly to look at my poor patient, and ponder the chances for her life. I came to the conclusion that they were very slight indeed. The naturally delicate organization had been fearfully practised upon. If I could only keep her long enough under treatment for her fall, to permit of her mind becoming stronger, it might be possible to prove ill-usage on the part of the step-mother, and take her out of her power; as she was, such a proceeding was beyond all possibility.

Mrs. Ferris and Mr. Parker had every thing their own way, and were quite conscious of the fact. If this state of things were to continue very long, the girl would soon become a helpless imbecile. Thinking over these things, I looked up, to find my patient lying awake, with her eyes fixed on my face.

"I remember you now—where am I?" she asked, in

a voice too low and weak to be heard by the nurse, with her head out of the distant window.

"You are in your own room, and you remember seeing me this morning after you fell."

"No, no, I have seen you some place before." She thought a moment, and then a bright smile broke over her face and lit it up. "I know now—the night papa died, and afterward, one day in the street."

"You must not let either your mother, or anybody else that you see here, know that you remember me," I whispered. "Speak very low—the nurse is in the room."

"I understand you," she replied. "Oh, if you could only know what I suffer! They make me drink things that set me wild, so that I don't know what I am saying or doing; people think I am insane, you know better. Please take me away from them."

"If you will do as I tell you, and try to grow strong, that is the only way before you. I can do nothing without your help, and I must be able to prove that you are perfectly sane before I can take a single step for your benefit."

"What must I do?" she murmured. "Why did papa leave me to her? She hates me, and always did."

"Yes, but she deceived him completely. You must stay here as long as you can; don't let them think that you can walk or be removed. Make the most of your fall until your mind is steadier; don't walk till I give you leave."

The handle of the door turned at this moment, and I put my finger to my lips. She closed her eyes as Mrs. Ferris entered. Mr. Parker evidently had his part to play; to the mere spectator he was only an admirer of Mrs. Ferris, not at all interested in her unfortunate daughter. Having explained to her how much better her child was, and left directions for her treatment during the night, I went out for a stroll in the fresh air, **perfectly astonished at what** had just passed. **After all those years, this child had known** my features; my name she probably had never heard. I concluded that her mind was still strong enough to insure a perfect recovery, much more so than I had dared to hope, and that her wild fits were the effects of the stimulants they made her swallow. How long I remained out I don't know; I thought of schemes and plans without number by which to circumvent the designs of this **extraordinary** woman, who had surely sold herself for the coveted prize, her husband's entire property.

Going back to the house, I looked in on my patient. She was sound asleep. Mrs. Ferris was reading, and the nurse was sewing, so I retired to my room satisfied with the course of events. The next morning Miss Ferris was much **better, but quite unable to walk. I** left orders for her treatment that day, and then went out for a long ramble, feeling sure that she was safe for a short time from further attempts on her mental health, owing to the remarks I had made; and wishing, besides, to lull all suspicions of what I might think that would naturally arise in such cunning minds. I knew that, once they suspected me of understanding or doubting them, my power was lost forever. Thus matters went on for some days, and that they were afraid of me I saw clearly. Miss Ferris still remained unable to walk, but her eyes were soft and natural, and I knew that she was improving fast, altogether too much so for them. We had been too closely watched to allow of any private conversation together, and so, a quiet pressure of her hand, and a significant glance every time I felt her pulse, were all the secret signs of our counterconspiracy that we could venture upon. In speaking to her, I spoke as if to a person of weak mind, and loud enough for all in the room to hear me.

One day, about two weeks after her fall, I went into the room and found her sitting in an arm-chair near the window. Her hands lay idle in her lap, and the whole expression of her face was one of intense weariness and listlessness. As she saw me, it suddenly changed to a bright, eager one; every feature was lit up with intelligence, while a smile, beautiful in its effect, dimpled for a moment her flushed cheeks. For the second that it lasted she was again the same pretty child who had thrown me that bright glance years before; the next moment Mrs. Ferris came in, and my patient sank back the listless, weary victim, I was accustomed to seeing.

"Why haven't you a book?" I asked quietly, as I took her hand and sat down beside her. Mrs. Ferris standing thinking in a distant window, did not hear the question.

"I can't read," was the answer; "I have had no teacher since papa died."

"Is it possible?" I remarked, almost unconsciously, in my surprise.

"Is it a wonder that I am nearly crazy? But for you, and what you have promised me, I would feel like doing again what I tried a short time ago. Sometimes I am mad when I think of myself, and the terrible trap I am in; then again, I feel that there is no hope for escape, and I long for death to end this misery. Mrs. Ferris will tell you that they are the two phases of my insanity, as she tells every one that sees me."

"My poor child," I said, "only be patient. Try and control yourself, and I will do all that I can; see how much better you are already for these two weeks of rest."

"Yes, but how long will it last?"

She put her hands over her face and cried softly, completely overpowered by the sense of her own hopeless, helpless position.

Mrs. Ferris, attracted by the sound, now came toward us with a sharp glance at me.

"Miss Ferris has been too much alone," I remarked, "she is dispirited with her long confinement in this room. We must try and get her out for a short time; the change will be good for her."

The sharp look changed to one of studied concern. Mrs. Ferris put her arm round the shrinking figure.

"We must take her for a ride, doctor, if you think she will be able, this afternoon."

"By all means," I said, "and repeat it every afternoon, if this does not fatigue her too much."

Miss Ferris now looked up, and with a few cheerful, encouraging words, I bade her "good-morning."

For three or four days after that interview I was unable to secure a word alone with my patient; the watch was sure, though unobtrusive. However, she steadily improved, and rode out every afternoon, her mother beside her in the carriage, her nurse opposite. At last, one morning, having made my accustomed visit, Mrs. Ferris followed me out of the room, and having thanked me for my attention and skill, asked for my account. I was not surprised; it was just the move I anticipated. Having complied with her request, my visits to Miss Ferris ceased, and our old positions were resumed. Miss Ferris, however, was very quiet when at the public table, acting very much as those around her did, and now and then we interchanged a few words on general topics; but once the meal was over, I only caught glimpses of her for the rest of the day. Mrs. Ferris, on the contrary, took particular pains to talk to me, and always met me with a fascinating smile and an agreeable manner, never leaving me without going over what I had done for her dear child, and thanking me again and again for the visible improvement in her health, caused by my skilful treatment.

One fine morning Miss Ferris did not come down to

breakfast. "She was not at all indisposed," her mother said, "only tired and unwilling to make any exertion." Her breakfast was sent to her, and after walking irresolutely up and down my room, debating some means of obtaining an interview with her, I took my hat and left the house, passing purposely the window generally chosen by Mr. Parker and Mrs. Ferris for their daily council of two. They saw me, as I intended they should, and as I raised my hat Mrs. Ferris bestowed on me one of her most fascinating smiles. I remained out a longer time than I had intended, for, rambling along, cogitating many things in my mind, I lost my way, and in trying to retrace my steps I came upon so many new beauties of scenery, wild flowers, and artistic effects, that I forgot myself in my almost childish delight, and remained contemplating them, entirely unmindful of the time that was passing away. At last I reached the hotel tired out, and sat down for a rest in the hall-way. My communicative friend, the waiter, coming along with the gong in his hand, gave me an inquisitive look before he commenced his artistic efforts on its surface. At last, having given the concluding touch with a graceful flourish of his arm, he drew near me and caught my eye.

"They're all gone, sir."

"What! Who are all gone? What do you mean?" I asked, struck by his remark.

"Why, Mrs. Ferris and her sick daughter; they left just after breakfast."

For a moment I was too much surprised to speak; at last I found understanding and breath at the same time.

"Where did they go? did you hear?"

"No, sir, not a word; they did it all very quickly and very quietly," was the answer.

"Who took them to the station?"

"One of our men; he is in the stable now."

"Did you notice Miss Ferris, whether she looked strong?" I asked.

"She had such a thick veil on, sir, I couldn't catch a sight of her face, but James says that he knows she didn't want to go, because she cried all the way to the cars; however, as the poor thing is mad, perhaps she didn't know where she was going, or what she was crying for."

I didn't answer this last proposition, but went to the stables in search of James. I found him in the centre of a group describing how he drove "the poor young woman that was out of her mind entirely," to the cars, and how they had to lift her in by force, while she kept calling on the doctor to save her. Seeing me, James lowered his voice at once and came forward. I drew him aside, and learned that the trunks had been checked through for New York. This was all I cared to hear. I started for Buffalo that afternoon, arranged for a longer absence than I had at first intended, and leaving my shooting and fishing apparatus in care of Mrs. Marks, I took the first train going east, with a bitter feeling of having been outwitted very cleverly. I heard of them all along the route till we reached New York; there I lost them. In that busy, noisy, rushing place, a small party, probably divided on purpose, would attract no notice whatever.

My first point was Mr. Master's office, so I put up at a quiet house, looked out his number in the directory, and then started for the place. I found no one in but a nice-looking lad of fourteen, who was dusting out the place. He told me that Mr. Masters had been travelling all summer, and was not expected home till November; Mr. Price, his partner, would attend to any thing I might have to say. Here was a dilemma. Of what use could Mr. Price be to me? Probably he had never heard of Mrs. Ferris. I explained that it was private business, to which Mr. Masters alone could attend. "Well, he could give me an address, but it was very unlikely that the letter would ever reach Mr. Masters, as he was never in one place for any length of time." There was a pile of letters, directed to Mr. Masters, on his private desk, awaiting his return. However, I determined to risk it, and so I wrote a short, distinct account of what had taken place during the few weeks just past, recalled myself to his memory, and begged of him to return at once to New York, where I would await him. Having directed it, I posted it at once, and then commenced a general search at every hotel and boarding-house in the city likely to contain Mrs. Ferris and her unfortunate step-daughter.

CHAPTER III.

IN WHICH MY SUSPICIONS ARE CONFIRMED..

For three weeks I spent my time as follows: visiting Mr. Masters' office, only to learn "that he was not at home nor had they heard from him;" examining hotel registers, going to every house that contained any one named Ferris, according to the directory; and peering into every carriage and under every bonnet that I met in my long walks. All without success; I was becoming thin from anxiety and disappointment. The boy in Mr. Masters' office must have concluded that I was a harmless sort of lunatic. At first he condescended to answer my inquiries, and proposed Mr. Price as an adviser. Finding his counsel of no use, he gradually ceased in his attentions to me, until at last, he would look up from his occupation as I would open the door, shake his head in anticipation of the usual question, and then return to it without bestowing on me another glance.

Fortunately for myself, I had recognized, one evening, in a gentleman standing on the steps of the St. Nicholas

Hotel, an old chum of mine, Harry Weston by name, who was on from Richmond for a few weeks of New York entertainment. We spent an evening together very often, comparing experiences, and amusing ourselves with reminiscences of old times. In my anxious state of mind I was always glad to meet him, for being a light-hearted, merry fellow, without a care in the world, he generally relieved me of a portion of my despondency, and succeeded in imbuing me with some of his own buoyancy of spirit.

One morning, in the early part of November, I opened the door of Mr. Masters' office, and looked up in anticipation of the usual negative shake to which I had become so accustomed. To my joyful surprise, there at his desk sat Mr. Masters, looking very fresh and ruddy, as though his vacation had agreed with him. He was so intent on a letter which he held before him, that I had advanced almost to his side before he looked off it and glanced at me.

I held out my hand and asked him, "Do you remember me?"

He hesitated a moment, as if trying to place me; but the instant I mentioned the name of Ferris, a bright smile broke over his face, and he grasped my hand with a warmth of manner and a word of welcome, that no doubt astonished the office-boy, who happened to be the only witness of the scene.

"You are the very man of all others that I wanted!" he exclaimed. "You find me puzzled to death over

3

a letter from our old acquaintance Mrs. Ferris. It would take me a month to tell you of the life she has led me these last six years. What do you think she has done now? I have been trying for three years to see Arthur Ferris's child, without success. Here is a letter in which she tells me, 'that her poor unfortunate child is in such a broken state of health, that it is necessary to take her to Europe for two or three years,' and she is gone a month! This letter has been lying here all that time."

I was so shocked, that the expression of my face caught the old gentleman's attention.

"There is something the matter," he said; "you suspect something—what is it?"

I told him what had brought me to New York, and detained me in the city so long. The effect of my story was terrible on him. All at once the plot lay clear before him.

For years she had so managed, that Mr. Masters had never once seen his ward. Now she had taken her completely out of his reach, as there was no direction given in the letter to which he could write; the apology being, that her plans were unsettled, and that as soon as possible she would communicate with him again. I read her letter over and over very carefully. It was cautious, and apparently perfectly open in its tenor. She explained that Arabella's health was very unsatisfactory; that she had travelled all over the country to benefit her, but without success, and that a celebrated physician of Buffalo, whom she had consulted, had at once recommended a sea-voyage, and a residence in the south of Europe, until her health should be completely reëstablished. On arriving in New York she had been unable to see him (Mr. Masters), but Mr. Parker, whom she had consulted all through the affair, approved of the plan. She would have awaited his return, but in view of the rapidly failing strength of her daughter, she had been obliged to waive all her own wishes, and think only of Arabella.

The perfect plausibility of the letter made my heart sink within me. How long would the child live where there was no human being to take her part, or stand between her and her two unscrupulous guardians? What might they not attempt and accomplish? We two men sat looking at each other in the little office, conscious of the misery and suffering before the poor girl, and utterly powerless legally to save her out of their hands. At last Mr. Masters looked up with a faint ray of hope breaking over his face, and spoke:

"My wife and I will start for Europe at once; she is used to travelling, and likes it. It won't take us any time to prepare for the voyage. If it is possible to overreach that woman and conceal the child for three years, until she is of age under her father's will, I shall take the responsibility on myself; in such a case as this, deception becomes a virtue."

"Had we not better find out whether or not Mr. Parker is with them?" I asked.

"That is the first move," was the reply. "I shall go now and decide the question. Will you dine with me this evening, and explain your views of the case to my wife? I should like her to hear it from your own lips; and in the event of our being successful in gaining possession of the child, we had better form some plan for her protection with your assistance."

I agreed to his proposal with pleasure ; so he handed me his card and we parted—I going up-town, and he to Mr. Parker's place of business. While passing up Broadway, I felt a hand laid on my shoulder, and turning, met Harry Weston's bright eyes and pleasant voice.

"Why, Jack, you're looking a hundred per cent. better than you did yesterday. Has she consented? or has the board declared a dividend?"

"Neither the one nor the other; but Mr. Masters has returned—the gentleman I have been waiting so long to see."

"Well, the sight of him has had a very good effect upon you. I start for home to-morrow evening. To-morrow morning, I think of joining a party on a visit to some of the city institutions. Will you come?"

I hesitated for a moment.

"Now don't refuse, Jack; the air and scenery will do both of us good. Of course, as far as the institutions and their inmates are concerned, there is not much novelty about them. Such misery is only too common and familiar to us. However, I can promise for the party

being a pleasant one, and you shall have an introduction to three of the prettiest and most agreeable girls in
the world."

The allusion to the three "prettiest and most agreeable girls in the world," recalled to my mind the form of
another girl, who, under happier circumstances, might
have been ranked in the same category. Seeing how
grave and preoccupied I was becoming, my companion
drew my arm in his and turned the conversation on
other topics. By the time we had reached his hotel, his
genial manner had produced its usual effect upon me,
and I had promised to meet him at the house where the
pleasure-party would assemble, by ten o'clock the next
morning. That evening I kept my appointment with
Mr. Masters, and was introduced to his wife, whom I
found a pleasant, warm-hearted little woman, if any
thing too impulsive; she having formed already in her
own mind some impossible scheme that she was very
impatient to accomplish without any further discussion.
We sat till a late hour, a council of three, planning
ways and means. Scheme after scheme was proposed,
and abandoned as impracticable. Mr. Masters had ascertained that Mr. Parker had been out of the city for
over a month, and was not expected home at any given
time. So we concluded that he was not far removed
from Mrs. Ferris and her charge, wherever they might be.
Mrs. Masters remembered the year of Miss Ferris's
birth; and having brought down from a high shelf of
the bookcase an old portfolio, she took a letter out of it

which contained an allusion to the circumstance, and the day of the month on which it had occurred.

"She was seventeen the 5th of last September," the good little woman announced, laying her glasses on the table, and pushing the old letter toward me.

"And she won't be of age until the day she is twenty. Two years and ten months of misery if she lives, and if we don't do something at once to take her out of that woman's power," remarked the old gentleman, in a determined tone of voice.

"This happens to be the 5th of November," I observed.

"Yes, and we can't sail for a week. I couldn't procure a passage to-day in next Saturday's steamer for love or money," Mr. Masters said, impatiently.

"Well, well, Joseph, don't fret. It may be all for the best," Mrs. Masters observed, with a bright smile directed toward her husband's face.

He was walking up and down the room with quick, impatient steps, annoyed at the delay and inactivity forced on him by circumstances. Catching the smile, he stopped to caress the good, kind face raised to his, and remarked:

"Ah, Sallie, if we could all possess your faith and patience!"

When leaving, he invited me to stop at his house during the remainder of my stay in the city, proposing that I should wait and see them off for Europe. As we had arranged that he would keep me informed of every thing that might transpire during his absence, I declined the invitation, and made up my mind to start for home the next night, feeling that I had neglected my patients long enough, and could be of no further service to Mr. Masters.

The next morning I presented myself at the appointed time and place, met my friend, and was introduced to a number of young people, whose manners and appearance quite astonished me. They were dressed in the gayest colors; feathers, ribbons, and ornaments of the most showy and, to me, extraordinary kind, danced and flashed in all directions. They laughed, they chattered, they appeared to enjoy every second of time to the very fullest extent. The pinning on of a veil, or the knotting of a ribbon in a becoming style, seemed to be the only care in life, the very summit of their ambition. They treated me most politely, no doubt for my friend's sake; paid me every attention, and listened with deference, and bright, attentive looks, to all my remarks. Before many hours passed, I became convinced that the light spirits, which had at first appeared to me exaggerated and assumed, were really natural and usual to them. I concluded that the fault, and need of something, I could not tell what, lay in myself. In fact, my youth was gone, with all its light-heartedness and lack of care. My profession was a saddening one in its effect, taken at its best, and, joined to my natural disposition, had served to make me graver and more thoughtful than most men of thirty-four. Besides, want of means had

kept me out of company when young, and by the time
that want was no longer felt, society had lost for me all
its attractions. Thus it happened that I stood on the
deck of the little steamboat, in the midst of this merry
party, with the feeling at my heart of not possessing
one thought in common with them.

The "three prettiest and most agreeable girls in the
world" were standing at a little distance off, looking
at the scenery, and passing remarks on every object
that attracted their attention. Harry Weston stood,
partly leaning against the railing of the deck, listening
and answering, his bright face all sparkling with pleasure and animation. He gradually drew me into the
conversation, which now turned on the islands, and
their respective buildings just coming in sight.

"Cousin Edith says that she will not go inside the
doors of the Lunatic Asylum, Mr. Weston," observed
one of the three girls, a tall, stylish-looking young lady,
with flashing eyes, and a bright smile that displayed
two beautiful dimples.

"Indeed, Mr. Weston," replied the young lady referred to as cousin Edith, "it would be no pleasure to
me at all. I should like to see the grounds and buildings for the sake of knowing that the poor creatures
are well cared for; but as to looking at human misery
in that form, oh! I couldn't do it; it makes me shudder
even to think of it."

"Papa says that they don't allow visitors to see
any thing very disagreeable—I believe only those whose

insanity takes a mild form, and who are perfectly harmless—monomaniacs I think he called them.   Those who
are dangerous are kept apart in some other building."

"Yes, Edith," remarked the third young lady, "and
Uncle William insists that plenty of them are no more
insane than we are.   He says that their relatives place
them there, very often, because they are poor and in-
firm, and not able to support themselves; and as it is a
city institution, and free, it relieves them of all expense"

"But, Carrie, how can that be? Surely the physician in charge would not receive them unless they had
some form of insanity," asked Miss Edith, unconvinced.

"Well, he thinks so.   What he means is this: they
may be a little weak on some one point, and perfectly
harmless; of course, if they were rich, it would be
passed over and concealed, or else called eccentricity;
but being poor, it is made an excuse for putting them
out of the way, where they can give no trouble."

"Do you believe what Cousin Carrie says?" asked
Miss Edith, with an appealing look at Harry Weston.

"Most decidedly," was his reply.   "The private
asylums throughout the country contain many such
cases. If people in good circumstances are unwilling
to take charge of their relatives so afflicted, we can
hardly wonder if those of a lower rank in life take advantage of this free institution to rid themselves of such
a responsibility."

Miss Edith Fullerton looked shocked, and Harry
3*

quickly began speaking on some other subject. When it was time to go on shore, he placed her in my charge; and during our stay in the different buildings, I was pleased with her sensible, well-chosen remarks, and surprised at the interest she exhibited in every thing shown us. The day was fine and sunny, and remarkably warm for the season. Every thing in nature was perfect, and exhilarating in its effect, tending to make the heart sadder as we wandered through these huge edifices telling of crime and degradation, and gazed on their wretched inmates.

We were a large party, gay and merry in spite of all these fearful surroundings. How almost impossible it is to bring the miseries of others home to ourselves! My companions laughed and chatted on, looking with curious eyes at the figures, in convicts' garments, passing and repassing, as if they belonged to another world and order of being. As we left the workhouse, accompanied by the warden, we came upon a procession of women on their way to it. My companion shivered, and clung closer to my arm as we stood aside to let them pass. Would any one believe that they had ever been young, ever been innocent, and yet some of them had not reached their eighteenth year! Just as they had been taken off the streets the night before, and placed in the station-houses, they were put on the boat in the morning and sent "to the island." They passed before us with lowered heads, the personification of moral degradation.

"They look upon this as their home," the warden remarked, in answer to some observation that I did not hear. "The same ones are sent here over and over again. You see they have no home nor character, they can't find work, nobody will have any thing to do with them ; so as soon as their time is up, and we send them back to the city, they begin to drink and fight on purpose to be put up again."

"And can nothing be done for them in this large city, so full of churches and benevolent societies?" asked Miss Fullerton. "Surely there are ways by which a reform could be effected."

"Well, there are several clergymen doing their best to be allowed to visit here, and I hope they will succeed in their efforts. Some such influence is sadly needed, but you have no idea of the difficulties attending such a work. The evils they will have to contend against are beyond description. Where the moral degradation is so complete, an appeal to the reason becomes impossible; you can only hope to reach them through their feelings, and they have grown so blunted by neglect and misery, that how to touch them is a question. They have lost all faith in humanity, and they have no knowledge of a higher Power."

The warden spoke feelingly and with emphasis, sincerely deploring the wretchedness which he had neither power nor authority to ameliorate. We pursued our way toward the lunatic asylum, admiring the grounds and the situation of the various buildings connected

with it. On reaching the entrance, we were met by one
of the assistant physicians, who politely offered to show
us through the building, and explain any thing that we
might like to understand. Miss Fullerton refused to
enter the place, and proposed remaining in a small
summer-house, that had caught her attention, standing
not far from us in the midst of a flower-garden. Finding it impossible to overrule her objections, we left her
admiring some plants not yet out of bloom, and proceeded on our tour of inspection. We were shown one
hall, with little dormitories opening out of it, in which
were a number of women of various ages. Some were
singing, others sewing, many walking back and forth
with quick, decided steps, clasped hands, and bent heads.
They appeared to be engaged in deep thought, but we
were assured that their minds were quite vacant, their
understanding gone forever. A few attempted to attract our notice, but entire indifference to us was almost
general; they had, no doubt, become quite accustomed
to being gazed at by parties of gayly-attired, sight-
hunting visitors. The place was scrupulously clean,
light, and airy, and they appeared to be furnished with
means for occupation and amusement. On our way out
we stepped into a little museum, supplied by good-heart-
ed contributors with many interesting curiosities, intended for the amusement and instruction of the afflicted
inmates of the institution. While there, Harry Weston
entered into a conversation regarding the social condition of the people committed to the asylum. The young

doctor was very explicit and communicative on the subject. He informed us that the head physician had made insanity his study for years, and was considered the very highest authority in that branch of his profession in the country. For that reason, people of wealth and position often intrusted their relatives to his care, because, while his skill was undisputed, he could have no object in detaining them longer than would be necessary in order to effect a cure, the institution being a charitable one. In private asylums, the temptation to prolong a patient's recovery was not always resisted.

"Then you discharge the person as soon as you consider him or her perfectly recovered?" said Harry.

"Yes, there is no object to us in keeping them here, they are only an expense to the city. If they are incurable and poor, they remain here, or we send them to their relatives if desired; of course, we have no power to detain them, if their own people are able and willing to take charge of them. In many cases they are left with us by persons apparently well off, whom we never see or hear of again. Poor, harmless creatures, who might as well be cared for at home as far as their being dangerous is concerned, but then they are a trouble, and so they end their lives here with us. There are some who have been here over twenty years."

The announcement that we "just had time to reach the steamboat," broke off the conversation at this interesting point, and gathering up shawls and parasols we hastened down to the entrance, just beyond which stood

Miss Fullerton, looking very pale and thoughtful. She put her arm in mine without speaking, but as soon as we were out of the garden and on the road she gave a quick glance around her and said abruptly:

"I believe now what Cousin Carrie said. There was one of the prettiest young girls I ever saw, gathering flowers in the garden, and from the way she spoke I believe she is just as sensible as I am."

"Probably she is one of the doctor's family—I believe they reside on the island," I said.

"Not at all; she told me that her own people had placed her here, and that she feels happier here than with them, as long as she is allowed to go about and amuse herself alone with the flowers; but she thinks it is dreadful to be put among those who are really insane at other times."

"I think," I remarked, "that it is a symptom of insanity, that of believing one's self sane, and all around us mad."

"I only wish you had seen her, as it is impossible for me to convince you that she is perfectly rational."

"She may be a monomaniac, and you, probably, didn't touch on the subject likely to arouse her. Was she quite young? In that case there may be hopes entertained of her complete recovery."

"I should say, if asked, that she was about sixteen; she is very childish both in manner and appearance, and I never saw such eyes except in a picture."

Miss Fullerton sighed, and we pursued our way toward the steamboat landing in silence. The little she had seen appeared to be quite enough for her, and had visibly affected her spirits. We reached the boat and were about seating ourselves comfortably on deck with the rest of the party, when she suddenly exclaimed:

"Oh! Dr. Wilmer, I have lost my shawl and parasol. I must have left them on the bench in the summer-house, for I don't recollect having them since."

The shawl was a large, extra one, provided in case of the weather becoming colder on our return trip. I had carried it on my arm all the morning, but curiously enough had neither missed it nor thought of it after leaving the asylum.

"I shall have time to find them," I answered, and I made my way off the boat and up the narrow road as fast as I could.

As it happened, I met no one who appeared to be employed in any official capacity about the place, and I hastened toward the summer-house, trying to catch a glimpse of the bright-colored object of my search. I had my hand on it when I heard a rustling sound, and a cry of joy, and the next second Arabella Ferris was clinging round my neck, breathless with surprise and delight. I don't know what I said, I know that I sank on the bench, and clasped her in my arms, completely overpowered by emotions that I can neither explain nor express. When I looked up she was sitting with clasped hands, her soft eyes fixed on my face, and an expression of perfect faith and peace on her own. That my presence was all-powerful for her release and protection was her firm belief. I sat looking at her without speaking. What to do was the question that I was resolving in my mind. Moments were precious, a wild plan flashed through my brain and I determined to risk its attempt. She was dressed in a dark material not unlike what Miss Fullerton wore, and her hat lay beside her on the ground. I folded the shawl and fastened it on her in a way to hide her dress, drew her arm in mine, opened the parasol and held it over her head as we left the summer-house. Once outside, I glanced around; no one was observing us that I could see, and we walked through the garden toward the road leading to the boat-landing. We had gone but a short way when we saw the boat out in the river, steaming in the direction of the city. My companion hitherto had not spoken; she only followed my directions and clung to my arm firmly, endeavoring with all her strength to keep her trembling steps up with mine. That she was very weak I could tell by looking down at the thin, white hand grasping my arm. Now, when I stopped short in the road, disappointed and almost despairing, she looked up suddenly, and exclaimed:

"I know what to do: come to the boat-house, and the 'admiral' will take us across the river in the rowboat."

I looked surprised. "What do you mean? who is the 'admiral?'"

„He belongs here, and has charge of the boat; very

frequently visitors go over to the city that way; I often sit and watch it going across."

She had turned, while speaking, in the other direction, and we walked as rapidly as possible toward the northern end of the island. It did not take us long to reach our destination, a little boat-house, near which, in the water, lay a boat about pushing off. It contained several gentlemen who had been inspecting the island, and who were, fortunately for us, returning to the city by this agreeable way. Catching sight of us, an old man who stood in the boat, touched his hat, a most comical affair, ornamented with faded artificial flowers, and waited for us. He assisted Miss Ferris into the boat, and the gentlemen politely made room for us among its cushions. The old man with the ornamented hat gave an order in an important nautical tone of voice, as if his little sail-boat were a three decker, and then seated himself at the helm. The next moment we were gliding through the water toward the opposite bank. My companion had sunk on the seat in an almost fainting condition; the mere hope of liberty was enough to excite her at any time; now that the hope seemed about to be fulfilled, she was completely overcome with joy. Feeling afraid, lest one of the gentlemen in the boat might belong to the institution, and recognize her, I sat with one arm round her waist supporting her, and the other holding the parasol over her face. The gentlemen, who were all very stout and ruddy looking, talked without ceasing on various subjects, mostly political ones. My attention was more or less attracted by them, and I felt rather amused than otherwise at some of the opinions they expressed. After a while they all lit cigars, and began discussing a dinner-party about coming off on one of the islands. They became so interested on the subjects of salmon, turtle-soup, and champagne, that I turned without feeling any further uneasiness to my companion and the consideration of her position. She was too weak and frightened to utter a word, and I tried to reassure her, and imbue her with the courage necessary to a successful termination of our adventure. We were rapidly approaching the shore, when I observed with dismay a small party of gentlemen awaiting our arrival. They were standing on a platform, or kind of piazza, attached to a public house that stood on the bank fronting the river. Their voices and merry laughter were wafted toward us by the wind, and attracted the attention of the gentlemen in the boat.

A number of loud salutations now ensued, among which the words "doctor" and "governor" were very distinct. In the midst of it all I felt Miss Ferris trembling, and, looking at her face, saw that it was white with fear.

"That is the doctor who is talking; I know his voice. What shall I do? please don't let him take me back again!" Her voice was so low that I could hardly catch the meaning of the words. Just then we touched the wharf, and the men put out their hooks and steadied the boat alongside for us to land.

"Courage," I whispered; "don't give up yet, we are nearly safe."

The gentlemen sprang out first, and up the wooden steps, joining the other party at the top of them. Here was a dilemma. It would be rather a difficult matter to pass, unobserved by the vigilant doctor, this watchful group. One gentleman came to my rescue; who he was I have never found out, but I owe him many thanks. I was assisting Miss Ferris out of the boat, painfully conscious of the glances fixed on us, yet not daring to let her observe my fears, when he called out, in a full, cheerful voice: "Come, gentlemen, we are not going to part this way; let us have a bottle of wine." The next minute he had turned in the direction of the house, followed by the whole group. To lift Miss Ferris up the steps, and half carry her across the platform, was the work of but a few moments. The carriage, in which the doctor and his party had driven out from the city, stood in the street, near the side of the public-house. The driver, who was preparing to return to the city, jumped off his box with alacrity on observing my signal, and opened the door. I lifted Miss Ferris into it, gave him the direction of Mr. Masters' house, and then threw myself back on the cushions with a long-drawn sigh of relief. That over, I made a pillow of my overcoat and put it under my companion's head; wrapped Miss Fullerton's shawl around her, and enjoined strict silence.

She slept very quietly after a little while, and I sat watching her, with curious emotions, caused by mingled

joy and thankfulness, swelling in my heart. It was a long
and, to me, entirely unfamiliar road, which we traversed
that chilly November evening. Anxiety on Miss Ferris's account, without doubt, made it appear even more
tedious; and, when at last the driver stopped his horses
and opened the door to announce our arrival at our destination, my fears for her had increased alarmingly.
Miss Ferris, though still sleeping, was talking incoherently and burning with fever. The driver rang the bell
of the house, and as soon as the door was opened, I carried her up the steps, through the hall, and into the parlor, where sat Mr. and Mrs. Masters awaiting the announcement of dinner. They started from their chairs
on seeing me, and heard with speechless amazement my
first words:

"This is Miss Ferris. Don't ask me any thing," I
continued, "until she is in bed, and don't wait a moment, but get a room ready for her at once."

Mrs. Masters hurried away without another word,
and her husband stood looking with tearful eyes at the
slight, wasted form on the sofa before him. Miss Ferris lay regarding him with a curious expression of half
recognition on her face. From him her eyes wandered
to me, and she murmured the words, "Don't leave me."

"You are safe now," I said, soothingly; "you are
with your father's old friends. They will take care of
you."

Mr. Masters by degrees brought himself to her recollection, and she listened with a smile on her face while

he talked over days long since passed away, when she
had sat on his knee, and eaten candies out of his pocket.
I let him talk on, knowing that it was necessary for her
to fully trust in and love these kind people, the only
ones to stand between her and her dreaded step-mother.
She was Mr. Masters' god-child as it turned out, and
had always been very fond of him in the old happy
times before her father's death.   So he chatted on, bringing to mind various pets and toys that she had owned,
and different little expeditions to bookstores and candy-
shops that they had undertaken together.   Listening to
them, I began to question whether it would not be better to take up the threads of her life just at this happy
point, from which they had been so cruelly turned away,
and by never mentioning what had passed in the last
six years, try to make her forget all its later miseries.
She had been, on the whole, a happy little child; in
knowledge and feeling she was one still.   She knew
nothing of books, her whole study for six long years had
been the characters and impulses of the two women
who had controlled her life during that time.   Of that
phase of human nature her experience was a sad and
minute one.   She might live to an old age, and never
meet with it again.

When Mrs. Masters came back, she found Miss
Ferris sitting up, with her hand in Mr. Masters', smiling
at the story of some childish prank of hers that he was
telling.   The good woman took the young girl into her
heart at once, kissing her and almost crying over her.

Seeing that her fear of these new friends was dissipated, I at once prescribed rest, and no more talking. However, I had to promise to go up and see her before leaving the house, so as to satisfy her mind, and then she went away, with Mrs. Masters' motherly arm around her, and a servant with a very good-natured face following them. Mrs. Masters sent us down word that she could not think of leaving the poor child, at least until she slept, so we dined without her; and I gave Mr. Masters a circumstantial account of my day's adventures. The good man was more astonished than even I had been.

That Mrs. Ferris should trust the child out of her own keeping seemed incredible to him. I accounted for it easily enough in my own mind. She had no doubt come to the conclusion that making away with the girl, by the means that I had discovered her using, was a highly dangerous undertaking—one open to a great risk, and not very easily accomplished. There was no fear of any one that she knew ever meeting the child, or recognizing her, in a lunatic asylum, provided for the poor and friendless of another class. Besides, she had left her to live or die there, careless of which it might be. She had abandoned her entirely, feeling quite sure that release was impossible except by death; a result very probable, as in case she did not sink under physical weakness, the blue waters were spread out on all sides around her inviting her to bury her cares forever in their depths. Mr. Masters was inclined to think that

Mrs. Ferris would communicate with the head physician, and learn in time of her daughter's strange disappearance. I held to the contrary opinion; but Mrs. Masters came down, and having heard all the particulars, agreed with us, that Miss Ferris should be removed from the city as soon as she was able to travel. It was best to be prepared for all emergencies, Mr. Masters thought, and it was necessary to conceal the fact of Miss Ferris's existence in the United States, for at least two years and ten months.

"The day she reaches her twentieth year, Doctor Wilmer, will be a merry one for us. We shall have a jollification of some kind, as sure as my name is Joe Masters."

"I only hope she will be alive on that day, and I shall be satisfied," Mrs. Masters answered, with a doleful look and an ominous shake of her head.

Mr. Masters gave me a questioning glance.

"Miss Ferris is not strong," I said, in answer to his eager gaze in my face; "but I don't think she is any worse than when I saw her in September. Now she has a bright prospect before her, and that will do more to restore her to health than any thing I could prescribe."

"You must understand her constitution better than any doctor could that we might call in," remarked Mr. Masters; "still, if you would like a consultation—"

"It will not be necessary," I answered. "Her nervous system is terribly weakened; rest and freedom from all excitement, and especially from all recollection

of what she has suffered, are positively required. I
should advise, after a little while, taking up her education just where she left it off, and treating her exactly
as you would a child. If it be possible, let her have her
girlhood, with all its innocence, and freedom from care
and knowledge of the world."

"I don't think it would ever do to send her to a
boarding-school," said Mrs. Masters; "the girls would
laugh at her ignorance, and increase her nervousness."

"And we can't keep her here," Mr. Masters replied.
"If Mrs. Ferris hears of her escape, we shall have a
whole force of detectives watching every movement we
make. Come, doctor," he went on, "concoct some
plan for hiding the young lady, and at the same time
providing the means for educating her properly. She
will have the spending of ten thousand a year, and she
must be prepared for the position she will occupy, if all
goes well."

I sat lost in thought, debating a point in my mind.
I had formed a plan, and it seemed a feasible one, and
yet I was diffident about proposing it. I was questioning my own motives in regard to it.

"Out with it, doctor!" cried Mr. Masters; "you've
thought of something, I can see that by your face. That
is a wonderful head of yours for strategy. Come, don't
be bashful—let us hear it!"

So I explained to him that my mother and sister
were living alone in a very quiet little village near
Albany; that the house was roomy, and the neighbor-

hood all that could be desired ; that my sister had been
educated for a teacher, and had been a very successful one for many years, until our mother's health failed,
and it became necessary for her to undertake the management of the house. Before I was half through, Mr.
Masters was shaking my hand, and declaring that nothing could be better; Mrs. Masters was equally delighted; and it was agreed that I should write at once to
my sister, and make all the proper arrangements.
On going up to visit my patient, I found her asleep,
with the good-natured-looking servant keeping watch
beside her. Promising to return and finish my stay in
New York at Mr. Masters' house, I started for Harry
Weston's hotel, and caught him just about leaving it for
the cars, his valise in his hand and his overcoat on his arm.
He was surprised and delighted to see me, they all having concluded that I was on the island for the night.

"But what have you done with yourself?" he exclaimed, giving me a long look. "I never saw such a
change in a man as that sail has made in you; it was
very effective. Upon my word, Jack, you do me credit
—I shall put that down among my wonderful cures."

"Harry," I said, "if you will have patience for
three years, I will let you into a secret. It is not my
own, or you should know it now."

"So you want to make me believe that it is some
stupid secret, and not my sail, that has affected you so
powerfully. Come, Jack, don't be jealous of my superior skill; but remember, three years from to-day I shall

4

come North and hear your wonderful mystery." I accompanied him to the cars, and having procured Miss Fullerton's address, bade him a hearty "good-by."

On returning to Mr. Masters' house, I heard that my patient was awake, but delirious. True enough, meeting me so unexpectedly, and escaping so successfully when almost despairing, had been too much excitement for the weakened nerves and brain. We passed a terrible night, listening to her curiously mingled ravings. Niagara, her fall, and our few conversations together, were inextricably confounded with her journey to New York, her arrival at the lunatic asylum, and her escape from it. Mrs. Masters listened attentively and cried bitterly over the sufferings and cruelties she had endured; and Mr. Masters had to go down to the parlor, where he vented his rage against Mrs. Ferris, Mr. Parker, and Susan, in a most audible manner. The weary ravings at length were hushed, and Miss Ferris slept a quiet, refreshing sleep. In the afternoon of the following day I called on Miss Fullerton and requested permission to keep the bright shawl and fringed parasol, as mementoes of the preceding one. They are hanging up now, in an old cabinet not very far from where I sit writing. I rather think that, at the time, Miss Fullerton thought, very naturally, that I had not succeeded in finding them; however, she don't think so at present. For two weeks I remained at Mr. Masters' house, and while my patient slowly regained strength of mind and body, Mrs. Masters superintended the cutting out and fitting of a most remarkable wardrobe, which from its extent and costliness must have slightly turned the heads of the quiet villagers for whose benefit it was afterward displayed.

Mr. Masters had gone up the river, seen my mother and sister, made all the arrangements, and was now engaged in sending numerous articles up there, destined for the use and comfort of his adopted daughter. Among the rest was a magnificent piano-forte, whose grandeur quite eclipsed the old one that stood in our quiet parlor, and whose tone and volume delighted my sister. When at last I decided that my patient was able to travel, my sister came down to New York, and was introduced to her future pupil. The change that a few weeks of happiness and freedom from care had effected in Miss Ferris, was quite remarkable. I felt rather amused at the surprise exhibited by my sister on seeing her; she had no doubt formed a very good idea of her from my first letters, but I had not thought of telling of the alteration which had since taken place in her health and appearance. Therefore, when Miss Ferris came into the room, with light steps and eyes shining with pleasure, dressed in a rich dark silk, with soft lace shadowing her neck and arms, and her hair falling around her in long, bright curls, she quite astonished my sister, who was totally unprepared for such a pretty vision.

The next moment, to the still greater surprise of that quiet lady, Miss Ferris threw her arms around my neck, and kissed me, exclaiming—

"How long you have been away! Oh, I am so glad to see you!"

Then she turned, and was introduced to her new teacher and guardian, going through the ceremony in a very different manner, she having a morbid dread of all strangers.

When we were alone again, my sister expressed her surprise at such strange behavior on the part of a young lady of seventeen, and took me to task for permitting it and appearing pleased with it.

"You forget," I remonstrated, "that Miss Ferris is a perfect child in all but years, and acts impulsively as her feelings prompt her. She has had such a bitter experience thus far, that it would be cruel to check the few childish qualities remaining with her. Mr. and Mrs. Masters were delighted to find her exhibiting some of the gayety, and if you will call it so, silliness, natural to her age."

My sister laughed, and patted my arm.

"John," she said, "to hear you talk, one would think you were about eighty. Don't play you are so old, at least, until you look it. It would never do for Miss Ferris to lose her heart to you, and just at present you are the first object in her thoughts. She makes no secret of the fact; it shines in her eyes, and shows in all her actions."

"Which proves exactly to what the feeling amounts," I said. "It is gratitude, and childish admiration. Being the first one to protect her, she naturally clings to me, and invests me with qualities that I do not possess.   At present I am her hero; it will not last very long.   Three years from now, when she is prepared to take her place in society, young, beautiful, and fascinating, her feeling for me will be the same—only modified; enthusiastic admiration and affection you may call it, but certainly not love."

"And would you have it otherwise, John?" my sister asked.   "Remember her wealth, and the difference in age between you."

"Exactly so," I answered.   "When she is beginning life, surrounded by all the influences that render it attractive, I shall be a gray-haired, old doctor, poring over my dusty books, and going my usual rounds without a thought of any thing outside of my profession."

"Ah, John, if you would only marry some nice girl suited to you in age—but there is no use in proposing such a thing to you.   You are a more confirmed old bachelor every time we meet."   And my sister left me, without having penetrated or even suspected my secret.

CHAPTER IV.

My sister spent several days in the city, making necessary purchases of books, drawing-materials, music, and so forth, calculated to make a very learned woman out of my innocent little patient, who still ran to meet me whenever I came in after being away for some hours. Mr. and Mrs. Masters had become so attached to their ward, that considerations for her safety alone could have induced them to part with her. A warm feeling of affection was already forming between her and my sister, so that they appeared to regard each other as friends rather than as teacher and pupil. I almost envied my sister the pleasant task of cultivating the talents, and forming the tastes of this young girl, whose naturally ardent temperament and inquiring mind had received new force, and were asserting themselves in a high degree. We formed a very pleasant, very happy party, and, notwithstanding the coldness of the season, thoroughly enjoyed our sail up the Hudson to Albany. We found my mother anxiously awaiting

us, and prepared to give us all a warm welcome, especially Miss Ferris, for whom her deepest sympathies
were excited. The latter danced about the house, examining with interest all her new possessions, and promising to be very good and patient in making the best
use of her time. I explained to her that neither of her
friends could visit her often, and the necessity for this
precaution. She acquiesced silently in all our plans,
and promised to be as happy and contented as she
could. However, in spite of all her good resolutions,
she parted from us very reluctantly, and the last
glimpse we had of her, as we drove away, she was
leaning against the gate, crying bitterly.

I returned to my house and practice, to the great
delight of my patient and much-enduring professional
brother who had so kindly performed my duties
throughout my long absence. To say that the house
was duller and gloomier than ever, does not express it.
It was only by throwing off all recollections of the
weeks just passed, and pursuing my work with re-
doubled energies, that I could at all content myself in
my chosen mode of living. The secret which I had hid
from others was torturing me. I had made up my mind
to bury it, and in time overcome it. A matter easier to
imagine than to accomplish. In spite of her wildness,
her misery, and her ignorance, Miss Ferris had taken
possession of my whole heart. If I had loved her in all
her wretchedness, her present altered condition had not
served to lessen the passion. As she had been, some

wild hope of one day possessing her had seized upon
me. When I pictured her to myself as she would be at
some future day, not very far off, I felt the hope fade
and die out of my heart. "The feeling must be overcome," I said to myself; "action and study will drive it
away." But it was not overcome; nothing I undertook
had the power of dispelling or modifying it. So I carried it about with me as a memento of something past
and done with, and allowed no ray of hope to shine
upon it, or color it with aspirations which could never
be realized.

My sister corresponded with me regularly, and spoke
in glowing terms of her pupil's progress. From Mr.
Masters I received monthly bulletins, telling of Mrs.
Ferris, and the means she was taking for Arabella's
complete restoration to health. The old gentleman's
letters were perfect studies. Mrs. Ferris little knew
the amount of enjoyment afforded us by her long, care-
fully-worded communications. Mr. Masters quoted
from them largely, and added his own criticisms. I
came to the conclusion that the dear old man was
growing younger on account of them. Meanwhile he
forwarded to her all the money required for her
daughter's support, as calculated by her, and kept a
memorandum of the same in his desk. Fortunately for
Miss Ferris, her money was completely under the control of this good old man, and Mrs. Ferris had never
interfered in the management of it, fearful of exciting
suspicion against herself. These accounts of Miss Fer-

ris's health, transmitted from various cities in the south
of Europe, were quite curious and very well planned.
Sometimes she had improved so much, that Mrs. Ferris
felt very sanguine about her; then again, she would
sink visibly, and cause them great uneasiness. The
charges for medical advice were surprising, and far exceeded any thing of the kind ever heard of before, at
least by me.

My sister's reports, on the contrary, were all that
could be desired; and Mr. Masters, who frequently went
up to see her and her pupil, always concluded his letters
to me with a postscript, thanking me for the wonderful
plan that I had suggested. He also was in the habit of
informing me that "little Belle's progress in music was
quite astonishing." As I had left my sister strict injunctions to watch Miss Ferris's health, and give me accurate
reports about it, I was able to gather from a comparison
of the two accounts a very good idea of how she lived
and spent her time. Evidently she was very happy,
childlike, and free from care. "To her past troubles,"
my sister wrote, "she never alludes, and I don't think
that her mind reverts to them at all, she has so many
new occupations, and they are all so strange and novel
to her. As for mother, I shall soon become jealous for
she is completely wrapped up in the child."

Occupied by my duties and other cares, the winter
passed by almost imperceptibly to me; and I remember
being surprised, one day in spring, at finding some early
violets peeping up from a hedge by the roadside. Dur-

4*

ing the summer which followed, I returned my friend's kindness, and took charge of his affairs while he enjoyed a long vacation. I had made up my mind to resist, for a while at least, all temptations, and therefore refused my sister's repeated invitations for "just one week's pleasure of my company." I was trying to determine if the old maxim, "Out of sight, out of mind," held good in my case, but thus far it had decidedly failed in doing so. I had even accepted numerous invitations during the winter just past, and had been introduced to many beautiful and accomplished girls, rich in all the attractions that wealth, beauty, and knowledge bestow on their happy possessors. Even while listening to their soft voices, and catching the merry glances thrown on me from their bright eyes, I would find myself comparing with them, almost unconsciously, the slight form and delicate features of the one so constantly in my thoughts. Recollections of a voice whose tones were still sweeter, and of eyes whose loveliness none could equal, would come over me at all times and in all places, filling my heart with hopeless longings for that which was so impossible to attain. But for my professional duties, which were at that time very much increased, and their great responsibility, I do not know what would have become of me.

Mr. Masters and his wife did not leave the city that summer, as Mr. Parker had suddenly reappeared in New York, exciting their fears by his curiosity and watchfulness. He had given some plausible excuse for his long

absence from his business, and professed complete ignorance of Mrs. Ferris's movements, after having placed her
and her daughter under the care of the captain on whose
ship they had sailed for Europe. He was very particular in examining all the papers and deeds connected with
his ward's property, and expressed himself in terms of
great satisfaction at the result of some of Mr. Masters'
investments, complimenting him very highly on the
manner in which he was discharging his trust. His surprise at the large sums asked for by Mrs. Ferris, for the
support of her daughter, was well affected, and quite
amused his suspicious partner, who was rapidly forming
a very unfavorable opinion of this joint guardian of Miss
Arabella Ferris.

In September Mr. Parker again left New York, and
my friend, Doctor Miller, for whom I had been doing
duty, returned to Buffalo. Another winter passed away,
during which Mrs. Ferris's letters continued in the same
strain, and my sister's became more and more extravagant in their descriptions of the beauty and talents of
her interesting pupil. How little my sister guessed of
the fresh torture given me by every letter of hers that
I received! How little she would have understood the
contradictory passions they stirred up within my heart!
I exulted in the idea that my conception of Miss Ferris's
powers of mind had not been a mistaken one; I gloried
in the thought that she had so totally overcome the disadvantages of her childhood, and was realizing all my
fondest hopes, and yet—yes, it must be acknowledged,

I felt that the barrier between us was each day growing wider and deeper. I must endeavor to subdue these foolish fancies, and be content to see her, loving and beloved, the wife of some younger man, one more suited to her age and temperament than I could ever hope to become. I reasoned, or rather tried to reason, myself into the belief, that after a few years I should be quite willing to settle down into the position of a trusted friend, respected and loved as such, with my chair at the table and my place by the fireside, happy at the sight of her happiness, and resigned to the conviction that another, and not I, was the cause of her peace and contentment.

Before another September came, I had almost made up my mind that my feelings for Miss Ferris had assumed this quiet, passionless state, and I concluded to take a trip east and see my friends. As nearly two years had gone by in the interval, I anticipated a very warm reception, and determined not to tell them of my expected visit, but to enjoy their pleased surprise. One sultry afternoon, in the first week of October, I opened the gate of my mother's pretty front garden, and sauntered up the pathway toward the window of the little room in which she usually sat at work. Looking in, there she was, knitting a soft, white stocking, destined for my next winter's comfort. My sister sat on a low chair near her, sorting seeds into various little papers laid on the carpet before her. I looked around the room in vain for the other figure, which, I am afraid, generally

occupied the chief place in the home pictures I was so
accustomed to forming in my imagination. Overcoming
the disappointment as quickly as possible, I raised myself by means of my hands to an old position of mine
on the window ledge—quite a favorite one in my
boyish days—and bade my mother and sister "Good-
afternoon."

The next minute their arms were around me, and between hugging and kissing I at length reached the floor
in safety, while they stood, breathless with surprise and
delight, looking at me.

"How well and handsome you are looking, John!"
exclaimed my sister, pushing my hair away from my
forehead; and then, as usual, throwing her arms around
my neck and leaning her head against my breast, with
tears of joy standing in her eyes.

My dear sister, she believed I was a hero—and we
had not met for two long years.

"I should like to know when John didn't look handsome, the dear boy!" my mother answered, giving me a
glance of mingled love and pride from the soft, clear
eyes that had always met mine thus lovingly.

"It's well I only let you see me at long intervals, or
you would spoil me. What would my patients say if
they should behold their dignified Doctor Wilmer being
hugged and kissed to such an extent, and hear him
called 'a dear boy'? Consider my age—thirty-six, am
I not, mother?"

"Nonsense, John! never mind your age;" and my

mother kissed me again, calling me her own "dear, *dear* boy, no matter how old I might be."

"John," said my sister, "all this time you have never thought of asking after Belle."

Hadn't I, though, my dear, unsuspicious sister?

"Where is she?" I asked.

"Gone down to the village, to see one of her friends who has been very ill for two weeks. She goes to sit an hour or two with her every afternoon."

"I miss the child very much," remarked my mother; "but it is pleasant for her to know some nice young people; she would feel it very much if deprived of their society."

"Why should she be deprived of their society?" I asked.

"Well, there really seems to be no reason why she should not enjoy their little parties and gatherings; but you know how it is—Mr. Masters is so afraid of her being recognized, that we have to be very careful about where she goes, and with whom she meets."

"Mr. Masters is perfectly right," I said. "The consequences would be dreadful; in another year she can go where and meet whom she likes."

"She is not remarkably fond of society," my sister said, "and when she took a fancy to Pauline Lecount I was delighted. Pauline is so very bright and gay, she infects every one that comes under her influence with some of her own lightheartedness."

"Is she the only child in the family?" I asked.

"Oh, not at all; there is an immense family of them, any number of brothers and sisters. I believe a new one turns up every week or so, that has been spending a year with some relative or another; and these relatives appear to live in every State of the Union."

"Quite a family they must be," I said; "does Miss Ferris only fancy one of them?"

"Oh, she likes them all more or less; but Pauline is decidedly the favored one of the lot. They are of French descent, and I suspect their means are rather limited. Mr. Lecount is a lawyer, and one of his sons is in the office with him. They are very talented and sociable, and cultivate such pleasant home amusements! I often wish they were rich; for as it is, they are very hospitable, and every one likes to visit at their house."

"Yes," went on my mother, taking up the subject where my sister dropped it.—"Belle told me last night that there was another brother home on a visit that she never saw before. He practises law in Philadelphia, and very seldom has an opportunity of seeing his family. It must be a very pleasant thing," mused my mother, "to own such a fine set of children, all out in the world doing for themselves, and still coming back every now and then for a sight of the old home and their parents. Now the girls might all help, there are four of them, but the old folks are too proud to let them try. I wanted one of them to teach Belle French, but when I spoke of payment, the old lady blazed up, and said that she was willing to have Belle join them in their French readings, and conversations, but 'Do it for money? oh! no; it was hard enough for her sons to have to work, the girls were ladies, and no matter how poor they might become, ladies they should remain.' I pity their old aristocratic ideas in this republican country. Of course, the girls expect to marry well, and so they ought, handsome and accomplished as they are; but suppose they don't, what will become of them? The young men will marry, and although Mr. Lecount owns his place, what would it be, divided among so many? Very foolish, very foolish of them indeed!" concluded my sensible republican mother.

While she had been giving vent to her opinions of the Lecounts, I had retaken possession of the window-seat, and, although listening to her words, had been watching with interest two persons coming along the road toward the house. One was a young man of twenty-five or six, tall and well-proportioned, with an easy, graceful carriage, and glossy black curls, shaking and shining under the broad-brimmed, low-crowned hat that he wore. He was pulling a rose to pieces, leaf by leaf, while talking earnestly to the young girl walking at his side. This young girl's face was concealed from my view by the broad leaf of her straw hat, the crown of which was ornamented with natural flowers, evidently picked from the basket half full of them that she carried on her arm. She had on a soft, full, white muslin dress, ornamented at the neck, waist, and wrists by knots and ends of lilac ribbon. It was looped up over a shorter under-skirt with more ribbons of the same delicate shade, displaying two very pretty little feet, cased in the most elaborately trimmed boots that I had ever seen. To my surprise, they stopped at the gate, and, while he opened it, she invited him to enter the house and be introduced to Mrs. and Miss Wilmer. I recognized the clear, sweet voice at once; this pretty vision, then, coming tripping up the path, was no other than my once wearied little patient, so tired of life and all its miseries! At present, the bright side was turned to her, tinged with its fairest coloring. She was much taller, and her figure had become round and graceful in the two years that had passed since I left her, leaning over the gate with tears in her eyes, watching our departure. She stopped in the path to point out a carnation pink to her companion, and my sister, catching sight of her, remarked:

"There is Belle now, and that must be the brother from Philadelphia; I have not seen him since he was a schoolboy. Shall I tell her that you are here?"

"No, don't," said my mother; "let us see how she will behave. Latterly, she has hardly mentioned you to us; either your continued absence has offended her, or else she has gradually lost her interest in you. The first year she was with us she talked of you incessantly, and longed to see you every week as impatiently as a child of six years would; indeed, though she is nineteen now, I don't know any child more innocent and impulsive."

"That poor young fellow seems entirely fascinated," said my sister, turning from the window; "I only hope he won't put her down for a perfect little flirt."

"Why should he?"

"Why? Simply because she is so childish, that she is pleased with every one she meets, takes their attentions, becomes interested in them, and tries to make them as happy as possible. Claude Lecount has lost his heart to her, and she thinks no more of him than of any of his brothers. As for teaching her prudence, it is out of the question. Mr. Masters thinks her perfection, and begs of us not to let her understand the world and its ways. Of course, to us, who know all the circumstances, her manner is not unreasonable or unnatural; but could you convince a young man, brought up in a large city like New York, that a young girl could reach the age of nineteen, in this century, and remain so innocent as she is? Certainly not; those two brothers will be at daggers' points about her in a week, and will mutually agree in the end that she is a finished flirt."

My sister's prophecy was suddenly cut short by hearing the hall door open, and the next moment Miss Ferris stood on the threshold, ushering in Mr. Louis Lecount. She did not see me at first, as I sat on the window-seat; and while introducing her escort in her pretty, original style—"Mrs. Wilmer, this is Pauline's brother Louis"—she removed her hat, thereby displaying her bright eyes, and a mass of curls shading them and her throat. Crossing the room to hang up her basket, she suddenly saw me. For a second she stood pale and mute with surprise; the next, she had her arms round my neck, laughing and crying for joy.

Mr. Louis Lecount looked rather astonished, while my sister tried to explain what great friends we were, and how we had not met for two years. The young gentleman rose after a few minutes, and took his leave, promising to call again. I quite admired his good taste, particularly as Miss Ferris had become almost unconscious of his presence in the room, and was sitting near me, with beaming eyes, pouring out question after question relating to the circumstances which had prevented me from coming home for such a "long, long time."

I found it difficult to make excuses for my absence, it being impossible to tell her the real one; and sitting thus, looking into her clear, truthful eyes, and listening to her sweet voice as she met and put aside, as utterly ridiculous, my best arguments, I felt that my good resolutions had all vanished, and that, instead of having overcome my foolish love, it was mastering me more strongly than ever. I determined to shorten my visit; it would be misery to see her happy in the attentions of these two young men, one of whom would probably succeed in gaining her heart. If I were older, I might be enabled to view it all with the best wishes for her happiness, and without a regret for my own disappointment; if I were younger, I might enter the lists as a rival of these two attractive admirers. As it was, my cause was hopeless. Would she have run into my arms, every feature lit up with joy and affection, had she regarded me otherwise than as a dear friend, holding to her the place of an uncle or an elder brother, who could appreciate these marks of love without placing too high a value on them, or in any way misunderstanding them? Decidedly, her feeling for me was the same as it ever had been—enthusiastic, demonstrative, unconcealed; but it did not satisfy me. Its very exhibition only caused me to draw comparisons between it and the expression of that deeper sentiment for which I longed in vain. Thus, while she exerted herself to make me happy, and talked unreservedly of the progress she had made in all her studies, and of the heavy debt of gratitude she owed me, she unconsciously added to the weight of bitterness that was overpowering me.

We had wandered into the parlor, where her books and music were scattered about; and my sister was busy preparing supper in the other room. Miss Ferris drew my attention to a stand of exquisite flowers in one of the windows. Turning to make a remark about them, I was surprised to find her leaning against the wall, with her face hidden from me. Something dejected and strange in her attitude struck me, and I bent to catch a glimpse of her face. She was crying silently, in the old way that I had so often noticed at Niagara.

"What is the matter, Belle," I asked; "what troubles you?"

"I can't tell; I am silly, but you are so changed, so

cold and distant—did I offend you?" As she spoke, she put her little hand on my arm, and looked in my face with the old sorrowful expression in her eyes.

What was I to do? put aside all ideas of honor—tell her how I loved her—and accept from her deep gratitude the assent not prompted by her heart? No, better she should think me cold and indifferent, than that such a sacrifice should be made; better be misjudged, than cause her any future unhappiness. So I only took her hand softly in mine, and assured her that she had not offended me in the least, and that she must make a little allowance for my surprise at finding so much alteration in herself.

"You have grown into a young lady," I went on in a jesting tone, though I had never felt more sad in my life, "and I left you quite a child; are you sure you are quite strong now and happy?"

"Yes, very strong; my head never troubles me, and I am so happy that sometimes I tremble lest it should not last. Every time I see my dear guardian I feel more and more what it would be to have my step-mother discover me. I would rather die than go back to her treatment. Do you know that I count the days as they go by, and time flies too slowly for me! There are ten months yet to come before I can feel free and at ease."

"But you are safe here; certainly out of danger of any recognition by your old friends and acquaintances. This is such a quiet place, people never come here for either business or pleasure."

"Very few, but still one would be sufficient, provided that one was a friend of ours. It would all be done innocently, because nobody knows what you do. All our acquaintances thought that Mrs. Ferris was 'passionately attached to her little daughter.' How often have I heard that expression, while standing or sitting in the room with company! It always made me shiver, and once I had an indistinct idea that 'passionately attached' was only a fine expression for 'hate'—indeed I had."

"And what idea have you about it now?" I asked.

"I don't like the expression at all; it always meant so little to me, that even now, when Pauline Lecount tells me that she is passionately attached to this or that person, I can't feel that she cares for them at all."

"And is she 'passionately attached' to you?" I asked.

Miss Ferris smiled, and colored slightly.

"Yes," she answered, "that is what she says, and she told me last evening, as a great secret, that her brother Claude was—"

"Was also passionately attached to you—is it not so?"

I expected another blush, but, instead of coloring or looking down, Miss Ferris raised her eyes to my face, and clasped her hands on my arm.

"You know it don't mean any thing, and if you are sure that you are not angry with me, I will tell you just what I think."

I shook my head at her, and she went on in her old childish way, smiling and sighing in turn, as her heart prompted her.

"I like Pauline, and I like your sister and mother, and I am very sure that I like my dear guardian and Mrs. Masters; how can I help loving them?—think of all I owe them, all they have done for my happiness—and as for you, I can't tell you how I feel toward you. Nothing I could do or say would repay you for all the care you have taken of me. All I can do is, feel your goodness, and think of you alway. Do you know that I can sit quiet and see before me, just like a series of pictures, every thing that has happened since I first saw you the night my father died? You don't know how I have longed for you to talk to in these last two years; I had ever so many questions, written out, that I wanted you to answer. I always feel that I can be as childish as I like with you, and say just what comes into my head first. You will not misunderstand me, I am sure."

"No, never," I said gently, longing, as I looked at her, to stroke the soft curls that fell on her neck. No wonder she thought me cold and strange; I was struggling to overcome myself, and no doubt, in the effort, became ten times sterner and more silent than I intended.

"About Claude Lecount," she continued—"how could he care for me? I never did any thing for him except to sing a song, or play a piece that he likes; and all he ever did for me was to give me a few flowers out of the garden, to trim my hat with. He is very pleasant, and as kind to his sister as he can be, and I like him for that, wouldn't you?"

"Decidedly I would," I replied, looking down at the earnest eyes.

"Claude is going to New York soon," she went on, slowly rolling and unrolling her sash as she spoke, "and Victor, the youngest brother, will go into his father's office in Claude's place. I believe all the sons are lawyers; they study with their father, and then settle in some other place to practise their profession. I think that is a very good plan. Mr. Lecount jokes about it, and says that it is the reason why they are all such good friends with each other. I think, if I had a brother or a sister, I should never wish to part from them at all."

"And yet, Belle, I live far away from my mother and only sister, not because we could not agree together, but because circumstances have rendered it necessary. A large family, like your friends the Lecounts, could hardly find enough to do in a little dull village' like this. You will miss Claude very much, will you not?"

"No, not much, I have so many things to occupy my time; and then he says he will be able to run up every Saturday night, and spend Sunday at home."

"And his brother that was here, just now?"

"Oh! I never saw him until yesterday; he very seldom comes home, he has so much to attend to in Philadelphia."

"Have they ever showed any curiosity about you?" I asked.

"They never ask me any questions. Miss Wilmer, when she introduced me to them, told them that I was an orphan under Mr. Masters' guardianship, and they have never tried to discover any thing about me—they are too polite. I wonder what they would think if they knew all?" The poor child blushed painfully and trembled visibly. Was it possible, I thought, that, in spite of her silence and gayety, the past with all its misery was weighing on her heart?

"You must not think of those things," I said gently; "look upon all those past troubles as trials sent to you for your own future good; there is no shame attached to your part in them, and you must never allow yourself to fret for what was inevitable. Some day you will see why you were tried, and never cease to acknowledge the great blessings you enjoy at present, and the great field for doing good that your wealth and position will throw open to you in the future."

"And do you think I ever will be able to be of use in the world? At present I am more like a wax flower under glass than any thing else. Mrs. Masters frets if I get my feet damp, and Mr. Masters watches me as if he feared every breeze would carry me off."

"Mr. Masters has taken a great responsibility on himself, and I can't blame him for being over-careful of you."

"John, here are Mr. and Mrs. Masters coming up the road!" cried my sister at the door.

Away flew Miss Ferris out of the house and down

5

the garden path. I followed leisurely, and found Mr.
Masters breathless from the embrace she had given him,
and Mrs. Masters undergoing a like greeting. Mr.
Masters nearly shook my hand off, and, in the midst of
declarations and exclamations of delight, informed me
that I always arrived at the right time, and that he had
the most wonderful piece of news to tell us.

"But, I won't say a word until after tea, and then,
when we are all together, you shall have it. It will take
more breath than I am possessed of at present, owing
to the hill and this saucy young lady on my arm." The
"saucy young lady" pulled his face down and gave
him another kiss and a merry smile. It was a pleasant
sight to witness the happy confidence existing between
the old couple and their bright little ward.

Tea over, we waited patiently for the "wonderful
news," and Mr. Masters, having taken from his pocket a
large European letter, laid it before him on the table
and introduced its contents, thus:

"Now, Miss Ferris, here is a letter, full of long
expressions of grief and trouble, which announces
your death and funeral, and even a model, in pen and
ink, of your grave and tombstone, with the inscrip-
tion complete. What do you think of that, little
Belle?" and he kissed her gently, for her face had
become suddenly grave with surprise and fear at the
words.

"Well, what will that woman undertake next?"
asked my mother, recovering first from her surprise.

Whereupon Mr. Masters opened the letter, and gave it to us at full length. After a minute account, in the most high-flown language, of all she had done to benefit her dear child's health, she gave a history of her last hours and death, which she described as having been most touchingly serene and happy. She also enclosed a copy of the doctor's certificate of death, and all the bills incidental to the mournful event, which was supposed to have taken place in Florence. In conclusion, she begged Mr. Masters to communicate the tidings to Mr. Parker; as she had found it impossible, in the state of grief she was in, to write any more on the subject. She also trusted the charge of every thing to them, knowing that they would do right by her in her desolate condition; and, as she intended remaining abroad until her health should be entirely reëstablished, she hoped they would communicate with her frequently, and let her understand, as far as she was able to do so, how her affairs were managed. Mr. Masters laughed heartily at the concluding injunction.

"I should like to know what part of the management of her affairs she couldn't comprehend. Why, she can tell you to a fraction what her interest should be, and as for making investments, she is as sharp as a needle in that line."

"Where is Mr. Parker at present?" I asked.

"In New York, of course. I need not tell you how astounded he was at my news, but you will be amused when I inform you that, feeling deeply for Mrs. Ferris

and the loneliness of her position, he is making preparations to join her in her retirement at Florence; the
ostensible reason for the trip being, the necessity of
setting before her and explaining to her the exact state
of her late husband's affairs. Of course, I appreciate the
great necessity of the voyage, and I have no doubt but
that we shall receive wedding-cards before six months
are over."

"I do believe that this affair has taken ten years off
Mr. Masters' age," remarked his wife, with a bright
smile on her face. "Before it happened, he was always
complaining; now there is nothing too difficult for him
to undertake, and he is as active and bright as I ever
remember him."

"Well, little one, what do you think of it all?" Mr.
Masters asked, turning to Miss Ferris.

She had been sitting, listening attentively to his
story, her eyes raised to his face; now she colored and
looked down.

"What do I think?" she repeated; "I think that,
only for Doctor Wilmer, part of that letter might be true.
When he first met me at Niagara, I should have welcomed death gladly in any shape, as a blessed release.
He is the only one here who can realize the truth of
what I say; he knows what I was suffering, and how
his kind words and anxious care alone gave me the
courage to wish to live."

"My dear child, don't think of that time, if it makes
you nervous," Mrs. Masters said, softly, putting her arms

round the trembling girl. "Come with me, and show
me those wonderful orange-blossoms that you have
written so much about; I don't know when I saw any
growing on the tree."

"They are curiosities, and quite a credit to Belle, I
can assure you," my sister said, rising and following the
other ladies into the adjoining room.

"I am sorry I said any thing about that letter before
Belle," Mr. Masters remarked, turning to me, "but I
had no idea that it would have such an effect on her.
How very nervous she is! the least allusion to those old
troubles seems to recall them to her so vividly."

"It would be much better not to refer to them
at all before her," I answered. "Seeing me was sufficient novelty for one day, and, for some years at least
to come, any over-excitement will have a very bad
effect upon her. I dread the idea of a meeting between her and Mrs. Ferris, although I suppose it will
be necessary."

"Yes, for this reason Mrs. Ferris enclosed an obit-
uary notice for me to send to the different morning
papers. Of course, I don't intend helping her scheme
by doing any thing of the kind; but as soon as she is
able, if she has not done so already, she will write to
her friends in New York a full account of this imaginary
affair; and as I can't attempt to contradict it for ten
months, it will of course be fully credited, and all the
acquaintances she ever had will have time to hear the
report, talk it over, and make it an established fact in

their minds. The only thing to be done is just to invite
all these people to the house as soon after Belle comes
of age as possible, and contrive a meeting between the
two; otherwise I shall have difficult work to establish
her identity. You see, I couldn't prove it, I had not
seen her in six years; and no doubt they have laid their
plans so as to be ready for any movement that I might
make against this fabrication. Your testimony and my
own recollection of the child are all I have to work
upon. We must attempt strategy; and if Mrs. Ferris
in her surprise should prove our assertion true, why, the
whole affair would be settled—I am pretty sure she
would retire from the field without a word, quite
satisfied if we did not prosecute her for her actions,
although I think such a case would stand alone in the
records of crime."

"They would have to frame new laws of punishment
to meet it," I replied. "But if we only succeed in establishing Miss Ferris's identity, and restoring her to
her proper position in perfect health, I believe we can
be satisfied to leave Mrs. Ferris in the hands of a higher
power. Such people don't die without their sins coming home to them in some form, even if the retribution
is unknown to any but themselves."

"You are right, Doctor Wilmer, quite right;
though I have felt a strong desire to retaliate on that
woman some of the misery that she made my poor
friend's child undergo. However, as you say, ten
months from now we can turn round and laugh at her;

and if she has any conscience—which is an open question—we will leave her to its mercy."

Having shaken hands over our agreement, the honest old gentleman lit his evening cigar and strolled out on the lawn to enjoy it, while I rejoined the ladies in the parlor.

CHAPTER V.

I FOUND that the two brothers, Louis and Claude Lecount, had arrived, and were using all the arguments in their power to induce my sister to allow Miss Ferris to join a large picnic which was to come off the ensuing week. While Mr. Louis sat near her, enlarging on the beauties of the proposed picnic ground, and the very agreeable company invited, Mr. Claude leaned over the piano and explained his wishes to Miss Ferris, who sat trifling with some music and listening attentively, with sparkling eyes raised to his face. Having gone through an introduction to Mr. Claude, I took a chair near Mrs. Masters, and, while hearing the discussion, surveyed my supposed rival.

He was taller and handsomer than his brother; more graceful, if that were possible, and possessed that easy elegance of manner, that faculty of always knowing exactly what to say or do at the right moment, which, some people declare, springs from self-conceit and pride, but which, I think, is inborn and belongs to certain persons naturally. At least, I have known many to spend their lives trying to acquire it, while the envied possessors of it remained unconscious of their rich gift. However that may be, Mr. Claude Lecount was very much at home in my mother's house, and appeared to be on terms of the closest friendship with Miss Ferris. Occasionally she would throw me a bright glance, which I observed him follow with surprise; and when at last, driven from want of further excuses to appeal to me, my sister turned and asked me to decide the question, he put down the music he was holding, and regarded me with a look in which curiosity and dislike were largely blended.

"I don't think it would be quite sensible," I answered. Of course it was a new idea to them, the refusing such a pleasure to a young girl; and knowing that it would be impossible to explain the motives controlling us, I made every allowance for their evident disappointment and wounded feelings.

"Miss Belle is anxious to go, and my sisters have made all the arrangements. If you are afraid of her taking cold, Miss Wilmer, I don't think there can be any danger. Pauline is going, and of course will start for home before it becomes damp, and Miss Belle is to ride in the carriage with her."

Mr. Claude Lecount said this with an assured manner, as though it was quite conclusive. Belle twisted her pretty hands together and looked toward my sister.

"Some friends of ours, the Barrows, are coming up

5*

for it," broke in Mr. Louis. I noticed Miss Ferris tremble, and look at me appealingly.

"What 'Barrows' are they?" I inquired, with a quiet gesture, imposing silence on her.

"They live in Sixteenth Street, in New York; Mr. Barrow is a lawyer, and his sons are with him. Are you acquainted with them?"

"No, I am not," I replied; but I could see that Miss Ferris was.

"They are such nice people," Mr. Louis went on, "some of mother's oldest friends, and she has not seen them in years. We expect a great deal of pleasure from their visit, and mother wished very much to make them acquainted with Miss Belle. Miss Barrow will be married next month, and the girls are going down to the wedding."

"Can't you alter the decision?" asked Mr. Claude, turning to Miss Ferris, and speaking in an undertone.

"Doctor Wilmer knows best, and I always do as he says," was the clear, innocent answer.

The two brothers looked at me, and my sister, rising hastily, proposed some music. Mrs. Masters, who had not taken part in the question, joined in the request; and so Miss Ferris sang some solos, and then some duets, in a clear, sweet voice, which harmonized perfectly with Mr. Claude's full tenor. I cannot tell whether admiration or jealousy rose strongest within me—I fear the latter. When at last the gentlemen took their leave, I was in such a state of torture that I could hardly command my voice sufficiently to answer Mr. Masters' remarks on Belle's wonderful love and talent for music.

The next morning, when I rose, I heard the birdlike tones coming to me from the parlor directly under my room, where she was practising. Some of the words were distinct, and it struck me at the time that she sang them with a great deal of expression for one so young. It was Franz Abt's exquisite melody, " When the Swallows Homeward Fly," then new to me, but since become my favorite song. The words,

> " Hush my heart, why thus complain ?
> Thou must too thy woes contain,"

found an answering echo in my heart. After all my struggles and decisions, I came to the conclusion that they had been of no avail. One evening in her company had scattered them all like straws before the wind, and I was as far from peace as ever. I determined to go on to New York, spend some time there seeking distraction in its amusements, and then return to Buffalo, without trusting myself to another visit home. Having come to this heroic resolve, I went down-stairs, and met Miss Ferris in the hall with her hat on her head and a basket and scissors in her hand, about going to cut fresh flowers for the vases. She exclaimed, with delight in every feature of her face, that I must go with her and carry the basket. Half way down the walk she caught my arm, and, looking very grave, asked—

"What am I to do if the Barrows come here and stop at Mrs. Lecount's? They were very intimate with Mrs. Ferris, and she exhibited me to them as if I were a wild animal the day before she took me to that asylum. They would be sure to recognize me; and even my name, if they hear it, will excite their curiosity."

"It is to be hoped that something will detain them in New York for the next ten months; but in case they do arrive, you must stay in-doors and refuse yourself to all visitors. Taking you away for a week, unless it might be down to the city, would be almost as dangerous as remaining here; there are so many returning now from the watering-places, the cars and the boats are all crowded. We must consult Mr. Masters. Does he know this family?"

"That I cannot tell, perhaps not; I don't remember seeing them in the house before papa's death. I think they belong to Mrs. Ferris' set altogether."

It turned out that Mr. Masters had never seen one of the Barrows, and only knew them by reputation. They were probably just as ignorant of his existence; so we concluded to remain at home, and trust that no recognition might occur. That afternoon Miss Ferris went to spend a few hours with her friend, and Mr. Masters and I took a long ride in the country, leaving the three ladies to a social conversation over their knitting. On returning we found an urgent invitation to spend the evening at Mr. Lecount's; so, after tea, to which Miss Ferris did not return, we strolled down there in the twilight.

The house was one of the oldest in the county, and built of stone, strong and substantial enough in material and extent, but with an aspect of decay hanging around it, most observable in the out-houses, which, though very picturesque, hinted at limited means. The garden trees were overgrown, and their branches joined above the path, rendering it quite dark on leaving the open road. The grass was rank on the lawn, the flower-beds so overspread by weeds and tangled vines as to make the plants in them undistinguishable. I had leisure to note these things as we picked our steps slowly over the neglected pathway, and reached at last a long, low piazza, half hidden by a trellis, which was entirely covered with luxuriant vines of various kinds. As we approached, voices were audible; and as we crossed the piazza the fluttering of her white dress drew our attention to Miss Ferris seated on a rustic bench, listening to the low tones of Mr. Claude Lecount, who leaned against the lattice-work. Some rays from the fast-declining sun had penetrated the thick foliage, and were darting about her head and face, bringing out the rich coloring of her hair, and making it shine like threads of gold.

She rose hastily to meet us with an exclamation of pleasure on her lips. I thought her companion hardly liked the interruption. However, he smoothed his forehead and came forward, welcoming us most gracefully. The parlor, which we entered through the low windows opening on the piazza, was a large, square room, filled with massive old-fashioned furniture, placed in such a way as to form little nooks and corners, where two or three persons could sit and converse quite independent of other groups near them. At the far end of it such a little group was gathered round a table, on which a very brilliant lamp was burning. They put aside their various employments as we entered, and rose to receive us.

Mrs. Lecount was a tall, elegant woman, from whom, without a doubt, the sons had inherited their singular beauty and grace. Miss Pauline had resumed her reclining attitude on the sofa with a deep sigh, as if exhausted by the effort she had made in rising; and while answering the various questions concerning her health put to her by my anxious mother and sister, I could perceive the close scrutiny with which she regarded us all in turn.

She was a most beautiful brunette, with bands of shining black hair framing her face, and large almond-shaped eyes, which appeared to darken and lighten according to the varied feelings she was experiencing. That Miss Ferris admired her was most certain; she took her accustomed seat, a low chair, near her friend's sofa, and listened attentively to the conversation that followed.

As I anticipated, they commenced with the picnic. As we had no good reasons with which to meet their combined arguments, I could not wonder at the perplexed glances thrown at me from all sides, particularly from Miss Pauline's searching eyes, when, as on the previous occasion, Miss Ferris again left the decision to me.

During the remainder of the evening I found myself an object of great interest to that young lady. She was evidently trying to place me with regard to Miss Ferris, and felt rather puzzled as to the right I possessed of controlling the latter's actions. Once the picnic subject was dropped, I became silent, and, leaning back in my corner of the sofa, amused myself contemplating the others in the party, and trying to make sense of the various scraps of conversation that reached me. Another lady, Miss Marie Lecount, whom I judged to be the eldest daughter, now joined the circle, and commenced an animated discussion on zephyr wool, double and single, with my sister. Mrs. Lecount and my mother were deep in the mysteries of household economy, and I could easily observe how Miss Pauline was working her plans. Mr. Lecount, a tall old gentleman, with white hair and a kindly manner, was talking politics with Mr. Masters and his son Louis.

Thus the young people were left to themselves, with only Miss Pauline, as it were, to make up the pleasant little group of three. Miss Ferris, from her low seat by the sofa, could pay attention to her friend, and at the same time hear every word addressed to her by Mr. Claude, who occupied the other corner of his sister's sofa. Mr. Louis at last made a diversion in the room, by taking up a flute and proposing some music. His brother escorted Miss Ferris to the piano and turned over her music while she accompanied him in a very pretty duet.

I was listening to it attentively, when a touch from Miss Pauline's fan drew my attention.

"Excuse my seeming rudeness, Doctor Wilmer, but I have been quite ill, and am only now commencing to go about again."

She had changed her seat for one quite close to me, and was gazing earnestly into my face. I answered her, saying, that Miss Ferris had told me about her, and that I had not expected to meet her.

"I had heard so much about you from Belle, I could not resist the temptation of coming down to see you. I believe you have known her a long time, and she speaks of you with such enthusiasm!"

"I remember her since she was quite a little girl," I replied.

"She seems to regard you somewhat as a guardian, or elder brother. Poor little dear! to think she is an orphan, with neither brother nor sister; how sad it appears to me, for I am surrounded by near relatives."

"You have great reasons to feel thankful," I answered; "Miss Ferris' position is a strange, and I hope an uncommon one. However, she is not unhappy, and I think she possesses talents which will in a great measure make up to her for the want of relations."

"I never saw any one so passionately fond of flowers; she and Claude never tire of taking care of them, and as for music, their tastes in it agree perfectly."

I fell into a fit of musing after this last speech. It occurred to me that I too was a great admirer of flowers and music. Before going to college, I had always taken care of my mother's flower-garden. I had planted and watered it, and visions of numberless slips that I had set out, great geraniums and oleanders that I had transplanted, and wreathing clematis and woodbine that I had trained over the windows and porches, rose before my eyes. Then, too, had I not played the organ and led the choir in the village church; and had not more than one of the congregation remarked on the sweetness of my voice, and the clearness of my touch? Looking back, it seemed as though another, and not I, had been the actor in those scenes. The busy years of college-life, and the sharp struggles which succeeded them in the race for reputation and fortune, had almost blotted from my memory the recollections of the dear old days of home and boyhood. Would Mr. Claude Lecount, twelve years hence, after battling with the world and its corroding influences, be as fond of these innocent amusements as he was at present, particularly when pursued in the society of a beautiful, artless girl, whose every impulse was instantly visible in the clear, confiding eyes, and unaffected manner? I doubted the fact; Mr. Claude Lecount was only human. Very few men come out of the conflict with feelings as fresh, with hearts as generous and open, and confidence in their fellow-beings as strong as when they enter the arena of life. And yet Mr. Claude was displaying great wisdom, for surely if there is any earthly power which tends more than another to make a man retain his trust in human nature, it is the love and companionship of a true woman, whether she be his wife, his mother, his sister, or only a tried friend. Therefore I did not blame Mr. Claude for discovering in Miss Ferris the charms that I admired so much, nor did I envy him his advantage of youth; I only felt settling down, as it were, over me, a dull weight of despondency, which I feared I would never be able to shake off. Miss Pauline's voice again broke in upon my reverie.

"You reside altogether in Buffalo, Doctor Wilmer. Do you like it there?"

"Yes, I have become attached to the place and people; it would be like commencing life again to leave my practice there."

"How uncomfortable that must be for your family here! they cannot hope to enjoy much of your society; and then, I should think, as Belle's guardian, you would prefer being nearer to them."

"Do not remain under a false impression, Miss Lecount? I am not guardian to Miss Ferris; Mr. Masters was left trustee of both her and her property, under her father's will."

"That I was aware of, your sister explained it to us; but still I thought you might have something to do with her education or property, along with him."

"Nothing whatever," I answered.

"Then, how very romantic your mutual friendship is! Belle always quotes Dr. Wilmer, your judgment is quite conclusive with her; and hearing your name so frequently made us very curious to meet you, and I certainly expected to see a much older person."

Here Miss Pauline laughed affectedly; and having penetrated her motives, I felt rather amused than otherwise at her last remark.

"I believe I hardly look venerable enough for a Mentor, and I have never tried the position," I said. "No doubt, hearing me referred to very often by my mother and sister, has given Miss Ferris the habit of doing the same thing."

I saw that Miss Pauline suspected an unusual understanding between Miss Ferris and me, an idea which the former had unconsciously helped to forward by so constantly mentioning my name. The secret of our mutual confidence, however, was one not easy to penetrate, and Miss Pauline's attacks remained unheeded though understood.

After the music was ended, the conversation became more general. I particularly noticed that, in speaking, the whole family mentioned " Belle and Claude " in the same breath, as if they were understood to be equally interested in the subject under discussion. It annoyed and pained me. I could see clearly how the others present were quietly forwarding Miss Pauline's scheme, and I knew how easily a young girl, completely withdrawn from the world, might be induced to engage herself to a gentleman, fascinating and handsome, like Mr. Claude. Once her word was passed, she, so truthful and conscientious, would not recall the promise given, while too young to understand the wants and yearnings of her own nature.

I determined to talk the matter over with my sister, but was I the one to do it? Could I conscientiously say that my feelings were disinterested? Was I a proper judge of Mr. Claude Lecount, his heart, and his motives? If Miss Pauline saw that her brother's happiness depended on the love of this young girl, so strangely thrown among them, was she not only doing a sister's part in trying to secure that happiness to him? Had she not a perfect right to view in me a dangerous rival, to be met and defeated with the weapons of artifice, so powerful in the hands of a woman of depth and shrewdness?

I think that from that first evening she was thoroughly convinced that the fascination of her great beauty would have no effect on me. In a measure she read me as truly as I did her; only that, where I understood her whole position and its advantages, she could not comprehend mine. She could not penetrate the powerful scruple which prevented me from meeting her brother on equal grounds, namely, my great claim on Miss Ferris' gratitude. Therefore, the very cause which held me back, quiet and constrained, effected in her the greatest uneasiness. She could not attribute bashful-ness to me, and my silent, undemonstrative manner gave the impression of the consciousness of power possessed.

On rising to take our leave, she promised to return the visit as soon as her health would permit; and Mr. Claude, taking up his hat, drew Miss Ferris' arm through his own, and they sauntered before us down the path. It was some distance to the gate, and when we reached it, he was bidding her good-by, holding her hand in his, while he addressed to her some earnest, parting words. He wished us " good-night" pleasantly, apologized for not going all the way with us, and, raising his hat, returned up the path toward the house. Miss Ferris took Mr. Masters' arm and remained silent for some time, a very unusual thing with her.

"A very nice young fellow," Mr. Masters at length ejaculated. " What do you say, Belle ? "

"I like him," was the quiet answer.

"I wonder he didn't escort you home, he used to do it," my sister remarked in a style peculiar to herself, half serious, half satirical.

" He is tired, and besides he has to pack his trunk, he is going to New York to-morrow," Miss Ferris explained in a low tone.

"New York ! " my sister exclaimed; " why, he was so anxious about that picnic, that he couldn't talk of any thing else last night."

" I know that, but he says that it has lost all its attraction for him since I am not going, and so the sooner he begins business the better for himself."

"Dear me, I am sorry; but indeed, Belle, it would never do for us to give our consent to your going; the risk is too great, isn't it, John?"

"Decidedly so!" I answered.

"What a beauty Miss Pauline is!" remarked Mrs. Masters; "I never saw such a perfect brunette. Joseph, we must invite her down to the city this winter, and she will grow accustomed to us and our ways. Then, next winter when we have our pet home, perhaps she will be willing to stay some time with us. Our house would be very lonely after her own."

"Not if we had the doctor on with us," Mr. Masters replied, with an arch glance at me. "I think she took quite a fancy to you, and possibly you may return the compliment; certainly neither of you paid much attention to any one else in the room."

"I don't wonder at any one admiring her; she might turn an older and wiser head than even Doctor Wilmer's," Mrs. Masters went on.

Between admiring Miss Pauline, and arranging a fishing expedition for the next day, we at last reached the house.

The lamp in the sitting-room was turned quite low, and, before my sister could reach it to raise it, Miss Ferris had said good-night and was leaving the room.

"Oh! Belle, don't go yet; get some cake for us. Why! you have been crying," exclaimed my sister, as the light suddenly flashed on Miss Ferris' face.

"Why! little one, you surely would not cry about

a picnic party," Mr. Masters said, putting his arm round her waist. "Only wait till you are twenty, and you shall have picnics by the dozen, and Mr. Claude at every one of them."

"I was not crying about the picnic," Miss Ferris said in a low tone, at the same time hiding her face on Mr. Masters' shoulder.

He kissed her gently. "Well, well, pet, whatever the trouble is, better go and sleep now, and forget it all until morning; perhaps it won't seem so terrible then."

He let her go, watching her out of the room and up the stairs, walking in a slow manner, not at all natural.

"It can't be possible that Mr. Claude has stolen our pet's heart," Mr. Masters said, closing the door and addressing us all at once, with a puzzled expression in his face.

"It wouldn't be at all surprising," answered Mrs. Masters. "He is so handsome, and you all must have noticed the attention he paid her this evening. A stranger would have said at once that they were engaged."

"Dear me, dear me!" exclaimed my sister, looking horrified; "how silly I have been!"

"Not at all, my dear Miss Wilmer, not at all. The young man lacks nothing but money, and if he has any talent he won't be long without it. In this country that is no objection, and besides, she has plenty. We have no right to quarrel with what appears unavoidable. There is nothing to be said against the young man or his family. The only thing I wish is, that no engagement be entered into until after she comes of age. If possible, Miss Wilmer, try and make her agree to that arrangement. They are both young enough to wait a few months, although Sallie and I had our minds made up before she was eighteen."

"Yes, Joseph," Mrs. Masters answered, pressing his hand in hers, "and I don't think we ever regretted it."

"And we hadn't ten thousand a year ready to step into, had we, little woman? Well, if we only live to see Arthur Ferris' child happy, we may die contented. There is one thing certain: this young man may suspect that she is rich, but he cannot be sure of it, and, from what I have seen of him, I think he is disinterested in his love."

"Belle is quite worthy of being loved for herself alone," said my sister, "but at the same time, the Lecounts are shrewd enough, when they think of all the different little things they have heard and seen, to suspect that Belle is either rich in her own right, or is considered your heiress. Her dress, and the luxuries of all kinds that you have surrounded her with, would justify the conclusion. However, she is her own mistress in the affair; no one here will prejudice her either in his favor or against him. Of course, he will have a strong friend in his sister Pauline, and if you think it best, we might by degrees break off the intimacy."

"Not at all," was Mr. Masters' answer. "Let the girl's own heart decide the matter. Of course she has as yet seen nothing of the world; she has had no opportunity of comparing this Mr. Lecount with other young men equally well educated and fascinating; but the trouble is this: once in her own house, surrounded by new friends and old ones, she will be a mark for every brainless young fop, in search of a rich wife, that she may meet. New York abounds with them at present— gay, thoughtless fellows, **brought up with** expensive tastes and extravagant habits by their silly parents, without any legitimate business, and afraid of soiling their white hands with hard work. Why, when they do succeed in obtaining a position in a bank or a mercantile house, the salary don't suffice to support them. 'A rich wife' is the watch-word at present. When I was young, a man felt proud when he knew that he could support another and himself comfortably. A wife then was a precious prize, to be worked for and won by the use of the talents and energy that a man possessed in himself. If his home were only two rooms, they were his, and she was mistress of them. Now, all that is changed. Our young men are quite willing to marry before they can honestly support themselves, and 'live home,' as they term it, with their wife's father and mother. And some of them think it quite a condescension on their part to accept a comfortable home, in exchange for the trifling attentions they bestow on their wives, when it suits them to be kind and thoughtful. I don't like to think of giving Belle to one of these aristocratic idlers." Mr. Masters had grown quite irate in his anticipations of Miss Ferris' suitors, and walked up

6

and down the room with heavy steps, whilst delivering his opinion of the young men with whom he was in the habit of meeting.

"Don't borrow trouble, Joseph," remarked his wife. "Mr. Lecount, at least, cannot be quite so objectionable as the young men you are speaking of, and Belle might go farther and fare worse."

"Belle has a great development of firmness," said my sister, smiling; "she will not marry Claude Lecount unless she likes him, and up to the present time I don't think such an idea has ever come into her head. Perhaps we had better wait a little before we trouble our minds about Belle's husband. She is as yet a mere child, and likely to continue so for some time to come."

"I hope you may be right," said Mr. Masters, shaking his head prophetically, "but her manner to-night was not very childish."

"Ah, well, Joseph," said Mrs. Masters, as she lit her lamp, and was leaving the room, "these things are beyond us; we must wait and be patient."

The next morning, long before Miss Ferris was accustomed to make her appearance, Mr. Masters and I had started on our fishing excursion. It was deserving of the title, for we fished all day and caught nothing but sun-burned necks and hands. So we set out for home, voting the expedition a complete failure. Miss Ferris was just taking leave of her friend Miss Pauline, as we passed the Lecounts' gate. We stopped and had a merry greeting from them, and some very dangerous

glances from the oriental eyes, which, though aimed at
me, struck Mr. Masters. That good-natured gentleman
immediately commenced weaving in his brain a wonderful romance, in which I was to be the hero and Miss
Pauline the heroine. That young lady was arranging
when she would come and spend a day with us, and as
we turned away I offered Miss Ferris my arm. But
she had taken Mr. Masters' hastily, and was making
some absurd remarks to him on the amount of fish he
had caught. Her manner was curious, a forced gayety
and petulance, under which I detected a nervousness
and a tendency to the old excitability. I lingered behind them pondering over the change in Miss Ferris'
manner toward me. Even my presence made her act
unnaturally with her guardian. The light laugh, and
the tones of her voice that reached me, might deceive
another, particularly one so unsuspicious as honest Mr.
Masters. They did not mislead me. My innocent, impulsive darling was trying to act a part, trying to
appear happy, when, in truth, she was troubled and
miserable. I determined to find out from her what it
was that caused her uneasiness, feeling sure that she
would tell me, seeing that a few days before she had
opened her heart to me in the old confidential way. To
my great surprise she avoided me during the remainder
of the evening, refusing to walk with me; and having
found some intricate needle-work, she sat down near
Mrs. Masters, and became so interested in it as to appear indifferent to the general conversation around her.

Once, having dropped a ball of wool, I picked it up and handed it to her. She colored as she met my eyes fixed on her face, but made no remark, and more puzzled than ever I resumed my conversation with Mr. Masters.

The possibility of the Barrows arriving troubled Mr. Masters exceedingly, and he determined to remain and mount guard over Miss Ferris during their stay in the neighborhood.

"Yes," said my sister, "you can take Belle off early in the mornings and explore the country, and John and mother may entertain them if Pauline brings them here. Perhaps it would be better to call and invite them to the house so as to ward off suspicion, Belle's absence will then appear accidental."

"The task of entertaining them will fall on you," I answered, "for I shall leave for home to-morrow."

In the general surprise that followed my announcement, and amid exclamations of dismay and disgust at my obstinacy, Miss Ferris escaped from the room.

"Poor Belle," said my mother, after I had overcome their united arguments, and decided upon leaving by the early train on the following morning—"poor Belle, she has enjoyed very little of your society, after all. The poor child didn't know what to say to you, and so she left the room without a word."

"John, you are such an obstinate creature," went on my sister, "what do your patients think of you?"

"They think as I do, that, being strong, and having

seen you all well and happy, I ought to be in Buffalo attending to them and their whims."

"What could have come to Belle this evening? Her work is ruined. What could the child have been thinking of?" exclaimed my sister, lifting up Miss Ferris's needle-work, and holding it for Mrs. Masters to inspect.

"Oh, Mr. Claude Lecount, without a doubt," replied Mr. Masters, shaking his head; "the child is in love as sure as I am alive," and the old gentleman went up-stairs, humming some lines from "Love's Young Dream."

I opened the window and strolled up and down the piazza in the cool night air, trying to realize my position and reason myself into the belief that I was contented with it. My visit home had not helped me to bear my disappointment any better. It had only served to make my love for Miss Ferris more intense, and to increase my jealousy and doubts of her feeling for me. In trying to account for the change in her manner toward me, I never thought of how much my own conduct had to do with it. I forgot that I had become cold and distant, and I blamed her for the loss of the old confidence and warm affection that had existed between us. I attributed her reserve and avoidance of me to the new feeling for Claude Lecount, which I believed was absorbing all her thoughts. Jealousy had so taken possession of me that I seized upon every trifle, a glance or a word that had passed between them, as

proofs of her love for him, and attached no importance
to her assertions to the contrary, made on the first day
of my visit. I argued that she was not conscious of her
own sentiments for him then, but that his departure and
absence had caused her to realize them, and that so
suddenly, as to render her unable to conceal from us
their effect upon her. In my blind jealousy I made up
my mind to leave her with our estrangement unex-
plained, forgetting that by so doing I was playing into
Miss Pauline's hands, and leaving her in possession of
the whole field. Deprived of my advice, Miss Ferris
would naturally turn to her for consolation; and while
still hurt with me, it would be an easy task for Miss
Pauline to instil into the innocent mind a doubt of me
and my sincerity. Once doubted, could not all my
words and acts be misconstrued? I never gave these
things a thought, I only hugged to my heart my own
trouble, and determined to return to my work, call
pride and indifference to my aid, and drown all recollection of my own romance in the busy wear and tear
of every-day life.

I was about to enter the house, when a low sob
struck on my ears, and, turning in the direction from
which it came, I caught a glimpse of a white dress fluttering in the air. There was an old rustic bench in
that part of the garden, and hurrying toward it I found
Miss Ferris seated on it. She was crying passionately;
her face hidden against her hands, which were clasped
round the twisted branch that formed the side of the

bench. My first impulse was to put my arms around
her and pet her, as I would a spoiled child of six years,
but I remembered Mr. Claude Lecount, and realized
that she was no longer a child, but a woman who possessed a more than ordinary depth of feeling and sensitiveness.

She started as I spoke to her, and, raising her head,
showed me a pale face, with sad, tearful eyes, and
quivering lips. She ceased sobbing at once, but trembled visibly, when I drew her arm through mine and
led her toward the house, telling her the danger she
ran of contracting a heavy cold. I did not dare to
question her as to the cause of her grief, feeling that I
had no right to seek her confidence in a matter where
her love was concerned, unless she offered it voluntarily.
I told her to confide in Mr. Masters, and tell him what
troubled her, assuring her that he thought only of her
happiness, and would do every thing in his power to
secure it. She appeared to listen to my advice, but
made no remark that could give me an idea of the current of her thoughts. She did not so much as allude to
my intended departure, but I could see in the moonlight
that her face wore an expression such as I had never
before seen on it. Her lips were compressed, and the
sad look in her eyes had given place to a quiet, cold
expression, denoting self-control and calculation. Her
whole manner reminded me of what she had been fast
growing into before I met her at Niagara, and shook
her, by my interest in her and the force of a strong will,

out of the dull apathetic despair that was stealing over her so sadly.

Hers was no common nature. Joined to ardent affections and quick impulsiveness, she possessed a quiet, cautious, unsuspected firmness, which, if exerted, could entirely control the passions which appeared on the surface, and seemed to denote her true disposition. Finding it impossible to gain her confidence, and afraid to demand an explanation of her coldness, lest I should forget myself and let her see my own heart, I took leave of her on reaching the house, where we had found my sister, lamp in hand, about making a search for us. For a moment, while her hand lay in mine, she gave me a glance, bright and searching, as if she felt inclined to tell me something, but either my face or her own thoughts made her recall the desire, and, having wished me a safe trip, she left us standing in the hall together. I was disappointed, and my sister was astonished.

"How strange Belle looks, and how very unnaturally she acts! John, dear, do you think she is quite well? don't you feel anxious about her? Where did you find her? I went in to see if she was asleep, and, when I missed her, you can't tell what a feeling of dread came over me. The idea of her going out in the damp air in her thin dress! I declare, for the last three days she has been a perfect enigma to me. Can you understand her?"

"Not very well, unless, as Mr. Masters says, she is in love, and has suddenly become a wise little woman,

instead of a bright, spoiled child. Another thing, the
only childhood she knew was over before she was six
years old. From that time until she came here, she
was denied all childish pleasures, and forced to think
and reason far beyond her strength. I suppose the old
habit of thinking and fretting comes easy to her, now
that Mr. Claude's attentions have given her subject for
meditation."

"I think you take it too quietly, John," replied my
sister, looking still more anxious. "If she don't improve, I shall send for you, and I wish you would put
off your return home, and stay with us a few days
longer. I am very uneasy about her."

"You must see," I said, "that my presence has no
good effect upon her. I think, on the contrary, that it
tends to increase her trouble."

"And yet, John, at one time you were every thing
to her."

It was well that my sister was too much engaged
with the lamp at that moment to look at me. My face
might have told her a secret. I turned away, that she
should not observe the effect of her words, and she mistook the movement for one of impatience.

"Well, well, John, since you are so anxious to be
back at your work, I shall not try to keep you from it;
only remember," and here my sister put her arms round
my neck and looked into my eyes, "that mother grows
older every day, and longs to have you near her. I

6*

wish you would think seriously of trying to establish yourself here, or else, as you are determined not to marry, why not save some money, and retire from your profession? you could find enough here to amuse you, without attending to business."

"You think so," I answered; "but I know better. I have enough now to satisfy my own tastes and wants, but I should be miserable without my every-day work to occupy my mind. Besides, I love my profession, and I shall never give it up until I feel myself unable to practise it faithfully. I will, however, see what can be done, so that after Miss Ferris comes of age we may be together again."

"Yes, John, we have no one but mother; let us study only her comfort while she is spared to us."

After my sister had kissed me good-night, I began to think of all she had said, and thought very seriously of it, too. In Buffalo I had far greater chances of making a name and reputation than in a small village, where, instead of many, I was likely to have only one rival to compete with. Still, a doctor can find subjects for his skill, and meet with new and strange cases in any field where he may choose to employ his talents and use his knowledge, whether it be among the narrow, dirty streets of a crowded city, or among the scattered houses of a country village. Suffering and misery are about equally distributed in both; and where poverty and ignorance may exist on the one side, pride and meanness will balance them on the other. The "bubble reputation" had lost its principal charms for me. To enjoy a thing that we earn, in the true sense of the word, is impossible, unless there is some one near us who can appreciate, not only the labor and its reward, but also the laborer. Hereafter, I might work for the work's sake, but not for the added respect and fame that success should bring me.

I determined to establish myself near my mother, if not in her own village, as soon as Miss Ferris should be safe in New York. The next morning that young lady did not come down to our early breakfast, so I left the house without seeing her. I had been home but a few days when my sister wrote to me, to say that "Belle had taken a heavy cold that night before I left, and had been confined to her room ever since." The next news was, that, while Miss Ferris was still sick, the picnic had taken place. The Barrows had arrived in good time, and the whole affair had been most enjoyable and satisfactory. Owing to the care Miss Ferris required, my sister had remained at home, and had not met any of the people from New York. Pauline, however, had been with Belle every day, and had read Claude's letters aloud for her. They were very witty, and contained graphic descriptions of all that passed of much moment in the metropolis.

Before Mr. Masters went home, Belle had confided to him the fact that Claude had asked her to be his wife, and she had told him that she had never thought of such a thing. Claude, however, pleaded hard to be

allowed to address her, and wished to correspond with
her. She had been too timid to promise such a favor,
without her guardian's sanction, and, as Mr. Masters did
not approve of it, Claude had urged it no further, con-
tenting himself with sending her long messages in his
sister's letters. Mr. Masters' opinion and my sister's
agreed. Both were sure that Belle was in love with
the young man, but had not realized it at the time
he proposed, which explained her curious answer. I
gathered from all the accounts I heard, that Miss Ferris
and Miss Pauline were more intimate than ever, and
that, whenever Mr. Claude paid a visit home, his attentions to the former were exclusive. My sister thought
that Miss Ferris was pleased and flattered by all this
devotion, but felt quite. sure that Mr. Claude had not
risked another proposal. She would tell me at times
that "Belle appeared to be more timid and retiring
every time she met Claude," and in the next letter I
would read a long account of a sleighing-party, for
which he had run up from the city, and at which Belle
had looked prettier and enjoyed herself more than any
one else.

Another time he had arrived with some beautiful
skates of an entirely new design, and was going to
teach Belle how to use them. In spite of the bitter
pain these reports caused me, I read them over and
over again, trying to find in the descriptions of Miss
Ferris's manner something on which to build fresh hopes.
I was unsuccessful. My sister concluded that Belle's

love for Mr. Claude deepened daily, and Mr. Masters wrote fine reports of the young man's character and business qualifications.

So time rolled by—days, weeks, and months—until early in the summer, when Mr. Masters received the long-expected announcement. Mrs. Ferris and Mr. Parker had been married at the chapel of the American embassy in Paris, and were about setting out for Switzerland, where they proposed remaining for some months. This intelligence made Mr. Masters feel quite easy in his mind, and I heard soon after that my sister and Miss Pauline were on a visit at his house for a special purpose. In view of the fifth of September, now drawing near, a day ardently longed for by the whole band of conspirators against Mrs. Parker, Mr. Masters was refitting his house to suit the tastes of the young people whose pleasure lay so near his heart.

He intended giving a large party on that night, to which should be invited every friend and acquaintance of the late Mr. Ferris. Miss Pauline's taste was most exquisite, my sister informed me, and Mrs. Masters was delighted with all her suggestions. As my presence might be necessary on that occasion, I made my arrangements accordingly, although anticipating more pain than pleasure.

I had been for some time negotiating with a gentleman who wished to succeed me in my practice; and my mother already, in imagination, saw me once more living contentedly in my old home. Every one in our little circle had a great joy in anticipation, and each depended on the other for its fulfilment. Mr. Masters was turning his house upside down for Miss Ferris, and mother was employed in the same way for me. Meanwhile my sister and Miss Pauline divided their time between both houses. Miss Ferris was building fairy castles in the air, and I never stopped to analyze my own feelings, once I had determined to sell my practice and return home. My own air-castle being demolished, I concluded to help my mother in realizing hers, by taking possession of my own apartment in it.

I had intended starting for New York before the first of September, so as to be able to help forward Mr. Masters' arrangements, he having urged me to be in good time. However, one of my best friends was taken dangerously ill the very day on which I had intended to leave home, and I determined to remain with him until there were some signs of improvement in his condition. At last I felt that I could leave him with safety, and I started.

I arrived at Mr. Masters' door, valise in hand, on the party night, about half an hour before the guests were expected to assemble. The ladies were in their rooms, the servant informed me, and so I went up to the one prepared for me without seeing any of them, although I anxiously wished for a few moments' conversation with my sister. The parlors were quite full when I descended, and I hastened to pay my respects to the hostess, who stood at the end of them receiving her guests. Many of them were entire strangers to her, and Mr. Masters was introducing Mrs. Barrow when I joined them.

CHAPTER VI.

AN UNEXPECTED GUEST.

HAVING apologized for my late appearance, I turned away in search of some one that I knew. The rooms were certainly most beautiful, and did full credit to Miss Pauline's taste; although I could detect traces of Miss Ferris in the decorations. Her favorite colors, white and violet, were visible wherever they could be introduced, and were particularly noticeable in the arrangement of the flowers. White rosebuds, camelias, and tube-roses, contrasted with heliotropes and violets, were scattered in profusion throughout the rooms. Every ornament that could be made available contained natural flowers, whose beauty and mingled perfumes added to the influence of the scene. From various opinions that reached me as I made my way through the little groups, I gathered that the affair was considered rather strange and mysterious. It was too early in the season, some thought; others wondered at the costliness and display so opposite to the usual taste of Mrs. Masters. Many walked about as though per-

plexed at having received invitations; and those I concluded at once were Mrs. Parker's own friends. At last
I caught a glimpse of a figure which seemed familiar;
but, on having a full view of it, I felt that I was mistaken. Surely my staid sister, with smooth hair and
high dress, never could have so changed her identity.
Yet in spite of the low-necked evening toilet of ruby-
colored silk, covered with lace ornaments, and the hair
arranged in the latest style, all puffs and coils, it was
my sister; for she turned at that moment and came to
welcome me, her face lit up with pleasure. I always
had an idea, amounting to a belief, that my sister's features and figure were very handsome; but that night I
felt that she was indeed a beautiful woman in spite of
her forty years. Time had seemingly forgotten her, or
else it had but little effect on one who led such a quiet,
unselfish life.

My mother next claimed my attention, also looking
very happy; and I laughingly read her a lecture on her
extravagance, for she, who had talked about economy
for years, was fairly gorgeous in black moiré, with point
lace at her neck and wrists. For the first time in my
life I beheld my mother dressed as I had often imagined
her in my boyish visions. It had been my great ambition to give her such luxuries, but she had ever resisted my expressed wishes, saying that it would be wrong
to waste on such unnecessary things the money I earned
so hard. Now, when I declared that I would be obliged
to reconsider my plan of selling out my lucrative prac-

tice, she only said, "Think of the occasion! surely that will warrant the expense."

I must say that I felt very proud of my little mother; when, after some coaxing, she condescended to take a turn round the room, leaning on my arm. The violet ribbons trimming her lace cap gave a brightness to her soft eyes, and I found myself admiring the little hand shaded with lace that lay on my arm. My sister had volunteered no remarks about Miss Ferris, and I had felt myself unequal to asking any questions. I determined to await events patiently; and while still practising that virtue, Miss Pauline Lecount entered the room, hanging on her brother's arm. Her appearance, which was dazzling, caused a general buzz of admiration, which followed her as she swept through the rooms toward a group which I had not before noticed, composed principally of her own family.

Her dress of white tulle, soft and graceful, was interwoven with silver, and trimmed with wreaths of dark-red roses. They caught up the overskirt, peeped from the folds of the corsage twined over the graceful neck and rounded arms, and shone in the black braids of her beautiful hair. Certainly Miss Pauline's taste was beyond question.

The other members of her family were attracting much attention, owing to their decided beauty. I recognized her mother, Miss Marie, and the two young gentlemen to whom I had been introduced. As I was about going over to renew my acquaintance with them, there was a slight confusion in the room, and Mr. Masters called my name. Drawing me to his side, and demanding attention by a slight gesture, he asked to explain the meaning of the party so strangely given. There was a general pressing toward him, and then the guests became silent. His impressive manner affected all in the room.

He commenced, and told in a few touching words the story of Miss Ferris, and the wrongs she had suffered. Laying his hand on my shoulder, he presented me as his witness to the truth of all he had said. He appealed to the old friends of Mr. Ferris, and particularly to those who had known his first wife, to stand by the cause of their orphan child. His voice shook at times with emotion when referring to the sufferings heaped on the innocent girl; and then amid the general hush, caused by astonishment and doubt that followed his words, he left the room. A few moments passed; people began to find words in which to express their surprise. Several declared that they would recognize the child anywhere; others looked at me suspiciously, and spoke of Mrs. Ferris's devotion to her step-child. A general interchange of opinions was going on when Mr. Masters reappeared with Miss Ferris leaning on his arm. Certainly a lovelier vision had never before met their glances. She was dressed in white tulle, that floated around her slight, elegant figure like a cloud. Her beautiful hair lay in long, soft curls on her neck; and the excitement of the affair had brought a delicate

color, like the pink of a sea-shell, into her cheeks. For
a moment there was complete silence, such as had succeeded Mr. Masters' announcement of her existence.
Then a cry of " Belle, little Belle ! don't you remember
me ?" broke the spell. The speaker, a tall, fine-looking
woman, who had stood near me, rushed forward and
caught Miss Ferris in her arms, kissing her fondly.

"You are Mrs. Lester, papa's cousin," was the answer, and it carried conviction to many hearts.

Mrs. Barrow, strange to say, was a strong witness.

"Now that I see her eyes, I am quite sure that it
is she. I saw her the day before she was put into that
terrible asylum."

"Oh yes, mamma, I remember her perfectly," exclaimed Miss Barrow.

It was some time before I had a chance to speak to
the heroine of the evening. She was passed from one
to another, to be kissed and petted like a valuable curiosity. Others seized upon me and plied their questions, which, I am happy to say, they were delicate and
thoughtful enough not to press on Miss Ferris.

I received more invitations to dinner during that
evening than I ever had in all the years of my life put
together. The Lecounts were certainly the most amazed
people I had ever seen. My mother and sister found
themselves surrounded by eager questioners, and gave
their experience of Miss Ferris over and over again to
the delighted listeners. Mr. Masters went about rubbing his face, which was rosy with delight, and endured

any number of congratulations and endless handshaking. For that night he was a greater diplomatist than even Metternich.

Mr. Claude Lecount had at last succeeded in drawing Miss Ferris's arm through his, and was walking in triumph with her around the rooms. His handsome head was bent down, while he poured his delicate compliments into her ears. Her manner was curious, shy, and retiring, as if only half liking this exclusive attention. Her eyes were fastened on her fan, which she opened and shut nervously, and the bright color was mantling in the transparent cheeks. As I turned from observing her, to answer a question of Mrs. Lester's, I caught Miss Pauline's eyes fixed intently on my face. We bowed rather confusedly, each so well understanding the other. I felt that the dark-eyed beauty was a powerful antagonist.

Mr. Masters coming toward me, pointed to the musicians, who had taken their places behind a screen formed of large tropical plants, placed in ornamental boxes, and invited me to commence the dance with Miss Ferris. I found her conversing with Mr. Claude in a little room which had been turned into a conservatory for the evening. She started when she heard my voice, and turned as if to welcome me in the old, impulsive manner. The next minute she had controlled the feeling, and blushing deeply, without raising her eyes to mine, she held out her hand, stammering some words to the effect that she was glad to see me, and was sorry for my detention. Then she glanced toward her companion, and intimated that we had met before. We bowed distantly, and I offered her my arm and made my request.

She blushed painfully, it seemed to me, and, very much embarrassed, looked at Mr. Claude.

"Miss Ferris is engaged to me for this, Doctor Wilmer," said that gentleman, in a tone of ill-concealed triumph.

"The next one, then—I think it is a polka," I went on, looking at Miss Ferris.

She appeared more and more confused.

"Miss Ferris has been kind enough to promise me that one, and the next, also," said Mr. Claude, with sparkling eyes.

"Is your card entirely filled?" I asked.

She detached it from the chain of her fan, and put it in my hand, with fingers that trembled visibly, in spite of her newly-acquired self-control.

I ran my eyes over the list of dances. Mr. Claude's name was down for the first three, and then appeared at intervals on the card; his brother Louis had also secured several. I felt, if any thing, more hurt at the want of good taste exhibited in Mr. Claude's conduct, than at my own disappointment. I wrote my name down for two dances, and then went in search of another partner. If I suffered, they should not be aware of the fact. Miss Ferris's appearance, leaning on Mr. Lecount's arm, was the signal for a general choice of

partners, and I was fortunate enough to secure Miss
Pauline's hand, which she put in mine, with one of her
most fascinating smiles accompanying the favor. In
the course of the dance, which happened to be the
Lancers, I frequently had to take Miss Ferris's hand.
The heightened color and confused manner proved her
consciousness of my presence each time; but her eyes
never once met mine. I had to be content with admiring the long, dark, curling lashes that shaded them so
completely. My brilliant-looking partner rallied me on
my seriousness, and exerted her conversational powers
to entertain me. I confessed to feeling rather tired,
having travelled day and night from Buffalo without
obtaining much rest. When the dance was over, I
joined the group, composed principally of her family,
and answered as well as I could the numberless questions put to me by them. Their interest in Miss Ferris
had increased to a great degree, and Mrs. Barrow was
expressing her opinions of Mrs. Parker in a way any
thing but complimentary to that lady. I was quite
glad to rest during the second dance, and having secured Miss Marie's hand for the third in order, I resigned myself gracefully to the attentions of which I
became the object.

Mr. Masters was exerting himself bravely to complete the effect of his stratagem already so successful,
and Mrs. Masters had as much to do as she could well
attend to, finding partners for the young people. Meanwhile I never turned my eyes toward Miss Ferris with-

out being conscious that Miss Pauline's were on me. I
felt a slight relief when Miss Marie and I had taken our
places in a quadrille; and when not dancing, I followed
the movements of the graceful, fairy-like figure of Miss
Ferris, with eager eyes. She was dancing in the set
next to the one I was in, and, although unconscious of
it herself, was attracting the attention of all in the room
by her beauty.

I had just completed my share of a movement in the
dance, when a piercing scream paralyzed every one in the
company, and, darting through the amazed group, Miss
Ferris flung her arms around my neck, and hid her face
against my shoulder, shivering and gasping with fear.

"She is there! there, by the door!" was all I could
make out from her confused, incoherent words. We all
turned in that direction. There, leaning against the
wall, as if for support, stood Mrs. Parker. Surprise had
for the moment rendered her motionless, but, before we
had time to speak, she advanced rapidly toward me, her
eager, wild eyes fixed on Miss Ferris, and her hands
outstretched, as if to grasp her.

As I caught her arm, she glanced at me for the first
time. The effect was most strange and instantaneous.
The wild glare died out of her eyes, she turned pale, and
would have fallen but for her husband, who rushed forward and caught her as she fainted. Mrs. Masters sent
for restoratives, and while some gathered round Mrs.
Parker, others pressed around Miss Ferris, reassuring
her, and begging of her to compose herself. I was sur-

prised at the effect that the sight of her step-mother had upon her, although no one in the room understood so well the delicacy of her constitution. Without losing consciousness, she became so faint as to be unable to walk without support, and so I carried her into the little conservatory, where I left her with my sister and mother, while I returned to assist Mr. Masters, if necessary.

Mr. Parker had, very sensibly, refused to allow the affair to be discussed that night, not thinking his wife equal to the effort. Mr. Masters proposed a meeting the next day, at which I would be present, and suggested that all claims on both Miss Ferris and the property should be then settled.

Mr. Parker would give no answer until his wife was able to take her share in the discussion, and Mr. Masters agreed, assuring them that he had no intention of prosecuting them for their treatment of Miss Ferris, as such a proceeding would be opposed to the young lady's own wishes. He, however, alluded to the powerful witness he would have in the person of Doctor Wilmer, and the remark had a decided effect. The conversation had been carried on in tones loud enough for all in the room to hear. Mrs. Parker, having regained some of her old firmness, listened attentively, without speaking, as though weighing the principal points in her own mind. Mr. Masters' quiet dignity, as if conscious of the strength of his own position, was a marked contrast to the affected coolness and the attempted arrogance of Mr. Parker. Possibly the man felt thoroughly ashamed of himself

7

for the part he had played in the affair, which, dramatic as it might appear to many, proved very nearly tragic to one of the actors in it.

Mrs. Parker's feelings, on finding herself surrounded by the very persons among whom she had intended to reside on terms of friendship, may be imagined but not described. She had to look only in the faces present, to know in what estimation they held her. With them her power was lost forever. A sigh of relief followed her as she left the room for her carriage, and then every one commenced giving his opinions on the whole affair, which certainly could not have happened more opportunely. No greater proof of Miss Ferris's identity could have been given, and her triumph and Mrs. Parker's punishment had been effected simultaneously.

From what we afterward learned, the circumstance was easily explained. Mr. and Mrs. Parker had returned from Europe the evening before, and had taken the earliest occasion to call on Mr. Masters. Being in dinner dress, the servant had naturally mistaken them for invited guests, and had at once ushered them into the room, causing a scene as strange as it was unexpected. It had not the effect of breaking up the party, and after supper every thing wore its usual aspect. Miss Ferris took my advice, and remained quiet during several dances, but I could hardly approach her at those times owing to the number surrounding her, and so all hopes of a conversation were over. It happened that the dances for which she was engaged to me were the ones that I had prohibited as too exciting, and instead of having her company to myself while they were in progress, I had to share it with Mr. Claude and Miss Pauline, as neither of them would think of dancing when she had to remain quiet. At every turn I found myself met and defeated by my smiling antagonist in white and red, and certainly her devotion to her brother was most admirable. It was an early hour in the morning when the last carriage left the door. The young ladies did not appear at breakfast, being "too tired to think of such a thing," my sister told me.

My stock of patience was large, and I read the papers in the library, wandered about the parlors, settled matters with my mother and sister, listened to their plans—they were projecting a great shopping expedition, from which I begged to be excused, not caring particularly whether the new curtains were crimson or black—and killed time to the best of my ability until two o'clock. That was the usual hour for luncheon, and I waited for the young ladies before descending to the dining-room.

Mr. Masters, who had been busy in the library all the morning collecting papers relating to Miss Ferris and her property, now came in with a note just received from Mr. Parker.

"Just as I suspected—she is taking time to rally her forces," he exclaimed; "they cannot make any appointment now, as Mrs. Parker is quite sick. Well, we must not allow Belle outside the door, without two of us at least near her; and after lunch I am going to search for the register of her mother's marriage, and her own birth. That woman has every paper in her possession, and she may deny Belle's age. I must have a lawyer's advice on the matter, and the quicker we collect our documents the better."

"John is waiting for the girls," said my sister, amused at my impatience.

"So Miss Pauline is bashful," laughed Mr. Masters, with a side glance at his wife. He rang the bell. "Tell the young ladies that we are waiting."

"If you please, sir, they won't be down; they had breakfast brought up to them late," was the servant's answer.

Mr. Masters laughed, and enjoyed his lunch more than I did. We were more fortunate in what we had undertaken outside the house. The doctor's book was at our service, and the church register was perfectly clear. The lawyer took copies of all the papers necessary, and gave it as his opinion that we would meet with no opposition from Mrs. Parker. Mr. Masters returned home in high glee, and we found the family party assembled in the parlor. Mr. Claude, having a standing invitation to dinner, was on duty beside the piano, where Miss Ferris was trying over some new music. We told of our successful search, and were complimented on our wisdom. I went over to Miss Ferris.

"I hope you are not very tired after last night. You are unused to so much excitement."

"Not very," she answered, "but you must be strong. Pauline heard you going out this morning before eight o'clock."

"Did she, indeed?" I asked.

"Yes; I thought you would have slept later, after such tiresome travelling. We both wondered what important business could call you out at that hour."

"And what have you been occupied with all day?" I asked.

"With nothing of any use. Pauline darkened the rooms, and made me sleep very late. She was afraid I would be sick after what happened last night, and, indeed, I am sure I acted very foolishly; but you can't imagine how frightened I was, when I looked up and met Mrs. Parker's eyes fastened on me, they were so wild and wicked, and the whole thing was so sudden and unexpected."

"I can understand your feelings very well. It would take a person with stronger nerves than you possess, to bear such a shock with coolness," I replied.

She looked up at me as if relieved of some doubt, and her face brightened.

"I was afraid you thought me both silly and affected."

"Did I ever say or do any thing that could lead you to believe that I had such an opinion of you?" I asked.

She flushed, and was about answering, when Miss Pauline's voice, close beside us, inquired—

"Belle, love, did you speak to Doctor Wilmer about the concert?"

"I never thought of it," was the answer.

I turned to look at my fair antagonist, in white muslin and crimson ribbons, who did not scruple to use deceit in gaining her ends. She at once described the objects of the concert to which they were going that evening, with her two brothers; and Mr. Masters, joining the group, proposed that we should all go in a party, if there was any thing worth hearing to be sung.

At dinner, and at the concert afterward, Miss Ferris was completely monopolized by the two gentlemen, and I devoted myself to Miss Pauline and her sister. The two young ladies were to spend a month with Miss Ferris, as Mr. Masters was afraid of her becoming homesick if deprived of all her friends at once. My sister and mother intended going home the next day, much to the disappointment of our kind host, who was never happier than when completely surrounded by company. I only awaited the conclusion of the difficulty with the Parkers, feeling more and more convinced of Miss Ferris's growing indifference to me. Her words were pleasant enough, when now and then, for a few minutes at a time, I found an opportunity to converse with her. But the old warmth of manner and childish confidence were gone. She was perfectly polite, but guarded and reticent, as if fearing herself. Even with Mr. Masters and his wife, her playful looks and pretty petulance were giving place to a more womanly and quiet style of showing her devotion. I argued that this was a natural and usual alteration, characterizing the

change from careless childhood to thoughtful woman-
hood. Mr. Masters, if he was conscious of the difference in her, did not mention it.

I could not help thinking that Miss Pauline was in
some way accountable for the change in my once warm-
hearted little patient.

One day I met Harry Weston in the street, and I
fulfilled my promise to him by explaining my curious
conduct during his former visit to the city. His astou-
ishment was intense, and his congratulations most sincere. He also had something pleasant to tell me. He
was about to be married to Miss Edith Fullerton, and
insisted on my being present at the ceremony. We
strolled down to Mr. Masters' office, and I introduced
him to the good old gentleman. The friendship which
resulted from their meeting has grown into a warm at-
tachment between the two families.

I renewed my acquaintance with Miss Fullerton
that evening, and she expressed a strong desire to meet
again the pretty girl who had attracted her attention
that memorable day on the island. She heard with
astonishment the useful part taken by her shawl and
parasol in the proceedings of that afternoon, and did
not wonder at my wish to retain them. Miss Ferris
remembered the meeting, and was quite anxious to
see Miss Fullerton when I told her of my visit the
morning after. Several visits between the ladies of the
two families took place before Miss Fullerton's marriage, and I saw with pleasure that Miss Ferris regarded

her new friend with feelings of real admiration and love.
As Harry Weston intended spending some months in
New York with his bride, I felt more satisfied about
leaving it; the companionship of a sensible, intellectual
woman, like Mrs. Weston, could not but have a good
effect on Miss Ferris, and might serve to counteract the
influence exerted over her by Miss Pauline. From my
former knowledge of Mrs. Weston, I felt that she was
conscientious, and firm enough to uphold her own convictions; I very much doubted Miss Pauline's truthfulness, and Miss Ferris trusted in her. How far she
might venture in order to accomplish what she had undertaken, was a question difficult to answer.

I would not think of poisoning the delicate, sensitive
mind with suspicions which I could not prove, and, although, as the days went by, I disliked Miss Pauline
more and more, I kept my doubts in my own heart.
Miss Pauline displayed a tact and a knowledge of stratagem quite wonderful to me. She was prepared for me
at all points, and she worked so quietly and cleverly
that no one ever suspected her designs. It was only
on looking back, after being thwarted in some pet
scheme, and trying to see why I had failed in effecting
it, that I could trace her influence in frustrating it. If
I purposely remained in the house with the hope of enjoying Miss Ferris's society, there was always some
excuse for the young ladies to go out; some shopping
had to be done, or a visit must be returned. If I proposed a party to a picture-gallery, or a public institu-

tion, a severe headache was sure to attack Miss Pauline or her sister. My time hung heavy on my hands, Mr. and Mrs. Parker still remained silent, my mother and sister were home, Harry Weston and his bride were out of town, and Mr. Masters was busy looking after the progress of some of his recent speculations. In the evenings we were sure to be joined by visitors if we remained at home, and if we went out Mr. Claude always made one of the party.

At last, when my patience was nearly exhausted, Mr. Parker called on Mr. Masters and begged to have a settlement arranged without the necessity of his wife appearing in the affair. Mr. Masters insisted on having the large sums refunded which Mrs. Parker had drawn during her absence in Europe. A considerable delay and many arguments ensued. Mr. Parker threatened to claim possession of Miss Ferris, on the plea that she was not yet of age, and firmly refused to give up his trusteeship of her property. Mr. Masters showed the proofs of her age, and referred to her father's will, which allowed her to make her own selection with regard both to the persons she would live with and her choice in marriage. He declared his intention of standing a lawsuit, which would involve a terrible exposure, as far as Mrs. Parker was concerned, rather than withdraw one of his points. How far Mr. Parker had been connected with the plot we could not tell; there was no positive proof of his knowledge of it whatever. We might suspect him, but we could not charge him with

7*

complicity in it. Owing to the curious provisions of the will, the business connection between the two trustees could not be dissolved, unless one should resign voluntarily, and appoint a successor acceptable to the other. The property could not be sold; the interest alone was to be equally divided between the two legatees, the trustees, of course, having the power to invest it for their benefit. Therefore, as long as they both lived, the two ladies would have an equal amount from the original estate every year, although the value of their separate investments of that amount might vary. Hitherto, Mr. Masters had made those investments for both parties, and the results had been about equal. He declined, in future, having any thing to do with Mrs. Parker's share, further than was required by the provisions of the will, not wishing to meet that lady under any circumstances.

I was present at every interview between the two gentlemen, and, although I took no active part in the settlement, I could see that my presence carried its weight with Mr. Parker. Considerations for his wife, against whom I would be a very strong witness, made him agree in the end to Mr. Masters' proposition. The money, amounting to several thousand dollars, was returned, and the agreement signed. Mrs. Parker gave up all claims on the custody of Miss Ferris; and we, on the part of that young lady, promised that no prosecution for past ill-treatment should be undertaken.

I must confess I felt sorry that Mrs. Parker escaped

without any punishment save the loss of some money.
Still, on the whole, we had great reasons for being
satisfied with the arrangement. When we told the result to the assembled family that evening, Miss Ferris
was the least excited of the whole party at what had
happened. She only said:

"I am so happy at present, that I cannot wish any
ill to her. Perhaps, too, she is sorry now for what has
occurred. We should try and forget it all."

"You are too good-natured, Belle, darling," Miss
Pauline said, throwing her arms around Miss Ferris,
and kissing her.

"Belle is trying to do right," said Mrs. Masters, in
a low tone; "the rule is, never to remember an injury,
nor forget a kindness."

Miss Ferris colored, and looked at her fan.

"I should like to know who ever kept up to it?"
asked Miss Marie Lecount, smiling.

"No one," answered her sister; "some remember
both the injuries and kindnesses, and some think of the
injuries only, because they always make the deepest
impression. Others forget both—the whole thing is a
mere question of memory."

"Then you doubt the possibility of the rule being
practised?" I remarked.

"Yes, taken in its literal sense. A memory strong
enough to recollect every kindness experienced by its
possessor, will surely retain also the impression of an
injury received. I think it means this: we can remem-

ber the injury, but we must not act upon that recollection by seeking to revenge it."

"That is the spirit of the law, decidedly," said Mrs. Masters.

"And it needs a strong will to practise it," remarked her husband. "A man who can perform it by overcoming himself deserves, in my opinion, a great deal of credit."

"Yes, much more than one who is kind to those who have wronged him, simply because his memory is too poor to remember in what they offended him. I would not give much for his gratitude for past kindness," remarked Mr. Claude Lecount.

"Nor I either," said his sister Pauline.

"In that case a poor memory would be the easiest to go through the world with, because one wouldn't have to be always fighting against an evil spirit, even if it is good for self-discipline," Miss Ferris said, in a low tone; "but surely there is something more than mere memory involved in the question. I think the whole nature and temperament exert an influence in the matter—don't you, Doctor Wilmer?"

"Yes, I do," I answered. "I think that some people are more charitable and readier to find excuses for a fault, even when committed against themselves, than others; and by them, of course, forgiveness is more easily exercised than by persons naturally morose and vindictive. The latter class will brood over a thoughtless slight, until, to their morbid minds, it becomes a

serious injury; whereas, the very same offence would be
either altogether unnoticed, or passed by as totally insignificant, by the former."

"And do you think that these people, who from
their nature can forgive easily, are always grateful for
a kindness?" asked Miss Pauline, giving me a searching glance from her magnificent eyes.

"Most decidedly, from their very generosity and
warm-heartedness, they are, if any thing, more likely to
magnify a favor, and attribute to it effects of which it is
not always the true cause."

"Such people are very rare. I never met with any
of them," said Miss Pauline, smiling rather sneeringly.

"Which does not prove the fact of their non-exist-
ence. They may be the exception to the general rule;
but, remember, that such a character takes time to de-
velop itself, and is in danger of being frequently, if not
altogether, misunderstood. I have a theory that the
finest natures are the least appreciated in this world,
because beyond the comprehension of the mass. They
seldom meet with kindred spirits capable of satisfying
them; and so their deepest and best emotions remain
hidden in their own breasts—felt, but unexpressed."

"Dear me, I should not care to know any so difficult
to understand; I should be forever wounding them unconsciously; I prefer people who show their true natures
on the surface, people that I can read at a glance," said
Miss Pauline, taking Miss Ferris's hand in her own and
softly pressing it. Miss Ferris was apparently too much

interested in the conversation to notice her friend's devotion.

" Of course, you practise what you admire so much," I remarked, looking at Miss Pauline. She blushed confusedly, and turned away, without replying.

" What a comical thing it would be if everybody were obliged to say exactly what they thought, and not even allowed to give a wrong impression ! " said Miss Ferris.

" I know what I think now," said Mrs. Masters, smiling.

We all looked at her expectantly.

" Come, Sallie, give us your opinion," said her husband.

" Well, I think the sooner we begin to forget our grievances, and think only of our many blessings, the better. That is what Belle has resolved to do ; and now, if you please, dinner is waiting.—Give me your arm, Doctor Wilmer. I think," she added, in a lower tone to me, "that the conversation was becoming unpleasant to Miss Pauline—she seemed annoyed."

I looked into her face, amused at her shrewdness ; surely this quiet, good-humored little woman saw more than people supposed.

During the dinner-hour Mr. Claude talked a great deal to Mr. Masters about his own prospects. I sat between the two gentlemen, and, as Mr. Masters constantly turned to me for an opinion, I became quite conversant with the business affairs in which Mr. Claude was engaged. The gentleman, in whose employment he was, had formerly been a lawyer of some reputation, and still devoted a part of his time and talents to his legitimate profession. Latterly, he had been operating in stocks to a large extent; and, according to his young clerk's opinion, was rapidly amassing a fortune.

"He is about entering into a new speculation," went on Mr. Claude. The topic under discussion by the ladies having become exhausted at this juncture, they all turned their attention to Mr. Claude's conversation.

"What is it?" inquired Mr. Masters; "does it promise to pay well—any chance of a dividend within ten years?"

"Oh, yes! the expenses are not heavy; after a few months they expect to pay seven per cent. I wish you could meet the gentleman who knows all about the quarry."

"Oh! it's a quarry, is it?" answered Mr. Masters, with a dubious smile. "Where is it?"

"Down South somewhere. Soapstone."

"Soapstone!" repeated Mr. Masters. "Well, what do they propose doing with it?"

"Oh, quantities of useful articles can be manufactured from it—slate-pencils, griddles—"

"Griddles!" echoed Mrs. Masters. "Well, that is something new. I should prefer an iron one."

"These that we propose making will be much better. Owing to the greasy nature of the stone, no butter will be required in the baking, and the cakes will be much healthier."

"Well, they find out something new every day," said Mrs. Masters with a sigh. "The world will soon be too learned for me."

"Mr. Walker is to be president, and Mr. Parker treasurer.

"What Parker is that?" asked Mr. Masters, becoming suddenly interested.

"The same one that was here the other night," answered Mr. Claude.

"I gave Parker credit for more wisdom," Mr. Masters said, slowly; "although I remember that at one time he was interested in a coal-mine. Well, he is shrewd; there may be something in it worth the venture. I hope you don't intend to invest. A young fellow like you had better put his money where he is sure of finding it when he needs it."

Mr. Claude colored.

"As yet," he answered, "I have nothing to invest. Mr. Walker has been kind enough to propose me for secretary; and he offered, yesterday, to give me an interest in the firm after January."

"What kind of a person is this that you say knows all about the quarry? What is his name?"

"Hammond—S. Y. Hammond he signs himself, perhaps you know him. He is a tall, elegant-looking man, well educated, and knows all the first people in the country intimately. You can't mention a subject that he is not thoroughly at home upon, and his manners are perfect."

"Is he a New-Yorker?" asked Mr. Masters, thoughtfully, as if trying to bring the name to his recollection.

"No, he is a Western man. He stops at the Metropolitan at present."

"As a general thing, I don't much like these strangers who stop at hotels, and are concerned in speculations. There's a lack of solidity about them that is rather doubtful. They are here to-day, and off, no one knows where, to-morrow. If you have any influence with Mr. Walker, I should advise you to speak to him. Tell him to think seriously on the matter before undertaking it. It is rather an expensive affair to put in operation without due foresight."

"The company is already pretty well established. The first meeting of the shareholders is called for to-morrow, and Mr. Walker expects the work to be commenced in a few weeks."

Mr. Claude Lecount was evidently very much impressed with the beauties of speculation; and, after our return to the parlor, he entered into an explanation of how such matters were conducted, for the benefit of Miss Ferris, who hitherto had been in blissful ignorance of their existence. I saw that Mr. Masters viewed his new ideas with distrust, and felt uneasy about the infatuation which had taken such hold upon his thoughts. He talked on about the wonderful luck that some men had. One gentleman was driving his own horses, who, two years before, was not worth a hundred dollars. Another, the president of a mining company in South America, was building a magnificent country-seat on the Hudson, after plans sent to him by his family from Europe, where they were then travelling. Ten years before, he had been going about the city living on his wits, or, as Mr. Dickens has it, "the absence of wit in others." Mr. Masters shook his head, and argued the instability of a fortune made in such ways. He considered that it only rendered men careless; that money so easily acquired was never properly valued, and was very likely to be squandered even more rapidly than it had been gained. These arguments had no effect on Mr. Claude Lecount. He met them with the specious ones so artfully dwelt upon by the head movers of the speculation. His mind was evidently made up, and he no doubt considered Mr. Masters as being rather behind the age. He pitied him for his willingness to plod along in the old beaten track, when fortunes were to be made in a day by the exertion of mere shrewdness or cunning, instead of being acquired only after a lifetime of steady, honest toil.

As it was my last evening, I determined, if possible, to reach the cause of Miss Ferris's coolness toward me; and with that intention I drew my seat near to hers, and led the conversation to my proposed removal from Buffalo and establishment in my native town. She appeared interested, but there was no visible return to the old manner. The presence of Miss Pauline seemed to

cast a spell over us. I felt that she was constrained,
and I was sure of my own lack of self-confidence.

"Belle, will you try this air from 'Ernani?'" asked
Mr. Claude, approaching us.

Miss Ferris blushed; and, murmuring an assent,
rose and went to the piano.

He detained her at it, going over old songs and trying new ones for some time. I strolled into the library,
threw myself into an arm-chair, and gave up to the
jealous despair that had seized upon me. I had not
only to lose all hope of gaining her love—even her girlish friendship and her trust in me had been undermined
and destroyed. And yet what a contradiction of what
I had once supposed her true character to be! Could
this quiet, dignified, self-controlled Miss Ferris, who
weighed her words before speaking, as if afraid of com-
mitting herself, be indeed the warm-hearted, impulsive
child who had once thrown herself into my arms, and
wept with joy on seeing me? Should I ever forget that
day, or the light that shone in every feature of her face
when her eyes met mine? Could I not yet feel the clasp
of her hand on my arm, and hear the low, appealing
tones of her voice? Had she not, but a few short weeks
ago, fled to me for protection when frightened, although
her lover stood at her side? Was it possible that we
were all wearing masks, hiding our true sentiments, living in a state of cold constraint and studied indifference? Were we unconsciously bringing on ourselves
a future of misery and vain regrets? Was I wrong in

my determination not to possess a love given in gratitude? Was I really insuring her happiness by trampling
on my own heart, and crushing its love and hope?

I asked myself these questions over and over again,
each time becoming less satisfied with my own conduct.
Under an impulse, sudden as it was strange, I wrote my
sentiments, described all my feelings toward her from
the first time I saw her by that strange deathbed, until
that very night when I left her at the piano with one
whose claims I dared to question. I told her all my
doubts, explained my silence, and the motives that had
caused it. I said that I would not be satisfied with a
love springing from gratitude; that if for a moment she
doubted her feelings for me, independent of all that had
passed before her meeting with Mr. Lecount, that doubt
must decide my answer. I begged of her to think well
before she decided, to remember the difference in our
years and means. I urged no claim; I only told her
that I loved her, not for her beauty, not for her youth,
but for the mysterious, indescribable quality which she
alone possessed of all the women whom I had ever met
—that strange power, in which heart and intellect are
united—that capability of comprehending one intuitively, of understanding one's thoughts and wishes, even
when unexpressed, owing to that quick innate percep-
tion which unites, in secret, sympathetic hearts and
minds. I arranged that, if she decided against me, her
silence would be understood; if, on the contrary, she
felt that I might hope, I should expect a letter, if it only

contained one word. By this plan I would spare her the pain of writing a refusal.

Having sealed my letter with a ring on which my initials were engraved, and directed it, I debated how to convey it to her. Her book, which she had been reading before we went to dinner, was lying on the table near me, with its pretty mark in the place where she had left off. I remembered seeing her arrange it and close the book as we came in. I opened it and put my letter beside the mark, on which the words "Remember me," worked in gold beads, and "Pauline," in smaller letters of crimson silk, caught my attention. She haunts me, I thought, as I closed the book and returned it to its place.

When I went back to the parlor the ladies had retired, and Mr. Claude was gone away. Mr. Masters was standing near the window in deep thought. He had turned out all but one jet, and started, as I approached him, in the dim light.

"Oh, Doctor Wilmer, it is you!" he exclaimed, reassured. "I was just thinking over all Mr. Lecount said about that new quarry speculation. What a hold it has taken on him; I feel sorry for it. His profession is a good one if properly followed; but it seems to be irksome to him already. He wants to make money quickly, and is impatient of any thing that demands time and labor. However, he is young, and may see the folly of the thing after a while. He has nothing to lose, and arguments are thrown away upon him. This flinging away the substance and grasping at the shadow is the common disease at present; all the young men are infected with it. You won't find one in a hundred willing to do what his father did before him; work for the luxuries of life, and attain them in his old age by denying himself in his youth. He must have them at once, while, as he says, he is young and can enjoy them. That is all very well in its way, provided he has the money and can honestly afford to spend it. The trouble is, that not one young man in a hundred, or I may say a thousand, possesses the means of gratifying his luxurious tastes conscientiously, and so, as soon as he saves a little money, he begins to speculate. If he succeeds, every one he knows follows his example; and the result is, that hard work is at a discount, and speculation on the increase."

"A poor prospect for the country," I remarked.

"Oh, it will all end in a grand crash! Somebody must furnish the money that these presidents, directors, and treasurers are squandering; for I am very sure that the investments themselves have not realized it as yet. The shareholders will all be ruined—not because the speculations are bad, but because their money is misused. Instead of working these mines and quarries with it, and thus giving employment to hundreds, it goes toward buying houses, furniture, and fast horses for the heads of the companies. The sight of all this style and magnificence is enough to turn the head of a young fellow like Lecount. He thinks he can do the same."

"You don't think he will succeed," I remarked, hardly knowing what to say.

"I do not. He is not shrewd enough for the business. He might become a very good lawyer, and I think his own good sense will show him the wisdom of applying himself to his profession. It is one of the best in the country, I am sorry to say ; but then, as long as people will go to law about trifles, lawyers will fill their own pockets. I learned by experience, years ago, that the majority of lawsuits help only the lawyers who carry on the case. I am afraid this connection with Walker will injure him very much. Walker is one of your sharp speculators. He always manages to take care of himself, but I don't think his partners usually fare as well. He will excite Lecount with his descriptions of money, and of how easily it is made, although I don't think he would be very willing to enter into the details of the transactions. Such men are nuisances in a community. They upset a man's principles, his standard of honesty becomes gradually lowered, and his ideas of right and wrong grow confused, owing to their crafty arguments and specious excuses. Their offices are more to be feared than the gambling-saloons. A man goes into a regular gaming-house with his eyes open, and knowing what he is doing ; he enters blindfold into speculations, without the slightest idea of what they are leading him to."

I felt that Mr. Masters was fretting for Mr. Lecount's future, believing that he would endanger the comfort and fortune of his wife ; and certainly, if Miss Ferris were to occupy that position, the old gentleman's anxiety for his darling's happiness was not unfounded. I did not dare to give an opinion on Mr. Lecount, as my knowledge of that gentleman amounted to very little, and I could hardly be considered an impartial judge.

CHAPTER VII.

DEFEAT.

THE next morning I took my leave of the family. They were all assembled in the parlor, and I found no opportunity of speaking to Miss Ferris apart from the others. I felt sure that my letter would be in her hands before many hours, and I knew that it would explain every thing that might have seemed strange in my manner and conduct toward her. She bade me good-by in a nervous, timid way, and in a voice so low, that I could hardly catch the words. Miss Pauline, on the contrary, overwhelmed me with expressions of regret at my departure, and with hopes of my safe arrival at home. They followed me out to the door, and when I reached the corner I turned to take another look at them. Mrs. Masters and the two sisters were bending over a vine that twined on the balcony, quite forgetful of me. Miss Ferris was looking after me, her hand shading her eyes from the sun, that shone full on her slight figure and pretty hair. How often did that picture come before my eyes in after-years, the graceful form, the small upraised hand, and the curls, gleaming like gold in the

8

sun's rays, that fell round her neck! As I raised my hat, our eyes met, and for a moment one of the old smiles lit up her face. Then she kissed her hand to Mr. Masters, who accompanied me, and shook her head at him as she turned to enter the house. But the smile was mine, and for months the recollection of it made me happy. I regarded it as a ray of hope, and when most despairing it comforted me. Once at home, my business negotiations employed a great portion of my time and thoughts. Week after week went by, until at last I was ready to leave Buffalo. Nothing but the certainty that I was making my mother and sister happy could have recompensed me for what I was about to do. In ten years I had formed many pleasant friendships, and my prosperity had attached me to the city. I had none but happy recollections to carry away with me, and I left my position with regret. Mrs. Marks, my faithful housekeeper during my residence there, was to remain with my successor; the only living thing that I took away with me was my friend Dash, an immense New-foundland dog, that I had owned for some years. It had been given me when a mere puppy, by a little boy whom I had attended in a long sickness.

The boy was away at school when I left Buffalo. We had become great friends after his recovery, and I valued the dog for his sake as much as for its own. My mother was amused when I presented my travelling companion to her, and rather frightened when he placed one of his huge fore-paws on her lap, and offered her the

other to shake. However, his honest eyes reassured
her, and in spite of the resentment at his intrusion exhibited by her Maltese cat, and his immense size and
voracious appetite, he soon became a general favorite.

My mother had fitted up a room for me, on the door
of which the word " Office," in large letters, attracted
my notice. The report of my intention to establish myself in the place had spread over the town, and before
many days were over it was as much as I could do to
attend to the calls I received. Every case that had
baffled the skill of the two doctors belonging to the
place was at once put in my hands, and I was fortunate
enough to treat many of them successfully. I found
myself fully established, and quite famous in a very
short time, much to my own astonishment; but then I
had my reputation made before going there, and was
comfortably off besides. People concluded that I could
afford to give an honest opinion, and some sound advice,
very often far more needed than medicine.

Meanwhile, how did matters progress outside of my
professional labors? As the days passed by, and no letter reached me, I was alternately hopeful and despairing. My arguments for and against myself varied with
my temper, and the struggle still continued. I corresponded with Mr. Masters, and my sister received letters
regularly from her old pupil. Miss Pauline had been
home while I was still in Buffalo, but when I reached
my mother's house, she was gone back to New York to
spend the winter with Miss Ferris. Mr. Claude's visits

to his home had ceased, but he wrote every week. According to all accounts, they were enjoying themselves beyond description. Balls, parties, concerts, and the opera, monopolized the attention of the two young ladies. They were rival belles, the difference in their styles preventing jealousy. Mr. Claude's letters, the substance of them being always communicated to my sister by his admiring mother, were filled with glowing descriptions of the beauty of Miss Ferris, her talents, the admiration called forth by them, the wonders of her toilets, and the attention she received. Miss Ferris wrote more about her friend than about herself; either she was not inclined to be confidential, or my sister was not the one to whom she would express her deeper feelings.

I had called once or twice on Mrs. Lecount with my sister, and had been most warmly received by the family. As their conversation was principally on the subject that engrossed the greater part of my thoughts, I listened to it eagerly, as it gave me a good idea of how Miss Ferris passed her time. One morning I was present at the arrival of a packet of letters and papers, which called forth various comments.

"Pauline says that she never saw such a girl. It is as much as they can do to make her accept invitations," began Miss Marie, referring to the open letter in her hand.

"That is curious," said my sister. "To judge from the number of places she goes to, I should think she must be perfectly in love with society."

"Well, no," answered Mrs. Lecount. "Pauline has complained of her dislike to fashionable amusements all along. She thinks that Belle enters into them more to please her guardian than herself. I am sure that at home here she thought more of flowers and books than of any thing else. Pauline says that she likes to read, and would never pay a visit but for her."

"I always thought that Belle's tastes were domestic," said my sister; "but of course her life here was necessarily a quiet one, and a person could hardly form a correct opinion of her. Society has charms for all young people, and she must resemble other girls more or less."

"According to Pauline," remarked Miss Marie, "she does not care for the attention of gentlemen. She avoids them as much as possible, and gives them no encouragement."

"That is very easily accounted for. Belle is not a flirt. She finds no pleasure in giving others pain by inspiring sentiments which she feels she cannot return," answered Mrs. Lecount, in a significant tone, and with a meaning glance at her daughter.

My sister looked conscious. "Belle is truly honorable," she said.

I remember that visit so perfectly! It was a cold, wintry day. The snow lay deep on the ground, dazzling our eyes with its brilliant whiteness in the sun's rays. I had driven my sister over in a sleigh, and she intended riding around with me to the different places where I had to make calls. She often accompanied me in this way, sometimes leaving the sleigh to warm her feet, but generally remaining in it, wrapped up in the robes, while I paid my short visits. As we drove up the long avenue leading to Mrs. Lecount's, I noticed the house and grounds particularly, and the aspect of decay hanging over every thing struck me more forcibly than ever.

The green foliage of the vines, that served to cover the house in summer, besides adding to its picturesqueness, had all disappeared, and nothing remained of them but the lifeless branches that shook and rustled in the wintry wind. The sunbeams, as if in revenge for being shut out during the warm weather, now darted in and out unchecked, bringing to light the broken chimneys, the dilapidated shutters, and the general need of paint and new wood. I found myself thinking that Mr. Claude might better invest his spare money in the old homestead, thereby making it comfortable for his parents and sisters, than sink it in a soapstone quarry. However, he was a business man, and I was a doctor.

Several times after we left the house my sister rallied me on my silence, and tried in vain to engage my attention on the subject uppermost in her mind—the visible lack of means in the Lecounts' home. My thoughts were so filled with Mrs. Lecount's little speech, that I heard my sister's words without answering them.

"I wonder," she went on, "why Claude is not able to assist them more. Before he left home, his mother anticipated great things from his settling in New York.

So far, his departure has not benefited her much. She tells me now that it takes a great deal of money to support a young man in such a large city, and particularly where it is necessary for him to go into society constantly. She herself had no idea of the expenses it involves, but she says that it is absolutely essential to his future success, and she will deny herself and the girls rather than let him want for the least luxury. It is a pity about Marie. She is so fond of gayety, but as it is impossible to dress the two sisters for a winter in New York, and as Pauline is the most brilliant and beautiful, Marie gives way to her, and remains at home —buried, you may say, for her accomplishments are entirely thrown away here."

"Miss Pauline dressed expensively while I was in New York," I ventured to remark.

"Yes, I know, but Mrs. Masters is continually making her the richest presents, out of gratitude for her kindness to Belle, and here at home they practise the closest economy, so that she may queen it in New York this winter."

My sister woke me out of a reverie by shaking my arm, and exclaiming—.

"John, I wish you would take it into your wise head to fall in love with Pauline. I have often felt sure that she rather fancied you, and mother and I would both be pleased with your choice."

"So, after giving up Buffalo, and all its attractions for the sake of being near you, no sooner am I settled,

than you form a plan to get rid of me again. Pray, is
the office disagreeable, or the smell of drugs, or do you
object to the appearance of my poor patients?"

"Now, John, do be serious for a moment," she went
on, little thinking what a very disappointed companion
she had, or how forced was his pleasantry. "You know
mother and I cannot live forever, and your happiness is
something to us, especially when we consider what you
have done to secure ours. I can think of nothing more
delightful than for you to be happily married and settled here beside us; if the house should, indeed, prove
too small for your mother and wife together, you
know, we will make every concession—a wife has the
first claim."

"Yes, I know, but I think it would be hard in me
to put your amiability to such a test, for I can assure
you that there is no house in the county large enough
to contain my mother and Miss Pauline as my wife. So
put all ideas of that connection out of your head."

"Why, John, what has poor Pauline done to you?
You are prejudiced against her."

"Who was there to prejudice me against her?
Sister, she is universally admired."

"Well, then, what is the trouble?"

"Simply this—I don't fancy her at all," I answered.

"I am sure you could not find a more beautiful girl,
and her accomplishments are endless. Then her manners are perfection, and a graceful hostess is a fine addition to a doctor's house."

My sister took my hand and pressed it in her own for a few moments, as if collecting courage to say something still stronger, as an argument. Presently she commenced again :

"John, sometimes when I sit looking at you, I feel very unhappy. I begin to think that, after all, we have caused the sacrifice of your happiness. When you were young you had to struggle for yourself, that was well enough ; but as soon as you were able, you asked me to give up the school, and trust to you for the means to furnish mother with the luxuries it secured to her. I know that you argued mother's failing health, but I can see now that you thought of my strength, and need of rest. Do not be angry with me if I tell you that, on looking back, I think I can see where my own faults were. I should never have given up my independence unless forced to do so by circumstances. In doing so I became a burden on you, and the effects of it are visible now. In your unselfishness you deprived yourself of the means of marrying, and gradually overcame your own wishes and hopes. After all, John, it is false pride for a sister not to work because her brother can support her."

I kissed away my sister's tears and lifted her head that I might look into her honest, fearless eyes.

"Sister," I said, " believe me, when I tell you that, as far as money is concerned, I might have married six years ago. Other circumstances, beyond the control of means and position, have influenced me. Can you not trust me that this is so ?"

8*

"Yes, John, but only for us you might have married twelve years ago. Do not try to convince me that we have had no effect upon your life. If only I might see you with children round you, loving and happy, and a wife so devoted to you, that she might make up to you, with her love, for all the struggles of your early life, I should die much easier, feeling that the mischief was repaired, and your life not altogether wasted."

"And yet I was instrumental in saving Arabella Ferris," I murmured, almost unconsciously.

"Yes, John, but she was a mere child, and you saved her for another. Even her old gratitude and devotion are fast disappearing—they are completely replaced by her love for Claude Lecount."

I made no reply to my sister's last observation, not being able to command myself sufficiently. I turned to arrange the robes, that she might not see my face, and stopped gladly at the gate of a house where I was expected. The conversation was not renewed between us after I rejoined my sister; she probably thought that it was distasteful to me. It did give rise to a train of thoughts that led me to ask myself the question, "What am I living for?" I had accomplished the objects that I had set before me when starting in life. I had succeeded in my profession, and through that success had become able to provide liberally for my mother and sister. My work was no longer necessary to them. If I were to die, they could only miss my love and com-

panionship, but such a possibility had never entered
their minds. On searching deeper, I realized that my
love for Miss Ferris had been for many years the domi-
nant feeling, influencing all my thoughts and actions.
If my hopes of possessing her were destined to be shattered, then I must set before me another object, capable
of demanding all my talents and energies for its attain-
ment. I must confess, however, that I did not allow
my mind to dwell on the possibility of such a necessity
occurring. I am afraid that I was too fond of picturing
to myself a visionary home, in which Miss Ferris was
the central object, with all its sweetest attractions and
highest influences springing from her presence in it.
To such a home I should never weary of returning.
Its peace and brightness would dispel my anxiety or
gloominess of mind caused by the labors of the day; its
love would serve to increase that spirit of charity which
a doctor should possess in a high degree.

To a man possessed of a deep mind and extended
views of life, added to a warm heart and quick feelings,
there is something most satisfactory in the practice of
medicine. He gains an insight into human nature such
as no other calling can afford. He sees people as they
are, not as they seem to be. In sickness, the mask,
worn for the world, is for the time cast aside, the physician reads the true character of the person before him.
If, at times, he is disheartened and appalled by the
miseries and suffering of mind and body disclosed to
him, he is, at others, softened and overcome by the ex-

hibition of all those higher and holier affections, closely
concealed from the outside observer, but revealed to
him almost unconsciously when called forth by sorrow
or death. If he speak the word that deals despair and
agony that cannot be expressed, does he not also whis-
per of hope and recovery? Will not the heart-felt grasp
of the patient's hand, and the smiles that denote the
gratitude too deep for words, of an anxious family,
recompense him for the broken rest, the exhausted
strength, and the weary, throbbing brain? Surely there
is something noble in the spending of one's self, that
another may reap the benefit and rejoice.

I rode home one evening, feeling very tired and very
happy, having just relieved the fears of a mother for her
only child. I had been attending the boy for hours,
and the cool fresh air was very welcome to my aching
head after the heated atmosphere of the sick-room. It
was near the end of March, and I remembered with
pleasure that the gay season was over in New York,
and indulged myself in the hope that with the spring-
flowers would come Miss Ferris to enjoy country air
and scenery. As I passed Mrs. Lecount's, I noticed a
boy wheeling a barrow, on which a trunk was placed,
up the path toward the house; but without paying any
attention to the circumstance I rode on, while the air-
castle I was building assumed immense proportions.

My sister was seated near the parlor window, and
as that fact generally denoted company, I went into the
sitting-room and threw myself into an arm-chair for a

short rest. A moment or so afterward the hall door was shut, and my sister followed me and stood in front of my chair, her eyes on my face.

"What do you think I have to tell you? John, guess the news; but then you would never think of it, although it don't surprise me. Pauline is just gone, and Belle is going to be married in a few months; Claude has won her in spite of all—"

My sister suddenly stopped, and threw her arms around my neck. My face had told its own tale—my secret was mine no longer.

"Oh! John, John, my own dear brother," she sobbed, "that I should have told you this, that I should help to break your heart! How blind I have been! Oh! John, John," and she kissed and petted me, and smoothed the hair from my face, and tried to comfort me.

"Never speak of this again," I said, when I could command my voice. .

She promised, and then kindly left me. For a few minutes I felt stunned; I began to realize how much I had hoped for, and counted upon in spite of all arguments and appearances to the contrary. Had I not been deceiving myself for months, refusing to accept the evidence of her indifference to me, which I had agreed upon, and proposed myself. Truly, I had none to blame but myself for the bitterness of the pain caused by this sudden announcement. Still the blow was all the heavier, and, as I walked up and down the room, I felt a strong desire to go away by myself, among new scenes

and interests, where I might overcome by degrees the
passion in which henceforth it would be wicked to indulge—if I could but go, without the cause of my sudden departure being suspected by any one, save my
sister.   I feared Miss Pauline; my pride was great, even
though it had just received that terrible check.   If I
made no delay, my absence might not excite suspicion.
To remain where I was, and hear all the discussions
which would naturally follow the report of her engagement; to be invited to her wedding, and to be obliged
to attend it, with bright smiles on my face, congratulations on my lips, and with an aching heart—the mere
thought was insupportable; I trembled at the vision it
brought before my mind.   I resolved to come to a decision at once, while pride was sustaining me, otherwise
I feared the actions that blinded passion might attempt.

For years I had been comparing the workings of the
two systems of medicine, allopathic and homœopathic.
I had been trained in the old school, and had imbibed
all the prejudices felt by its faculties against the arguments advanced by the new school of practitioners.
Practical experience at length convinced me that my
prejudices were wrong, and that a reform was not only
needed, but was actually going on, quietly but surely,
among the more enlightened members of the old system.
Without acknowledging it—a thing they were unwilling to do, because men in the majority don't like to own
that they are in error, and blind to reason—they were
modifying their treatment and questioning its laws.   I

was often astonished at the obstinacy exhibited by some of the old practitioners, and their adherence to ideas long since abandoned by even the advocates of their own system. They spoke in glowing terms of the advances made of late years in the various arts and sciences with which they had nothing whatever to do; but it was totally impossible to convince them that the science of medicine was capable of improvement. As they had learned it they practised it, and argued that the mode of treatment which had sufficed human nature thirty or forty years ago was quite good enough for the human nature of the present day. In many cases they, when called to attend a consultation, either thwarted or completely stopped, by their narrow-minded opinions, the efforts of a younger and more progressive colleague.

I had once been called to consult on a case of this kind, and the barbarity of the treatment had taught me a lesson never to be forgotten. The patient was a middle-aged man, naturally healthy, not inclined to consumption, and not suffering from any chronic disease. He was a singer, and, as far as I could learn, of an easy temperament, not excitable or irritable, and possessed of a patient, gentle, uncomplaining disposition. Returning home one afternoon from a long rehearsal, he was caught in a heavy shower, and contracted a cold which at once settled on his lungs. One of these non-progressive practitioners was called in. He was accustomed to working in the old beaten track, without glancing aside to the right or left; and merely considering the case, which he named congestion of the lungs, and without giving a thought to the other conditions of the patient's constitution, which had been weakened by excessive practice, he ordered the most severe remedies.

When I was summoned, the patient was sinking rapidly. Deprived of the strength with which to battle against the disease, from the effect of successive cupping, bleeding, and leeching, and denied all nourishment that would support the system, he was then past hope—reduced to this pitiable condition by the practice of that very science which professed to relieve suffering, not to increase it!

For the first time in my life I felt disgusted with the profession that could countenance such a barbarous proceeding. In the eyes of the law, and of the medical fraternity, this doctor stood clear of all guilt. He had obeyed the rules prescribed by the books, out of which he had learned all he knew of medicine. Those books were his authority; he followed them mechanically. Others might imbibe new-fashioned theories, and use the gifts bestowed on them by Providence, in combining practical experience with the knowledge gained by reading; such ideas were to him and to all like him perfectly ridiculous. He practised medicine, as he had studied it, by routine. His heart and mind had nothing to do with his profession; it was a mere machine, which, when worked, brought him in his daily bread. He had spent some years acquiring the little he knew of it; if that little would carry him through the world, he was satisfied. His diploma gained, he was no longer a student; his business from henceforth was to exercise what he had learned to the best advantage, without adding to his own stock of knowledge. The experience of today taught him no lesson for to-morrow. In a word, he had mistaken his vocation. There are many throughout the world in the same predicament; they are to be found among all trades and callings; but in the medical profession they are to be most feared, because in that they are permitted to injure their fellow-beings with perfect impunity.

This case, which, in my opinion, was licensed murder, filled me with a desire to know more of the system which insists that a patient requires all his strength to battle with disease, and ignores depletion except in extraordinary cases. I knew that the European hospitals, where it was allowed to be exercised, would afford the best opportunities for an extended insight into its workings. I might judge for myself in testing the disadvantages that I had heard urged against it.

I had come to a conclusion when the tea-bell rang, and no sooner was the meal over than I electrified my mother and startled my sister by announcing that I was going to Europe. As my sister understood me, she offered no opposition, and rather sided with me, though quietly, so as not to excite suspicion, as I met and overthrew my mother's arguments against my proposed trip.

"As if it were necessary for you to study homœopathy in a French hospital, John, you who have been so successful already! If you have new theories, why not put them in practice here at home?"

"Because my theories reduced to practice would be called experiments. I may find them in successful operation where I propose going."

"And what will become of us? Just as we were beginning to feel happy, and, as it were, settled for years!"

"Oh, mother!" broke in my sister, "only beginning? Surely, we have been happy all our life."

"Mother, you can pack up, let the house, and see if there is not something to interest you and sister in the Old World."

"What! at my time of life?" screamed my mother. "No, no, John; we will stay home and keep the fire on the hearth for you. I think you will soon grow tired of your wanderings in search of theories."

"John has the theories with him," said my sister; "he wants to see them carried into practice."

"Well, well, theory or practice, they're all the same to me when they take my boy from me, that I reckoned on keeping beside me all my life. What will Mr. Masters say, and our little Belle? Pauline says they are arranging the marriage already."

My sister looked at me sorrowfully.

"Are they?" I managed to murmur, with a glance at her that forbade interruption.

"Yes; it will be a very grand affair. Six bridesmaids—Pauline and Marie among them. White and pink I think she told me. The young couple are going to their own house—Mr. Masters thinks it best when there is money enough. He is looking out for one to buy for them, and Claude is in partnership with Mr. Walker. Pauline says they're making heaps of money. The ceremony will be at Trinity Chapel, and we are all expected down for it. Marie and Pauline are going to New York next week to help with the preparations. You never saw any thing like the joy they are all in. Pauline says that Belle is perfectly happy, and as shy as ever. The dear, dear child; what a lovely bride she will make! I am anxious to see her. I hope she will be happy; certainly she deserves to be, considering all she went through some years ago. Come, John, forget your theories, and promise not to go away until after Belle's marriage. She would be dreadfully disappointed if you were not there. But, of course, you have no idea of not being there."

And, as if the matter were fully determined, my mother drew her shawl over her head, and went down to the gate to meet Mrs. Lecount, who was just then stopping her horse at it, with the hope of another discussion.

"What torture you have just endured, John, and how bravely you stood it out! What will you do?" asked my sister, putting her arm round my neck.

"Go as quickly as I can arrange matters here!"

"And Mr. Masters? Oh! John, how can you leave the country without seeing them?"

"I intend to see them. I must stand one more heart-ache, and then you shall admit that I can conquer myself; but not here, where every thing reminds me of her, and keeps my misery fresh before my sight. Try and convince mother that I am determined, and find some trace of the silver lining in this cloud that will comfort both her and me."

"John, it may take years for us to see that lining; at present, I can't find it. Mother's happiness is disturbed, and your heart almost broken; but you know what is right, and I feel that you ought to go away."

The next morning I followed my mother into the kitchen, and while she tossed up eggs and beat sugar, and manufactured a cake, I urged every reason, plausible and ridiculous, that I could think of, in behalf of my trip. At last I noticed that one argument had some effect on her. When I mentioned the number of years that I had been working and studying, with but few intervals of rest, and urged the incalculable good that travel and freedom from care would do me, not to speak of the years such a change might add to my life, she stopped her work and sat down to consider this new view of the case. The result was, her full and cordial consent, and I went to work at my preparations with a heart very much lightened of care on her account.

By a few skilful retreats I escaped an interview with Miss Pauline, feeling myself as yet unequal to it. A week after her departure for New York, I called to bid her family farewell, and, in view of making my visit to

Europe as important as possible, my mother and sister accompanied me to New York to see me off. I had written to Mr. Masters, telling him my intentions, and leaving him to communicate them to the family. I had planned it so as to have only one night in New York to spend at his house, feeling that my courage and pride would bear no more. In spite of my determination, I felt my heart beating rapidly, as we drove up to his home, and discerned several figures on the balcony and at the door ready to receive us. Shall I confess that I was disappointed when I found, on alighting from the carriage, that Miss Ferris was not among them? As we reached the parlor door, Mr. Masters began apologizing for her absence. She had made the engagement before they knew exactly what night we would arrive, and found it impossible to break it. Of course we accepted the excuse. My mother and sister explained my motives to the ladies present, and Mr. Masters attacked me on my unkindness in not staying for Belle's wedding. I parried his remarks, conscious that a pair of dark eyes was fixed on my face. How I envied my brave sister her coolness and self-command as portions of her conversation reached me! "Poor John has worked so hard for years! I begged of him to think of this trip, and it must do him good. Last winter he had such a hacking cough. You know a doctor's life is a very hard one; obliged to be out at night in all seasons of the year." These, and many more of such remarks reached me, as I listened to Mr.

Masters telling his kind-hearted, thoughtful arrangements for the happiness of the young couple. As he
made no remarks about speculations, and talked as if
Mr. Lecount were engaged wholly in his legitimate
business, I concluded that the gentleman had given up
that branch of money-making, and was pleasing Mr.
Masters by his quiet attention to the profession of which
he was a member.

In spite of my own wretchedness, I could not help
feeling pleased at the evident happiness of my kind
friends. That they were bound up in their adopted
child, and concerned in every thing that affected her
interest, was plain to all. If only the one absorbing
feeling were overcome, how contentedly might I go
away, leaving her to the love and care of these honest
protectors! Once I would have relinquished all hope
of ever seeing her again, for the certainty that she was
happy, and secure from her cruel stepmother; now, I
would give years of my life to be able to regain that
feeling, seeing that she was in the position I had then
coveted for her.

We were yet conversing, the watchful eyes still
searching my face, which I knew was stony and impassive, in spite of my efforts to look natural, when a night-
key was inserted into the hall door, and from my position I saw Miss Ferris enter with her accepted lover.
As she stood for a minute under the brilliant light in
the hall, her whole figure and face impressed me with
the idea that a great change had been effected in her,

whether a natural one, the result of her experience of
the world during the past winter, or a false one, forced
upon her by circumstances, I could not determine. The
air of perfect self-possession, and the immobility of the
delicate features were the peculiarities that struck me
most, and I began to feel some misgivings as to her
state of intense happiness. In fact, my ideal had lost
her identity, and was but one among the many beautiful and apparently worldly-minded girls so frequently
met with in our community.

She was expensively dressed in a most becoming
style, and rustled into the room, holding out her two
hands to my mother and sister, and uttering some
commonplace exclamation, expressive of her pleasure
at seeing them. She turned to me in exactly the
same manner, and with like words of welcome, but
as her eyes met mine, they died away on her lips, and a
faint color rose to her cheeks.

" Let me take your bonnet, Belle," said Miss Pauline,
rising hastily and coming forward.

Miss Ferris dropped my hand as if startled, and
blushed still more as she turned away.

"Thank you, Pauline," she murmured, almost inaudibly. "I shall run up-stairs with it; no, don't
trouble yourself"—for Miss Pauline would have followed her—and she left the room.

This little by-play had passed unnoticed by the others
present, Mr. Lecount being engaged talking to my sister
and mother, and Mr. and Mrs. Masters being unsuspicious.

It was some time before Miss Ferris reappeared, and then her manner was nervous; her face also showed traces of agitation. I believed that this was the result of meeting me, after having declined my offer, an act which must have given her some pain. I determined to reassure her, not liking to cause her gentle nature to feel any sorrow or self-blame for my disappointment. I assumed a gay, talkative manner, and succeeded in deceiving her. She resumed the quiet, self-possessed air, and received the attentions lavished on her by Mr. Lecount, who had taken his place beside her, with a coolness and ease remarkable in one so young. Her winter in society had certainly done wonders for her, or, perhaps, she owed these new accomplishments to the teachings of Miss Pauline. Then again, it struck me that she felt as I did, and thought that these lover-like attentions were in rather bad taste, considering our presence, and the motives which had brought about our visit.

Her manner indicated indifference rather than bash-fulness or fondness, and at times she turned from him with a wearied look in the soft eyes, to hear what Mr. Masters was saying, or to throw a faint smile to my mother. Meanwhile Mr. Claude played with her pretty hand, on one finger of which a diamond was sparkling, twisted the soft curls, and whispered low-toned remarks in the accustomed way, with tender glances from his fine eyes accompanying them. Had she given him one answering token of love, he would have driven me wild with jealousy, but her generous, pitying heart could find no pleasure in giving me fresh pain.

At last Mr. Lecount rose to take leave, and Miss Ferris gave him her hand quietly, after he had wished us all good-night and me a pleasant voyage. He either did not, or would not understand her, but placing his arm round her waist, drew her into the hall and detained her some time at the door. When she returned she sat down on the sofa between my mother and sister, and, throwing an arm round each with some of her old impetuosity, asked and answered questions without number. She had made them promise to stay with her a week, before it was time to separate for the night.

The next morning Miss Pauline was in the dining-room when I went down, alert and watchful. Had I wished for an opportunity to speak to Miss Ferris alone, she would have prevented the wish being gratified. However, she need not have feared me; I had no intention of trusting myself to such an interview. I firmly believed that Miss Ferris had told of my letter to her friend, not being able to account in any other way for her extreme vigilance. I had some purchases to make in the city, and intended leaving the house after breakfast with Mr. Masters, it being understood that my mother and sister would meet me at the pier. As I was bidding Miss Ferris good-by, Mr. Masters called out—

"You will see them again, they will all come down to the ship time enough to inspect your quarters, and

9

keep up your spirits till the last. I only wish you would postpone your trip until after Belle's wedding, and then we might all join you, and have a good time. Travelling alone is dull work."

"And so I had better go first, and be ready to receive you all when you come, and teach you the language and customs of the country."

My sister laughed, and I ran down the steps and called gayly to Mr. Masters.

We had transacted our business and reached the ship long before the carriage came in sight. At last, from my place on deck, I caught a glimpse of my mother's face, and we joined the party on the pier. As I had anticipated, Miss Ferris was not among them. Mr. Masters expressed his astonishment. Mrs. Masters explained that Belle could not find courage to watch the ship disappearing that carried away one of her best friends.

My mother said that Belle was crying as if her heart would break when they were strapping my trunk on the carriage; and that Pauline wished to come, but could not possibly leave Belle in such grief.

"Belle has not been like her old self lately," remarked Mr. Masters. "It all comes of being in love, I suppose."

As my sister was leaving my little state-room, I drew her back, and asked what caused Miss Ferris's grief.

"That is what has been puzzling me ever since we

left the house. After her indifference last night I hardly expected such a scene. She threw her arms around my neck, and cried, and said that she was sorry for having been so cool to you, and you her best friend. She begged me to tell you that she could not bear to see you going away, and that she would pray for your safe return. Altogether she is the most unaccountable girl I ever had any thing to do with."

"She is sorry for me," I thought, as we joined the rest of the party. A few moments after, I was leaning over the side of the ship, watching the dear forms fast becoming more and more indistinct in the increasing distance.

CHAPTER VIII.

THREE YEARS AFTER.

DURING the three years that I remained in Europe I heard very few details of what was taking place among the people in whom I had felt so much interest. My sister was either ignorant of their movements, or she was purposely silent about them. I inclined toward the latter opinion, and never made any but general inquiries when I mentioned them in my letters. Mr. Masters kept up an irregular correspondence with me in his old happy style, and, to judge from his way of alluding to his ward and her husband, every thing was progressing in the most satisfactory manner.

I knew that the young couple had a very pretty house in New York, and that a little son had come to them, who, according to Mr. Masters, far exceeded in beauty and intelligence any child ever before born into the world. Owing to these reports I was perfectly satisfied of the complete happiness of her whom I had so hopelessly loved. I gave my whole attention to the subject the study of which I had set before me, and with the most satisfactory results. I returned home invigorated and light-hearted, feeling that my long absence had done me an incalculable amount of good. I had gained in health and experience, and I felt a strong desire to return to my work and prosecute it with more vigor than ever. My mother and sister were overjoyed at my arrival, and before I had been home a week I was as well informed on the affairs of every family in the place as one who had never been absent from it a day.

The Lecounts, both at home and in New York, were acting in a manner totally unaccountable to my sister and mother. The young couple had never been in the village during their three years of married life. My mother and sister had never been invited to stop at their house, and had only seen them occasionally, when visiting in New York at Mr. Masters'.

"Perhaps their house is too small to admit of visitors staying over night," I urged, rather puzzled at the whole affair, so utterly contrary to young Mrs. Lecount's affectionate disposition.

"The house is a very large one, and Belle always has one or two of the family from here stopping with her. Pauline is almost a fixture there. I know they entertain other company at the same time, for Mr. Masters has often alluded to the fact, both here and in his own house."

"He seems to think they are rather extravagant," remarked my mother.

"But surely you have been in the house, you have

seen Mrs. Lecount in her own home. Could you not judge what her reason might be for neither coming here nor asking you there?"

"No, I could not. At the first visit, Pauline was present all the time. She is one of the family, and I suppose had a perfect right to receive us when we called; still she contrived to throw a restraint over us that was quite inexplicable, and yet decided. Belle has changed somewhat; she is less cordial, more dignified and reticent, than you can imagine. I felt so chilled, that I called her Mrs. Lecount when we were taking leave. Would you believe it, she caught my hand, and begged of me not to do so again. 'Call me Belle,' she whispered, as she kissed me. We were alone in the hall. I put my arms round her, and she shook all over; the next moment Pauline came out of the parlor, where she had been showing some flowers to mother, and Belle changed again instantly to the cold, dignified Mrs. Lecount."

"When did that happen?" I asked. "It sounds strange; you never mentioned it to me in your letters."

"Why should I? It would do you no good, and besides, Belle did not appear unhappy. On the contrary, she was surrounded by luxuries, for the house is perfect, and she was looking very handsome. That was about six months after her marriage. We did not pay her a visit again until after her child was born. Mother and I went down expressly to see her. Mrs. Lecount had been with her all through, and Belle told us that

no one could have been kinder. That visit was a very
pleasant one. Mrs. Lecount left us with Belle, and she
was more like her old self in her manner. She was so
perfectly happy showing us the baby! Her delight
was more like a child's over a pretty new doll than any
thing else. Mother was afraid she would let the little
thing fall, or injure its spine, the way she was playing
with it, and we both felt relieved when the nurse came
in and took it from her. She talked then of coming
up here as soon as she was strong, but she never did,
and that was two years ago. We have only seen
her once since then, and under the circumstances we
could not ask her true reason for never visiting us.
Mr. Masters gave a large dinner party on the anniver-
sary of his wedding-day—the thirty-fifth, I think—and
we went down for it. Of course, we expected to see
Belle that day before dinner, but she did not come in
until it was nearly over. Claude made some excuse for
their late appearance, and I was struck by the curious
way in which they acted toward each other. Pauline
was not present; I forget what prevented her accepting
the invitation. Belle was pleasant and talkative, but
not inclined to be confidential, and she was so surrounded by admirers, that I found little opportunity to
speak to her. Both she and Claude looked remarkably
handsome that night, and they attracted universal attention. Belle asked us to call the next day, and
after she was gone, mother said to Mrs. Masters that
she thought there was something wrong between the

young people. Mrs. Masters said, not at all, that Belle
hated demonstrations before strangers, and would not
permit them. As it was the first time I had seen them
together since their marriage, I concluded they were
very happy, as Mrs. Masters thought so, and she, of
course, had plenty of opportunities for judging them."

"Did you call the next day?" I asked.

"Yes, but we did not see Belle. Pauline received
us, and excused her. She had a terrible headache, and
could not bear the least sound in the room. We asked
to see the baby, but he was out with his nurse; so we
left our love for her, and started for home that night.
We have not seen Belle since."

I commenced walking up and down the room.

"Now, John, please don't go to work and worry
yourself about Belle's happiness. If you do, I shall feel
sorry for having remembered and told you all these
things. I never wrote them to you, because I wanted to
give you time to forget all your old troubles. Mother
thinks it a good sign when the new friends have super-
seded the old; although it is not pleasant to be forgotten so entirely. However, they are young, and may
find more congenial companions than two old women,
shut up in a country village, and totally ignorant of the
latest fashions and the new amusements. I used to picture to myself Belle on a visit to us, occupying her old
room, and going over the old pleasures that served to
entertain her when society and its charms were unknown
and uncared for. Pauline, when she does come to see us,

always dispels my illusions by describing Belle as she lives now, surrounded with company, and taking her part in every gayety that is planned or thought of."

"Yes," I said, "at twenty-three the world is very bright, and particularly so for those who have the means to enjoy it. We must not be severe on Mrs. Lecount. She feels these pleasures the more for having been debarred of them so long."

"Yes, and then nothing is too extravagant for the family she has married into. They uphold her in things that her own judgment would disapprove. You will be astonished when you see the old house. It has been repaired and refitted from top to bottom. Of course, we know where the money came from, and they even tell us that Belle loves the old place so dearly, that she insisted on having it put in order at her own expense, and refused to consider the money they expended as a loan."

"And yet she has not visited it since she was married?"

"No, but then Belle is generous enough to do that and more for the comfort of others, and I have no doubt but that the old people will thank her every day for what she has done for them."

"She is a warm-hearted, good little girl," said my mother, coming in, "if she does seem to have forgotten us; and I am almost sure that there is something at the bottom of all this, and that we will find out what it is, if we have patience."

This conversation had been the result of my inviting

9*

the two ladies who composed my family to call with me
on Mrs. Lecount. They both demurred, feeling ag-
grieved with the whole set. They had paid the last
visit, and anyhow it was the Lecounts' place to call on
me. I had no great desire to see the family, and so the
weeks passed over, until I had been back a month without meeting one of them.

One afternoon, as I was riding home, I came upon a
strange figure of a female walking along the grass by
the roadside. Her curious costume was not new to me;
I had seen numberless women dressed in the same style
in Europe, but she looked quite remarkable and out of
place when met on a country road in the United States.
As I expected, when I drew closer, I found that she was
a young, bright-looking French girl, with rosy cheeks,
and dark hair, half hidden under her stiff white cap.
Walking before her, and supported by an embroidered
strap that she held in her hands, was a pretty boy, about
two years of age. His hair fell on his neck in a shower
of golden curls, and as I passed he raised his head and
disclosed a pair of soft brown eyes shaded by long dark
lashes. The horse attracted his attention, and he pointed at it, and then turned to his nurse, about to cry.

"Does it frighten him?" I asked, stopping short in
the road.

"No, sir," was the reply, in very good English;
"but he wants to get on it. His father often rides him
up and down the street.

"Let me take him," I said, and she lifted him up to

me, while he laughed and clapped his hands in glee. He patted the horse, and played with its long mane, shaking it in front of the animal's eyes and leaning over it fearlessly, while the nurse walked along, holding the long band which was still fastened around his waist.

"What is his name?" I asked, at last, wondering where the child could belong.

"Charles Arthur Lecount," was the quick answer, the last names pronounced with a strong French accent.

For a moment I felt giddy, like one in a vivid dream; then, as thought returned, I understood the meaning of the child's appearance.

"You are from New York?" I said.

"Monsieur is quite right. Madame not find herself very well, and we all come here."

I asked no more questions, and when we reached Mrs. Lecount's gate, she stopped and took the little boy down, but not without a great deal of coaxing and promises of sugar-plums. She spoke to the child in French, and held him up inside the gate to bid the kind gentleman "good-by," which he did in his childish way, kissing his little fat hand to me, and waving his cap.

When I reached home, my sister was waiting for me at the gate, her face bright with joy.

"I know all about it!" I cried out.

"What do you know?"

"Mrs. Lecount is here," I answered, gayly.

"Yes, that is it; did you see her?"

"No; I met with an adventure, in which I made the acquaintance of her little son and his nurse. What have you heard?"

"Why, Pauline ran over to tell us, and was more astonished than we were when she heard that you were home. Your letter must have gone astray. However, they are all here, that is, all but Claude; he had business to attend to, and so Belle started with Pauline and the baby and servants. She wasn't at all well, and the doctor there told Claude to send her inland, in preference to a watering-place. Pauline says that Belle cried to come here, and so Claude allowed her to, but she wanted to spend the summer at Newport or Cape May, of course; she wouldn't be Pauline Lecount if she wished any thing else."

"Don't get so warm," I said, patting my sister's hand.

"Warm, indeed! I don't see how I can help growing hot, when I hear of such things. The idea of Pauline dictating where Belle should go for the summer, and Belle having to cry before they would allow her to come where she might see her old friends! It is well they did not know of your return, or she might have cried in vain. I am sure our living here has something to do with the matter, in spite of Pauline's warmth and friendship."

"Very probably it has; but we can do no good either to ourselves or Mrs. Lecount by quarrelling now. The mischief is done, and we had better be friends if that is possible."

"Oh! there is no danger of them; they are too politic to say any thing against us to Belle. We shall always be friends on the surface."

"Then let us search no deeper. For Belle's sake we will avoid all unpleasantness."

"Yes, John, you have always considered her happiness, and I suppose you always will."

"As long as I live," I answered.

My sister bent her head for a moment to kiss my hand that held hers; and then, shaking the tears from her eyes, she called out to me, in a gay tone of voice, as I rode off, to make haste, for the tea was nearly cold.

About three o'clock the next morning, my sister awakened me with the words—

"John, you are sent for. Victor Lecount is downstairs."

"Well! who wants me? what is the matter?"

"Belle's child is in convulsions, and they are all terrified out of their senses."

"Perhaps you had better come over as soon as you can," I said, as I hurriedly threw on my clothes. I found Victor waiting for me, and together we hastened down the road, while he told me all he knew about what had happened. It didn't amount to much; the child had been restless in the early part of the night, and its mother had insisted on sitting up to watch him. Shortly after two o'clock he had been seized with a convulsion, and his mother, in her fright, had roused the house with screams that he was dying. Her terror was natural, as she had never witnessed such a sight before, and Victor had hurried off to me. The worst part of it all was that Mrs. Lecount was confined to her bed with rheumatism, and wholly unable to render her grandchild any assistance except by giving orders, which the girls were too frightened to carry out properly.

I found the house in a state of hopeless confusion. Young Mrs. Lecount was sitting on a low chair with her baby in her arms, watching with dilated eyes the convulsive movements of the small, waxen limbs. Pauline and Marie were standing near her, begging of her to put the child on the bed, and declaring that she was making him worse by holding him so tightly. The servants had lit every lamp in the house, and then collected in a group, to exchange opinions. Mr. Lecount was scolding the French girl, and demanding what she had done to his grandchild; while the poor creature sobbed, and shook, and declared in loud tones, and with many gestures, that she had done nothing to hurt him. The only silent ones in the room were the tearless young mother and the suffering child.

"Send those servants to make a fire, and get a warm bath ready at once," I said to Miss Pauline the moment I had glanced round the room and taken in the state of affairs.

The servants disappeared with Miss Marie to see that the order was obeyed, and comparative silence succeeded their departure.

Mrs. Lecount, roused by the sound of my voice,

stirred slightly, and looked up in my face, as I bent over the child, with a dumb misery in every feature that went to my heart. I saw, in a single glance, the change in her; she was thin and worn, and her voice had acquired a sadness of tone that startled me.

"My only hope, my only comfort!" she murmured, as I still watched him.

"Let me take him," I said.

For a moment she clasped him tighter, and a wild look came in her eyes, then, as a softer expression dawned on her face, she held him toward me, saying:

"Yes, you will do right; you know best."

"And you must help me—you and his nurse. If you will be strong and hopeful, there is no cause for fear. The little fellow will be running about as gay as ever in a week."

My words had the desired effect. With a strong effort she regained her self-control, and, knowing that it would satisfy her, I called upon her for every little assistance that was necessary. What a change a few words of hope had effected! This young mother, whom I had found sitting cold and motionless, watching, as she supposed, her child's last moments, was now an entirely different creature, moving with soft, elastic tread about the room, anticipating my words, and looking for happy results from what I was doing, with a perfect confidence in my skill and knowledge.

When at last the child opened his eyes and called "mamma," in a faint, fretful voice, she clasped him in her arms with a joyful cry, while the expression of her face was in itself a thanksgiving more powerful than language could offer up.

She paced the room back and forth for some time, trying to lull the child to sleep, almost indifferent, in her great happiness, to what was taking place around her. I turned and spoke to Miss Pauline for the first time, wishing to give her the directions what to do in case of the child being seized again during my absence. She had remained in the room all the time, a quiet spectator, not offering either advice or assistance, for which I thanked her, feeling sure that Mrs. Lecount preferred doing every thing herself for her own child. The nurse had gone to tell the baby's grandmother of his safety, and her low tones were intended for me alone.

"What could have caused all this?" she asked.

"There are various reasons for it. Do you know what he ate yesterday?"

She shrugged her pretty shoulders, and a rather contemptuous expression came over her face.

"How should I know? His mother and his nurse attend to that. He is a charming child," she went on, afraid that she had lost ground in my opinion—"a lovely boy; only we all fear that Belle will spoil him. She will allow no one but his father to interfere, and, of course, a man occupied with business cares can't attend to the forming of his child's disposition."

"Nor is it necessary; the child had better be left to his mother for some years to come."

"But he is so passionate he is wearing Belle out. We are all anxious about her; she is far from strong."

I looked for a moment at the slight figure bending over the child, now sleeping quietly in his little cradle.

"I can't think it any thing more serious than a slight loss of vigor, caused by the over-fatigue and late hours of a gay winter. Mrs. Lecount will regain her strength after a few months of country air and quiet."

I spoke in the coldest, most indifferent tones possible, aware of the jealous eyes fixed on my face, and the quick ears drinking in all my words.

Mrs. Lecount joined us.

"Do you think he is quite over it now?" she asked, in low tones, careful of disturbing the distant sleeper.

"I hope so; I have given Miss Pauline all the necessary directions in case of a recurrence of these attacks, and I shall call in during the evening."

"Must you go away?" she asked, clasping her hands.

"Yes, the necessity is imperative; but I don't anticipate any more of them. He is very much weakened, and I should like to ascertain what he ate yesterday."

Of course the mother knew, and she named over what he had had, but they were all perfectly harmless. I began to look for some other cause for his sudden illness, when my eyes fell on a large lemon, half hidden among some toys that were scattered over the sofa. Several small portions of the rind were missing, and the rough edges round the holes told of little teeth having been at work. I picked it up hastily, and at that moment the nurse entered the room.

"Did the baby swallow the pieces he bit out of this?" I asked, holding the lemon before her.

"Yes, he did, before I could take them out of his mouth; but, surely, monsieur doesn't think that such a little thing would hurt him."

"It has nearly killed him," I said; "it would injure a much older child than he is. Mrs. Lecount, you must be more careful; such playthings are totally unnecessary."

"Indeed, I didn't give it to him; I didn't know he had it," Mrs. Lecount answered, her eyes filling with tears.

"Why, no!" said the nurse, "Mademoiselle Pauline gave it to him."

Mrs. Lecount turned to her with a reproachful look in her soft eyes that said more than words.

"Well!" and Miss Pauline's dark eyes grew darker, while the color rose in her cheeks, "he was crying for nothing, and I gave it to him to pacify him!"

"Mademoiselle forgets she slapped his hands for upsetting her work-basket; he never cries for nothing;" and the French girl's face grew crimson with indignation.

Mrs. Lecount laid her hand on the angry girl's shoulder, enforcing silence, and then turned away with a deep sigh. Miss Pauline left the room, darting a threatening look at the nurse, and I followed the mother's steps, and listened for a few minutes to the child's gentle breathing.

"I think he will do well now, and you require rest; let the nurse watch, and do you try and sleep."

She pressed my hand and assented; but I felt that she did not trust herself to speak, lest she might blame her sister-in-law.

When I opened the door, the day was just breaking. The whole scene was a contrast to the one I had just quitted. All was still in the gray, hazy light; not a sound broke the silence of nature. I had just witnessed the expression of nearly all the passions of humanity, grief, love, joy, jealousy, and anger. A few hours in a sick-room had served to arouse them all to their utmost extent. The calm out of doors was very acceptable, and I walked slowly down the lawn enjoying it. I noticed the improvements my sister had spoken of. The former aspect of decay had disappeared; every thing, from the garden-plants to the new weather-vane on the roof, looked trim and handsome. There was an air of unostentatious wealth and comfort about every thing that gave a charming appearance to the old place.

Three years had done wonders for many in the way of comfort and freedom from care; but I had my doubts whether, after all, the happiness of the one had been effected whose welfare should have been the uppermost thought in all hearts. As I walked home, I pondered deeply on the immense influence for good or evil that one life exerts over others. I looked back on the years that had passed since I first saw the little child held for the last time in her dying father's arms. How strange the after-events which the young life, so frail and uncertain, had linked together in one strong chain, uniting such opposite interests, and binding in close friendship so many antagonistic natures! Without possessing any remarkable talent, or great powers of mind; thrown, by force of circumstances, and often against her will, into strange positions and among curious people; and, having no self-proposed aim in life, she had yet done more good than many who, starting without her disadvantages, attempt to compass by dint of their own strength and intellect what her gentle innocence had unconsciously effected.

Her childish smile had exerted an influence over me beyond the power of words. It had been my beacon-light for years. Her helplessness and sad suffering had called forth my deepest feelings, and roused all my energies in her defence. Her presence and love had increased her guardian's happiness, and brightened my mother's lonely life. Even her rejection of me had taught patience and resignation. In her unselfish generosity, she was forwarding by all the means in her power the happiness of her husband's family. If her wealth brought bodily comforts, her gentle forbearance was softening the proud, ambitious hearts, and filling them with better and higher aspirations.

It was nearly six o'clock in the evening when I returned to Mrs. Lecount's. My sister was in the parlor

with the family, and, from the merry tones that reached
my ears through the open windows, I judged that the
baby was much better. I was ushered into the midst
of them by the servant.

"I am so glad to see you, Doctor Wilmer," Miss Pauline exclaimed. "Arthur has been quite lively all the
afternoon, but nothing that we can say will satisfy
Belle. She will fret, and she must have your opinion
before she will believe that he is out of danger."

"She was asleep when I went up last," said Miss
Marie; "I will go and tell her you are here."

"Belle don't appear very strong," said my sister.
"I hope she will stay with us all summer. Little
Arthur will enjoy it so much."

"I can't tell how it will be," answered Miss Pauline.
"Claude had not decided when we left home. I expect
him up, however, either to-night or to-morrow morning.
Perhaps you can persuade him to remain here, but I
know he had a wish to go somewhere in Connecticut.
He wanted to see some mills there, that a friend of his
has an interest in. I believe it would be a very good
investment, and Claude had his mind nearly made up.
However, Mr. Masters insisted that he should go there
and examine every thing about them first. Of course,
it would take some time, and the place is very pretty
and healthy, so that Belle and Arthur could go with
him."

"So Mr. Lecount is not over his love of speculation
yet," I thought, on my way up-stairs.

I found Mrs. Lecount sitting at the open window with her baby in her arms, and the nurse building a block-house on the table for the young gentleman's amusement. The little fellow was languid and dull, and inclined to go asleep, which he did in a few minutes after, with his head on his mother's shoulder, its bright rings of golden hair mingling with her dark curls. She was, as my sister had told me, reserved and cold. Once assured of her child's safety, the bright light died out of her eyes, and the life and enthusiasm of her manner went with it. Her thoughts all centred in him; her eyes wandered over the sleeping form, as if seeing nothing beyond, while I talked to her on indifferent subjects, trying to arouse something of her old interest and curiosity.

"You have not been out of the house to-day," I said, noticing her pale cheeks and drooping figure.

"No, I could not leave Arthur; he wanted me with him all the time."

"Trust him with his nurse now, and go out for a little while in the garden, before it becomes too damp. You must consider your health for his sake, if not for your own."

To my surprise she rose at once, put the child in his cradle, and drawing a shawl hastily out of a box, wrapped it round her, with a slight shiver, and walked to the door.

"You are very obedient," I said, laughingly; "and Arthur is so well that I shall pay him no more doctor's visits. Will you come in?" I asked, as we reached the parlor door.

"No, no, I shall go out on the piazza for a few minutes; don't disturb them, I prefer being alone."

She turned away, and I found the young ladies in the midst of a noisy argument, which must have reached the ears of the silent woman pacing up and down the balcony outside. I tried to stop it, but found the effort almost impossible. The subject under discussion was, how Belle was spoiling her child by injudicious indulgence, and how she was sacrificing her own health and comfort in humoring his whims. As I knew none of the merits of the case, I could offer no opinion, though called upon to do so by Miss Pauline. The conversation had been brought about by Victor declaring that Pauline was in fault about the child's sickness, while she insisted that the whole trouble arose from his being allowed to have his own way in every thing.

"It is just the same in New York," she concluded, with flashing eyes, and in an excited tone of voice, which did not speak well for her temper. "The whole house must give way to him, father, mother, servants and all. I am determined that he shan't rule me. Claude ought to take him in hand; he is already entirely beyond his mother's control, and she has herself to thank for it."

I don't know which astonished me most, Miss Pauline speaking in such terms of young Mrs. Lecount before my sister and me, or the idea that a boy not two

years old was a terror to all around him, and beyond
the management and influence of his mother. Nothing
in the child's appearance could warrant such an assertion, and I suspected that Miss Pauline's wounded feelings were to blame for her thoughtless speech.

When I left the house, Mrs. Lecount was not on the
piazza, so I went quickly down the lawn to the gate,
presuming that she had returned to her room. I was
rather surprised to find her near the end of the path,
where it branched off toward an old summer-house
covered with vines. She turned to meet me on hearing
my steps, and I saw tears glistening in her eyes, though
she tried to keep her face in shadow.

"You see how hard it is, Doctor Wilmer, to please
every one." She attempted a gay manner, but failed
utterly.

"Then you heard—"

"Heard—I came down this far that I might hear no
more. Thank you for trying to turn the conversation
to a more interesting subject. If you only knew how
tired I am of hearing my child's faults discussed, and
how old the theme is, you would not be surprised at my
taking it so coolly. At first, I did what you probably
expected to-night. I became warm and excited, and
defended myself and my actions; now I take no part in
the argument. Mr. Lecount is quite willing to leave the
child to me, and I am responsible to no other person."

"I was more astonished at Miss Pauline's want of
taste—"

"Oh! don't misjudge her. She means no harm. Custom has made the subject so common that I am always prepared for it, no matter who may be present. The child is a general pet. Pauline is really very fond of him, in spite of all she says against him; voluntarily she would not hurt him. Now and then, when he troubles her, she loses her temper with him. I am sorry Victor mentioned the affair to her. Surely the sight of the little creature's sufferings was punishment enough."

The noise of the gate opening made us turn in that direction. A gentleman in a slouched hat and linen duster, with a valise in his hand, was coming in. His eyes fell on us instantly, and as his wife started forward, with the cry, " Why, it is Claude !" his features darkened perceptibly. She saw it, and the words of welcome died away on her lips, while the bright color rose in her face. I extended my hand, but Mr. Lecount drew himself up without noticing it, and looked from one to the other with an angry glare in his eyes. The whole scene was unaccountable to me.

" What brings you here, sir ?" was his salutation.

His wife caught his arm, her eyes dilating and brilliant with wounded pride.

" Claude! oh, Claude! Doctor Wilmer has just saved Arthur's life. How can you speak so to him? Our child has been very sick," and the tears came in her eyes while she trembled with weakness and fear. Why should she be afraid of him? Yet it was certainly a sensation of dread that was stealing over her, creeping

10

into her eyes, and blanching her cheeks. Her husband shook her hand off roughly, and uttered an oath.

"What did I know of Arthur's sickness? And what has it to do with all this anyhow? But no doubt you can explain the affair to your own satisfaction, if not to mine," he said rudely.

Mrs. Lecount raised her head and looked at him with an expression of speechless horror, which changed to one of sorrowful reproach. The same idea had suddenly struck both of us—Mr. Lecount was not quite himself.

She held out her hand to me, without making any reply to his last remark.

"Doctor Wilmer," she said in a low voice, "forget all this for my sake. Think of the circumstances."

Her husband caught the words.

"Don't apologize for me, madam; I am quite capable of arranging my own affairs. I am never ashamed of making an apology where it is due. In this case I can see no necessity for one." His tone was sneering, and affected her strangely.

"Nor do I ask one," I said; "you did not insult me. If Mrs. Lecount is willing to overlook what has passed, in view of all the circumstances, I have no desire to speak or think of it again."

He turned away up the path and she lingered a moment with her hand pressed tightly over her heart, before following him. I walked home with a new subject for meditation before me. As I had never given Mr. Lecount cause for jealousy, I could only suppose that

she had acquainted him with the contents of my letter.
And yet, even that would not explain his brutal rudeness to her. In marrying him she had fully proved her
indifference to me, and rendered all suspicious and jeal-
ousies on his part totally unjustifiable and contempt-
ible. She had chosen freely and fearlessly, and I made
up my mind that something had obscured Mr. Lecount's
usual good sense and reasoning powers. When my sister returned a few hours after, I was afraid to ask any
questions, but there were none needed.

"You just missed Claude," she began. "He came
in a little after you left. I never saw him look so
strange, and he acted and talked almost wildly. Pauline, of course, gave him a long account of Arthur, commencing at the very beginning, and I was astonished at
the little effect it had upon him. He didn't even go up
to see Belle all the evening. Only the Lecounts are
such temperate men, I should say he was intoxicated."

"Perhaps he was," I answered.

"Well, it is not improbable. He came up on the
cars, and of course a very little of the wretched stuff
they sell along the road would affect him, particularly
if he were unused to it."

"It is strange," I said, musingly; "I never thought
any of the family inclined that way."

"The strangest part of all was, that he was so cross
and quarrelsome. Naturally, he is always good-tempered and quiet."

"Three or four years in New York, among the stock

brokers, don't tend to make a man more amiable.   I
think it has an opposite influence."

"Well, if stocks make such bears of men, I hope you
will never touch them, John."

"I don't think I will," I replied, laughing.

"I don't know what you are laughing at, John.   I
feel in any thing but a gay mood.   When I went up to
bid Belle good-by, I left Claude sitting beside Pauline,
muttering something that I knew she didn't want me to
hear.   She was trying to stop him ; but just as I passed,
I heard him say, 'It was nothing but an excuse to see
the handsome doctor.'   Now, I should like to know his
meaning.   He looked savage enough, and she put her
hand over his mouth and affected to laugh, as if he had
said something witty.   There was nothing amusing
about his appearance, and Belle —" She stopped, as
if she had gone too far, and would have recalled her
words, if possible.

"Well, what about her ?" I said, for my sister was
folding up her work with an energy quite uncalled for
by the pieces of linen.   "Come, tell me what you mean;
don't keep me in suspense."

"Why, when I went into the room, I found her lying
on the bed, burning with fever, and her hair and the
pillow damp with her tears.   The room was dark, the
lamp turned entirely out, and at first I thought she was
asleep, she was so quiet.   However, she heard my steps
and called out to me, and when I went to her and asked
what ailed her, she threw her arms around my neck and

sobbed as if her heart would break. Then she made me promise not to speak of it down-stairs, and so I lifted her baby out of his cradle, and put him in her arms; and then I had to go back and speak pleasantly to the others, knowing that she was up there all alone, and in trouble."

"Rather a hard task to you, my impulsive sister; however, at times, we are all obliged to control our hearts and tongues."

"That is true; I felt like telling them all, and him particularly, that they were breaking her heart between them, with all their declarations and protestations of love for her. I wish I had now."

"And I am delighted that you did not. Whatever her trouble is, she wishes to keep it from the family, and it would increase her misery if she were obliged to answer all their questions."

"I wonder could it be, that Claude not going up to see her made her unhappy? He may have thought that she should have run down to welcome him in her old way. Men have such fancies! But even if she did annoy him, he shouldn't have been indifferent to the child. She could hardly take him down so soon; and one would suppose that he would have been anxious to see Arthur. No doubt they both felt hurt, and of course she frets the most."

"Of course; and as long as the trouble lies between the two, the less the family know about it the better. No doubt, by this time, they have forgotten and forgiven the whole affair, and are surprised at their own foolishness in letting such a little thing do so much mischief."

"Little things cause all the unhappiness in the world. They reach the heart quickest, because too small to be noticed by any but the one that loves. Straws show which way the wind blows, and no doubt Claude's indifference to his child was more painful to Belle than his disregard of her. If she is too proud to let him know what she suffered, he will feel worse, and accuse her of still greater coldness. Who can tell what will come of such a misunderstanding? That is why I approve of thunder-storms in the family, now and then; they clear the domestic air. They often do good by bringing to light the little causes that are apt to lead to such great effects."

" Belle is too truthful to allow a misunderstanding to exist for any length of time. I don't think you need fear for her domestic happiness."

My sister left me, quite reassured.

CHAPTER IX.

A DINNER-PARTY.

The next morning, as I was quitting the house, I met Victor Lecount. He had come purposely out of his way to leave a note with me, which contained an invitation to dinner for the following day, and also an apology from his brother for what had occurred the night before. Mr. Lecount gave no reason for his curious conduct, no doubt considering such a proceeding as totally beneath him. The wording of the message was stiff and cold. It was evidently written under compulsion. There was none of the warmth or impulsiveness in it that denotes a generous spirit, quick to acknowledge its own fault—it was merely an apology, and nothing more, the least that could be offered. I turned back to give my sister the other note, wishing very much that I could decline the invitation it contained. However, I had no real excuse, and I felt that my absence from the party would give pain to Mrs. Lecount, as she would naturally conclude that I had not accepted her husband's apology. My mother and sister were delighted with the idea. Any amusement that promised to relieve the monotony of their life for a few hours was always welcome. I left them discussing the never-failing topic, what they should wear, and started again on my long round of visits.

When I reached home that evening, I found Mr. and Mrs. Masters seated comfortably in their old places, and every thing looking so like the old times, that I could hardly realize the changes that had taken place since I had seen them last. They were so delighted at meeting me, and we had so much to talk about, that my sister concluded we would sit up all night. However, as they had come up for the dinner-party, to please Mrs. Lecount, and intended remaining with us for a week, we wished each other a reluctant good-night before twelve o'clock. Mr. Masters had altered very much in the three years. He was careworn, and I thought preoccupied, although he attempted a gay manner, which was too forced to be like his own old one, so genial and happy. Several times during the evening he seemed about to tell me something; but after a moment's reflection, in which he would brush his hair back nervously, a favorite motion of his when thinking, he would change the conversation by making a remark wholly foreign to the subject under discussion. There was evidently something on his mind that gave him much uneasiness, and I at once connected it with his ward and her affairs, because, strange to say, neither Mr. nor Mrs. Lecount had been mentioned that evening by any of us.

My own reasons for not alluding to them I did not

care to analyze, but Mr. Masters' silence regarding them was curious; because his ward and her happiness had been favorite themes with him for years, and ones that called forth all his eloquence, and his best and deepest feelings. Hitherto I had shared his confidence in all matters relating to her and her welfare. An absence of three years was calculated to weaken that desire of his to impart to me all his thoughts and misgivings concerning her. He could hardly suppose that my interest in her affairs was as deep as ever; it was natural for him to believe that late events had excluded all thought of her from my mind, and that what affected her was a matter of perfect indifference to me. I was satisfied that he should have those opinions. I disliked the mere idea of hearing any thing that might weaken my belief in her present happiness. I was the last person in the world to whom such doubts should be confided, and I did my best to keep the conversation on other matters at breakfast the next morning. Fortunately for me, I had to leave home as soon as the meal was over, and I begged of them to go without me to Mrs. Lecount's, promising to be present as early as possible, but the chances were that I should be detained beyond the dinner-hour.

They were gone, as I had expected, when I returned that evening; so I made my toilet as rapidly as possible, and started to join them. The party assembled in the large parlor was much more numerous than I had anticipated. Several gentlemen, strangers to me, were standing in a group near the mantel-piece, talking and

10*

laughing among themselves, without paying any attention to the other persons present. Miss Pauline, looking brilliant as usual, was in the act of introducing another to my sister. Mr. Masters was talking to Mrs. Lecount, and several ladies belonging to the neighborhood were scattered through the room, amusing themselves in the various ways customary on such occasions. The place was well lighted, the ladies in full dinner-dress, the apartment handsome and luxurious in its new furniture and decorations. Over all there was that restrained stiffness which generally pervades a dinner-party before dinner is announced. This evening it was especially noticeable. The young couple, in whose honor the party was given, had not yet made their appearance. The group at the fireplace seemed all in all to itself, and quite adverse to becoming sociable with the others in the room. Miss Pauline, though talking and laughing with her usual grace, was not quite at ease; I could detect anxiety in the restless manner, and the quick glances thrown now and then in the direction of the staircase. There was a something, not to be explained, that affected all the family, in spite of their gayety, and became the more apparent to me owing to their persistent efforts to conceal it. I was so well known to many in the room, that I only waited a moment for an introduction to the strangers. As it did not take place, I sat down near Miss Marie, and entered into conversation with her.

"It is so awkward, Doctor Wilmer," she observed;

"Claude has not come down yet, and those gentlemen are strangers to us. Pauline was alone when they arrived, and she didn't catch their names distinctly when they announced themselves. I begged of her to ask for them again, and introduce them to us properly, but she let the time slip over, expecting Claude every minute; and so here we are in a dilemma. Mr. Masters is not sufficiently acquainted with them to be of any use in the matter, and Pauline is so distressed that I pity her."

"They don't appear to mind the awkwardness of the affair themselves," I answered, as a general laugh from the group saluted our ears.

"No, and I am sure I am very glad of it. They must think it very strange, however, and Claude's absence is worse than all."

I made up my mind that "Claude's absence" was the secret of Miss Pauline's strange lack of self-possession. I began to wish as heartily as any one for his appearance. It was long past the dinner-hour, and every one in the room looked prepared for the sudden development of a great mystery. At last a rustling sound on the stairs drew the general attention in that direction, and the next moment Mr. Lecount entered, with his wife leaning on his arm. Nothing that my sister had told me, of the curious change in young Mrs. Lecount's manner at times, prepared me for such a transformation as I witnessed that night. That she was beautiful no one could dispute, but to me such beauty only caused pain. Every tinge of color had left her face; every expression that was pleasing was gone. Her features were set and rigid, as if cut in marble, and there was a stony, defiant look in her eyes that brought back to my memory visions of scenes that made me tremble. Even the dark, heavy silk of her dress, trailing on the ground, gave an unnatural height to her figure, and the absence of all the usual puffs and trimmings, while it added to her dignity, completely removed from her all traces of girlish grace and youthfulness. She went through the introductions, and spoke to her guests in a manner so polite as to leave no chance for complaint, yet so cold and distant as to repel all ideas of familiarity or future friendship.

Mr. Lecount talked loudly, and laughed gayly, as if to make up for his wife's coolness. He apologized for their late appearance in an off-hand, careless way, and with some words about the known length of a lady's toilet, that caused a general exclamation, and some gay sallies in reply. Dinner was announced, and one of the gentlemen offered his arm to Mrs. Lecount. She took it, with a slight shudder, as if disliking the contact, and hearing a half-repressed sigh behind me, I turned to find Mr. Masters, with his eyes fixed on her face. I touched his arm, for which he thanked me with a nod, and we took our places at the table as careless and happy-looking as any in the room. The gentlemen from New York ate their dinner like men accustomed to enjoying that meal. There was a gravity and premeditation about all they did, that to a mere looker-on was highly amusing. They spoke but little, and what they did say was addressed principally to Mr. Lecount, and was all Greek to me. I observed, however, that Mr. Masters listened attentively, and seemed to follow them in their remarks. Young Mrs. Lecount was seated between two of them; one, a tall, dignified-looking man, with a bald head, and spectacles, paid her a great deal of attention, and talked fluently on various subjects of interest. He was evidently more of a lady's-man than the others, and much more cultivated in his manners.

While they talked of stocks and bonds to the husband, he conversed on the topics of the day with the wife. She listened politely, replying now and then, when required, in monosyllables. Her plates were removed almost untouched, and I detected the sigh of relief with which she rose from the table when the long, formal dinner was over. The ladies gone, the gentlemen drew their chairs together, and, filling their glasses, renewed the conversation with increased vigor.

I learned that the tall, dignified man was Mr. Hammond. The short, stout one, who had sat on Mrs. Lecount's left, was the president of a new mining company. The other three, one of whom was Mr. Walker, were thin, sharp-looking men, with overhanging brows, compressed lips, and a certain hard, shrewd expression in their eyes, which spoke volumes. Had I been a speculator, I might have learned much of the inside machinery set in motion by these arrangers of joint-stock companies. As it was, their terms and expressions were quite new to me; and I looked at them, and listened to their schemes for making money rapidly, with as much amazement as if they were the real originators of the designs that they sought to carry out successfully.

That there was any thing but money worth having in the world seemed a most preposterous idea, to judge from their conversation. They spoke of thousands and millions in the same tone that I would mention tens and hundreds; and it did appear strange that I should work hard for years in order to amass the sum that they talked of realizing by the operations of a single day. Still, on looking at their hard, careworn faces, out of which all that spoke of youth and feeling had entirely disappeared, I felt that I would not be willing to change places with one of them. I noticed several things that evening, although it was some time afterward when I understood their full meaning.

Mr. Lecount seemed irritable and restless. He filled his glass quite often, and drank in a careless, hasty way, as if only half conscious of what he was doing. His father had left the room to attend to some law business, and Victor had joined the ladies in the parlor. Mr. Masters was a quiet, observant listener, and appeared to be weighing well every word that was uttered, and I felt a conviction that his presence was causing Mr. Lecount's uneasiness. Meanwhile, the short, stout gentleman enjoyed his wine and the dessert, stopping now

and then in the midst of a story to crack a nut or put
a fig in his mouth. There was something very unpre-
possessing about his face and in his manner. I disliked
the studied laugh with which he ended his remarks, and
he told some stories that were not only coarse in themselves, and calculated to lower a man's opinion of
women in general, but, in view of the fact that he had
just been introduced to the wife of his host, were certainly in the very worst taste. The style in which
he told them added to their unpleasantness, and I felt a
great desire stealing over me to throw him out of the
window which was open behind him. His facetiousness
and levity contrasted well with the gravity and bu-
siness-like air of the others. They laughed at his
stories, and encouraged him to proceed, but I was not
much astonished when I heard afterward that he was a
mere puppet in their hands. Mr. Hammond sipped his
wine slowly, and built little pyramids of orange seeds
on the table-cloth, casting curious glances at Mr.
Masters, and making but few remarks. Now and then,
when referred to by Mr. Walker, he would explain
fluently and elegantly the properties of certain kinds
of earth, and the wealth that lay hidden in them. He
knew the value of land in all the different States, and
talked so well and learnedly on the subject, that I did
not wonder at the influence he exerted over Mr. Lecount.
He was certainly most fascinating, both from his extended knowledge, and the graceful manner in which
he dispensed it. He was a fine theorist. Having heard

him describe how fortunes might be made by skilfully
uniting science with labor, it seemed the easiest thing
in the world to be worth millions.

I began to wonder if the practice of his superior
knowledge and fine theories had placed him in the possession of unbounded wealth.   Surely, if he could tell
others just what to do in order to turn every thing they
touched into gold, he himself must be a perfect Crœsus.
His appearance would warrant such a supposition.   His
clothes were costly, and his hands white and soft as a
woman's.   They had never been soiled by manual labor—his head had saved them from such a necessity.
I felt myself sharing in the general admiration that he
excited, and I could not help wishing that all Mr. Lecount's friends were equally gentlemanly and well-in-
formed.   That any one could associate with the short,
stout gentleman, whom they called Phil, and not be
contaminated, was out of the question.   I feared the
effect of such an intercourse on a character like Mr.
Lecount's.   He lost dignity in the companionship, a fact
which was already visible when we rose from the table.
Mr. Lecount was flushed and unsteady, with a reckless,
daring expression in his face, and an unpleasant glitter
in his eyes.

"Come, Phil!" he shouted.   "Come into the parlor, and the ladies will give us some music."

Happily, Phil, or rather, Mr. Hunter, to give him
his proper name, knew more of his own condition than
Mr. Lecount did.   He obstinately refused to move, so

we left him sitting near the window, with the pure, fresh air blowing on his heated face.

We had to cross the broad hall to reach the parlor, and the doors being all wide open, I caught sight of young Mrs. Lecount, seated near one of the windows. She looked up quickly on hearing our steps and voices, and Mr. Masters and I noticed the dull, despairing expression that settled on her face when her eyes fell on her husband, as he came through the hall, looking quite wild, and switching his handkerchief in the air. With an exclamation of disgust Mr. Masters turned away and went out through the open door. Mr. Hammond took a seat near Mrs. Lecount, and began a conversation on the new opera company promised to them in the fall. He had heard several of the singers in Europe, and he discussed their voices and styles, described their relative merits, and explained their chief attractions, using numerous musical terms in Italian with the ease and fluency of an old manager. Mrs. Lecount listened, assented, and disapproved, while he gave his recollections of Grisi and Mario, compared Formes and Amodio, criticised Alboni, and lavished encomiums on La Grange. In spite of his powers of conversation and the interest of the subject, Mrs. Lecount often made absent-minded replies, and her eyes wandered constantly toward her husband, where he stood talking earnestly to Mr. Walker in rather loud tones. The words "fifty per cent.," "poor stock," "going up rapidly," "none in the market," "humbug," "credit," fell on our ears, mingled

with opinions on "Norma," "Belisario," "Ernani," and
other operas, in the low, measured tones of Mr. Hammond.

"Claude, will you never become tired of stocks and
bonds? Do come here and tell us which opera you prefer," Miss Pauline at last remarked, with a significant
glance which was quite unheeded by her brother.

"I am so fond of music! will you favor me with
some?" asked Mr. Hammond, looking at Miss Pauline.

She went to the piano and played an air with brilliant variations. It had an effect. Mr. Hammond was
bending over her the next moment, watching her slender fingers as they touched the keys. Stocks were forgotten for the moment, and Mr. Lecount approached
his wife.

"I want you to sing that little song from 'Mari-
taña,' 'The memory of the past.' Mr. Hammond was
speaking of it the other day."

It was the first time that Mr. Lecount had addressed
his wife that evening, and his manner of doing it was
rather curious. · She clasped her hands and looked in
his face.

"Not that song; don't ask for that to-night, Claude,"
she said, imploringly, and in a softened tone of voice.
For the moment she was like her old self.

"And why not to-night? What is there in that
any more than in any other song, *now?* They are all
alike. I hate sentimentalism!"

"Then, if all songs are alike, I shall sing something

else," Mrs. Lecount answered coldly, with an instant
return to her haughty manner.

"You will sing what I asked for first," Mr. Lecount
said, offering his arm. She rose and walked to the
piano without touching it or looking at him. Miss
Pauline made room for her smilingly, and every one in
the place became instantly silent. Mr. Hammond listened with astonishment at first, which gave place to
admiration, as the clear, sweet voice filled the room.
She sang with an expression born of real feeling, and
with a passionate sadness that proved to me the presence of true sorrow in her heart.

Mr. Masters had entered the room, attracted by the
music, and Mr. Hunter also appeared on the scene.
Mrs. Lecount sang again and again at the earnest en-
treaties of Mr. Hammond and her husband's requests,
which were, in reality, commands. It was a late hour
when the party broke up, and Mr. Masters walked home
without opening his lips, a very bad sign with him. He
took his lamp and nodded good-night to us in the same
manner, and Mrs. Masters followed him with an expressive glance and a sorrowful shake of her head. Altogether it was the most curious dinner-party that I had
ever assisted at, and had signally failed in giving pleasure to some of the guests.

"Don't tell me that Belle is happy, John!" said
my sister, the moment my mother had left the room.
"If you like to think so, you may, but it will take a
great deal to make me believe it. I never saw any-

body so changed as she is; and as for Claude, if that is all New York has done for him, he might better have remained at home here. Mrs. Hope says he looks ten years older than he did when he was here last, and that was just before his marriage. It is well that none of the neighbors knew much about Belle; they would be more astonished at the alteration in her. I was glad that Mr. and Mrs. Lecount and Marie were so pleasant; they made the affair go off well. As for Pauline, she was nearly crazy, and I can't wonder at it."

"Then you think that no one noticed any thing odd about young Mr. Lecount and his wife?"

"I didn't hear any remarks of that kind. They all thought Belle very beautiful and very distant. However, they seem to think that the latter quality belongs to city people, and I did not undeceive them. I suppose you know that the gentlemen are all going away next week to examine some water-power in Connecticut, and Belle has to go along with them. Claude intends to remain there two months at least, and it is decided that she and Arthur will stay with him."

"And Miss Pauline?"

"Oh! she goes too. She is in raptures with the place already. Mr. Hammond has described it so beautifully, they anticipate a great amount of pleasure. It is very wild, and so picturesque; just the place for picnics and boating-parties."

"Mr. Hammond is quite fascinating," I remarked.

"Yes; he is a gentleman as far as we can see. I

wish that the same might be said of Mr. Hunter. Poor
Belle actually shivered when he took her hand in his.
Imagine having to spend some time in his company, and
sit down to dinner with him every day! I do wonder
where Claude makes the acquaintance of such people."

"And I wonder how he dares to introduce them to
his wife."

"That is a fact. If I were Belle, I should refuse to
receive them."

"If you were Belle, you might discover that you
couldn't always carry out your own ideas. As long as
she remains under her husband's protection, she is bound
to obey him, no matter what the effort to do so may
cost her. The fault lies with him altogether; he has
no business to invite such men to his house, just because
it is his, and he can bring whom he likes into it. He
should respect her tastes; and he must know that persons
of Mr. Hunter's stamp are entirely beneath her notice."

"Well, John, it all comes of these stocks and bonds.
Mr. Masters says he cannot help meeting with these
men in business connections, and he is so absorbed in
the matter that he is not satisfied with seeing them out
of doors, but must have them home in the evening. No
wonder Belle looks changed; she must be thoroughly
tired of entertaining speculators. Claude has lost his
taste for music; she has hardly a new song, and she
don't speak as if she visited much. I can't imagine how
she amuses herself, unless it is in taking care of Arthur.
She is neither old enough nor worldly-minded enough

to throw herself into fashionable amusements as other
women do when their husbands desert their society for
that of these fascinating stockholders. She is just the
girl to place all her affections on her husband, and depend on him for all her happiness. If he fails her, she
will fret and mope; but it will be some time before she
undertakes to find amusements for herself that he can't
share in. I don't understand the matter at all, and I
never think of it without pain. After all our efforts and
successes, we have failed in accomplishing the chief-end
that we had in view. Belle is not happy; nothing can
convince me to the contrary."

CHAPTER X.

A TALK WITH MR. MASTERS.

My sister's opinion, so freely expressed, caused me much uneasiness, and Mr. Masters', when I heard it, only augmented my fears. The next day, after dinner, he called to me to join him in the garden, where he was walking without his usual accompaniment, a good cigar, and its absence was a very bad sign with him. His manner was nervous and irritable, and his eyes searched my face with a troubled, restless expression in them, as if he needed help, but saw no way of obtaining it. I had been absent since the morning, and was ignorant of how he had spent his day.

"What am I to do?" he began, drawing my arm through his and looking around to see that no one was within hearing distance. "What can I do? What did you think of Mr. Hammond yesterday?"

"I rather admired him," I answered. "He is a gentleman in manner and appearance, at least, and his knowledge is very general and correct as far as I can judge."

Mr. Masters sighed, and shook his head.

"That is the trouble. I cannot succeed in exciting the least suspicion of him in any one, and I can prove very little to his discredit, although my own mind is fully made up about him."

"What do you fear?" I asked, looking and feeling astonished at his words.

"Fear? I fear every thing that is bad for Claude Lecount. He is in the hands of an unprincipled set of men, but I dread Mr. Hammond more than all the others together. His very plausibility and modesty are, in my eyes, his worst features. But, to make you understand what I mean, I must tell you how things have been going on for the last two years. I think that Mr. Hammond's influence has controlled Claude for that length of time. I know that he was inclined to speculate before he married Belle. Mr. Walker's success gave him a taste for it. At first he was governed by Walker's advice, and he always told me what he had in contemplation. The schemes were generally good ones, but very slow in bringing in returns for the sums laid out on them. He sunk in that way a great deal of the money that I had realized for his wife. It had been made by the investment of part of her yearly interest from the estate, and, as it was outside of her regular income, I was satisfied to let him use it as he pleased. When it was all withdrawn from where I had it paying interest, and sunk in his speculations, I thought that he would be satisfied to await the results, and, in the mean time, prosecute his legitimate busi ·

ness. I was mistaken. Mr. Hammond all at once gave up Mr. Walker, and attached himself to Mr. Lecount. What they are doing I cannot tell, being no longer admitted into their confidence. It is quite enough for me to know that during the last two years their income has not met their expenses, and I have had to advance money to Belle before her own was due, so that she could pay her house bills. In all justice, they should be able to live well, and save every year some thousands of dollars. The money is paid into Mr. Lecount's hands, and I know that Mrs. Lecount is not personally more extravagant than is allowable; still it all goes—how, I cannot make out. It is a hard task to warn a wife against her husband, and so far I have not been able to make up my mind to do it. Last week I made a discovery which convinces me that Claude will squander all she has unless I interfere. It was that discovery that brought me up here now. This morning I tried to tell it to my ward, but I found it utterly impossible to break it to her. I went up to the house for no other purpose. I felt sure that the gentlemen would be out, and I was right—they were all gone fishing. She came down to me, looking so sweet and innocent, with her child in her arms, and so bright and happy, that I could not bring the words out. They would have choked me; and yet the attempt must be made, and that at once."

"Then you thought she looked happy," I said.

"Yes, totally different from yesterday. She was gentle and childish, as she used to be. I think, if she

11

had been in the same mood that she was in last night, I could have explained every thing to her without an effort; she would have seemed ready to hear it; but the change in her destroyed all my plans, and although the ladies left us, and I had a fine opportunity of opening my mind to her, I came away without even hinting at the subject that interests me."

"And you say that it is necessary for her to know it?"

"Let me tell you, Doctor Wilmer. Last week I found out that Claude had been indorsing for Mr. Hammond to the extent of ten thousand dollars. That startled me. Next I heard that Mr. Lecount was negotiating for a heavy loan, for which a mortgage would be given on a valuable piece of her property that is at present free of all encumbrance. I connected the two things at once. She is only a woman, and she loves her husband; if Mr. Hammond cannot take up his own paper, Claude must, and she will sacrifice every thing to preserve his credit. All this is under the supposition that she understands the whole affair; but, if Claude don't care to let his wife into his secrets, a very little persuasion on his part will suffice, and she will sign every thing that he puts before her without having the least idea of the importance of what she does."

"Have you made any inquiries about Mr. Hammond?" I asked, feeling more and more the reasonableness of the old man's anxiety.

"I have; it was my first move; and the more I

learned of him, the more cause I had for uneasiness. So far she has not signed the papers. I have now to show her the reasons why she must not be induced to do such a thing, and obtain her solemn promise that she will not be urged or forced to put her signature to any paper without my knowledge and consent. It is a hard duty, that you must admit, and I fear I shall lose my friend; but Arthur Ferris's daughter shall not be ruined by these sharpers if I can prevent it, and I shall use all my influence to counteract their schemes. Will you aid me?"

"I will!" I said, grasping the hand he held out to me. "Courage! think of how many dangers she has escaped, and don't despair of saving her from this one!"

The old man raised his head, brushed a few tears away, and smiled brightly, as if imbued with fresh energy.

"You do me good," he said, with one of his honest glances searching my face. "I shall feel quite strong and able to meet them all if I have you to stand by me. Mrs. Masters always insisted that you had more influence over Belle than all the rest of us put together. If it comes to the worst, you must promise to test it again."

"I am afraid you overrate my powers," I said, thinking of the effort that such an interview would cost me.

"Well, I shall not call upon you unless it becomes absolutely necessary. The matter must be settled soon. I understand she accompanies her husband to Connecti-

cut; that affair depends on the other. He cannot em-
bark in the speculation without a new supply of ready
money, which money he, of course, expects to raise on
her property. If I succeed, that speculation will have
to be abandoned, and so what I intend to do must be
done at once."

"You should see her, then, to-morrow. A great deal
can be done in one day, and Mr. Lecount may wish to be
sure of the money before he examines the investment."

"That is true. I shall lose no more time in securing
Mrs. Lecount's promise. If I can only convince her of
Mr. Hammond's lack of standing or reputation, the matter will be easy after the first plunge. That is what
I dread. I went to the hotel where Mr. Hammond
stops, and inquired about him. You would be amused
at the answers I received. It seems that he sometimes
sleeps in the house, but he has no regular room. He
calls every day, however, for his letters, which are directed there, and meets gentlemen very often by appointment in the reading-room. He has given some
dinners there, and the clerk seemed very much impressed with his importance, and has an idea that, when
not there, Mr. Hammond is stopping by invitation at
the house of one of his very numerous friends."

"The idea is a true one at present," I said, laughing.

"You're right. For once, at least, the clerk is not
mistaken. The trouble is, that the man could give me
no further intelligence, except that he came from St.
Louis. I went at once to a friend of mine who has busi-

ness connections there, and asked him to make inquiries about this Mr. Hammond for me."

" Well, and the result—"

" Justified all my fears. Mr. Hammond represents himself as a man of property and position. The only person of the name that my friend could discover any thing about was a well-known gambler and sharper who left there some years ago. He belonged to a respectable family, was well educated, and started in life with some means left him by his father. My friend met several old residents there, who knew all about him, and their description of him answers for this gentleman who has acquired such an influence over Claude. There is no doubt in my mind but that they are one and the same person. These people even mentioned his amount of general information, and said how extraordinary it was that a man possessed of so much knowledge had made so little use of it. They attributed this to his natural indolence and his early association. When he left college he joined a fast set, and lived on his money till it was all squandered. By that time he had grown so accustomed to a life of ease and pleasure that application to any one pursuit required a steadiness and energy that he had outlived, allowing that he had ever possessed them, which I doubt very much. The result is, that he lives partly by gambling, and principally by attaching himself to men of means, winning their confidence by his polished manners and agreeable information, and borrowing money from them by representing that he is rich and willing to pay a heavy rate of interest for the loan."

"And is there no way of convincing Mr. Lecount of his true character?"

"So far I have been foiled in every attempt that I have made. Mr. Lecount is young, and, if I must say it, lacks foresight. The fact of having a rich wife is likely to ruin him if some change is not effected in him soon. It will take him years to make the sum that he has committed himself for, and I am quite willing that his money should go in that way, if he would only earn it by practising law. In time he would master his profession and have the means to indulge in these rash speculations, although I think that if he had to work for the money he would not risk it so foolishly. As it is, his business is neglected, and he seems to think that his wife's fortune is inexhaustible, and quite at his disposal to throw away and lend as he pleases."

"He is still very young," I said.

"Yes, and his youth may excuse his rashness, but it does not excuse his presumption and want of respect for older and wiser heads. I told him, before he married Belle, that I was satisfied that she should marry a poor man, provided he had a good calling in life that he was willing to pursue honestly and steadily. It made no difference to me what it was, so long as it might be named as fair and legitimate. I told him that she had enough and to spare, and could assist him whenever he saw a good opportunity for investing money. I knew

that Belle only valued her money for the good it would
do, and I did not like to hurt his pride, or let him feel
for one moment that his wife was conferring any favors
on him.   For that reason I showed him all that I was
doing, and explained every thing connected with her
affairs to him.   I placed all her income in his hands;
she would not have it otherwise, and the first thing she
requested him to do for her was to put his father's
house in perfect order.   Her delicacy was almost morbid in every thing relating to money; every dollar she
spends passes through his hands before she has it, and
she is careful in every way about offending his pride.
No one would ever suppose for one moment that the
money he uses so lavishly comes from her, and that
his complete power over it is the result of her perfect
trust in his good faith.   One might think that her carelessness proceeded from ignorance; but it is not the
case.   She understands her own position thoroughly.   I
was determined that she should.   I made her apply all
she had learned about interest, dividends, and per cent.
by comprehending her own affairs.   If she signs these
papers, however, before I see her, the probability is that
she will not fully understand them; if she does it afterward, I shall know that, at any rate, she is fully conscious of the importance of the action."

"But you hope to prevent such an unfortunate thing
being accomplished?"

"Yes, I hope it.   When I look back on the last three
years, and think how Mr. Lecount has abused the confi-

dence placed in him by his wife and her friends, I lose all compunctions about showing her her husband's character in its true light."

"It is a difficult thing to do under any circumstances, and particularly so in your case. Is there no alternative? Can you not reason with him?"

"Reason with him, Doctor Wilmer! I have tried every argument applicable to the case. I even told him that I considered these transactions dishonest when carried on with his wife's money. I said that, even if he had earned it himself, it would be wrong to risk her comfort and the means of supporting her by such doubtful speculations. He answered me rudely, and declared that, if we were to remain friends, it could only be through my paying no attention to his affairs. I said that I considered it my affair in a measure; and his answer was, that, once I paid the yearly income into his hands to use for his family's good, all my interest in it ceased. I blame myself now for giving him so much power in the matter, but, at the time, it appeared to be the best thing for their happiness that I could do. This last year he has been worse than ever; as I told you, I have had to advance money to them to meet expenses. If he makes any thing in his business, it goes with the rest, and if he were to succeed in what he contemplates at present, she would be ruined before the time that her father appointed for her to come into full control of her property. She is now nearly twenty-four, and at thirty-five all my interest in the matter ceases.

Then she can do as she pleases. Mr. Lecount may start what speculations he sees fit. One of his recent investments is a diamond-mine in Brazil, and most of his others are just about equally sensible and profitable. They sound amusing, and I might laugh at them if they concerned a stranger, but I cannot take the matter easy when Belle is to be the loser.

"Any thing I can do to help you I will," I said. "Arrange some plan for speaking to her, and we will assist you in accomplishing it."

"I need not tell you that Claude no longer likes me; you must have noticed last evening how restive he was because I remained after dinner with his friends. I knew he did not want me there, but my suspicions were aroused, and I was determined to hear all I could. He attempted to stop them several times, but they let enough drop to satisfy me. He has tried to quarrel with me more than once, but he did not succeed. I understand him. He would be delighted to prevent me meeting his wife. However, I shall put up with any thing from him for the sake of seeing her now and then, and watching over her. She seldom comes near us now, never in the evening except by invitation. Only for her morning visits, when she brings her child and his nurse with her, I don't know what would become of my wife and me. We have grown so used to her and so fond of her, that the idea of gradually losing her is very hard to bear. I know that she feels the influence that is separating us, but she does not like to ac-

11*

knowledge it to herself, and she tries to hide it from us.
In some things she is but a child still. Now, my idea
is this. Let us all go up there to-night for a short time.
I ought to leave for home to-morrow, and if I can succeed
in warning her it can pass for a farewell visit, as there
is a necessity for my presence in New York, and nothing but this affair to detain me here. Of course, I shall
remain longer if not successful to-night, and shall depend on you to keep Miss Pauline engaged in conversation in another part of the room."

I promised, and we returned to the house to prepare
for the visit.

When we reached Mr. Lecount's, there was a noisy
party assembled at the dinner-table; we could hear their
voices and loud laughter before we caught sight of the
gentlemen themselves, which we did through the open
blinds as we approached the house. When we entered
the parlor, young Mrs. Lecount was absent from the
family circle gathered round the centre-table. Our
coming caused no surprise, as it was the custom for
neighbors to drop in upon each other whenever they
felt like it.

The ladies looked very bright and handsome, and,
with their various pieces of gay fancy-work in their
hands, were quite ready for visitors and a long gossip.
The formality of the preceding day had disappeared,
and the usual ease and graceful merriment, always so
enjoyable, were in the ascendant. Mrs. Lecount had
nearly regained her health, and was, if any thing, more

fascinating than her handsome daughters. My admiration for her was an understood thing, so she made room for me on the sofa, with a bright smile, and, placing her skein of wool over my hands, went on winding it as if my holding it were the most natural and regular thing in the world.

"Where is Belle?" called out my sister, with a glance that took in all the recesses in the room.

Mrs. Lecount looked at her daughter and then at me, without answering.

"She is not quite well—" commenced Miss Pauline.

"Now, Pauline, why do you say that to frighten Mr. Masters and every one else?" said Miss Marie, in her own straightforward manner, and looking full in her sister's face. "The truth is," she went on, lowering her voice, "Belle does not like one of Claude's friends well enough to meet him again at the table, and so, under plea of a slight headache, she has remained upstairs all the evening. I think she is quite right—I would do the same thing myself. That Mr. Hunter is not a gentleman, and she cannot put up with his impudent familiarity. Her head must ache enough now, for her chamber is over the dining-room, and his voice is loud enough to be heard all over the house. If he goes with the others to Connecticut, I can't imagine what Belle will do. She told me distinctly, this morning, that she would not meet him again."

"Let me go up to her," said my sister; "Mr. Masters thinks of leaving us in the morning, and I am sure she will want to see him. I know she will come down for me."

"Tell her Mr. Hunter is still at the table, and not likely to leave it for some time. She may venture down for a few minutes," Miss Marie said, half laughingly.

"And if Arthur is awake, tell her to bring him down too—I want to see him," added Mrs. Masters.

My sister left the room, and Mr. Masters waited impatiently for his ward's appearance.

Miss Pauline seemed ill at ease, and cast longing glances toward the open door of the dining-room, as if wishing for the presence of the gentlemen in the parlor. Her answers to my remarks were quite vague and absent-minded, and I felt that she dreaded a meeting between Mr. Masters and her sister-in-law, without knowing exactly what to do to prevent it.

In a few minutes young Mrs. Lecount entered, with her child half asleep in her arms. She gave him to Mrs. Masters, fondly kissing the old lady as she did so.

"I was just rocking him to sleep when you came in," she said; "I am so glad to see you all! but why must you return to New York to-morrow?" and she put her hand on Mr. Masters' arm, and looked into his face appealingly, as if afraid of losing a certain support with his departure.

He drew her arm in his, and walked off to the end of the long room, with some gay answer as to satisfying her curiosity. They stood for some time near a distant window, and then sat down, almost concealed from

view by its heavy curtains, and the shadow of a large
book-case that stood near by. Miss Pauline watched
them suspiciously, but suddenly becoming conscious of
my observation, she joined in the conversation caused
by little Arthur's baby-prattle and mischief. He was
sitting quite contentedly with Mrs. Masters, flourishing
about an expensive fan of his aunt's, that he had
snatched off one of the little tables. My sister was
making quiet efforts to take it from him, as it was
threatened with speedy destruction, and the young
gentleman seemed just as determined to retain possession of it. His attempts to open and use it in imitation
of his aunt would have been quite amusing, if the toy
had been less costly. At last his movements attracted
Miss Pauline's attention, and she forgot for a time Mr.
Masters and his ward!

"You little mischief," she exclaimed, rising hastily.
"Give it to me this instant!"

Master Arthur only clutched it the tighter as she
spoke, and began to scream for his mother. Miss Pauline caught his hands and rescued her fan, while his
cries rose higher and louder, and in the midst of the
excitement the gentlemen sauntered into the room.
Mr. Lecount looked around him as if astonished.

"Have done, sir!" he said to his child, in a decided
tone. The little fellow choked back his sobs, and
obeyed instantly; then he fixed his eyes on his father's
face, while the tears trickled down his pretty cheeks,
but without moving or attempting to say a word.

Mr. Hammond stopped to look at him, with some remark on his beauty.

"Where is his nurse?" asked Mr. Lecount, turning to his sister, as if weary of the scene.

"I shall take him," answered a soft voice, and young Mrs. Lecount came forward, followed by Mr. Masters. She took her child in her arms, bowed distantly to all in the room, and went up-stairs. Her face was white and rigid, and her eyes looked as if she had been crying. Mr. Lecount, for a moment, stood confused, and an angry glare flashed in his eyes; but he recovered himself quickly, and spoke to us as usual. We did not remain long that evening. Mr. Masters was not in a sociable mood, and refused to join the other gentlemen in a game of *vingt-et-un*, which they were enjoying very much. I felt that we were a restraint on them, and I think that they were relieved when we rose to say good-night. When we reached home, Mr. Masters took my arm and told me the result of his interview with his ward, while we walked up and down the long piazza.

"You would hardly have given her credit for so much sense and spirit," he said. "Her husband wished her to sign those papers in New York, and he has urged her to consent repeatedly, since they came here. She refused steadily to do it, unless I approved of the measure. She wanted him to show me the papers the other day. His anger at the proposition raised her curiosity, and she discovered that I knew nothing from him about

the matter. Then she told him that she disliked the
friends that he has with him, and felt that their influence over him was injurious, and could only lead to
evil. She says, that only for Hunter, she thinks she
would have signed them some days ago, but she overheard him asking Claude if they were all right, and
her dislike of the man made her suspicious. She said,
very innocently, that she did not think any thing he
recommended could be good for Claude. She tried to
screen Claude all she could, but I know that he has
been very rough with her, and I intend to tell him what
I think of this affair before long. When I explained
about Hammond's notes, she begged of me to think of
some plan for saving her husband's credit. She knows,
as well as I do, that neither party will be able to take
them up. So I consented to get possession of them for
her, and she promised that she would sign nothing
without my knowledge. She feels as I do about these
speculations, and is just as much opposed to sinking
good money in them. Of course, she realizes the waste
that has been going on, and, what is more, she has
penetrated Mr. Hammond's designs, and distrusts him
entirely. She thinks he is too complimentary to be
sincere, and he annoys her with his attentions. She
quite astonished me; I did not give her credit for so
much shrewdness."

"I think," I said, "that she possesses the gift of
reading character, but what surprises me is, her lack of
influence with Mr. Lecount."

"I have often wondered at it too. After they were married a short time, she seemed to lose it, not gradually, but all at once. I have often noticed the change in his manner toward her. He shows neither tenderness nor respect, and yet she has not lost her claim on both. She has never lowered herself in his estimation, and she is still young and beautiful. I know that, womanlike, she has tried every thing in her power to wean him from these men, from gentle persuasion to downright opposition, as we saw to-night. One seems to be about as effective as the other. All the love in the world won't save a man from ruin if he is determined not to use his own reasoning powers. Nothing will stop Claude but want of means, and as long as his wife's property yields money, he will sink every cent he can gain possession of. She will have many a hard struggle to save what her father left her, and I anticipate a stormy interview with Mr. Claude after he hears of what took place to-night."

"What a position for her!" I said, almost unconsciously. Mr. Masters heard me.

"Yes, I was sorry for it, but what could I do? It was an ungrateful task to tell a wife to disobey her husband; but I should be false to my trust if I let him beggar her and himself; and it would take more money than I could furnish to meet his demands. He will be angry enough, for this Connecticut expedition must be given up, and how he will manage to excuse himself and his capital to the gentlemen, is more than I can

imagine. Only for her, I could laugh at the idea of
their faces when he tells them that he cannot par-
ticipate in their immense profits—and losses."

The next morning Mr. Masters left us for New
York. His wife remained, hoping to see more of her
darling, but for several days we saw nothing of the
Lecount family. We heard that the gentlemen from
New York were still there; and once or twice, when
returning home late at night, I had seen lights in the
house, and heard loud voices proceeding from it through
the open windows. My sister was busy making her
winter preserves, and besides, a little ceremonious.
She thought it was time for Belle and Pauline to call on
us. One morning, contrary to my usual habit, I was
in my office attending to a patient, when I heard a loud
barking, and considerable screaming. I looked out of
the window, and saw Master Arthur Lecount with his
arms around Dash's shaggy neck, attempting to climb
on his back. His mother was looking at him, half
frightened, half delighted at his courage, and his nurse
was holding him back with an energy almost ludicrous.
As usual, the child gained the day; he was lifted to the
coveted place on Dash's woolly back, and came in triumph up the path, refusing to be held on by either
mother or nurse. When I was at leisure, I went into
the parlor, expecting to find the family there, but they
were all gathered on the piazza, watching Master
Arthur enjoying himself. He was screaming with
delight, still perched on his dangerous seat, for Dash,

being quite unused to such treatment, was growing
restless under his young rider, and seemed disposed to
throw him on his head by a sudden rush to the kennel.
Young Mrs. Lecount was leaning against the nearest
tree, with extended hands, ready to catch her spoiled
darling if he should fall. She was looking remarkably
bright at the moment, and laughing at my sister's
remarks on the way she was ruining the boy. Seen in
repose, her face was careworn and sorrowful, and there
were large circles round her eyes, now dim and sunken,
though once so brilliant and full of expression.

My coming relieved her anxiety a little, for Dash
put his head under my arm and became quiet, and
Master Arthur grew tired of his play when there was
no longer any danger and consequent glory attached
to it, and ran off to gather my sister's favorite roses and
pinks. His nurse followed him, making vain attempts
to protect them. Mrs. Lecount sank with a low sigh
on her favorite old seat, a rustic bench, half hidden by
climbing roses and honeysuckles. Their slender, twin-
ing branches formed a bright-green frame for her slight,
graceful figure; and I never smell the perfume of their
blossoms without recalling the pretty picture that she
made so unconsciously, while listening, with a sad,
dreamy look in her face, to my mother's lecture.

"You are destroying your own health, my child,
forever running after Arthur, and fretting about him.
You should have more trust in Providence, and more
confidence in his nurse. If you think she is too young

and giddy for the charge, you should look for an older
person that you could rely upon."

"Mr. Lecount chose this girl himself; he was delighted with her accent, it was so remarkably pure,
and I know he would be very unwilling to part with
her; besides, I have no fault to find; she is both careful
and good-tempered."

"Then why sacrifice your own health for no reason?
It can do Arthur no good either now or in the future.
Besides, your unceasing anxiety shows a want of faith,
and yet your faith was once very strong." My mother
held out her hand as if to soften, by a caress, the apparent harshness of her speech.

Mrs. Lecount suddenly threw her arms around my
mother with one of her old passionate impulses, and laid
her young face against the worn, faded cheek.

"I have not lost my faith," she exclaimed, "oh, no!
I have not lost that. But if I ever had any self-reliance
it is all gone. I have lost confidence in myself; I am
afraid of not doing my duty to Arthur; if *he* should ever
reproach me for that, it would kill me. If I only had
you near me to tell me what is right! but I have no one
to guide me, and so many to please. It is hard to know
always just what is right to do; I try to be governed
by principle, but sometimes passion overcomes me, and
I fail. You can excuse me; you know what a mere
child I was when I left you three years ago. I was
young and foolish to undertake the cares of life, but I
met them bravely because I was so ignorant of all that

they required. I suppose I have gained wisdom by experience, but very often I feel as helpless and as childish
as I did the first day you saw me. I felt so this morning, and I came to you; I knew the sound of your voice
would do me good, and I will remember your advice
about Arthur." She rose as she spoke.

"Where are you going?" asked my sister, surprised.

" Going to bid you good-by. I promised to return
soon." She tried to smile as she spoke, but ended by
crying softly.

My sister could not repress her astonishment. "Why,
what do you mean, Belle? You have not stood in the
house for three years, and this is your first visit since
you came."

"Yes, and I left the bad news for the end. We are
going home to-night. Mr. Lecount will not remain
here any longer, so my first visit is my last. But I must
have one run through the dear old rooms so that I can
picture them in my mind, until I see them again."
She went gayly into the house arm in arm with my
mother, and I heard her lamenting the absence of some
old pieces of furniture, now replaced by new ones, more
fashionable and less enjoyable. She gathered flowers
from the plants that she had once tended, and exclaimed
with wondering delight at the size of some geraniums
that had grown from slips of her own setting. She
flitted from bush to bush, pointing out their beauties to
Arthur, and delighting my mother by recalling happy

recollections of the days that she had spent among them. Each was associated in her mind with some little incident trifling in itself, and possessed of no interest for others, yet it filled a page in the book of her girlish life.

At last the bright hour was over; there was a hurried, tearful good-by spoken, and the gate was closed on our welcome visitors. I felt that every thing surrounding me had lost a part of its attraction; the bushes were dusty, and the flowers drooped; the house appeared cold, and in want of repair; the garden-bench, so picturesque when she sat upon it, had retaken its old form; it was merely a worm-eaten board, darkened by wind and weather, and fit only for firewood. Her disappearance had the effect of the last stroke of midnight in the fairy tale. When next I looked at myself in the mirror, I felt that I appeared older and graver than I had before she came.

CHAPTER XI.

IN WHICH THE FIRST LINK OF A CURIOUS CHAIN IS FORGED.

THE following day Mr. Lecount's house settled into its usual habits, to his great relief, and we returned to our monotonous, happy life. Miss Pauline had gone to New York with the others; it appeared to be an understood thing that she should reside with them. I heard my mother and sister discussing the subject one night. They thought that the arrangement was a bad one, and not likely to lead to good results. To me the matter seemed unworthy of consideration, but I knew nothing of the small annoyances, so well understood by women, that often arise under such circumstances.

As the weeks passed, we heard little of what was taking place in the family. The winter that followed was dull, owing to the unsettled condition of the country. The political horizon was dark and threatening. Public credit and private fortunes were shaken. The men talked of failure, and the women of economy. I met gloom and despondency on every threshold. The saving of money was the theme of conversation, and the subject of deep thought. People hardly anticipated that the time was coming, when not only their money, but the lives of their children, should be demanded of them.

Political discussions were in the ascendant; and my sister, always ambitious of being my companion, by dint of listening and hard reading, became quite conversant with the questions that were agitating the country. Mr. Masters kept me supplied with the pamphlets and newspapers that discussed politics. We had all sides of the questions before us, and our little circle of friends was about equally divided on them. The Lecounts were for State rights decidedly; others were still hesitating as to which side was upholding the Constitution more were uncompromising Federalists. Our discussions, though noisy, were always friendly and interesting. Several of the opposing members of the circle were men of learning and deep foresight. They argued with this idea always in view, What is best for the future welfare of the country? Maps were looked up, the political opinions of the founders of the government were searched out and discussed. I learned more of the policy of the country that winter, its internal condition, and the aims of its opposing parties, than I had ever done in all my previous years put together.

In the midst of these agreeable debates I received a letter from Mr. Masters. He was quite sick, and desired to see me without delay. I went down to him at once.

He was confined to his room by a heavy cold, and its effects were only too visible in his altered appearance and weak voice.

"You see, doctor, I am growing old," he said, while the smile with which he had welcomed me faded from his face. "This winter has been hard on me; and anxiety wears more than work. Things have been growing worse and worse between Mr. Lecount and me. His wife has, so far, kept her promise, and he has not forgiven me for exacting it. He was here the other night, and had the coolness to ask me if I intended appointing him as my successor in the trusteeship of his wife's property. I told him no, decidedly; that in my estimation he was not fit for the responsibility. He became very abusive; happily, Belle was down-stairs with Mrs. Masters, and did not hear him. He demanded to know whom I had appointed, and I told him 'No one.' After he was gone I thought the matter over, and I begin to realize that it is time to make a choice. I need an honest man and one that feels an interest in my ward; you will tell me that you do not live here, and that you know but little of mortgages and real estate. You can learn enough of them in six months to understand her affairs; they are in good order. As far as the practical part of the business is concerned, it is in the hands of a fine lawyer, the one her father employed. He will confer with you when it is necessary, and you will judge honestly for her interest. I feel that I can trust you; that is why I have sent for you to ask this favor from you. It is a responsibility, but not one that an honest man should shrink from undertaking. She will have every confidence in you, and you know enough of Mr. Lecount to be careful of him. I dare not leave it in his hands, and I know of none but you that I am sure could not be overcome by his plausible arguments."

He looked at me earnestly for a few moments, and then held out his hand.

"Think it over to-night, doctor, and tell me your answer in the morning. After tea, if you are not too tired, I will just show you how her money is invested, and what you would have to do. Don't let my need of you overcome any principle of right that it might unsettle; do just what you feel to be correct. At the same time, don't be too modest in weighing your own abilities; don't let any idea of ignorance prevent you from saying 'Yes!'"

After tea Mr. Masters took a bundle of papers out of his safe, and went over them with me; explaining now and then what I did not understand, and often stopping in the middle of a sentence to figure up a sum or calculate interest. As he had told me, every thing was clear and concise; it needed but little effort to comprehend the state of Mrs. Lecount's affairs. The consideration that made me hesitate in accepting the trust was, the conviction that Mr. Lecount disliked me. His manner and conversation, whenever I was in his company, had convinced me of the fact. As jealousy was the only motive for this that I could think of, I disliked being

12

drawn into relations with Mrs. Lecount that might increase his mistrust, and cause her more trouble. I knew that she would have every confidence in my honesty and judgment, but that her husband would not. In the event of our opinions not agreeing, and discussions arising, the fact of having to side with me against him would be unpleasant for her, and injurious to her comfort. A greater stranger would, under such circumstances, make a more acceptable guardian.

On the other hand, Mr. Masters mistrusted the policy of putting all power into the hands of one not personally interested in her welfare. Then, again, Mr. Masters was not dangerously sick, and his constitution was naturally good; he might live for years beyond her thirty-fifth birthday. The very fact, of not being sure of a person that he trusted to succeed him, was wearing on his mind and spirits, and prolonged his illness. When I mentioned my reason for hesitating in the matter, he laughed.

"If Lecount's dislike is all that holds you back, you may make your mind easy. He will dislike any one that I appoint. He was silly enough to think that I would name him, and no one else will suit him. I told his wife that I would not do it under any consideration. She was saying one evening that she would willingly exchange money for peace, and I told her that with me it was a matter of principle not to allow her means to be squandered. This occurred only a month ago, and Lecount and I had some pretty sharp words between us. He wanted me to advance him some five thou-

sand dollars to invest in a gold-mine in British Colum-
bia. He began by reproaching me for breaking up that
Connecticut scheme; he told me that I prevented him
from realizing ten times what he wanted to invest.
Then he asked for the moderate sum of five thousand
for the mine. I refused, because I doubted the reputation of the men who were organizing the company.
When he found that he could do nothing with me, he
sent his wife to try and get it for him. I explained
my views of the matter to her, and told her, much more
gently than I had him, that I could not do it. Then
she spoke of sacrificing all for a little peace, and I had
to become very stern and determined with her, afraid I
might give in to her tears. I said that ten thousand a
year, besides what he made in his business, was quite
enough to buy peace, and that he should be satisfied
with squandering that amount. I did not think that
he had a right to complain, since he had never saved a
sixpence during his married life."

"And you found strength to resist her?" I said.

"Yes; when it became a question of conscience
whether every thing she owned should slip through
my fingers, I grew firm."

"And the gold-mine," I asked; "how has that turned
out?"

"Just as usual. The cashier suddenly disappeared
with all the funds, and the shareholders were left to
whistle for their money. I think there was quite a
sum collected, thirty or forty thousand dollars. It

proved a mine to him, at least, and he worked it successfully. Belle came to me when she heard of it, put
her arms around my neck, and told me I was a wise
man."

"And Mr. Hammond," I asked; "how is he?"

Mr. Masters laughed heartily.

"Very well in health, and very poor in pocket. He
has been Lecount's shadow the whole winter. According to his own story, he lost heavily in that gold-mine
scheme, and that, added to some previous losses, has
affected his financial affairs very much. His name was
among the list of shareholders for a large amount, but
I don't think he ever paid a cent into the treasurer's
hands. He almost lives in Lecount's house, and Belle
is tired of his constant society. He never comes here;
I keep those notes of his for an antidote. The idea of
a man, not able to take up his own paper, investing in
such a speculation! Any one but Claude Lecount would
see that the fellow is a complete humbug."

"Is the little boy well?" I asked.

"Yes, very well. That reminds me of another thing
that I want you to do for me. Belle has had a cough
all the time since she came home from Newport; they
went there after leaving your place last summer. Will
you call on her with Mrs. Masters before you return
home, and tell me what you think of her? You will
judge better than any one of the state of her health.
It gives me a great deal of uneasiness."

I consented, and the next morning Mrs. Masters

and I called on Mrs. Lecount. The house was quite near Mr. Masters', in a very pretty cross-street. We were shown into a large, dark parlor, with an arch and columns in the centre, and glass doors closing off the dining-room beyond. Although nearly eleven o'clock, there was a sound of knives and forks rattling on plates coming from it, mingled with laughter and conversation.

Mrs. Masters gave me an expressive look as she seated herself on a sofa, but made no observation whatever. A servant came and opened a blind to let in more light; then she drew a heavy curtain across the glass doors, that deadened the sounds from the dining-room, and left us, saying that Mrs. Lecount would be down in a few minutes. I had ample time to admire the costly furniture and exquisite ornaments with which the room was adorned. Every thing denoted wealth combined with refined taste. There was none of that stiffness observable, so common in many handsome rooms, making them look as if they were fitted up and kept for show. Here every thing was easy, and had the appearance of being used with appreciation and enjoyment. Some pieces of brilliant needle-work were scattered on an ornamental writing-table near where I sat, together with a half-finished letter. A basket full of envelopes, directed in a small, elegant hand, attracted Mrs. Masters' attention, and drew from her an exclamation of wonder.

"Another party this winter, and she in such poor health! Belle must be losing her reason."

A light step on the stairs, and Mrs. Lecount entered, with a bright smile of pleasure on her face.

"You must excuse my keeping you so long, but I was asleep when you came in," she said, at the same time throwing wide open the blinds, and letting the dazzling sunlight into the room. "I coughed so much all night that I was quite unable to rise this morning at my usual hour. Mr. Lecount has a breakfast-party, as I suppose you can guess, and Pauline had to take my place at the head of the table. However, that is a duty that I don't regret; I generally resign in her favor when I can with reason."

She spoke gayly, and delight at seeing us had sent a happy glow over her face, and an added brightness to her eyes. Her cheeks were pink with excitement, and the rich masses of her hair were disposed so as to hide their thin, wasted appearance. She drew her breakfast-shawl around her with a slight shiver, and sat where the sunbeams fell full upon her.

"Pauline tells me that the carpet is fading in this particular corner, because I am so fond of letting in the sunlight. But I love to feel it shining on me; it makes me warm and gay—don't you like it, Mrs. Masters?"

"I do, indeed, and with me the carpet would have to give way. This is your favorite corner, I know. I see you have been busy with invitations again."

"Yes, Mr. Lecount wanted another party; so I proposed having it before Lent began. It will be quite large, and I dread it already.—You must give me something that will cure my cold before it takes place," she said, turning to me.

At the same moment she commenced coughing terribly, and it was some time before she recovered sufficiently to go on with her explanation.

Then I listened while she and Mrs. Masters discussed the matter. With her, it was all throughout, "Pauline thinks this"—or, "Mr. Lecount says that." It was evident that she had little to do with the affair, except naming the one proviso, that it should not occur during Lent. That subject finished, she suddenly turned the conversation away from herself, and talked about my home and family with an eagerness that showed what a large share of her heart they possessed.

She seemed to fear my observation of her, and for that reason affected a gayety of manner quite unusual to her. I noticed the alteration in her, that was fretting Mr. Masters, but I knew that to remark on it to her would do more harm than good. Her little boy was out walking, and she wished us to remain to dinner, so as to see him. Mrs. Masters excused herself on the plea of her husband's health; and I declined, because I intended leaving for home that afternoon. Our visit was not interrupted; when we left her, the breakfast-party was still at the table. Before going, I asked her, laughingly, if she meant what she had said, about giving her a remedy for her cold. She replied, in the same tone, that she was serious, and had been waiting with the hope of seeing me before doing any thing to relieve it.

I wrote her a long prescription, and left it with a strict
charge to follow its directions implicitly. She promised,
and Mrs. Masters added gravely—

"Do it for Arthur's sake."

Mrs. Lecount colored at the words; then pressing
Mrs. Masters' hand, she said, quietly, "You may trust
to me."

"Was there any necessity for that last injunction?"
I asked Mrs. Masters, as we walked down the street.

"Surely you must have observed the difference in
Belle," she replied. "Did you not notice the apathy
and coolness that came over her when speaking of her
husband? There is some trouble between them. I can
detect desperation in her carelessness as to her own
health. I hope that what I said may affect her. Mr.
Masters is not as observing as I am; women naturally
see little things that men would attach no importance
to. I never speak of this to my husband—he frets
enough about her as it is. He thinks that her health is
failing on account of her natural delicacy of constitution, and that sometimes Claude's rash speculations give
her anxiety. I know that there is some deeper and
closer cause for the indifference to each other that I
have so often remarked. You heard her to-day, when
she said that she always resigned her seat to Pauline
when she could do it with reason. It is not the first
time that I have known her to remain in her own room
while her husband was entertaining his friends down-
stairs. Sometimes I think that Pauline's constant pres-

ence in the house has had a bad influence on both of them, although it would be impossible to say in what manner."

"It is strange to me that Miss Pauline is still un-married—she is so very handsome and attractive," I said, musingly.

"I feel sure that it is her own fault. She has had three brilliant winters, you may say four, in New York, with every advantage possible. I know that several very eligible gentlemen have paid her marked atten-tion, and it often surprises both Mr. Masters and me, how she remains so indifferent to them."

"She is at least not mercenary," I said. "For it is well known among us that her father is in very moderate circumstances. I think her conscientiousness is to be admired."

"It is, most certainly. Mr. Masters was afraid at one time that Mr. Hammond might succeed in gaining her affections, but I noticed that he was quite devoted to Belle, and neglected Pauline altogether. Mr. Masters inferred that Pauline's want of fortune was the drawback, as he is persuaded that Mr. Hammond is a mere fortune-hunter. Belle detests the man, in spite of his devotion and cultivation; and as for that Mr. Hunter, she keeps her room whenever he happens into the house."

"It is well she has her child to occupy her mind and time. He must be quite a pet of yours?" I said.

"He is a pet with everybody—except, perhaps, his father. Claude declares that he likes children when

12*

they are old enough to talk to and reason with, but he hates babies. I think his careless way of treating Arthur pains Belle more than she cares to say. She is almost too fond and indulgent. He is cross and fault-finding beyond reason. She makes an idol of Arthur, and tries to keep him a baby by her side, to be nursed and petted every hour in the day. Claude wants to make a little man of him at once. I think he would like to do away with his childhood and boyhood altogether, and have Arthur a precocious young gentleman, able to understand speculations, and the rise and fall of stocks. He insists on sending for him, to entertain these friends of his, by showing off the old-fashioned manner and expressions that he himself has put into the child's head against his wife's wishes. To see that little fellow standing up in a room full of people, all addressing remarks to him far beyond his comprehension, just for the amusement of hearing his shrewd, queer answers! He has a wonderful talent for arithmetic, and his father takes the greatest delight in asking him questions that tax his ability to the utmost extent. Belle is justly annoyed with it, and one night she put the little fellow asleep early, hoping he would escape the usual exhibition of his precocity. We were there at the time, and I congratulated myself when I heard that Arthur was safe in his crib, and that we would escape the infliction of his sharpness and his father's silliness for one night. Judge of our surprise when his nurse brought him into the room, rubbing his eyes that were half shut with sleep and red

with crying! His judicious father had insisted on having him awakened and dressed."

"No wonder Mrs. Lecount feels anxious. He will
ruin the child," I said.

"Then these parties. They cost immense sums of
money, and she has given several already this winter.
Not that Mr. Masters objects to them on the score of expense, though that is bad also. He thinks it all wrong in
view of the present dreadful condition of the country.
Property is depreciating, and things become more unsettled every day. He anticipates the worst, because he
meets with so many men from different sections of the
country, and from the tone of their conversation he says
that civil war is certain. He was saying last night that
he would like to arrange his affairs and buy a place up
near you, where he could enjoy the remainder of his life
in country pursuits. I think he will do it if every
thing goes right with Belle, but not unless that is
the case, for he has made up his mind to stay near her
always."

I thought over all that had been said to me the night
before while Mrs. Masters talked of Belle and her prospects. I concluded to accept Mr. Masters' proposal, and
I was repaid for my assent to it, by the improvement
that the taking of this care off his mind made in his
health.

He wrote, a few days after my return home, to say
that he was again able to go out, and that "Belle was
much better," owing to my good advice. The days

went over, and the public troubles increased. Private misfortunes were forgotten in view of the fearful danger menacing the republic. Opinions were divided; people talked of faults on both sides. Union and secession meetings were held in the same State. The people in the South went on with their preparations deliberately and systematically, and State after State passed the ordinance of secession. The people in the North watched and waited as if viewing a spectacle, and asked each other, "What next?" The government seemed to be paralyzed. Political demagogues of all parties stood confounded before the coming terror, which the unrestrained expression of their own prejudices had evoked.

Citizens of foreign countries, amassing fortunes in our midst, sneered at the troubles of the land that supported them, and taunted us with the instability of our boastful republic. Commercial failures were taking place in all parts of the country. There was a feeling of insecurity abroad; people wondered and questioned on whom to depend. The President was inaugurated under threats of assassination. The Confederates continued to possess themselves of the government property in the seceding States, with little or no opposition. It was felt that something was needed to unite the discordant elements in the North, before any decided steps could be taken by the Executive. That something came at last: Sumter was fired on—Americans attempted to lower their own flag, and trample it under foot. Then came the uprising of the North. Party feelings and differences were forgotten. The whole country was in danger; State questions were left for another time. Men, who had not spoken for years on account of some private trouble, were ready to march side by side for the defence of their common country. The President's call for troops to uphold the government, and preserve the integrity of the Union, was answered nobly and without delay. This action restored confidence; people felt that there was some effort necessary, and they were willing to make it, if only by so doing they might restore the former peace and prosperity of the republic.

Meetings were held and speeches made. Companies were formed and drilled in every village of the land. The governor was besieged by candidates for appointments. The whole country was in a state of unparalleled excitement. The ladies, not to be behindhand, were forming societies for knitting stockings and scraping lint. One evening I found my mother surrounded by bundles of old linen which she was assorting, and my sister busy winding yarn. Miss Marie and about a dozen other young ladies belonging to the neighborhood were in the room assisting her. I had come to be regarded as quite a middle-aged gentleman by the young people about me, and the exclamation, "It's only the doctor!" was not new to me. It was evident that they expected some one else; so I nodded in return for the smiles they threw me in a patronizing way, and was immediately requested to hold a skein of wool on my hands while one of my bright young friends wound it into a huge ball.

"We were expecting Victor," Miss Marie said, turning to me.   "He went to Albany yesterday."

"Any thing the matter?" I asked, wearily, for I was exhausted with a long day's work.

My sister looked up—

"He is raising a company for an Albany regiment, and expects to receive his commission very soon."

"Isn't he patriotic, Dr. Wilmer?" asked the young lady whose wool I was holding—Miss Susie Williams by name, a pretty girl, and quite a belle among us.

"He is, very."

"How dull it will be when the company goes away! Nearly every family is represented in it. The two Johnsons are going.   Mrs. Johnson says she feels more reconciled to their departure since they are together; each will look after the other in case any thing should happen."

My sister's last clause brought sad looks into the bright faces bending over the work-table, and I saw Miss Marie brush away some tears quickly, as if afraid that showing them would be unpatriotic and cowardly.

"I don't think there will be much fighting, do you?" asked Miss Susie again.

"I think there will be a great deal," I answered, slowly, making up my mind as I went along. In fact, the question had never before presented itself to my serious consideration. The events of each day, as it passed, had been sufficient for the thoughts to dwell upon. After tea, the elder Mr. Lecount came in with several others, and while they discussed the latest news, the young ladies worked away busily, listening with attention to the interesting theme. Victor Lecount had not returned yet, owing to the press of business at the capital. According to his letter, there were more candidates than positions, and he feared refusal.

At last he returned in triumph, and, after a short, hurried preparation, he took his company to Albany, where they would join the regiment. We saw them off, with music playing, colors flying, and the people cheering. How gay and bright they looked in their fresh uniforms and equipments! What noble emotions filled their breasts, and what brave, bright smiles played over the young faces! Disinterested and courageous, they only thought, "Our country is in danger; she has protected us. If she falls, what are we? Shall we not fight for her, and if need be die that she may live? What are our lives, compared to the hundreds of thousands that shall be after us? We will leave to them the heritage bequeathed to us by men who suffered as we expect to suffer." How sweet the flowers were that women, young and old, threw to them as they passed! How many bright eyes grew dim and blinded with tears! How many different emotions did they spring from—tears of joy, of pride, of heart-felt love of country—tears of sorrow! Could mothers be blamed if sadness mingled in the many feelings agitating them as they prepared their sons for the war, and ended in bitter tears of anguish at the moment of separation? As the regiment disappeared in the distance, Mrs. Lecount, who was standing near me, fainted away. She had kept up her courage and smiling face until the last line of men had passed; then the firmness and self-control that she had exhibited during the past few weeks gave way, and she sank into her husband's arms with a low, gasping moan. We were all asking ourselves the same question that had overcome her in contemplating it.

"How, and when, will they return?"

We heard regularly of the regiment's progress toward Washington, and the stocking-knitting went on with renewed energy, while the letters from our young heroes were read aloud to the assembled society amidst tears of joy and pride.

Toward the end of June I rode home one evening with my appointment as surgeon in a New York volunteer regiment in my pocket. I had been thinking of taking such a step for some time, considerations of my home duties alone withholding me. A conversation, between some neighbors just returned from New York, at last decided the question for me. They spoke of the extreme youth and consequent inexperience of the young doctors that were then receiving appointments, many of them having just obtained their diplomas. They gave, as a reason for this, the unwillingness of physicians of reputation to resign their positions and home comforts for the hardships and small pay of an

army doctor. Our town was well supplied with medical
men, most of whom had large families. I remembered,
with some bitterness, that I had neither wife nor child
to prevent me from giving my services to my country.
Besides, I had felt restless and discontented for some
months, and, strange to say, no sooner was my commission safe in my pocket, than a sensation of perfect relief
and peace came over me. I felt that I was doing right.

When I put the paper before my sister, she understood its purport instinctively; she had been watching
me closely for weeks, reading my doubts, yet afraid of
alluding to the subject of them. She rose without a
word, and, throwing her arms around me, laid her head
against my shoulder and cried, silently. My mother
coming in, stood for a moment surprised at our position,
then she threw a quick glance about the room, and saw
the folded paper on the table.

"John, John, you are not going to leave me!" I
heard her exclaim, and she stretched out her arms imploringly.

I caught her in my own and kissed her, unable to
answer her question.

"John is right, I am proud of him," my sister said,
bravely coming, as of old, to my assistance.

"I suppose I must not be the only selfish mother in
the place," she said, at last, after we had talked the
matter and its necessity over to her. In the end she
kissed me, and bade me go, with her blessing.

My arrangements were soon completed, my trunk

was packed so full of little comforts made by loving hands, that it was with difficulty that I succeeded in locking it. My mother and sister accompanied me to the cars; I can remember yet the appearance of every thing within and outside the house on that day. As we were leaving it, my sister drew me to a large mirror in the parlor, and laughingly demanded how I liked myself in a uniform. Then she pulled my cap on one side to give it an airy appearance, and lovingly stroked the dark hair beneath it. I had grown strong and muscular, owing to the amount of riding and walking that I did in the open air, and my black beard and mustache gave me quite the look of a stage brigand, according to my sister.

It was a lovely June afternoon, the roses and woodbine were in full bloom; there had been a slight shower in the morning, and the rain-drops yet glistened like diamonds on the soft petals of the flowers. The air was clear, the sky blue, the landscape fresh and bright in its tints of varied green. Bees hummed over the honey-laden plants, birds sang and chirped in the trees, and small colonies of ants were gathered in the garden-path, carrying away their winter store. I stood for a moment at the gate, to give one eager look at the dear home that I might never see again.

At the station we were greeted by many friends who had come to see me off, and wish me success and a safe return. Before we had said half that was intended, the whistle was blown, and the next moment I had

kissed the tears from my mother's eyes, and was in my
seat, gazing at the bright faces on the platform, while
the cars moved off amid the usual noisy confusion.

I had given myself a day to spend with Mr. Masters,
not having as yet informed him of my changed position.
I knew that he would be astonished, but, aware of his
patriotism, I felt sure of his approbation. During that
ride I reflected a great deal on my past life, and its
one bitter disappointment—a disappointment that I had
never completely recovered from. At times, it required
all the self-control that I was capable of exercising, to
overcome the strong emotions awakened by its recollection. I had determined to conquer myself, but the effort
cost me dear. I could despise myself for allowing such
a passion to master me in the face of such perfect
indifference on the part of its object. I felt that I had
sacrificed the best years of my life, first by indulging in
a bright hope, and afterward by regretting bitterly its
non-fulfilment. Even while endeavoring to forget the
object of my love, the thought of replacing her by another never entered my mind. The shrine might be
empty, but the place of its former image was filled with
sweet memories. It seemed to me that, feeling as I did,
love offered to another would have been perjury and a
mockery.

When I reached Mr. Masters' house late that night,
I heard that he and his wife were out of town. They
were at a pretty watering-place, within a few hours' ride
of New York, and I determined to follow them there.

I would have a short time to remain with them, and it was well worth the trouble of going.

I started early the next morning, after a refreshing sleep in Mr. Masters' comfortable house, and arrived safe at the hotel to which I had been directed by the servant. The clerk told me that Mr. Masters had taken his wife for the day to visit some friends in the neighborhood. Here was another disappointment. I made up my mind to wait until evening, if I only had an hour to spend in their company.

CHAPTER XII.

THE CHAIN IS LENGTHENED.

THE place was full that season. "Every hotel crowded," the clerk told me. I thought of going to the different houses with the hope of meeting a friend with whom I could pass a few of the hours until evening. So I wandered around until dinner-time, but without success. Among all the groups of gayly dressed people loitering on the piazzas, in the parlors and on the beach, I saw no familiar face. Dinner over, I strolled down to the water, and watched some merry children chasing each other along the sands, gathering shells and seaweeds, and digging holes to entrap some little fish that might be left behind by the retiring waves. Their light laughter and innocent prattle amused me greatly, and it was nearly five o'clock in the afternoon when I returned to the house to await Mr. and Mrs. Masters' arrival.

The rooms and piazza were filled with ladies, promenading in their rich evening dresses. There was the usual hum of voices, mingled with laughter and music. Old-fashioned, over-dressed little girls glided about in imita-

tion of their elders; while here and there a nurse was
visible, gathering her charges for their early tea. As I
passed along, a window opening on the piazza, from a
small private parlor, was flung back hastily, and a lady
stepped out, and stood for a moment in my way, gazing
around her—a queenly-looking woman, with flashing
black eyes, and handsome, decided features. She was
richly dressed, perhaps too gayly for perfect taste, but
the brilliant colors surrounding her contrasted well with
her heavy raven hair and clear olive complexion. She
had a crimson cloak thrown over her arm, and a soft,
white affair for her head, in her hand. A look of disappointment came over her face on seeing me, and giving
me a searching glance, she swept past me, and went slowly toward the more crowded part of the piazza. Farther
on, the place was entirely deserted, and a large arm-chair
attracted my attention. When I had taken possession
of it, I found that the approach to the house was before
me, and some closed green shutters at my back. The
quiet around me was remarkable, considering the near-
ness of the busy throng I had just passed through, and I
found myself after a few minutes sinking into a doze.

It deepened into a sleep from which I was aroused
by the curious sensation we feel when real noises mingle
with our dreams, and appear to take part in them. I
became aware that there were voices talking, so near
me, that the words were perfectly distinct. They were
raised and excited to angry tones, and came from within
the closed blinds behind me.

"I tell you that you are wrong. You shall not go!" a woman's voice said.

"Let me pass; you at least have no right to detain me," was the answer, in the low, rough tone of an angry man.

"Then I shall assume the right, as long as your wife is not able to take her own part."

"Let me pass; I am determined!" was the answer again.

"You will drive your wife into a lunatic asylum, if you go on like this."

"And it would be the best place for her. It's a pity she was ever taken out of the one she was in."

"Oh, Claude!" This exclamation, in a low, altered voice of painful entreaty and reproach, brought me to my senses.

As I started to my feet, surprised and shocked, there was a slight struggle in the room behind me, then a door clapped violently, and I heard a low moan and suppressed sobbing from the woman, whom I now knew to be Miss Pauline Lecount. I walked hastily, overcome by conflicting fears, toward the crowded end of the piazza, scarcely knowing where I went, and not caring much. I was just in time for another scene.

A beautiful little light wagon, drawn by a pair of spirited young horses, was standing in the road before the house, in sight of the assembled crowd, and various remarks, occasioned by its appearance, saluted my ears.

"I wonder he is not afraid of driving them! they look dangerous!" came from one side.

"He is a reckless sort of a fellow, anyhow," was the answer.

"Did you see him play last night? He must have a big pile somewhere!"

"Yes, I saw him in the early part of the evening; he was losing heavily then."

"He never wins. He is too impatient and irritable. I guess he only plays to kill time."

"I think he is killing his wife as well."

"Yes, she looks delicate; pretty little woman too. Quite a contrast to Mrs. Dimon."

"Yes, rather. I wonder what old Dimon can be thinking of, letting his wife go on as she does?"

"Thinking of? Money, of course! He knows she can take care of herself. All she flirts for is amusement. She loses nothing. I don't think she ever had a heart, or knew what feeling meant. She delights in attracting men, for the sake of annoying their wives. You should have seen the look of triumph she threw after Mrs. Lecount last night when she left the room unable to bear it any longer. Lecount was aware of it too, and he positively sneered at his wife's mortification. If I were Mrs. Lecount, I wouldn't remain here another day."

"She looks as if her heart were breaking. And that fellow named Hammond, he hardly lets her out of his sight. She don't appear to like him, and yet seems afraid of resenting his attentions."

"He is a friend of her husband, and one of Mrs.

Dimon's friends also. Yesterday I came across them walking together in the grounds, and she had her pocket-book in her hand, and was giving him money. Don't look so incredulous! I heard her say, 'You must be satisfied with one hundred for the present.' Of course, it looked curious, but he may be her brother for all we know, and might have found himself hard up. They are a curious group certainly, and quite interesting in their movements."

"Here comes the famous couple now. She looks magnificent."

The two gentlemen pressed forward for a better position, and I followed them. Mr. Lecount was leading Mrs. Dimon toward the wagon. He looked handsome, but dissipated and reckless. His whole attention was absorbed by the dashing-looking woman who had so fascinated him. Having adjusted her cloak to her satisfaction, he sprang to the seat beside her, caught the lines from the attending groom, with a proud, self-reliant glance around him, and the next minute they had disappeared in a cloud of dust. I had recognized in Mrs. Dimon the lady who had stepped from her room to the piazza a short time before, and I remembered the glance that she had thrown around her, as if expecting some one to be near. No doubt she had waited impatiently enough while the conversation that I had overheard passed between Mr. Lecount and his sister.

The excitement over, the crowd of fashionable loungers went in search of another, and I watched with anxiety every carriage that passed the house, hoping to see Mr. Masters' face in one of them. The secret of his presence in the hotel was now plain to me. Mrs. Lecount must be indeed unhappy when her guardian felt it his duty to remain so near her.

Later, at tea-time, I looked at the faces coming into the dining-room, and afterward searched the rows of people seated at the long tables, but without success. None of the Lecount family were present. As I left the room, Mr. Hammond was entering it alone. He recognized me, and I nodded slightly in return for his salutation, and passed out silently. My heart was too sore against him and his set to permit of my speaking to him. I felt that I never wanted to lay my eyes on the man again. I returned to the piazza and strolled impatiently up and down, endeavoring to think of something pleasant. I tried to set before me the duties and relaxations of the position I was about to occupy, and bring up to my mind the old tales of camp-life that I had been so fond of reading when a boy. I remembered imagining myself in the hero's place, and thinking what I should have done under the same circumstances. I even tried to laugh heartily, as of old, over the comical scenes and situations recounted in "Charles O'Malley" and "Harry Lorrequer," but without success. Try as I might, my thoughts would revert to the possible position and misery of Mrs. Lecount, in bad health, and neglected by her husband.

His wicked words, that he had used in speaking of

her to his sister, rang in my brain, and roused in me
feelings that were beyond expression. I refrained from
walking near the windows of their apartments, lest I
should hear more than I cared to know. Pity for her,
and indignation against the man who could find it in
his heart to ill-treat her thus cruelly and openly, had
taken possession of me. I paced back and forth, with
my strange-feeling cap set tightly on my head, and my
arms folded across my breast, with a pressure almost
painful. Meanwhile the scene was changing around
me. Night was falling, a storm was rising, and the
increasing dampness and chilliness in the air were driving the people in-doors. Still Mr. Masters did not come.
I began to fear that the stormy appearance of the sky
might prevent his return to the hotel that night.

It being too cold for pleasure outside, a dance was
improvised in the large parlor, and the crowd flocked
in there. In a very short time, the ball was in full
progress. I continued my walk with curious surroundings. On one side, a brilliantly-lighted room, filled
with richly-dressed people, all apparently merry-hearted
and enjoying themselves; music playing, fans rustling,
and couples whirling round and round in the mazes of
the waltz, "*à deux temps*," or flying up and down the
room in the exciting *galop*.

On the other side the elements were at work. The
stars were fast disappearing behind the gathering clouds,
the wind was rising and moaning round the corners of
the house. The roll of the distant surf was audible, and

gleams of lightning, followed by the long, low rumble
of thunder, opened and flashed through the thick, black
curtain, settling down like a pall over the landscape.
At last the storm burst, and the heavy rain descended
in torrents, with a rushing sound and a force that sur-
passed any thing of the kind within my recollection.
The trees bent and shivered with its fury; flower-pots
were upset, and plants beaten to the ground. Now and
then a gust of wind would sweep around the house and
down the avenue, carrying before it every thing that
lay in its path.

In the midst of this grand yet fearful scene, the
window behind where the arm-chair stood was opened
noiselessly, and a woman's form, muffled in a large
shawl, came out on the piazza. As she stood for a
while gazing toward the road, a flash of lightning lit
up the scene, and I recognized Miss Pauline Lecount.
In the momentary glimpse that I had of her face, I saw
that it was colorless from fright and suspense. Anxiety
was visible in every line of it. She drew her shawl
across her breast with a shudder, and began pacing
back and forth in front of the windows of their apartments. I resumed my weary promenade, going always
in the direction she did, so that our faces never once
met. At times she would stop, bend her head and listen for the sound of approaching wheels, then, with a
sigh of disappointment, take up her monotonous walk.

For almost an hour I listened to the light, firm tread
behind me, sounding like the echo of my own footfalls.

Then the storm gradually abated, until at length the rain ceased, the wind died away as suddenly as it had come up, and the only noise outside was caused by the drops that fell from the leaves of the swaying branches overhead. The moon and stars were again visible behind the light, fleecy clouds so rapidly disappearing from sight. We two weary watchers suddenly stopped short to look at them, probably with the same feeling— one of thankfulness in our hearts. At that moment we heard the noise of a horse's feet coming up the road, and Miss Pauline bent forward eagerly to catch sight of what was approaching. A rough-looking man, short and stout, came riding up the avenue at a quick trot, stopped his horse in front of the house door, and hurried into the bar-room. Miss Pauline turned away with a murmur of impatience, and I walked toward the parlor windows. Looking in mechanically, I saw the landlord crossing the room. Something in his face, an expression of shocked surprise, attracted me, and I followed him with my eyes. He went up to Mr. Hammond, who was bending over a lady, conversing earnestly as usual, said a few words to him, that brought a look like his own into that gentleman's face, and then they hastily left the room together. The lady, with whom Mr. Hammond had been talking, rose instantly, and communicated the news to a gentleman near by, and he as hurriedly as the others disappeared through the door.

I felt an undefined horror stealing over me, and the same influence seemed to be spreading through the oc-

cupants of the parlor. They were collecting in little
groups, exchanging ideas with eager faces, and in low
tones. In a few moments the horseman came out on
the piazza, surrounded by an excited crowd of people.
They seemed to be all talking at once, some questioning, others affirming. Two of them had stepped between
the man and his horse, and were listening eagerly to
what he was saying. I hastened forward and caught
the concluding portion of his story.

"You see, the wagon was just dashed to pieces
against the stone fence, and we found the horses standing quiet, but trembling all over with fright. The lady
don't know what scared them, but it was all done in a
second."

"How did he fall?" asked some one near me.

He was pitched right over the dash-board on his
head. You never saw such a sight."

"Who found him?" asked another gentleman.

"A lot of us from the house. The lady came as fast
as she could, but it was hard work in the storm, and she
couldn't speak for some time after she got in, between
the wetting she had and the fright."

"How did she escape?"

"She crept out of the back of the wagon, and it going at full speed, and let herself drop by her hands."

"How courageous! Are you sure that she belongs
here?"

"Yes, sir; she told us her name, and I can't remember it, but I know the gentleman myself; he passed the

house every day this month with the same horses. Everybody around knew Mr. Lecount."

"Are you sure he is dead?"

"Dead! he was stone-dead before she got to him. The doctors know it down at the house; they say he died instantly."

A long, heart-rending cry, and a gasping for breath, made us turn around. There, behind us, with wild, staring eyes and a ghastly face, stood Miss Pauline Lecount. I caught her as she tottered, and we carried her into a deserted little parlor, and applied restoratives. She struggled bravely to retain her consciousness, and succeeded.

"Don't tell her, don't tell his wife yet," she moaned, looking imploringly around her. I drew back, that she might not see me; but, sitting up suddenly, she caught sight of my face.

"You! are you here?" she screamed, burying her face in her hands, and shivering all over.

"Try and control yourself," I said, bending over her. "Remember how many are in the room."

She looked up in my face with a mocking laugh, and muttered hysterically—

"And for this, for this I have sinned! Oh! I am rightly punished."

. I began to fear that the shock was too much for Miss Pauline's brain, and that she was losing her reason.

"Shall I leave you?" I asked, in a low tone.

"Yes, yes, go away!"

Thinking that it might be best, I returned to the piazza, leaving her in the care of some of the ladies belonging to the house. The group outside was still collected, and as I joined them a carriage stopped at the door, and Mr. Masters assisted his wife out of it, and led her hastily up the steps.

"Be as quick as you can, Sallie. Let no one tell her but yourself," I heard him say to her.

Mrs. Masters hurried along the piazza, and disappeared through one of the many windows opening upon it. Her husband turned and saw me. He looked again, as if not trusting his eye-sight, and then grasped my hand.

"Wilmer, this is a terrible affair. Of course, you have heard it. Do you think my wife was in time? I thought we should never get here."

I told him what I knew, and of Miss Pauline's condition.

"But, how did you hear it?" I asked.

"We stopped for a light at the other house, and I heard them all talking of an accident. When they mentioned Mrs. Dimon, I asked further, with an idea that the gentleman was slightly injured, and she not at all. Judge of my surprise when I heard the truth, and realized its horror! First, they took me into a room and showed me—Wilmer, to think that this morning I left Claude Lecount looking as well as he ever did in his life! Oh, it is fearful! No one would recognize him. He fell with his head striking a rock. Oh, such a sight!

The doctors say it was all over in a moment. I don't know whether to be thankful or not. Sudden death is always terrible; what must it be where there is no preparation whatever for it?"

"His poor wife!" I said. "And we can do nothing to soften this blow."

The old gentleman wrung my hand, and sobbed aloud.

"Wilmer, pity me, when I say from my heart that I firmly believe, had Claude Lecount lived another year, his wife would have been in her grave before the end of it. His ill-treatment was killing her. You would hardly know her now."

"This will be a fearful shock, nevertheless, and her constitution is very frail."

"Yes, I know it, I know it only too well, but what can I do? No one realizes what she has suffered this past year, what misery of heart and mind. I have seen it in her face. This will be a deeper sorrow, but if she survives it we will do our best to guard her from any like it in the future. Poor child, her life seems fated to be one of unhappiness! When will her troubles end?"

"Did you see Mrs. Dimon?" I asked.

"No, she would not meet me. But I know all she had to tell. When she got out of the wagon, she looked for him, and found him lying just as he had fallen, quite dead. She went to the nearest house as fast as possible, and the people there sent a litter for him in the midst of all that storm, and two doctors, who hap-

13*

pened to be in the hotel, went with it. They saw that
nothing could be done. I have given the necessary
orders. He will be taken home to-morrow. It would
not be right to let his wife see him in his present condition. They tell me that he will look more natural after
a day or two."

"Then you will return to-morrow?"

"Yes, in the afternoon, if Belle is able to go."

"How strange it all appears!" I said. "I feel like
one in a dream."

"And so you may; events follow each other so rapidly now, that one shock is scarcely over before another
comes. Wilmer, I did like that young man, and, in
spite of all his faults, I never lost hope of him till
within this last year. Lately, however, he has been
perfectly mad in his recklessness. If Mrs. Dimon has a
spark of feeling left, this night's work ought to bring it
out. He is not the first young fellow that she has led
to ruin. If only this might be a warning to her, and
all married flirts like her!"

"She is a new acquaintance, is she not?"

"Yes, Hammond introduced him to her. There is
some connection between him and Mrs. Dimon. I can't
discover what it is. Sometimes I fancy that he is her
brother, but her avoidance of him when her husband is
present makes me doubt the fact. At any rate, it was
Hammond that suggested this place to Claude, and Mrs.
Dimon was here when we came. She went to work at
once to attract Lecount, and you see how she succeeded.

We could not induce Belle to return home. She insisted on remaining near her husband. Poor child! she hoped to gain him in the end. This is a sorrowful termination of her short married life, and it began so bright too. Well, we cannot look into the future; we must be satisfied with what comes, as long as we feel that we are not to blame in bringing the trouble on ourselves. Poor Claude! he never would realize the substantial means for happiness and the blessings that surrounded him."

Mrs. Masters joined us while we stood talking.

"How is Belle?" asked her husband.

"I can't tell. She appears crushed and utterly stunned. If she would only cry—but no, she just lies quiet, with her eyes closed, as if thinking. I brought Arthur to her, but even that did not rouse her. Pauline is with her now; poor girl, she controls herself wonderfully, and tries to comfort Belle. She wants to go with you, if you think of returning to the other hotel to-night. She says she feels able to see him, and I believe it will be better to satisfy her."

"Very well, then, I will take her; perhaps it is best for Belle not to have so many around her."

"Any thing that might increase her agitation should be avoided," I said.

"Then I will keep her as quiet as possible. But, Doctor Wilmer, I can hardly overcome my surprise at seeing you here among us. What does it mean?"

I explained my unexpected appearance, to their great astonishment.

"How long shall we have you with us?" asked Mr. Masters.

"Until five o'clock to-morrow morning. I shall just have time to join the detachment I am going with. Do not mention my presence here to Mrs. Lecount," I said to Mrs. Masters, as she wished me an affectionate good-by. "The singularity of the fact will only add to her excitement."

She promised, and, having wished me success and a safe return, she left us, to go back to her charge. For several hours Mr. Masters and I remained together, talking over the events of the day. About twelve o'clock Mrs. Masters joined us in the parlor where we sat, and reported that Mrs. Lecount was asleep, and Miss Pauline ready to accompany Mr. Masters. He went to make the necessary arrangements, and Mrs. Masters spoke to me about Belle's health, and the means to be taken for her perfect recovery.

I advised a removal to the country, and a total lack of all excitement.

"I think you are right, and, just as quickly as it can be done, we will find a pretty place somewhere in your neighborhood and remove to it. Mr. Masters has been wishing to do so for years, but we could not make up our minds to leave New York while Belle remained there."

"Mrs. Lecount seemed to enjoy country life some years ago," I said, musingly.

"Yes, she has spoken always as if it possessed the

greatest charms for her. Latterly, too, she has often reverted to little incidents that occurred in your mother's house, and once she said, with a sigh, that the years she spent there were the happiest of her life. However, there may be much pleasure in store for her yet. She is only twenty-five years of age—too young to lose all hope, and become tired of the world. Once the shock of this grief is over, the elasticity of spirit and brightness of youth may return to her."

"You are sure that she has no cough?" I asked.

"Quite sure; no, that is not the trouble now. For some time past her strength seems to have gradually decreased. Every day she is less inclined to make any exertion. Still, she has persisted in doing what she considered her duty. To me she is a complete enigma. She has borne little annoyances, too numerous to mention, without a word of complaint. Since we came here, no insult, that could wound a sensitive, refined mind, has been omitted. Every indignity has been heaped upon her, and yet nothing that we could urge would induce her to go home with her child, and leave her husband to his chosen companions. Perhaps we were wrong to propose such action, but he and Mrs. Dimon took particular pains to offend her, and we felt that the mortification was killing her. She has never said a word to either of us in reference to her husband's conduct, but we could tell by her appearance that his unkindness and neglect were breaking her heart. You would hardly recognize in her the bright young girl that left your mother's house five years ago! I can't remember when I heard her laugh, and the sad smile that she gives Arthur always brings the tears into my eyes. If I only had the key to all this that seems so strange! Mr. Masters insisted that it all lay in the fickleness of Mr. Lecount's nature. He argued that Claude's love was a mere passion, soon forgotten, and that the conviction of its utter worthlessness was destroying Belle, since she had perfect faith in its depth and sincerity. I cannot agree with him, and yet I cannot account for the trouble that certainly has weighed her down for years. That the marriage was an unhappy one is most certain; and that there was a cause for the misery they both suffered—some secret that lay between the two—is my firm belief."

"I cannot hazard an opinion," I said, in answer to her questioning look. "They seemed to be suited to each other, and she made her own choice; it is impossible for us to account for the change in their mutual affection. From all you say, I should judge that the fault was on Mr. Lecount's side, and that his wife's love for him had never wavered. Her patience and meek endurance would argue that she still hoped to regain his affection."

"Perhaps you are right. Still, your explanation does not satisfy me. I think that Belle was disappointed, and I will tell you why I think so. For six months after they were married every thing was as pleasant and smooth as could be desired. They were like two children together, unreserved and merry when addressing each other, and apparently the utmost confidence and harmony existing between them. If that condition of things had died away gradually, I might think as you and Mr. Masters do. Belle's feelings are deep and strong as well as impulsive, and Claude's affection might not answer all the requirements of such an apparently contradictory temperament. On the contrary, their unrestrained gayety and evident pleasure in each other's society ended suddenly, and without any apparent reason. That is why I suspect a mystery never confided to another. If such a cause existed, they were both too proud to mention it."

"And you remarked this alteration in them soon after their marriage? It is strange, but there must have been a foundation for it, for my sister noticed it at the same time."

"Yes, and mentioned it to me, but I was afraid to acknowledge its existence even to myself; and I made light of her remarks, and tried to make her believe that she was mistaken. Unfortunately, she was only too correct in her observations. The difference existed between them then, and has never been removed. I do not know what others may have suspected; I am sure that Mr. Masters, Pauline and I have been conscious of their unhappiness all along. I hope for her own sake, poor girl, that she was not the most in fault; if so, her grief will be all the more bitter, and this blow much harder."

"I will answer for her truth," I said, warmly. "Whatever was the trouble, I am sure that she never caused it."

"I sincerely hope that you are right. Her conscientiousness is so great, that, if self-convicted, her remorse would be lifelong."

"I cannot believe that she had any thing to do with it voluntarily. This sorrowful condition of things has been forced upon her; she never brought it on herself."

"Sallie," Mr. Masters said, coming in hastily, "I am all ready—let us go for Miss Pauline.—Wilmer, I shall see you before you start."

Mrs. Masters hurried away, and a few minutes afterward Mr. Masters passed the open door with Miss Pauline on his arm. I heard the carriage drive off rapidly, and then, leaving word with a servant to call me in time, I retired to my room for a few hours' sleep.

At five o'clock the next morning I found Mr. Masters pacing back and forth on the piazza, looking worn and weary in the clear, cheerful light. He had been up all night, and was only just returned from his sorrowful visit to the other hotel. After a few parting words I left him, promising to write from Washington, which I reached soon after, by way of Annapolis.

CHAPTER XIII.

THE regiment to which I belonged was stationed on Arlington Heights, and, during the few weeks that intervened between my arrival there and the movement of the army toward Manassas, I received numerous letters from my friends and family. Several changes consequent on the death of Mr. Lecount had taken place. Young Mrs. Lecount was lying very sick in her guardian's house, where she had been taken the day after her husband's funeral. His sudden death, and the very unpleasant circumstances attending it, had affected her in a manner far worse than was at first anticipated. My mother and sister had hastened to attend her at Mr. Masters' urgent entreaty, and her continued illness was causing them the greatest anxiety, a fact most visible in the tone of their letters. Miss Pauline had returned home, my sister wrote, in a sad state of depression, out of which her family found it impossible to arouse her.

To add to the general gloom, Mr. Masters was

shocked at the condition of Mr. Lecount's affairs. He had apprehended more or less trouble in regard to them, and suspected the existence of several heavy debts, but he was utterly unprepared for the real facts of the case as they were presented to him. He found himself beset by Mr. Lecount's creditors; claims of the most unforeseen nature were sent in to him, those classed as debts of honor being very numerous and large, and notes for heavy amounts were about being protested. In his first feeling of amazement and anger, he disputed them; but, upon searching Mr. Lecount's papers, he found that they were only too correct.

Immediate payment of all these liabilities was entirely out of the question, and their gradual liquidation in full, with interest, would require nearly the whole of Mrs. Lecount's income for many years. In his perplexity, Mr. Masters would have liked to propose a compromise for a small amount. He thought it great injustice for Mrs. Lecount to be obliged to pay debts contracted by her husband on the race-course and in gambling-saloons, inasmuch as they could not be collected legally. Observing the trouble that was weighing on his mind, she guessed the cause of it, and insisted on having an explanation of the whole affair.

In spite of her weakness, she examined every claim, decided the question for herself, and announced her intention of paying them all in full, with interest.

"But it will take years to do it!" Mr. Masters said.

"Very well; call a meeting of the creditors, tell

them my resolution, and the means I have for carrying it out. That will satisfy them, and they will be kind enough to wait patiently until their claims can be settled," was the answer.

" You will have to economize and live on very little," urged Mr. Masters.

"I am quite willing that it should be so; if only you will pay those who need their money, at once. I cannot endure the thought of any one suffering on my account, and I am certain that some of those tradesmen are really poor."

" This will make a serious difference in Arthur's fortune," went on Mr. Masters, " and as it is, you are losing money every day. Property is depreciating in value, and your rents must be lowered, if we expect to keep the tenants that occupy the houses at present."

" I should prefer seeing Arthur poor to letting him hear his father's name coupled with dishonesty."

" Then it shall be as you wish," Mr. Masters replied, as he gathered the bills into a bundle and left the room. In accordance with her desire, the pretty home was let, furnished, and Mrs. Lecount took up her residence permanently in her guardian's house. Shortly after the unfortunate battle at Manassas, my sister wrote that she was about returning home to attend to the domestic affairs; but that mother would still remain with " poor Belle," who did not recover her spirits, and was "still very helpless and weak."

During the inactivity that followed the fight at Ball's

Bluff, I was appointed to a position on one of the boards of examination then being instituted, to inquire into the qualifications of the officers forming the medical corps of the army. Thus occupied, I remained in Washington the greater part of the winter, seeking and finding a forgetfulness of the past, in the performance of the many duties presented to me. Just before starting for the Peninsula in the spring, I received letters from home of quite a pleasing character. Mr. Masters was negotiating for a house in our vicinity, and young Mrs. Lecount was so far recovered as to be able to take an active part in the hospital-work going on in New York.

"You will be surprised to hear," wrote my sister, "that she has mastered the art of turning a heel, and is knitting socks for our soldiers constantly. She also belongs to relief societies, cuts out work, visits the sick and wounded in the hospital, and has taken a helpless widow and her family of little children under her own special care. Mr. Masters thinks that this regular employment for head and hands is having a good effect upon her health and spirits, and he contributes large sums to carry out her benevolent schemes. I am looking forward eagerly for their arrival here; her example and influence will do wonders for our village 'aid society.' Pauline is going to Washington, to join the corps of nurses. Her people were very much opposed to the idea at first, but her continued lowness of spirits, and desire for a change of scene, at length overcame their dislike to her design. You would scarcely recognize

her, and I really believe that her quiet life here was
killing her. None of them have been the same since
Claude's death; it was a dreadful shock to his poor
mother, and sitting brooding over it was not the thing
for a girl of Pauline's active mind and energetic character. She was fast growing into a state of apathy and
indifference to all around her, most sad to witness. I
think her heart was bound up in her brother Claude.
Since his death, the great intimacy that existed between
her and Belle seems to have ceased; the news of Mr.
Masters' intention to settle here among us had no
visible effect upon her for good; it rather appeared to
increase her desire for going away. Of course, the
sight of Belle and Arthur would keep Claude's terrible end before her mind perpetually, and she realized its horror most bitterly and to the fullest extent.
From all I hear, it was a most awful affair. Victor
keeps the family in a condition of alternate delight and
despair—delight for his bravery and rapid promotion
(he is now a major)—and despair, lest he too should
never return. To-day, his mother wishes that he was
safe beside her, pursuing his quiet profession; and to-
morrow she will come with flushed cheeks and bright
eyes to tell us that she would not recall him for the
world. All our absent heroes are acquitting themselves
nobly, and, what with home duties, society meetings,
and the reading of army letters, we are in a state of
excitement in which pleasure and pain are so mingled,
that often it is impossible to tell which feeling is upper-

most. I wish very much that you were in the regiment with Victor and our other boys, but that is too much to ask for."

Thus wrote my sister; and the hopeful, enthusiastic tone of all her letters enabled me to set out with a light heart, and a mind free from all cares unconnected with the duties of my office.

The events that followed the arrival of the Army of the Potomac at Fortress Monroe have become fit subjects for the talents of the ablest historians of the day. That the army failed in achieving the object for which it fought, is beyond dispute. Perhaps the reasons for that failure will never be agreed upon; many of them may never be brought to light. It is to be hoped that, in the time to come, when the fog of prejudice, envy, dislike, and political partisanship, that always envelops and obscures the actions of the present, shall have been cleared away, due justice will be done to the talent and patriotism of the commanding general, and to the unexcelled bravery and enthusiasm of the men that fought under him. Let Antietam and South Mountain testify to their unflinching courage, after a bitter reverse, and their devotion to their idolized young leader. A man must deserve great respect, and be capable of inspiring strange confidence in the soldiers' hearts, when he can take the shattered regiments of a broken and dispirited army, and with them defeat the same enemy reënforced and flushed with victory.

During General Pope's campaign in Virginia I had the misfortune to be taken prisoner, and I paid a compulsory visit to Richmond in consequence. Our flank had been turned, and our men were in full retreat, perfectly careless of the wounded lying on the field. A small barn, that we had taken possession of for the accommodation of the unfortunate soldiers, was fired upon in spite of the hospital flag exposed to view, and a few minutes after a party of the enemy entered, and called upon us to surrender. The young surgeon who was assisting me burst into a loud laugh at the words. For a moment, the sound of his mirth grated on my ears; but on looking about me, the ludicrousness of the demand was apparent. Stretched upon the hay and straw, which we had hastily scattered over the wood flooring, were a dozen or more of our poor fellows, in postures denoting the intensity of their sufferings. Helpless and uncomplaining, they lay patiently awaiting their turn to be attended to. Hunger and fatigue, consequent upon their forced marches and desperate fighting, had weakened their constitutions, and when to this condition were added the effects of their recent wounds, their appearance was indeed pitiable. Not knowing what mercy to expect, they fixed their eyes on their captors with an expression in which curiosity and sadness were strangely mingled, and left the settlement of the affair to us.

I threw a hasty glance through the open door and windows, but no means of help were visible. Every one capable of retreating had disappeared in the wake of the defeated army. It was a hot, sultry afternoon in the end of August. The trees were white with dust and parched for want of rain. On one side lay a thick wood, through which had come the force that decided the fortune of the day. In every other direction were stretched uncultivated fields, with fences broken down, the ground torn up by cannon-balls, and rendered uneven by the deep tracks of the heavy artillery-wagons. Everywhere were scattered the *débris* of battle, and over all was shining the brilliant sun, rendering still more intense with its burning heat the sufferings of our deserted wounded, whose forms dotted the earth on all sides.

I asked in vain that we might be parolled, and left to care for the poor fellows around us. An officer in command of the party declared his intentions of taking not only us, but all of the wounded that he could collect, along with him.

"Here is one, then, that I'm thinking you'll never take," answered a soldier who was lying at our feet, at the same time raising himself on his elbow, and pointing to a slight form almost concealed in the hay near him.

I followed the movement with surprise, not having before noticed the figure he meant.

"He was brought in here quite early in the day, while you were on the field," Doctor Berry said, remarking my astonishment. "He was past hope then, and I thought it better to attend to those who might survive."

I pulled the straw aside, and raised the dying boy; as I did so, the light shining on his belt showed the number of his regiment and his company. For a moment my heart seemed to cease beating; then I brushed aside the heavy hair from the damp forehead, and looked at the thin features over which the gray hue of death was stealing. "Poor Mrs. Johnson!" I muttered, almost inaudibly. It was her youngest son that I held in my arms.

He opened his eyes, and looked in my face.

"Walter, my boy, don't you know me?" I asked.

He smiled faintly.

"If I could only see mother again!" he gasped. They were his last words.

"If you would like it done, some of my men will bury him, and you can put a mark near the grave, so that you can find it again," said the Southern officer, touching me on the shoulder.

I thanked him for his kindness, and accepted the offer. We collected some blankets to wrap the poor boy in, and Doctor Berry cut his initials in a piece of wood, that served for a head-stone to his grave. Some few little articles that were in his pockets I carried with me to send to his mother. That sad duty performed, we prepared the wounded men for a march to the enemy's camp, as well as it was possible under the circumstances, and started for our destination with heavy hearts. The possibility of the situation in which I now found myself had never given me much trouble. I had been so fortu-

14

nate hitherto in escaping both wounds and capture, that
I had grown quite careless about the danger we all ran
of meeting the two evils.

Doctor Berry walked beside me, assisting a lame soldier on his way, and the others of our party kept as near
to us as it was possible. Our captors entertained themselves by examining various little trifles picked up on
the field, comparing their treasures, and singing snatches
of songs, breathing fearful vengeance on the " Northern
foe."

The contemplation of the miseries of a prison-house,
and the feelings of those at home when they should hear
of our fate, completely put all ideas of singing out of
our minds, however patriotic we may have been at
heart. The knowledge of our defeat was also bitter to
us; if we had met with this disaster during the progress of a victory for our side, I really don't think that
the men would have cared about it; as it was, the low
curses, that I am sorry to say fell from their lips, were
all directed against the parties who in their opinion
were responsible for the failure of the day.

The officer in command strode on ahead of us, now
and then turning impatiently with an order to hasten
our steps. Once he joined me, and excused his severity
under the plea of having to carry out his orders, the
principal one being, to bring in all the prisoners he
could collect. He added that, personally, he had no
power to give a parole; but that, if his general were still
in camp, he would procure me an interview with him.

Unfortunately, we found upon our arrival there that the general had already gone forward with his command, and had left strict injunctions to "send all prisoners to Richmond." After a short delay, during which those of the wounded who were unable to march were placed in wagons, we set out on our weary journey, our number largely increased by more of our unfortunate comrades. The utter dreariness and the sufferings connected with that march, and the imprisonment that followed it, will never be effaced from my memory. The impressions left on my mind by the different scenes we witnessed will always remain with me. I can recall with painful minuteness the aspect of the desolated country, and the deserted, ruined homesteads; the appearance of our rough guards, with their worn uniforms and fine horses; and the confused crowd of which I formed a member. We were kept as close together as it was possible, and a strange sight we presented. Men from various regiments, and in tattered garments of all hues, were there, most of them suffering from slight wounds, and all haggard, sleepy, and hungry. Marching along thus, with gloomy, emaciated countenances and bent forms, their complete lack of energy and utter dejection struck me forcibly. We outnumbered our captors ten to one; and often before, when reading of like circumstances, I had wondered why the prisoners did not overpower their guards, and attempt to escape; it seemed to be an easy matter in such a wide extent of country. The question no longer troubled me; I realized the bitter effect of defeat on soldiers usually brave and self-possessed. I understood how quickly an army may become demoralized and uncontrollable. Deprived of their officers and their weapons, all other means of self-defence were forgotten; they lost all the ardor and impetuosity of a soldier; their hands hung helpless by their sides, and complete despair took possession of them.

On reaching Richmond, Doctor Berry and I, with the other officers captured, were separated from the privates and conducted to the quarters assigned us, a large room in the Libby prison, filled with our unhappy comrades. Our arrival served to break the weary monotony of the day, and they listened eagerly to all the news we had to tell. Sad tidings indeed, but still it supplied a subject for thought and discussion to the men, so tired of contemplating their own wretched condition. In attending to the descriptions of the movements of the past few weeks, given by the officers who had participated in them, their eyes brightened, their cheeks flushed and paled with alternate enthusiasm and sorrow, and their voices regained some of the old ring and depth of tone.

In the days that followed, I watched with surprise the amusements that occupied the long, weary hours of these full-grown men, and realized what they must have endured before resorting in desperation to these childish pursuits. Some played cards with an energy and interest almost ludicrous under the circumstances,

and the little pieces of pasteboard were subjects for a
collector of curiosities. Owing to the amount of service they had seen, they were about as easy to be de-
ciphered as Egyptian hieroglyphics. Notwithstanding
their disagreeable appearance, I found myself, after a
few days, making a fourth in a game of "old sledge,"
with great pleasure. Several of my comrades enter-
tained themselves by cutting rings and other little ornaments out of pieces of bone and wood begged from
the jailer. The pains they took, and the patience they
exhibited, in carving and polishing the objects of so
much industry, were almost incredible. I know many
a mother who wears with pride "the ring my son
made during his imprisonment in the Libby." Among
us were a few young fellows gifted with a talent for
sketching, and a spirit for fun not to be destroyed
under adversity. The caricatures with which they
filled every scrap of paper within their reach were always productive of merriment, and served to dispel
many a fit of dejection. Others kept diaries until their
materials were exhausted. Our condition, so intolera-
ble on the whole, taught us many good lessons. It
showed us human nature as it is; drawing out capabili-
ties for action, and expressions of deep feeling, which,
under happier circumstances, would have remained unsuspected and dormant till the end of time. Very few
could have left that prison-house without carrying
away with them kindlier feelings toward their fellow-
men than they had ever possessed before.

I was standing one morning near a window, watching Doctor Berry in his efforts to fashion a little cross from a piece of bone, when some one passing on the opposite side of the street attracted my attention by the steady glance he fixed upon us. As I looked down at him, he pulled his cap hastily over his eyes, and all I distinguished was a man in the well-known gray, with an immense beard, a thin figure, and a pair of very brown hands. Half an hour passed. I was sitting with my head bent on my arms, thinking of home with a longing to hear from it, that seemed to be eating into my heart; and the opening of the door, which usually caused more or less excitement, did not attract my attention. A moment afterward a hand was laid on my shoulder, and a well-known voice exclaimed:

"Jack, my dear boy, is this possible?"

I looked up and met Harry Weston's eyes, dimmed with tears, fixed on my face.

"How long have you been in this cursed place?" he exclaimed, before I had time to answer him, for he had given me an embrace that nearly took my breath away.

"Since August!"

"What! three months, and you never sent for me? Jack, I'm ashamed of you."

"I never supposed for one moment that you were here," I answered.

He understood me; for a second his eyes fell, then he looked me straight in the face.

"Wilmer, you shall not break our friendship without

hearing me. I regret from my heart the whole affair, and in my capacity as a surgeon I have rendered assistance to friend and foe alike. But I am a Virginian, a Southerner born and bred, with all the principles and prejudices that belong to us as a class. Whatever the result may be, I shall stand by my own State and people. I know all your arguments, but we have many good ones on our side. The questions we are defending have never been settled, and we have staked every thing we own that they may be decided now. Perhaps I am wrong; I am at least sincere. I can assure you that this struggle has ruined all my prospects, and nearly beggared me. May we not respect each other's views, and be friends?"

He held out his hand, and I took it in the spirit in which it was offered.

"Half an hour ago," he went on, "when I saw you at that window, I could hardly believe my senses. As soon as I had performed my errand, I returned, to satisfy myself of the truth of my eyesight. I am going now to try and get you out on parole; then we will go home and see Edith, my wife. I have kept her here with me all through—in fact, it is a necessity; my mother has not left her room for three years, and to remove her would be certain death. Perhaps, when you see all, and realize my position better, you will not think so badly of me."

He pressed my hand as he uttered the last words, with a choking gasp, and went away hastily.

"Go home!" How strangely the words sounded! How fully I realized their fond meaning now, their true significance! His very voice had softened in its tone as he said them. Who could calculate the happiness that this home had afforded him, or realize the blessing it had been to him? Only those who were equally fortunate in possessing one. I brushed off the tears that the thought "When shall I go home?" occasioned, and, pacing up and down the room, awaited his return.

He came back after some hours, looking flushed and tired, but happy at the success of his application. I was a prisoner on parole, with liberty to go where I pleased during the day, so long as I reported myself faithfully at night, and made no notes of what was passing in the city.

"That was all I could do for you, Jack, my boy; but cheer up—they are arranging for an exchange now, and you shall be included in the first detachment sent away." This he said as we left the "Libby" together, and proceeded in the direction of his house.

As we walked along, arm-in-arm, he entered into a description of what his life had been since I had parted from him shortly after his marriage. His voice, when he mentioned his wife, and the tender, joyous expression that lit up his face, proved that his domestic happiness was perfect, whatever troubles might have checked his professional career. He spoke with pride of his three little ones, and promised me a noisy welcome from them. The oldest child, a boy of four years,

was at the gate waiting for him. He bounded into his
father's arms with an exclamation of delight, and, resting his curly little head on Harry's cheek, surveyed me
with a puzzled expression, half wonder, half fear.

"Come, Harry, shake hands with Doctor Wilmer;
he is one of papa's friends."

Master Harry looked rather dubious, as if he doubted
the possibility of the thing.

"Him has a blue coat on," he answered, with a look
of contempt on his childish face that was most amusing.

We both laughed heartily.

"Harry," I said, "you are educating him in your
own principles."

"Indeed, Jack, I have never tried to impress such
ideas on his mind, he is too young; but, unfortunately,
the people who visit at my house are not so careful in
their remarks. He has picked up his notions from them,
not from his mother nor me."

"Harry and I will be good friends yet," I said.
"He will soon forget his dislike of a blue coat."

The homelike aspect of the place was quite refreshing after three months of prison-life. The house was
low and wide, with a pretty veranda around it, still
covered with the bright foliage and flowers of the
Southern vines. There was an air of life and activity
about every thing that exerted a strange, pleasant influence over me, and from the open windows came the
sweet sound of a woman's soft voice, and light laughter.

Harry Weston ran up the steps, his child still on
14*

his shoulder, and threw open the door of the sitting-room.

"Edith, here is Doctor Wilmer; I found him to-day in the Libby."

I looked into the room. Mrs. Weston was seated in a low chair, sewing a little dress, and rocking with her foot a cradle containing a beautiful baby of about two months. On the sofa, almost covered with shawls, was lying a delicate-looking old lady, with pretty features, and a sweet expression of face. As her son spoke, she dropped a coarse woollen stocking that she was knitting, and looked toward us with unaffected surprise. Mrs. Weston rose instantly from her seat, and the next moment was holding my hands in hers, and gazing into my face with tears of compassion in her eyes. When she spoke, it was in a voice of welcome and kindness that went to my heart. The old lady, on comprehending who I was, was quite pleased to see me, and a little girl of three summers peeped from behind her grandmother's sofa, and greeted me with a bright smile.

"That is my little Edith, Jack," Harry said, "and the young gentleman in the cradle is John Wilmer Weston, at your service. You see we have not forgotten you."

I bent over my little namesake with a feeling of gratified pride.

"Come in here, Jack!" Harry called out, opening the door of an adjoining room.

"Here is my wardrobe; suit yourself. I know I need

not tell you not to touch my best uniform; but you will find plenty of civilians' clothes there, and, if I don't make a mistake, some of them are blue; I bought them just before this trouble commenced."

"They are in the trunk, Harry," Mrs. Weston said, coming into the room. "If you like, I can fasten Doctor Wilmer's straps on the coat while he is dressing."

"I believe Edith has a fancy, felt, but unexpressed, for the blue uniform," Harry Weston said, throwing his arm around his wife, and looking in her face.

"Since you are both sincere, may I not respect the principles of each?" she answered, with flushed cheeks and glistening eyes.

"Between us, Wilmer," Harry went on, "there is very little of the rebel in my wife. She has her own opinions as well as the rest of us. Happily for me, the marriage service rises superior to political distinctions, and so my wife remains with me in spite of my gray uniform. Her two brothers are on your side in the contest, and for that reason party questions are never discussed in my house with my will. Mother is a hot little rebel, and spends her time, as you see her now, making up small comforts for our men. She never leaves her sofa without assistance, and she suffers terribly at times. This is one of her easy days."

"Is there no help for her?" I asked, looking at the quiet figure on the sofa in the next room.

"None whatever. Her health will never be restored,

but she is happy and cheerful in the midst of all our
troubles. The children are every thing to her in the
way of amusement, and for society and attention she
depends almost entirely on my wife. In fact, but for
this little Northerner, I do not know what would become of us."

"At this moment I wonder what will become of the
dinner," Mrs. Weston said, in a laughing tone, as she
left the room.

"Our best servants have run away from us, and
Mrs. Weston has to attend to nearly all the domestic
affairs herself. The few that remain here are working
under protest, just watching for a good opportunity to
steal off. Our old nurse is the only one that we can
place the least dependence on. She is invaluable with
the children, and she has taken a curious fancy to my
wife, and tries to relieve her as much as possible from
her household cares; still, they are too great a tax on
her strength."

Harry Weston was opening a trunk as he talked,
from which he took a new suit of blue-flannel clothes;
and having collected all the things necessary for my
toilet, he amused himself taking the straps off my old
coat, from which all brightness had long departed, and
conversing over the events of the day in his own earnest
manner. He had seated himself on a chair near the
window, and the rays of the setting sun, as they darted
into the room, shone full upon his blue eyes and fair
hair, and played over the bronzed cheeks and hands

that I remembered as white and delicate as those of a
woman. Whenever I think of him, I see him as he
looked that day, and bring to mind all his good-natured
actions. I recall him bending over his mother, and
easing her pain by his tender care and little attentions,
or with loving thoughtfulness assisting his wife in a
thousand little ways, too trifling, perhaps, to mention,
but they gave evidence of an affection which would
repay her for any and every hardship that she might be
called upon to suffer for his sake.

While I was dressing, he observed me glancing with
some curiosity from the floor to the costly mirror before
which I stood, and guessing my thoughts he commenced
laughing.

"The fact is, Jack, our carpets are gone to make
blankets for our soldiers. We have only those in the
parlor and sitting-room left. No doubt they will soon follow the others, and they could not go in a better cause."

"You fight under difficulties," I said.

"Yes, we are called upon to make a great many
sacrifices; loss of carpets is one of the least. I will tell
you what touches us the most; it is the lack of all the
nourishing articles of food that we used to have from
the North. We don't care for ourselves, but it is hard
to see our wives and children pining for want of them.
I know that my wife does not regain her strength as
usual, and I feel the fact keenly. She will not allow it;
but it is because she will not give me pain by confessing
it. Harry misses his fresh meat too. This continually

eating bacon is very unhealthy. We have fresh vege-
tables, of course, but they don't fill the place of beef
and mutton. I should take them all to Georgia if I
could remove my mother with safety, but that is impossible, and my wife will not hear of sending the two
older children away from her; she will not trust them
to distant relatives."

"And I cannot blame her; besides, if our plans are
carried out, Georgia will soon be as unsafe as Virginia."

"Say what you please here, Jack, but don't express
your opinions quite so openly in any other place this
side of the line. To tell the truth, if we don't gain some
more decided successes soon, this place will be unbearable
between high prices and lack of necessaries. If my wife
were only safe out of all this misery—but she declares
that she will never leave Richmond while I am in or
near it, and she means what she says."

"I wish," I said, looking into his face, which had
grown careworn and sad, "that you could send your
little ones to us. My sister would be delighted to have
the charge of them, and Mrs. Lecount would welcome
them heartily. She has never forgotten the debt of
gratitude she owes your wife. Besides, she has but the
one child, and since her husband's death her life has
been very quiet and lonely. Your Harry would be a
nice playmate for her Arthur; they are about the
same age."

"Yes, there are not more than eight months between
them, I believe," Harry said, musingly.

Then his eyes brightened, and he took my hand and pressed it warmly.

"Some day, Jack, I may remind you of this offer."

"You cannot do it too soon," I answered. "There is a large house, with only two women in it, and plenty of means. My mother would grow young again if she could hear children's voices about her."

"I shall speak to Edith," Harry said, in a voice hoarse with emotion. Then, with an effort that cost him much, he whispered—

"Jack, if we fail, I am a ruined man; and if I die, my wife and children will be entirely dependent on her father; and this war, for all I can tell, may have beggared him. She has no one here to look to for help; my relatives have all staked their fortunes on the result of the fight, and it will end for them the same as it will for me."

I took his hand, and put mine on his shoulder. Standing thus, we two men gazed for a moment each into the other's face, and understood each the other's heart. A knock at the door, and Mrs. Weston's sweet voice, announcing dinner, startled us. Harry recovered himself instantly, assumed his natural gayety, and as we left the room complimented me on the alteration in my appearance. During the meal, however, I felt convinced that the traces of his emotion were only too visible to his wife; her voice became even softer when addressing him, and her face borrowed some of the sad expression that remained in his. I watched her performing her duties of wife, mother, and housekeeper, with a feeling of respect that bordered on adoration. The war had almost impoverished her husband; his practice was swept away, his savings were invested in bonds, and they were living on the slender pay he received from the government. Owing to the high prices, and the difficulty of obtaining them, luxuries of all kinds were beyond their means. Their food was of the plainest quality, and not always sufficient in quantity. In spite of this and many other discomforts, Mrs. Weston was, in my opinion, far more beautiful than she had been as Miss Edith Fullerton. I remembered her in her bridal dress, glowing with youth, and radiant in the fresh loveliness of girlhood. I saw her now, a wife and mother, still young and handsome, but possessing the greater beauty of expression which the cares and joys of her married life had imparted to her face. I felt that the trials of her position had increased her fine qualities of head and heart, and strengthened her affections and powers of endurance. She was graceful, even elegant, in her dark cotton dress and linen collar, and the absence of all ornament seemed to bring into greater prominence the Grecian outlines of her head, with its coils of dark hair. Still, her beauty was her least charm. There was a naturalness and a lack of all affectation in her speech and manner that made her perfectly fascinating.

During the few weeks that I remained in Richmond after the day that Harry Weston found me, I spent most of the hours of freedom allowed me in his sitting-room. The children became fond of me, and even old Mrs. Weston would grow brighter on seeing me, in anticipation of an argument on the respective merits of the two armies. She was failing fast, a fact plainly visible to her son and daughter-in-law, who, under the circumstances, felt keenly their reduced means of living, and the impossibility of obtaining for the invalid many little luxuries that she fancied and wished for. Another anxiety was also weighing on young Mrs. Weston. There were rumors of an approaching battle; and the departure of some of the troops stationed in Richmond for the front was daily expected.

One morning, on going into the house, I found Mrs. Weston sitting crying on a low chair by the window. Her baby was on her knees, and the two older children, attracted by the sight of their mother's tears, were leaning against her, with their arms around her neck, trying in vain to kiss them away. She looked up with a faint smile on seeing me, and motioned to me to speak softly, so as not to disturb the old lady, who was asleep on her sofa.

"I have been trying to make up my mind to accept your kind offer, Doctor Wilmer," she said, taking my hand, "but it comes very hard on me. Separating from my children will be a bitter trial; one I never anticipated, although I thought that I had considered the very worst results that could arise from this unhappy war. Harry has been talking about it ever since you mentioned it to him. He has tried to make me understand its advantages, and of course I realize them; still I cannot part with them, they are such a comfort to us all here. If Harry goes away again, I do not know what I shall do. I have lost courage fearfully since baby came. Harry attributes it to my want of strength. He says I look too much on the dark side. Perhaps I do. Certainly the difficulties of our position seem to increase, and there is no sign of the war coming to an end. Perhaps some day I may be only too glad to ask you for advice and assistance."

I had never before seen Mrs. Weston give way to such gloomy thoughts; on the contrary, her cheerfulness and hopefulness had often surprised me. Drawing little Harry on my knee, I endeavored to lead her mind to other subjects. I spoke of my home, and our friends there, and, without intending it, I disclosed my own anxiety of mind, for, although I had written several times to my mother, no answer had ever reached me from her.

"Harry felt quite delighted last night," Mrs. Weston replied. "He thinks the exchange will go on at once, without further interruption. You must promise to write often after you leave here, and, if possible, I shall answer you."

The opening of the gate drew our attention, and, looking through the window, we saw Harry Weston coming hurriedly up the walk. He was equipped for a march, and his wife knew instinctively the meaning of his sudden appearance. She became deathly pale, and, laying the baby in the cradle, as if unable to hold it, she went softly out of the room, and met him at the door.

I saw her husband's face brighten when he caught sight of her, waiting on the veranda to welcome him. A moment after, when they came together into the room, she was begging him to lay aside his heavy knap-sack, and smoothing the bright hair from his heated face with trembling hands.

"He is going away," was all she could say to me, in a choking voice, as she motioned Harry to his usual arm-chair near his mother's sofa.

"I can't sit down, Edith, love ; I have only time to kiss the little ones, mother, and you. The regiment has started.—Wilmer," he went on, turning to me, " you will probably leave for Fortress Monroe to-morrow. I just saw the list, and your name is on it, old fellow —all right. Don't forget us here in Dixie, when you are safe again in Washington," he added, gayly, with an effort to recover his old light manner. "We are off to the front. This is worse than fighting," he said, a moment after, looking at his wife's face bent on his shoulder.

"Just an instant, darling," he whispered, releasing her hands from their clasp around his neck. He leaned over his mother, then, while she blessed him and wished him success in a feeble voice that shook with emotion in spite of her attempted self-control. My poor friend, I can see him now, bending over the baby-face in the cradle, and leaving passionate kisses mingled with bitter tears on the childish lips that he might never touch again. The remembrance of his wife's face, when he turned to her to kiss her for the last time, will remain with me as long as I live. She watched him until his form could no longer be distinguished in the busy street, and then, sinking on her knees beside the cradle, she laid her head on the pillow near the unconscious little baby-face, and sobbed convulsively.

"Edith, daughter!" the old lady called from her sofa, "do not fret like that. You never before gave way so much. Harry will return safe to you and his children. Come to me, your poor old mother, that may never see her son again."

"Poor mother!" Mrs. Weston said, rising hastily; then taking the quiet little figure in her arms, she soothed and caressed it, and tried, by comforting the helpless mother, to gain some hope for her own heavy heart.

"I never before felt so desolate and despondent, although Harry has often left us just as unexpectedly," she said, turning to me. "Do you think it foretells misfortune?"

"I think that you are not strong, and therefore disposed to imagine all kinds of horrors coming upon you. Your nerves are in a weakened condition, and you see only the troubles that may arise, not the blessings. Try and grow stronger for Harry's sake. If he has the misfortune to fall into our hands, I shall take care of him. We surgeons, as a general thing, run but little danger of wounds."

"Yes, but Harry has, more than once, led a company when its officers have all fallen, and I really believe that he enjoyed the danger it placed him in."

"Harry never knew what fear was," said old Mrs. Weston, energetically.

Her daughter sighed wearily, as if not so much impressed by the beauties of Harry's courage.

"There is hardly a house in our country where the women are not suffering as we are to-night. I only hope that we may have more victories. It inspires our men with so much enthusiasm!" the old lady exclaimed, warming with the subject.

Her daughter sighed again, and busied herself with the children, instead of answering.

Afterward, in view of my probable departure on the next day, Mrs. Weston wrote letters to her father and brothers, which I undertook to forward to them on my return to Washington. I bade the family good-by that afternoon with a heavy heart. In spite of the home-like surroundings, there was an air of desolation over every thing, and it seemed impossible to shake off the gloomy impressions that Harry's absence had occasioned. Mrs. Weston, with all her efforts to regain her usual cheerfulness, looked pale and crushed, and quite unable to sustain the cares of her position. Even the old lady's spirit had died away; and the children, awed by the sorrowful faces around them, had crept silently out of the room and down to the gate, to "look for papa," as little Edith said.

I returned to the Libby with sad forebodings, remembering Mrs. Weston's slight, drooping figure, and the baby-face she held against her own, as she stood in the window of the sitting-room watching my departure.

The next morning, as Harry had anticipated, I heard my name called off the list in the jailer's hand, and along with Doctor Berry, who was equally fortunate, I joined the detachment on their way to exchange and freedom.

One of the first faces I saw at Fortress Monroe was Mr. Masters'. He had been informed of my capture soon after it occurred, but not hearing further tidings of me, as my letters never reached home, he had at length started alone, determined on finding me, if alive. At Washington he could ascertain nothing definite, so he set out for Fortress Monroe, and was more fortunate in his search. He visited the hospitals, where many of our returned prisoners were lying sick, and one of them, who had been in the Libby with me, informed him of my presence there, and of my good health. Overjoyed at this news, Mr. Masters wrote home at once, but made up his mind to stay on, in the hope of seeing me exchanged.

CHAPTER XIV.

BETWEEN THE RIFLE-PITS AT FREDERICKSBURG.

WE went to Washington together, as I intended asking for leave of absence, and going home for a few weeks. I was disappointed in my calculations. Although near the end of December, another movement of the army was in progress. Every thing was in preparation for the coming fight, all furloughs had been recalled, and we were ordered to rejoin our regiments without delay. The division to which mine belonged was then at Falmouth, and, having consigned all my packages and letters for Mrs. Johnson and Mr. Fullerton to Mr. Masters' care, I started for that place, accompanied still by Doctor Berry. We were just in time for the opening of the ball, and our old comrades hailed our appearance with delight. The division was under marching orders, and at daybreak of the morning following our arrival we started toward the scene of the coming battle. We were halted on a large field about half a mile from the Rappahannock, where we awaited the orders to move forward.

Our men were attempting to lay the bridges under a murderous fire from the enemy's sharpshooters, who were stationed in the houses of Fredericksburg. They were picked off by dozens, yet the work went on. Before morning the bridges were finished, and our forces crossed under a heavy cannonade from the rebel batteries, and slowly drove the men out of the city and into their earthworks. ·

The main body of the enemy was strongly posted on the side of a sloping hill commanding the city—the batteries and rifle-pits, with the lines of infantry supporting them, being plainly visible to our soldiers as they advanced against them. Our lines of battle had been formed in a hollow back of the city, and under a hot fire the men marched steadily toward the first row of rifle-pits. Though terribly cut down, they carried it, and went into the second, but, being unable to hold that, they fell back on the first, and remained there all night. In marching up the slope, my regiment had been exposed to a heavy fire, and a shell had burst in the ranks, killing and wounding a number of the men.

That night, when out with one of the parties that were bringing in the wounded, I came upon a group of privates belonging to my own regiment. They had stolen out of the rifle-pit which our men were holding, and were searching for their own comrades who had fallen during the fight. They succeeded in finding a number of them, and carrying them off the field. Still later, I met them as they returned from burying those that were killed. It was a deserted part of the field, some distance from the line of sentinels, and they stopped to light their pipes, which they contrived to carry and save, under all circumstances.

" Is Lieutenant Williams safe ?" I asked. He was my best friend in the regiment, and I always thought of him first after a battle. He was daring and cool, and never hesitated to expose himself when it was necessary to encourage the men, though at the same time he was never reckless or foolhardy. The members of his company were fond of him ; he was just the man to gain their respect, and keep it when won. He had told me many things concerning his family and himself. He was an only child, and his mother had been left a widow before he had reached his seventh birthday. She had a small income, on which she had managed to give him a good education. When the war broke out, he held a fine position in a wholesale house in New York, one that promised rapid advancement, and he was engaged to be married. At that time he belonged to a militia regiment that was among the first to start for Washington; and when it returned home he thought it his duty to give up his place in the store and remain in the army. He enlisted as a private, and had been promoted for bravery and good conduct to the first lieutenancy. He had made quite a confidant of me, and often read to me scraps of news out of the letters that he received from his mother, and the young lady to whom he was engaged. He would sit for hours

15

with me, smoking gravely, while he discussed his future prospects, and the plans he had laid for himself, in case he should survive the war.

"For, Wilmer," he would say, "I am determined to see this thing out first, provided they leave me my limbs to do it with."

When I inquired for him, the man before me dropped his eyes on the ground, and shook his head.

"He fell outside our line, sir," he answered. "He was all right till we tried to take the second row of rifle-pits. I didn't see him in the retreat; the boys say that he is lying just between our sentinels and the rebs. Some of them tried to bring him off, but the fire was too hot, and they had to leave him there."

"Then he was alive?" I said.

"He was then, for he spoke to them. He told them to take care of themselves and not mind him, that he was not able to rise. They think his leg was broken. I wish we could bring him in, sir."

"It will be a hard piece of work," said another. "If the rebs see us, they'll fire on us, sure."

"Let us try," I said. "Does any one here know where he lies?"

"No, sir; but we can get one of the men that saw him. Perhaps he can remember."

With cautious steps and bent forms we crept into the ditch where our boys were lying, and found the one we needed. Then we picked our way among the dead bodies covering the ground around us, and at last reached the open space beyond our line of pickets. Our guide went slowly along, and we followed with our lanterns, and a litter destined for our unfortunate officer. It was a cold, windy night, and, happily for us, became quite dark, as the clouds drifted between us and the moon, and remained there until our work was over. We came at last upon the object of our search. He was insensible from cold and loss of blood, and it was some time before our efforts to revive him proved successful.

Then we raised him on the litter, and began our retreat as rapidly as we could move. We were quite near our own picket, and the men bearing the litter were already inside the line, when one of the party, in his haste, stumbled over a body lying on the ground, and, springing up with a quick oath, hurried after the others without looking back. I was just behind him, and a low moan from the form that he supposed dead reached my ear. I flashed my lantern over it almost mechanically, and saw that it was a soldier in the gray uniform. He was lying with his face hidden on his arm, and the life-blood was flowing from a small wound in the side. His attitude denoted perfect consciousness, as if he were sensible of his condition and approaching death, and awaited it with calmness.

Even as I bent over him he sighed heavily, and a choking sob that shook his whole frame met my ear.

" Can I help you ?" I asked, laying my hand on his shoulder, the utter misery and loneliness of his position awakening all my sympathies. He raised his head with an effort, and turned his eyes on me. Never shall I forget the sickening sensation of horror that rushed over me as I met that despairing look, nor the bright, happy expression that lit up the worn, sad face as he recognized me.

"Oh, Harry! Harry!" was all I could say, in my shocked surprise.

"Jack," he muttered feebly, "this is a mercy that I have prayed for, and my prayer is answered. Oh, how I have longed for the sight of a living face, and the sound of a friendly voice! What weary hours I have passed lying here, clinging to life with the hope of seeing some one that would tell my poor wife of my death!"

"Do not talk of death," I said, as gayly as I could; "let us see what our united skill can do for you."

"All the science and skill in the world would be useless here, Jack," he whispered, his voice growing fainter and fainter. "There is no way of stanching the blood, and in this position it runs slower than in any other. To move would be to hasten what is coming so surely. No human power can aid me now."

He lay without speaking for some minutes, and I leaned over him, holding his hand and watching the expressive features that changed with the color of his thoughts.

"My poor wife and children!" he groaned at last, gazing in my face as if wishing me to put into language the ideas that he was unable to express.

"They shall not want for any thing while I live," I said. "If Mr. Fullerton is unwilling to take charge of them, they shall come to me. In either case, I shall consider it a pleasure to protect them."

"They must not be dependent," he gasped; "teach them to work for themselves."

"I shall do exactly as you wish for them, if you will consent to trust them to me."

"I do," he answered; "I believe that you will do right by them."

"Then you will try and not feel any more anxiety for them," I said, looking into his face.

He understood me.

"Take my head on your arm, Jack," he whispered; "so; that is more comfortable than the hard ground, even if the change does cause pain. But there is no victory without a fight; no crown without its cross. In these last few hours I have appreciated more than in all the days of my life put together the beauty of our faith, and the comfort that it contains. The last time I attended church in Richmond, I heard the anthem sung, 'I know that my Redeemer liveth.' The words have floated in my brain ever since I fell, and their meaning has come home to me, I trust, not in vain."

He smiled faintly and closed his eyes, but a moment after opened them and fixed them on my face.

"Jack," he gasped, "how nobly your brave fellows fought to-day! They threw themselves upon certain death. If ever men deserved to win, they did. But they will not; our position is impregnable. And yet, how they struggle to maintain a principle, while we risk all to defend our rights and homes!"

"Is not the higher warfare," I said, "a struggle for a principle against the whole world?"

"Yes," he murmured, "the principle of truth."

He never spoke afterward. I laid his head against my breast, and took his hand in mine. Lying thus, his breath became fainter and fainter, until at length, with one last, shivering gasp, all was over, and my poor friend lay dead beside me. We had been boys at school together, chums at college, companions as men, good friends always. As I bent over the dead face, I realized that I had lost my oldest and dearest associate; the one that had understood me best and valued me the most. I smoothed the tangled curls, still bright and golden, over the sun-burned forehead, and covered with a handkerchief the thin, sunken features, whose sad, suffering expression was fast disappearing in the quiet peacefulness of death. I remembered, with a bitter pain at my heart, that I would never meet the glance of his honest, loving eyes again, never hear the cheerful tones of his kindly voice, never feel the warm grasp of his strong, friendly hand. I regretted leaving him thus on the frozen battle-ground, but on looking around me for help, I saw only the picket walking back and forward on his post. The men had all hastened away to the regiment, and my poor friend, like many other brave men on both sides, would probably fill "a nameless grave." The thought, I knew, had never troubled him; he had fallen in the cause to which he had devoted himself, and would be buried on the field for which he had fought. Lest strange and careless hands should place him in the ground, I took from his pockets the few things they contained and fastened them securely in my own. He had no watch with him, and very little money; but in one of the pockets of his old purse was a small colored photograph of his wife and a braid of her hair. Thinking that they might serve to identify him at a future day, I placed them on his breast, hoping that they would escape observation, and be buried with him.

That done, I looked on his face for the last time, and returned with a heavy heart to the city. There I ascertained that my regiment had been relieved, and was already in Fredericksburg. I found the boys, after a long search, in the act of preparing supper. They had stacked arms on the sidewalk, and were enjoying their rest from duty—a rest very acceptable after lying for thirty hours among the dead and dying on the battle-field. Later I sat by Lieutenant Williams, and wrote, at his dictation, to his mother. He was doing well, and was overjoyed at the thought that his leg would be saved, the doctors having at first feared the necessity of amputation.

The next day was occupied in removing our wounded across the river, and the men stationed in the city enter-tained themselves by going through the houses and enjoying in anticipation the pleasure of sleeping in them that night. They were, however, disappointed in their hopes, for at dark the evacuation was in progress, and the next day the troops were back in their old quarters at Falmouth.

As soon as I could take the time, I communicated with Mrs. Weston, and proposed her removal to the North. Her reply was long in reaching me. As I had anticipated, she refused to leave her mother-in-law in her desolate condition, but promised to consider my plan for sending her children, in charge of their nurse, through the lines. I had written the full particulars of the case to my sister, and she was quite ready to help me in carrying my ideas into practice.

The troops were in winter quarters, no important movement was in contemplation, and the old routine of hospital-work was again going on. The buildings assigned to the use of our wounded were all crowded, and, as fast as it was possible to remove them, the men were forwarded to the other cities. Mrs. Weston had requested me, if convenient, to see her father, and hear his opinion as to what she should do. I surmised, from what she said, that she had written to the old gentleman herself, and that his answer had not been entirely satisfactory to her. I concluded to accompany a detachment of our wounded to New York, and see Mr. Fullerton on the matter. It was now February. The calm that follows the storm had settled down over us. The soldiers in camp were mostly employed in arranging original amusements for themselves, and making merry over the boxes of good things sent to them by their families at home. The officers, as many as could, had received furloughs, and gone to their own cities, to be caressed, and listened to as heroes. The sick and wounded were looking forward with eager joy to the day on which they might start for home. Washington was dull to me; the daily sight of so much misery and death exerts a gloomy influence on those brought in such close contact with them.

Lieutenant Williams had recovered sufficiently to go to his mother's house, where, surrounded by every care and loving attention, he was rapidly regaining strength and spirits. It was, therefore, with a feeling of real pleasure that I started one morning, early in March, with a party of convalescents, for New York, having in my pocket a two weeks' furlough. Arrived there, I gave up my charge at the rooms of the New England Society on Broadway, and sauntered up to the St. Nicholas with slow steps, determined to enjoy every moment of my freedom from duty. Once there, in a cosy little room, with a hot dinner before me, I debated with myself what I should do first, in order to have the most time to spend at home.

It was necessary for me to see Mr. Fullerton, and I concluded to do so without delay; so I took his address from his daughter's letter, and left the hotel for his place of business. I found him at his desk, writing so busily, that he took no notice of me for some minutes,

15*

and I stood aside to await his leisure, in the mean time closely studying his appearance. I was in full uniform, and it struck me afterward that he had in glancing at me divined who I was, and my motive in seeking him; and that, while apparently studying the ledger before him, he was in reality forming his replies to my remarks.

He was a short man, and remarkably well preserved for his age, which must have been at least fifty-five. He was well shaven, and his hair was arranged so as to hide any sign of baldness. His clothes were of the finest black, cut in the latest style, and fitting admirably his neat, straight figure; even his neck-tie was of the most boyish pattern, and his whole appearance was decidedly youthful. His face, however, when at last he turned to me, was hard, cold, and impassive. There was nothing young or impulsive in his small, glittering blue eyes, and thin, firm lips. I argued badly for Mrs. Weston's case as I handed him my card. He read it slowly, as far as I could see not recognizing the name.

"And to what am I indebted for the pleasure of this visit?" he asked, fixing his eyes on my face, and moving his lips slowly; there was no other change of features.

I explained briefly my old friendship with his dead son-in-law, and the necessity of removing his widow and orphans from Richmond.

"I do not understand," he said, slowly, leaning an elbow on the desk to steady himself, and regarding me with a searching look from his high office stool.

"You must be aware of the increasing poverty of the Southern country, and of the complete helplessness of your daughter. Her youngest child is but five months old."

"Weston represented himself as being well off, when he married my daughter Edith."

"And he was so at that time; but you must recollect what has happened since then. He was not the only one that this war beggared. He, with others, staked all he owned on this contest—"

"The more fool he! Why the deuce didn't he sell out and come North, as others did?"

"You forget that, with his convictions, such a proceeding would have been most dishonorable. We do not respect those who live among us and yet sneer at us at the same time."

"I know nothing about that; a man should look out for his own. Honor is thought very little of, if there is no money to back it. He brought this trouble on his wife himself."

Mr. Fullerton was as cool as ice. I felt myself growing warm.

"If you please," I said, "we will leave Mr. Weston out of the question. The present position of his wife is what we have to talk about."

"What has become of Weston's relatives? He mentioned having a great number."

"They are all in the same trouble with regard to means. What they have is invested in Confederate bonds. A man can do much, even if involved, for his family; a woman, left as Mrs. Weston is, has no resources."

"She had a fine education, and was considered talented," he went on.

"Yes, but at present her knowledge is unavailable as a means of support. Her health is not very good; she could hardly undertake much work. She will not leave her husband's mother, but she can be relieved of the care and anxiety of her children. Her pride is such that, unless entirely unassisted by you, she will not accept any aid from me."

Mr. Fullerton thought for a few moments, and then commenced again.

"Doctor Wilmer, the facts of the case are these; I have lost heavily in this trouble, and do not feel myself able to undertake, at my age, the whole expense of so many persons. It is a duty or rather a kindness which I never anticipated being called upon to perform. My daughter kept house for me for some years, and when she married to please herself I was obliged to fill her place. In fact, I married again, and the present Mrs. Fullerton is, if any thing, younger than my daughter. Of course, she is mistress of my house, and such an addition to our family as you propose could hardly be acceptable to her, neither would a secondary position in my household be suitable for Mrs. Weston, my daughter. You see that such an arrangement is entirely out of the question."

"And Mrs. Weston's brothers?" I said.

"They are both married, and would hardly be able to undertake such a responsibility."

"Very well," I answered. "I wished to settle the matter at once. I thank you for your explanation."

I wished him good-by, and he accompanied me to the door most politely, regretting, as he did so, his inability to comply with his daughter's request. His perfect coolness and urbanity were striking. "If at any future time I can do any thing to further her children's interests, why, call on me," he remarked, as I quitted him. I bowed deeply in return for this condescension, and took my way to the hotel, pondering on my last lesson in human nature.

"So," I said to myself, "that is Mrs. Weston's father. How very unlike a parent and child may be! No wonder she was so much attached to my generous-hearted, impulsive friend."

On reaching my room, I found a letter there that had been forwarded to me from Washington. It was from Richmond, and contained news. Mrs. Weston, unable any longer to meet all the demands made upon her purse and strength, had consented to accept my proffered services. Her children, with their faithful old nurse, would leave Richmond on the first opportunity, and she begged of me to meet them on their arrival within our lines. She herself had concluded to retain two rooms in her house, and rent the others to transient lodgers, intending to maintain the old lady on the money she would receive from them.

I replied at once, telling her that I should leave directly for Fortress Monroe, and giving her, in as few words as possible, the result of my interview with her father. That done, I concluded that I could not go home; so I telegraphed to my sister to join me in New York, and then set about making the necessary preparations for the comfort of poor Harry's orphans.

The following day I met my sister at the railroad depot, and we started a few hours afterward for Annapolis. On our arrival at Fortress Monroe, I commenced my search for Mrs. Weston's children, as a number of refugees had entered our lines during my passage from New York. I could hear nothing of them, however, and so we remained there ready to receive them. I felt, as the days slipped by, that my chances for reaching home during that leave of absence were becoming less and less possible, and I was right in my calculation. It wanted two days of the expiration of my furlough, when we heard that a number of women and children were on their way to Fortress Monroe from Richmond. My sister and I were at the landing when the boat containing them arrived, and we scanned with eagerness the little groups collected on the deck. One at last fixed our attention. A short, stout colored woman, in a faded cotton gown, with a woollen shawl pinned close about her neck, and an old bandanna twisted around her head, stood holding on one arm a baby wrapped up in a large cloak, and on the other a little girl of three years whose hands were clasping her neck. Beside her, grasping her gown was a little boy dressed in gray home-spun.

"John," said my sister, catching sight of them, and turning to me with tearful eyes—"John, I think they are Mrs. Weston's children. See how their nurse, looks from them to the shore, as if searching for some one that she knows."

"I am almost sure of them," I said. "We will go to them at once."

Making our way with difficulty, we succeeded in reaching the little group. As we approached them, Master Harry recognized me, and bounding forward he caught my hand, his face, which was his father's in miniature, lighting up with pleasure.

"Mamma told me to do exactly as you wished," he exclaimed, "and, oh, how glad I am to see you!" he added, with a long sigh, which, under other circumstances, would have provoked a smile at its precociousness.

The nurse's face beamed with joy, and she expressed her delight in language almost unintelligible to my sister. The latter had taken little Edith in her arms, and, holding Master Harry's hand, I led the way off the boat. My time was nearly up, and so, after a very short rest, we started for Annapolis, at which place we would separate, I going on to Washington, and my sister taking the little ones and their nurse to New York, and from thence home.

On the steamer, nurse Flo, as the children called her, gave me the messages intrusted to her by her mis-

tress. From them I inferred that Mrs. Weston's own
health was causing her much anxiety, and that the old
lady was sinking rapidly. In her own odd language,
Florida told me, the terrible effect that her master's
death had had upon his wife. She had received intelligence of it the day after it occurred, and the shock had
nearly killed her. His mother, owing most probably to
her weak condition, had taken the news very quietly
and as if prepared for it. That her young mistress had
never looked the same since, but went about like a
shadow, speaking little, and crying when alone as if her
heart would break, did not surprise me. I could understand her grief, and appreciate its real sincerity and
depth.

Florida's fidelity was a touching tribute to the kindness of her owner, and a proof of her own honesty
and single-mindedness. She was sitting in the cabin of
the steamer, playing with the baby, and I was determined, before leaving them, to find out her ideas of her
own position, and whether I might trust to her remaining with the children. I told her that she was free to
go where she pleased, that there was no longer any one
to control her actions. She said that she knew all that;
her mistress had explained it to her, and told her that
others would pay her well for her work, whereas she
could afford to give her very little.

"Well," I asked. "Have you made up your
mind?"

Her answer was, "That money was no good to her;

what she wanted was to have food and clothes, and a place to live in. Besides, she had been born and brought up in the Weston family; they had taken care of her, and had been kind to her always, and if Mrs. Weston would let her, she would stay with her and her children as long as she lived."

As she spoke, her tears fell on the little waxen hands of baby Jack, that were grasping hers in play, and I felt that I could depend upon her faithfulness.

At Annapolis my sister bought her some bright, new bandannas, and pair of wondrous gold ear-rings, remarkable for their size, which threw her into ecstasies of delight; and having supplied the children with toys to enliven and shorten their tedious journey, I saw them off in high spirits, and in happy ignorance of their own sorrowful position.

Later, I received letters, telling me of their safe arrival in my mother's house, and of the warm welcome they received from young Mrs. Lecount, and Mr. and Mrs. Masters; together with a long description of the friendship already existing between Arthur and Harry, and of the merry games they played, into which even little Edith entered with joy, and at which Master Jack clapped his tiny hands with delight.

"Once more," my sister wrote, "the house is bright with the presence of little children, and merry with their childish laughter. Mother is growing active and energetic again, and looks better than she did since you went away. The 'pets,' as we call them, are always together, either here or at Mr. Masters', and Florida with her fidelity, her bandanna, and her ear-rings, is the wonder of the village, and the ' observed of all observers.' "

I forwarded my sister's letter to Mrs. Weston, and received a reply from her, in which she expressed her entire satisfaction with what had been done, and also mentioned her own improvement in health since being relieved of so much anxiety.

Toward the end of April she sent me information of her mother-in-law's death, and her own intention to proceed at once to the North, leaving her house at the disposal of some of her husband's relatives, who had offered to do the best they could with it for her benefit. A week after, I met her at Fortress Monroe, where she had arrived a day or two previously, and was waiting for the departure of a steamer for New York. We had a long interview, and I listened to the plans that she had formed in her mind with surprise. She intended to see her father at once, and ask him to assist her in establishing a school in New York. She was so hopeful and cheerful; so earnest in her desires to do all for her children alone; so determined to be independent, and so anxious to commence her new life without delay! Yet she looked delicate, and perfectly helpless; she had become thin and pale, and the expression of her eyes had changed; there was a timid mournfulness in them now, that they would retain always. She had the appearance of one who needed care and protection, rather than of a person ready to go forth and battle with the world and its disappointments.

I noticed how tender she was of her husband's memory; how carefully she refrained from saying the least thing that could reflect blame upon him, or impute to his actions the causes of the troubles that had fallen upon her. She seemed sanguine of obtaining her father's aid in spite of all that had passed, and I did not like to chill her hopes with my convictions to the contrary.

I placed her on board the steamer, in charge of an officer with whom I was acquainted, who was going home with his wife, and then returned to Washington, where I awaited intelligence of her safe arrival in New York, and the result of her meeting with her father.

As I had anticipated, the interview was not satisfactory; and my sister having joined her there, she hastened at once to see her children, from whom she had been so long separated. Shortly after the affair at Chancellorsville, I heard that she had been offered the teachership of the public school in our village, and had accepted it with pleasure. In addition, she had obtained a number of music-pupils, who came to the house for their lessons, and was improving daily in spirits.

CHAPTER XV.

"WHAT! Doctor Wilmer, is it you? How glad I am to meet you!"

It was early on the morning of the second day at Gettysburg. I was standing giving directions to some of the men, who were making accommodations for the wounded, when this salutation was uttered beside me. Turning quickly, I saw a fine-looking young fellow in a colonel's uniform, mounted on a powerful horse, bending toward me with outstretched hand. I did not recognize him at first, owing to the heavy black beard and mustache covering the lower part of his face, and the cap pressed down upon his forehead, to protect his eyes from the burning rays of the sun. The next moment I remembered him—the young fellow who, two years before, when a mere boy, had taken his company to Washington.

"Victor, is it possible?" I exclaimed, in my surprise. "How much you have changed!"

"Yes, I suppose I have; but you look the same as

over. When did you hear from home? I have been moving from place to place so much, that my letters have all missed me for the last three weeks."

"They were all well five days ago," I said. "How proud they must feel when they think of you! War agrees with you."

"Yes, I like it better than poring over musty old law-books in a dusty office. If I live to see this thing out, I shall try and obtain a position in the regular army. The life suits me."

"It is certainly more exciting than a quiet profession, and repays those who are daring, and fond of the glory attached to it; still, your promotion has been unusually rapid."

"Yes," he replied. "Our regiment has been all along doing good service, and our poor fellows were picked off before their straps were tarnished. I suppose it will be the same way with me."

"Have you escaped so far?"

"Yes, pretty well; I got a slight scratch at Antietam on my arm, but it was not enough to pension me for. I used to lie in the hospital there at Washington, and long for the sight of a home face."

"And your sister, Miss Pauline; was she not there?"

"No, not at that time; she was at Fortress Monroe, I believe she is there now. I have scarcely seen her since Claude's death; she took it terribly to heart. Do you know, Wilmer, I never could understand how all his misfortunes came about. He was always so steady at home—father had the highest hopes of him; but he told me one time, in speaking of Claude, that, once in New York, he seemed to lose his reason. Such a nice little wife as he had too; no one could have been more agreeable than she was to us all. She writes to me frequently such kind letters! Poor fellow, he might have done as I did, and fared far better. If killed, his death would at least have been honorable." He sighed heavily, and trifled with the hilt of his sword.

"Our boys suffered terribly yesterday," I said, to change the current of his thoughts.

"Yes," he replied. "The gray jackets made sad havoc in the First corps; but then it had no business to commence the attack with such a small number of men. We are going to have it, hot and heavy, again to-day. We must work hard if we would save the capital. Our men are pretty well exhausted now, and the whole of Lee's army is on the field. I must go, for I tell you the sight of the wounded don't tend to raise a fellow's spirits. Well—if you shouldn't see me to-morrow, just tell my family that I tried to do my duty. Good-by." He bent and shook my hand, then taking off his hat, he exclaimed: "The Union forever! Hurrah, boys, hurrah!" and the next moment was galloping off in the direction of a column of our troops forming the reserve.

The day wore on. Our boys, as fast as they arrived, were put into position, and the struggle was relaxed only to be renewed with fresh vigor and enthusiasm.

As regiment after regiment fell back to the rear, their places were instantly occupied, and all that long, hot July day the hand-to-hand fight continued. Foot by foot the ground was contested, and lost or won. Dense clouds of smoke rose over the fearful struggle, and floated away, only to be succeeded by others still heavier. The shrieks of the wounded were mingled with the roar of artillery, the whizzing of the dreaded shells, and the continuous rattle of musketry. The air was heavy with the smell of gunpowder, the smoke, and the dust; and still the work went on, as if each individual felt in his own heart the weight of the responsibility resting on the whole army.

About four o'clock in the afternoon, a regiment that had been relieved, and ordered to the rear, came straggling toward us; and the men having stacked arms, and unfastened their belts, quickly lit their pipes, and throwing themselves on the ground in attitudes denoting extreme fatigue, they gave vent to the feelings so long repressed, and discussed in noisy tones the progress of the fight.

Their tattered colors, shattered ranks, and torn clothes, gave evidence of the fierce struggle going on in the front, and I listened with interest to their various opinions. One of them approached me, supported by two of his companions, and, looking for the cause of his ghastly face and tottering steps, I saw that three of the fingers of his right hand were hanging, almost severed at the knuckles; the sickening sensation caused by the sight of them affecting him more than the pain. While I dressed his wound I asked him the number of his regiment.

"The F—th New York," he answered.

"Why, that is Colonel Lecount's regiment!" I exclaimed. "Is he safe?"

"That is more than I can tell, sir," he answered. "He didn't lead us off the field."

"I saw him go down myself," his companion remarked. "His horse fell at the same time."

"Then you don't know whether he was carried off or not?" I said.

"I think not, sir; the rebs were driving us at the time, and we did not recover the ground—"

"Yes, but the boys that relieved us did. I could see that before we left," remarked another of the men who had joined the group. "We were dreadfully cut up," he continued, in a tone of apology. "There's not two hundred of us left."

"We ought to go and find the colonel," said a powerful-looking man, rising from the ground where he had been stretched, listening to us, and commencing his preparations by slowly knocking the ashes out of his pipe, and replacing it in the band of his cap. Then clasping his belt, he looked about him, in anticipation of an assent to his proposition.

"I shall be with you in one moment," I said. A dozen voices immediately responded; and, guided by a captain of the regiment, we took our way toward the point where it had been stationed that morning. Our principal landmark was a group of rocks, in the shadow of which the men remembered having last seen their colonel. On that spot the fight was obstinate, hand to hand, and as the line wavered and broke, young Lecount had dashed between the opposing ranks, calling on his soldiers to rally around him. At that instant he was seen to fall, and in the momentary consternation which the loss of a trusted leader casts over a regiment, the rebels made a desperate charge, and the whole line was pressed back. At this juncture reënforcements arrived, and the exhausted men were ordered to the rear.

The captain gave me the particulars as we crossed the battle-field, where soldiers and horses lay dying and dead, in undisputed possession of the hotly-contested ground. My companion pointed in delight to the proofs of our victory; and we gazed with pleasure on the distant clouds of smoke, and listened to the thunders of the artillery, conscious that our brave boys were pushing back the heavy columns that had threatened to overwhelm us.

Arriving near the rocks, we found that the battle was still raging a little beyond them, between the left wing of our army and the right of the enemy. Stray bullets whistled over our heads, and the ground was torn up by balls from the rebel batteries posted on the rising ground, and commanding the open space over which we had to pass. The men hesitated, but only for

16

a moment, and then dashing forward, we reached a place of comparative safety in the shadow of the rocks.

The ground around us was covered with dead bodies. Friend and foe had fought with broken muskets and bayonets, and lay as they had fallen, locked in each other's arms. The clinched hands had not relaxed their hold; the stern faces yet wore a terrible expression of pain, mingled with fierce hate. Glaring eyeballs, started from their sockets, and covered with the glassy film of death, met us on every side. Even in death, the forms possessed an air of fixed determination, a steady, resolute look, as if they had made up their minds to conquer or die, then and there. I was not surprised, when I afterward learned that the two opposing regiments had met before, and had paid a heavy debt of vengeance at Gettysburg.

With many misgivings, we bent our steps to where the carcass of a large horse was lying, and, looking down, recognized the form crushed beneath it. The men carefully removed the heavy weight, and we found, to our joyful surprise, that the colonel was still living. He was lying on his side, his bridle-arm broken by a Minié ball, and several of his ribs fractured; the latter injury, however, was caused by his horse falling on him, a fact which happily preserved him from the bayonet-thrusts of the enemy.

"I thought you would never come," he said, very feebly, opening his eyes at the same time and looking in my face. "I did not speak before, not being sure of

who was assisting me. Sabre-cuts are not very agreeable, and if it had been a party of rebels I should have
played I was dead, and let them pick my pockets of
every thing. Your voice was a great relief when I
heard it. I recognized it at once."

"Do you think you can walk a little?" I asked him.

We raised him, but he was too weak. So, having
placed him on the litter, we prepared to return.

"My poor Stonewall!" he said, looking at his horse.
"That cannon-ball killed him instantly. I was struck
a few moments before, but I felt almost sure of taking
him out of this alive. What a place for a man to die
in!" He glanced about him with a visible shudder, at
which I did not wonder. The scene before me exceeded in horror any thing of the kind that I had ever
witnessed.

"How long will my arm be in a sling?" he asked,
as we commenced our retreat. I was walking beside
his litter, steadying it where the ground was rough, and
I turned to look at him, in admiration of his coolness.

"Better ask, how long before your side will be all
right. I think worse of that than of your arm."

"Oh, you are a regular Job's comforter, doctor;
come, give me an opinion."

"Well, six weeks, if the bone is not splintered."

He gave a long whistle.

"Why, the army may be in Richmond by that
time!"

"I sincerely hope that it will be; then you can go

home on a long furlough, and play hero to your heart's content."

We had reached the middle of the field, and he was saying something about his mother, when a loud report struck on our ears. Something whizzed over our heads and sank into the ground before us. The men recoiled, I heard an explosion, the ground trembled under our feet, things flew past my eyes, I felt a shock, and a burning sensation in my breast; I was falling, it seemed to me, in space, the ground receding as I neared it.

When I recovered consciousness I was lying down, and some one was bending over me. I opened my eyes, and saw Doctor Berry.

"Wilmer," he was saying, "are you conscious? do you understand me?"

The words had a confused sound. I felt myself trying to catch their meaning. He began again, this time with more effect.

"Wilmer, listen! try to keep your mind on what I am saying; it will become clear to you after a while."

"Yes," I moaned; "what is it?"

"Your foot is hurt badly. These fellows here want to take it off. They are strangers to me, surgeons from Boston. You must rally your strength and refuse to allow it. I have seen you save many a foot as much injured as yours is now, but they doubt the fact. I must go in search of the proper splints, and I am afraid to trust you alone with them. Can you comprehend what I say? Can you collect your thoughts?"

"Something presses on my chest," I said; "what is it?"

"You are hurt there, but not materially. Only find strength to look at these men, and words to speak to them. Moments are precious now; think what it would be to go through life lame!"

"Would it matter much?" I said, only half conscious of what he was saying.

He sighed heavily.

"Go and get the splints," I managed to say. "I will try and remember what you told me."

I heard him leave me, after having placed my foot in a position that satisfied him, and then a numbness seemed to spread itself over me. I felt immovable, inanimate, without the power of exerting thought or action in the least degree. From this state of half sleeping, half waking, I was roused by a sensation of acute agony, which thrilled through all my nerves and had the effect of restoring me to my full senses. I raised myself with much difficulty, and discovered the cause of my intense suffering. Two gentlemen, whose caps denoted that they belonged to some medical staff, were probing my foot, to their own great satisfaction and my extreme horror. Instantly, all Doctor Berry's injunctions recurred to me, and I realized their importance. To lose my foot, and be lame for life, or else to avail myself of an artificial one, seemed about to become a problem for me to solve. My obliging friends, having completed their examination, were spreading their instruments over the bed, and I lay quiet, watching them and wondering what would be their next move.

The idea of any person undertaking to relieve me of my foot, without first consulting me and obtaining my consent, seemed utterly preposterous; and, besides, I had not as yet made up my mind that such a proceeding was really necessary. I thought that, at least, I should like to look at it myself beforehand and give the subject proper consideration. Lameness might be quite admirable and hero-like in a soldier, but being merely an army surgeon, I did not think it would add much either to my fame or usefulness. I lay, therefore, in speechless amazement, watching with half-closed eyes the motions of the two medical gentlemen, and listening to their low-toned conversation.

I verified the old adage, "Listeners never hear any good of themselves." Still I felt that I had a right to be present at my own trial, and hear the verdict. I will do them the justice of saying that they sincerely believed in the wisdom of their own conclusion, and wished to do the best they knew how for me. Had I been their oldest friend, instead of a mere stranger, their decision would have been the same.

"Shall I apply the chloroform as he is, or shall we first explain the necessity of the case to him?" asked one of the other.

"If he were a private soldier," was the reply, "we should, of course, proceed to amputate the limb without consulting him. It appears that he is a surgeon him-

self, and, therefore, it will be only proper to tell him
what we are about to do."

"I am quite aware of your intentions," I said, looking at them in turn. "Thank you for your good wishes,
but I shall allow Doctor Berry, who is my friend, to
take charge of the affair."

"You do not know what you are saying," the elder
of the two answered, turning to me. He was a much
older man than I, a fact that I had noticed before addressing him. "Permit me to say," he continued, "that
I rank you in age, and probably in experience, and that
any man who tells you that he can save your foot is
not your friend."

"I would still prefer to hear my friend's opinion,"
I said.

"That is all very well, but you forget the time of
year it is. If it were winter, we might risk the consequences; but, considering that this is July, and the
weather extremely hot, such a delay will be highly
dangerous. Mortification may set in before morning,
and then nothing can be done. The only safety lies in
immediate amputation."

"The patient looks feverish already," remarked the
younger of the two.

"No wonder," I replied; "your conversation does
not tend to soothe my nerves."

"Still, we could not commence the operation without your consent," the elder one said, apologetically.

"Very well," I replied; "then it is all settled. I

shall not submit to any thing of the kind at present; and, if it should become necessary, my assistant here, Doctor Berry, will be quite competent to undertake it."

"He is rather young for the responsibility, I think," the old gentleman said.

"Excuse me for differing with you, but Doctor Berry has assisted me in the care of the regiment for nearly two years, and I have never heard the least charge made against him as regards incapacity for the position he holds."

I was growing tired of the whole affair, and wishing heartily that the gentlemen would leave me to suffer in silence, when Doctor Berry himself made his appearance at the opening of the tent, and my tormentors passed on, hoping that I would not regret my obstinacy.

"I believe they have driven you into a fever," my friend said, coming to me with the splints that he needed in his hand, and looking anxiously into my face.

"No, I am quite cool and ready for you."

"Very well, then," he answered gayly. "If I hurt you much, just cry out; it will be a great relief to you."

While he made all the arrangements, and tenderly dressed my foot, causing me the least pain possible, I took a view of my position, and found myself wondering how long I should remain in it. I was lying on a small mattress, placed on the ground in one of the hospital-tents, and on each side of me other wounded men were extended in the same manner. No better accommodation was possible, so we talked as merrily as we could under the circumstances, and made the most of our curious quarters. Colonel Lecount was in an adjoining tent, doing nicely; he had escaped all injury from the bursting shell; and so, being relieved from all anxiety, and having sent a few lines to my sister, telling her of my mishap, I sank into an uneasy sleep, which lasted during the night.

In the morning, while attending to me, Doctor Berry made me laugh heartily at his description of the gentlemen who had given me so much trouble the day before.

"They are both from Boston," he said. "I found out all about them last night. Williams swears that, if they ever come near here again, he will give the men leave to fire on them. He says that, if they had been allowed their way, there wouldn't have been a whole man left in the division hospital. One of them is a regular Doctor Sawbones, one of your real old fogies; thinks that the knife is the only instrument worth having in surgery. They say he is famous at cutting off limbs—does it with so much neatness and dispatch. He has quite a reputation at home, and came up here, as a great favor, to offer his valuable assistance. He became quite angry in the next tent; the surgeon there fired up and told him 'that he did not want his interference, and that we were all quite aware of the fact that it is much easier for us to take a limb off than to save it with care and attention.'"

"It must have been Allen who told him that—it is so like him. What became of them?"

10*

"Oh, they left at last in disgust. I heard that the young colonel, the one you went after, drew his sword on them. Nothing would do them but to take off his arm."

"That is just what Victor would do," I said, laughing at the ludicrousness of the scene, as I imagined it.

"It is sufficient to stop all enlistments," went on Doctor Berry. "A man may be willing to fight, and take the chances, but if he thinks that, the moment he is wounded, he is at the mercy of any ignoramus that may come along, with a saw in one hand and a tourniquet in the other, he is not likely to risk them. A wound received on the field, coming as it does at a moment of excitement, is easily borne; but to be chopped up leisurely in a hospital is another consideration, especially when a man feels that with a little extra trouble on the part of the surgeon the necessity might be obviated."

"It is a pity," I said, "that we are not better supplied with conscientious surgeons. Some of them have undoubtedly mistaken their vocation."

"Yes, particularly that old gentleman that was here yesterday. He should have been bred a butcher," said Doctor Berry, as he left me on his way to another patient.

For many weeks I remained in the field-hospital at Gettysburg. It was a dreary time to me, monotonous, and void of interest. The army had gone forward, and with it all the regimental surgeons that could be spared; among the rest, Doctor Berry. Many of the sick and wounded had been removed to Washington, Philadelphia, and New York. Those that remained were suffering from wounds received below, or in the hip-joint, and were not yet equal to the fatigue that a removal would cause. We were quite shut in from the outside world; the only news that reached us came through the daily and weekly-papers sent to the patients by their friends, and the reports which they contained relative to the army were not very satisfactory nor correct. Home letters were the greatest luxuries that could be received, and we longed for them as a child would long for a new toy, when they were detained by the irregularity of the mails.

To me, so accustomed to an active life in the fresh, open air, the confinement was irksome in the extreme. Minutes seemed like hours, hours like days. Then, too, my recovery progressed but slowly. My foot was very painful and tedious, and my chest troubled me greatly, a result that Doctor Berry had anticipated from the first. Owing to the low position of our beds, and the amount of rain that had fallen, making the ground damp and the air moist, a fever, accompanied with chills, was beginning to spread among the men with fatal effect.

Several near me, who had lost their limbs, and seemed to be recovering rapidly, were carried away by it, and I noticed that, in nearly every case where it supervened on amputation, it resulted in death. One example, in particular, made a deep impression on me. A young man, a fine, honest-looking soldier, had lost

his right leg below the knee, and had submitted cheerfully to the operation, which proved successful. He
bore his pain without a murmur, and I therefore was
surprised one day, on waking from a light sleep, to see
him crying silently, his face turned to me, and resting
on his arm. I spoke to him, and he told me what caused
his tears. A young lady, who was spending some weeks
at Gettysburg, visiting the hospitals and attending on
the wounded during the day, had just left his side. She
had been sitting near him for an hour, fanning him,
tempting his appetite with little luxuries, and brushing
the flies from his aching wound. Her kindness, and the
sight of a noble, good woman, thus ministering to him,
had brought tears of joy to his eyes—this powerful-
looking soldier, who had gazed on the miseries of battle-
fields for two years, unsoftened, and had met the surgeon's knife with composure.

After that I watched him, and became interested in
him. He had lost his knapsack on the field, and the
only thing that he possessed was a little picture of one
of his cousins, which he had put for safety in his pocket
before going into the fight. The young lady who visited
him supplied him with paper and a pencil, and several
times I saw him writing to this cousin, who lived in a
distant city. As his pain ceased, his spirits rose;
he even joked on his own misfortune, and I often fell
asleep while listening to him whistling popular airs,
which he did most beautifully.

He was looking forward with hope to his return

home, when the fever attacked him. He fought it bravely, but—alas!—it conquered him. Not many hours before his end, came letters from his family, bright and joyful in their tone, calculated to sustain his drooping spirits. The fever was on him at the time when his nurse read them to him—the kind words fell unheeded on his ears. He was "going home!"

"Tell them all that I died happy," he whispered to the chaplain, who bent over him in his dying moments. He did not speak again. A few hours after, he was buried in a little grove, not far from the town, and, his empty bed having been removed, all traces of him disappeared.

My sister had come to me immediately after hearing of my wound, and had remained with me for a week. Then my mother was attacked with a sudden and serious illness, and my sister had returned home to care for her. However, I did not lack attention. Nothing could exceed the kindness with which we were treated by the ladies attached to the corps of nurses, and others, who came to Gettysburg in order to be near their wounded relatives.

When at last I was removed with many of my comrades, to Washington, I foresaw but a short stay there, having determined, once my foot would permit me, to make my way home, if need be, on two crutches. I was little prepared for what then happened. The morning after my arrival in the city I awoke in a violent fever, and then I remembered, with dismay, the slight touches of it that I had felt while lying in the field-hospital at Gettysburg.

It was something that I had not made any preparation for meeting. I had trusted to my constitution, which was naturally good, to carry me safely over the effects of the wounds that I had received, and the possibility of contracting the fever in its worst form never occurred to me. With my burning head resting on my arm, I took a quiet survey of the room in which I had been placed, at dark, the night before. It was a long, narrow apartment—a regular hospital scene. The rows of neat little beds, standing near the walls, seemed to be all occupied. In the space between them nurses were coming and going with their noiseless tread, and doctors were bending attentively over their suffering charges. I looked through the open windows at the blue sky, and thought to myself—"If the fever does, attack me, this will be a better place to fight it than in the field-hospital that I have just quitted."

CHAPTER XVI.

HOW THE LINKS WERE JOINED.

AFTER arriving at that conclusion, I sank back on my pillow, and tried to turn my thoughts on other subjects. To my great horror, I found it impossible to follow out a connected train of ideas. A vague consciousness, that I feared to acknowledge to myself, became a sure conviction. I felt that my mind was commencing to wander, and in the effort that I made to overcome the weakness, and control my reasoning powers, I added to my own sufferings. For several days, I was aware of what took place around me, in spite of the high fever raging in my brain. I knew the doctor, and the nurse that attended me, and realized my own danger. After that I became delirious, and lay battling for life with the remnant of my bodily strength, which decreased hourly. During that fearful time I changed into a mere shadow of my former self. Dead to the present, the future a great void before me, nothing remained for me but the past, and that took entire possession of me. The scenes connected with it were forever passing before my eyes; the figures changing, and forming into new pictures, like the glasses in a kaleidoscope. In my disordered imagination I lived my life over again, and in my vivid fancy felt anew its former joys and sorrows.

With the touch of a soft hand still lingering on mine, with the low tones of a loved voice still sounding in my ears, I passed at length from the realms of sweet memories and wild dreams to the world of reality about me. I opened my eyes, and gazed around with a vague idea that I was sensible, and then closed them suddenly, with a sensation of horror spreading itself over me. Too weak to tremble, I lay unable to utter a cry, seeing through shut lids the vision that had paralyzed me. I tried to believe that my eyes had deceived me, and, summoning all my feeble resolution, I looked again. The thing was indeed there, a fearful reality, and not the creation of a disordered brain. There it stood, a dark screen surrounding three sides of my narrow couch, and shutting me off from the other occupants of the room, lest they should witness my dying struggles. "Then I am to die," I thought, "and this is probably my interval of consciousness before the end."

I lay gazing on the hospital-sign of death expected, and listened attentively for the rustle of a dress or the sound of a voice. The silence was terrible, worse than the roar and confusion of battle. It crushed me with its chilling weight. I wondered what caused it, I puzzled my mind for a reason. By degrees, I was impressed by the curious light in which the unpleasant object of

my thoughts was presented to me, and, turning my eyes
upward, I suddenly found an explanation for all that had
troubled me. The shadow of a hand, holding a book,
rested on the ceiling over my head, in immense proportions, and moved, now and then, as the light which
threw it flickered in the wind. I tried to look beyond,
hoping to catch a glimpse of the sky and the stars,
through the open window, by which the sweet night air
entered the room, but in vain. The screen shut out from
me all but the strip of white ceiling which the shadow.
darkened. Feebly and very slowly my weakened brain
and dulled perceptive faculties took in and realized the
position of affairs, and the probable scene beyond the
limits of my view.

It was night, and the patients slept; quiet and rest
were necessary to their recovery, those powerful medi-
cines that Nature provides—the quiet of night, the rest
of sleep. The stillness was accounted for. Here and
there, no doubt, the watchers were at their posts, but
why did one remain so close to me, sharpening the senses
to wakefulness by reading? The answer to my question, supplied by my own heart, thrilled through my
nerves. I was dying, and I had been delirious when last
visited by a physician. It was possible that I might be
given a short interval of consciousness, during which I
might take leave of earthly things, and prepare for the
unseen eternity.

Out of kindness, some one was watching near me,
attentive to catch the least sound or movement from

within the screen. "Alas!" I thought, "had that been only my mother, or my sister, how anxiously would she have hung over my pillow, and, watching every feature, known by inspiration the instant when sensibility returned!" In my desire to send a last message to the dear ones so far away, I attempted to call; but, although I exerted all my strength, no sound issued from my lips. Within reach of human aid, I was powerless to attain it. A dreadful sense of increasing weakness overpowered me; I felt an irresistible desire to scream, and yet was perfectly aware of my inability to make myself heard. The fear of death was stronger than the hope of life; and still I had a conviction that if the screen were removed, the thought of speedy dissolution would depart at the same time, and hope resume its power. Even while these strangely-mingled fancies chased each other through my brain, I was studying the shadow over my head, and wondering who the owner of the real hand might be. It certainly belonged to a woman; there was a delicacy in the outlines, and a peculiar gracefulness about the cuff rising from the wrist, that remained visible in spite of the increased size. As I looked, the hand assumed still larger proportions, and seemed to press closer to me, and at length rest upon me.

I sank into a doze. How long it continued I never knew. The sound of voices, conversing in hushed tones beside me, is the first sensation of which I have any recollection.

"Have you no hope whatever?" a female voice asked, and I wondered at the earnest agitation which its owner evinced.

"None whatever," was the answer, in a man's quiet, sententious style.

"And yet he has lingered for hours. Yesterday morning you gave him but six more to live. See how cool he looks! I thought it was a good sign. He sleeps quietly too, and has, ever since the gas was lit. May it not be the crisis of the fever?"

I could imagine the doctor shaking his head gravely, as he replied—

"I should be glad indeed to think so; but this, I fear, is the weakness that precedes death. I have seen it in so many cases, and we hospital doctors are not so easily deceived in the phases of a disease as those who are less experienced. Certainly if care could save, Doctor Wilmer ought to live, for you have done all in the power of human skill for him. You have been a most devoted nurse, and the country ought to feel deeply grateful to you, and other ladies, equally self-sacrificing and patriotic."

"And can I do no more?" came the whispered entreaty.

"If he wakens again you may give him some nourishing food, a little at a time. That is all that I can say to encourage you. To hold out hopes that appearances do not justify is something that I cannot bring myself to do. Many physicians think it allowable, I disagree with them entirely."

Having given his opinion, the doctor went away with soft steps to look at the other patients, and for a moment there was complete silence. Then a smothered sob broke the heavy stillness, and a sad voice murmured, "If he ever wakens again!" I felt tears falling on my hand, and, opening my eyes in surprise, met those of Miss Pauline Lecount fixed on my face. For an instant she gazed at me like one in a dream; then, instinctively realizing that I was conscious, she sank on her knees, and, pressing my hand convulsively in her own, said, in a choking voice:

"You shall not die without forgiving me!—Stay" —she exclaimed, as I made a faint effort to speak. "Listen to me. Do not answer me till you have heard all; let me justify her who cannot plead for herself. She was innocent—I alone caused all this misery. I alone injured you, and destroyed your whole life. If only you could realize the misery that I have endured these many years! You have suffered too, but you had wronged no one; yours was not the wretchedness that springs from a guilty conscience, struck with remorse, yet lacking the courage to confess its sin. But, alas! I am only trying to excuse myself, to palliate my own crime. When you know what I did in a moment of temptation; when you realize how I wronged you; then think of where we are at this moment, and as you are a Christian, and hope for mercy, try to forgive me."

She ceased for a moment, to recover her composure; and then, as if doubting her own strength to fulfil her resolution, she poured forth her story in a voice rendered low and distinct, with a great effort. I listened to her in a state of amazement, half questioning the evidence of my senses, trying to grasp the meaning of her words, and connecting feebly in my mind the chain for which she was supplying the links.

"The first evening that I met you," she said, "I read your secret, and I will confess that I wondered at it. Your love for Miss Ferris I never could understand. She was such a child in manner and knowledge, and so greatly your inferior. Your motives for concealing your feelings excited my curiosity for a long time, but when I afterward learned them, I could appreciate the power which they exerted over you. For months I watched Belle, and tried to sound her affection for you. But she baffled me; she either loved you passionately, and concealed her true feelings under a mask of indifference, or else she admired you as a friend, and did not care who knew it. I never could surprise her confidence in regard to you, and for that reason I concluded that something more than friendship governed her heart. Of course the secret of her position, which you were all guarding so carefully, would have given me the key to the whole affair. It would have explained the curious confidence existing between you two, and her tacit compliance with every thing you proposed, the very thing that excited my greatest uneasiness. However, I was a most unscrupulous antagonist, even at that time. Your silence I attributed to diffidence, and I took advantage of that, by representing it to her as indifference. Claude loved her; he was my favorite brother, and I would have attempted any thing for his sake. I inferred that she was rich from many circumstances, and I realized with bitterness in my heart that we were poor. What might not riches do for Claude? and, besides, he was disinterested in his love for Belle. Want of means was his only drawback; otherwise, they seemed well suited to each other. When you returned to Buffalo the first time, you left the field entirely open to me. I saw that, unconsciously, you had hurt Belle deeply; you had chilled her by your coldness, and thrown her heart from you. What you lost, I gained. She became quieter, less impulsive, more womanly, and shrank from mentioning your name. She felt that she had been too quick to give her affections where they were not sought for, and determined to drive away and overcome all thoughts of you. Without having the least clew to your motives, I saw the advantages to be derived from your conduct, and I hastened to make the most of them. I awakened her pride by hinting at your cool indifference, and then left the rest to Claude.

" His attentions flattered her vanity and soothed her wounded feelings. She was no coquette, and therefore tried honestly to return his love. Besides, Mr. Masters approved of the affair, and she liked to please him in every thing. Your continued absence and silence carried out what I had insinuated about you; and when we went to New York, every thing was progressing to my perfect satisfaction. All fears on your account were at rest in my heart. Belle seldom spoke of you, and even when she heard that you were coming to her party, I looked in vain for any trace of emotion in her appearance. Her dress for the evening seemed to monopolize all her attention.

"The night came; you can judge of my surprise, when, on the entrance of Mrs. Parker, I saw her leave Claude's side and fly to you for protection. I felt that, once in your presence, all your power over her returned; and the fabric I had taken such pains to build seemed about to dissolve in my very grasp. Mr. Masters' explanation also was calculated to recall memories too strong for me to battle with; and I realized that a meeting between you two without witnesses was all that was necessary to undo my whole work. A word from you would have revealed to her the passion lying dormant in her own heart, and the least sign of emotion on her side would have swept away your barrier of pride, and shown her the depth of your love.

"To prevent such an interview, I exerted every stratagem of which I was capable, and you know how well I succeeded. I had to enlist Claude on my side, and for that reason I imparted to him my suspicions of her real affection for you—alas! to my own future sorrow. He was jealous enough of you before I unfortunately aroused in him a corresponding feeling toward his wife; I sowed the seed of their future misery.

"Day after day I watched and waited for some movement on your part. I saw your efforts to meet Belle alone, and defeated them all. I noticed too how almost unconsciously her heart and thoughts turned to you, in spite of the check she had received from you. It would seem as if intuitively she knew the secret that governed you, and awaited patiently your time for revealing it.

"I see that you are astonished at my hardihood in confessing all this. You cannot be more so than I am myself. I can hardly realize that the hour, so ardently longed for, has come at last, and that here, on my knees, I am trying to repair the evil that I did, and obtain forgiveness for my sin. Pity me now—this is the worst part of all.

"One evening, after vainly attempting to talk to Belle undisturbed, you left us, and went into the library. I saw you writing, through the half-closed door, and guessed what it was that you were doing. That night, while you and Mr. Masters stood talking in the parlor, I returned to the library for the book that I had been reading before dinner. I had intended finishing it there, not feeling sleepy; but some of your conversation reached me, and I gathered from it that you were speaking of Claude. I did not care to listen, so I determined to carry my book to my own room. You will sneer at my scruples about eaves-dropping, when you hear what I afterward did. As I passed the table, Belle's volume of poetry attracted me, and knowing that she was not tired, I thought I would carry it up with me. As I lifted it very carelessly, something dropped from it. You guess what that was, and what I did with it. Do not look so sorry for me; think of the wrong I did to you. I looked at the address on the letter, and then at the seal. I had no pity for you, no compassion for your ruined hopes, your desolate, altered life. I only thought of Claude, my brother that I loved so fondly, his youth, his talents, and his love.

"I determined that Belle should never see the letter. Could I have foreseen what was to become of it, I should have hastened to put it in her hands. Looking back on that night, I think with wonder of my own coolness; but it was the foretaste of success that gave me courage to carry out my design. I returned up-stairs. I sat and read for hours with the fatal letter in my pocket, and discussed with Belle our plans for the succeeding day. After she slept, I went into the adjoining room, took your message from my dress, opened and read it with a sensation of gratified curiosity at having at last reached the cause of your long silence. As I perused it, I understood it perfectly, and all that had seemed strange in your conduct became clear before me. I appreciated the combined delicacy and pride that had controlled you, and I realized what an effect your explanation would have on Belle. The mere thought of her suspecting such feelings in you made me shiver, and for a moment I felt a strong desire to light the paper at the gas, and let it burn to ashes on the hearth. Something, however, prompted me to preserve it, and I placed it in a secret drawer of my writing-desk. The next day you

17

started on your return to Buffalo, where you awaited some sign from Belle. I recollect distinctly the expression of your face when you took leave of us that morning, and the sad, hopeless one that dawned in hers when again you left her, apparently cool, and without regret.

"Day after day passed, and we spent our time in a round of amusements. Belle was at first quiet and reticent, no doubt surprised at your conduct, and seeking in vain an explanation of it in her own mind. Then, as no letter came from you, her suspicion of your indifference to her became a settled, firm conviction, and with all the strength and energy of her character she battled with her own heart, and conquered. The struggle, however, took away the remains of her childishness, and left her what she has been ever since, a self-possessed, thoughtful woman. All impulsiveness and passion were gone, and it would seem as if they had never had any part in her being. She grew cheerful again and light-hearted, accepted Claude's attentions with pleasure, and, putting the whole past away from her, thought only of making those around her happy.

"As the months went by, she talked of you openly and unrestrainedly, as of a dear and valued friend; and at the same time grew more and more attached to Claude. When she accepted him, she did it voluntarily and with her whole heart. She respected and loved him, and he occupied all her thoughts. She was devoted to him and his interests, and showed it in looks and speech. None but a madman or a fool would have

doubted her truth. Claude once or twice complained of
her want of passion; but, had he been wise, he would
have thought more highly of her deep respect for him,
her steady love, and her faith in his goodness.

"A short time before they were married, he was talking about her to me, and he made the remark, that 'after
all, you had never cared for her.' I was foolish enough
to mention the proof of your love that was in my possession, and he demanded it, insisting on his right to see
it. I allowed him to persuade me, and I gave it to him.
He promised faithfully to destroy it, and assured me
shortly afterward that he had burnt it. Feeling that
all trace of my deception was destroyed, I ceased to
think of the matter, and lived in a state of perfect
security. You went to Europe as soon as Belle's engagement was announced, and I guessed your motive in
going, and saw you leave the country without a feeling
of pity for you, or remorse for what I had done. The
end seemed to justify the means, and the perfect happiness that Claude and Belle enjoyed entirely removed any
misgivings that I might have otherwise experienced.

"They were married, and for six months their life
was a dream of pleasure; they were like the lovers in a
fairy tale—happy in each other, and causing brightness
wherever they went. Then came the sudden shock that
brought confusion and misery into the house, and caused
all our future wretchedness.

"We had an invitation to a large party. How well I
remember the day! it was in November, and the weather

was remarkably mild and pleasant for that season of the year. We were sitting at the dinner-table, and Belle was about going up to dress for the evening, when one of the servants came in with a request. She wished to go out with a friend, and she wanted some money to buy a dress. You can see now what a trifling circumstance brought on our troubles.

"Belle gave her permission to go, and turning to Claude asked him if he had ten dollars in his pocket, as her purse was up-stairs; and then she added, laughingly, that she did not think there was so much in it.

"Claude replied gayly: 'Your flowers for to-night took every cent I had, but you will find a quantity of notes in the little drawer of my desk. Shall I bring you some?' He would have gone for them; but she laid her hand on his head and detained him.

"'I am just going up, so you need not stir,' she said, 'but I thank you for remembering my favorite flowers.' She bent over him, her eyes shining softly, kissed him lovingly, and then left the room.

"It was the last voluntary caress she ever gave him. We heard her light step on the stairs, and after a few minutes' conversation, Claude lit his cigar, and I went to my room to dress for the party. When I was nearly ready, I took my flowers in my hand and ran down to her with them. She could arrange them in my hair more gracefully than I could myself, and always did it for me.

"I pushed open the door of her dressing-room, and

went in. The fire was burning brightly, but the light
was turned low, and I was surprised at the silence, and
the absence of all disorder among her things on the toi-
let-table. At first I thought that she had dressed and
gone down-stairs; but while I stood thinking, I heard
something like a moan in her bedroom, and, attracted by
the sound, I went in hastily, fearing I knew not what.

"She was lying on the floor, her head resting on her
arms, and her face entirely hidden from me; but her
whole frame was convulsed with the agony that she was
trying in vain to suppress. In the utter extremity of
her grief she had thrown herself thus on the ground, forgetful of every thing but the remorse that had taken possession of her. I tried to raise her, too much surprised
to speak, and her blanched face frightened me; but what
were my horror and shame, my bitter despair, when an
open paper dropped from her hand, and I recognized
your letter! The whole mystery flashed upon me in a
second, and I began to tremble for the result of my cruel
treachery.

"While I was yet bending over her, trying to soothe
her, and promising to explain every thing, Claude sauntered into the room, and, supposing that Belle had been
attacked with a sudden illness, he hastened to assist
her, his face anxious and sad. Its expression changed
as his eyes fell on the fatal letter, and Belle noticed the
alteration in him. She caught it up eagerly, and then,
rising without aid, demanded to know what it all meant,
and how it came into her husband's possession.

"Her voice shook with emotion, and she gasped for breath as she spoke; still she listened patiently while I confessed every thing, and tried to take the whole blame on myself. She looked from one to the other of us until I had finished, and then suddenly catching Claude's hand, she asked—

"'Did you know of this and read it before you married me?'

"His answer in the affirmative seemed to crush her with sorrow.

"'All false!' she murmured. 'You that I respected and loved! You that I trusted entirely!'

"Her husband's want of honor and the wrong done to you were the two powerful griefs working in her heart. She had invested Claude with the finest qualities of humanity; she believed him to be up to the highest standard of moral integrity; and, when she found her image broken, she gave full vent to her despair. With a bitter cry she hid her face in her hands, and, sinking into a chair, she recalled the many kindnesses that you had shown her, and wept for your disappointment. I understood her grief, and the mingled emotions that caused it. I saw that she never thought of herself, that her whole heart was absorbed in the conviction of her husband's unworthiness, and the sad knowledge that her respect for him was gone forever.

"It seemed to me that Claude should have understood her also, and tried in every way to obtain her forgiveness and soothe her wounded feelings; particularly as I had been the most to blame, an excuse he might have urged in his own defence. Had he done so, the mischief might have ended there. Alas! he misconstrued the cause of her tears, and became angry with her. The seed of jealousy that I had planted in his heart sprang into life and bore bitter fruit.

"He worked himself into a furious passion, and accused her of having loved you first and best. Incapable of comprehending the refined sensitiveness of her nature, and blind to the claims that you really had on her gratitude and affection, he taunted her in a way that no woman of spirit could resist answering. In his insensate folly he taxed her with lack of candor in not having confessed to him her former passion for you. The idea of expecting a young, innocent girl to acknowledge the existence of a feeling to which she had never given expression by word or look, and shrank from admitting even to herself, was so utterly absurd and insulting, that I did not wonder at Belle's reply.

"She sprang from her seat and faced him. Her tears stopped, and her cheeks flamed with indignation.

"'You wrong me cruelly, Claude,' she exclaimed. 'You have no right to taunt me thus. You know I loved you, and you only, when I married you. I had nothing to tell you, nothing to confess. The wild fancies and romantic dreams of an impulsive, imaginative child would have sounded more than silly if put into language, and could have only excited your ridicule.'

"Her answer, instead of appeasing him, only added to the jealousy that was mastering him.

"'Then you acknowledge,' he exclaimed, in a threatening tone, 'that you did indulge in wild fancies and romantic dreams about this Doctor Wilmer?'

"'I cannot deny it,' she said, quietly. 'I suppose it was the natural consequence of my ignorance and loneliness. Unless you could have seen me as he found me, you could not appreciate his claims on my gratitude and affection, nor the deep admiration for him that took possession of me. My own folly I conquered long ago, but I cannot overcome the sorrow that this letter of his causes me, and I feel it all the more because I may not explain to him my coldness and silence. I dare not justify myself in his eyes, nor ask his pardon for the blow I have dealt him.'

"She was looking at the letter with tearful eyes as she spoke, and, before I could prevent the act, Claude seized it from her rudely, tore it in pieces, and then threw it on the blazing coals. She watched it burning, mute with surprise and dismay, and then covered her face with her hands.

"'You could not trust me even in that,' she said, in a stifled tone.

"'No!' Claude said, angrily. 'And in future, you must leave my papers alone. I would not have suspected you, who are so conscientious, of ransacking my desk.'

"'I opened the wrong drawer by mistake, and the

letter was lying before my eyes; I supposed it to be one of mine, and I wondered how it could have strayed among your things. After giving the girl her money, I unfolded it mechanically, and read it, too much surprised to speak. Its discovery was wholly accidental; I never suspected the existence of such a paper.'

"As Belle answered this last accusation, I trembled at the sound of her voice. It was clear and steady. Self-possession had returned to her. I felt that Claude was risking his whole future happiness in his foolish anger, and I left them, feeling intensely miserable, and dimly foreseeing the coming misfortune.

"The breach between them widened daily. I looked in vain for something capable of drawing their hearts together again. Claude was indignant, and took no trouble to hide the fact. His pride was offended, and he expected his wife to be the first to ask forgiveness. Belle seemed weighed down with the bitterness of her grief, and asked in vain for comfort or sympathy from her husband. He either could not or would not understand her mind, and her respect for him was diminishing under the heavy blow it had received.

"Their visible coolness toward each other excited much comment, and Mrs. Masters invented every imaginable excuse for it, the real one being entirely unsuspected by any one. We three holders of the secret guarded it faithfully. When Arthur was born, there was a change for the better that gladdened all our hearts. Claude softened toward his wife, and Belle seemed willing to

17*

forget every thing unpleasant that had passed and let the old love resume its sway. Unhappily, Claude's jealousy was not overcome; it still burned in his heart, and manifested itself on the most trivial occasions. It seemed to increase just in proportion as his true affection died out. I acknowledge that he was fickle; the love that I thought enduring was only a passion, destined to give place to others in their turn. The mere sight of your mother or sister would excite his anger, and the mention of your name drove him furious. Belle's love was insufficient to resist so many attacks upon it. She never offended him in word or deed, and avoided every thing that could arouse his jealousy; still I saw with despair that he was slowly but surely wearing out her affection.

"His passion for speculation gave her much uneasiness, and the low company that it led him into offended her refined taste and shocked her principles. Such a means for making money was, in her opinion, only licensed robbery, and she regarded his participation in it with perfect horror.

"His want of trust in her wounded her to the heart; he would not allow her for years to revisit her old home. You remember his anger the night that he opened the gate and found you talking with her. In his passion he forgot that you were unaware of what he knew so well, and insulted Belle with bitter taunts that must have sounded strange to you. He took her back to New York as soon as it was possible, and then, with the greatest inconsistency, neglected her for other women.

"The night that he was killed, your presence in the hotel seemed to me something almost prophetic. Had your heart been filled with a desire for revenge, nothing was wanting to satisfy it. He was lying a shattered corpse, and I was reaping the punishment I deserved, to its most bitter extent. When I realized that no such feeling brought you there at that time, that your coming was entirely accidental, then indeed it seemed as if Providence was at work, and that my sin had found me out. If only you might live now, live to repair the evil I did, and enjoy the happiness so long denied you! At least tell me that you forgive me. Have mercy on me! Forget that I had none for you."

Her voice died away in a low sob as she ceased, and she covered her face with her hands, while a convulsive trembling took possession of her whole form.

"As I hope for mercy," I said, "I do forgive you."

The words reached her ears in spite of the faint tone in which I uttered them, but she made no reply. I was shocked at the weakness of my own voice. I closed my eyes, and remained silent, dazzled by the flood of light that she had let in on my bewildered mind. A little while passed; then she rose quietly and went away. A few moments afterward she was bending over me, feeding me with the soup that she had gone to procure. Her manner had regained its usual dignified coolness, and her voice its old steadiness. No one would have recognized in her the passionate, impulsive woman who had knelt at my couch a short time before, asking for pardon in tones that trembled with sorrow and remorse.

I could have imagined the whole story a wild dream, but for the soft, happy expression that dawned in her eyes when they met mine, as if trying to imbue me with some of the hope and peace that were filling her own heart. I lay for hours in a delirium of joy that thrilled through my whole being, incapable of speaking, of thinking. Then I fell into a sound, refreshing sleep, out of which I awakened to find the screen removed, and Miss Pauline seated near me, fanning away the flies.

"The doctor says that you are out of danger," she whispered, bending over me with tearful eyes.

CHAPTER XVII.

THE QUESTION ANSWERED.

THIS joyful assurance answered the convictions of my own heart, and had a magical effect on my spirits. I began to improve with an energy that quite astonished the kind physician who had attended me so faithfully, and Miss Pauline communicated the news to my anxious mother and sister. She had written to them of my condition all along, until the day when the doctor had pronounced my case hopeless. Then her courage forsook her, and, happily for us all, she had found herself unequal to the task of sending them the sad intelligence. Perhaps the strong hope in my ultimate recovery, which had never failed her, partly controlled her silence. At any rate, they had remained ignorant of my extreme danger, and I was pleased to have it so. My mother was still so weak that she could ill have spared my sister's care, and her presence in the hospital could have done me no good, although it would have been a great comfort to me during my convalescence.

Those long August days passed slowly but not un-

pleasantly to me. One was but the repetition of
another—the only difference that marked them being
the gradual increase of strength which came to me so
gently, yet so surely. My mind regained its tone and
elasticity, while my body was still feeble; and as I re-
clined on my couch, or dragged my tottering limbs
from one corner of the long room to another, my
thoughts dwelt on the future, and revelled in dreams of
happiness far wilder than any that I had ever before
indulged in. Miss Pauline Lecount's revelation had, at
first, utterly confounded me; it was so strange and unexpected, so entirely at variance with all my former
reasoning on the subject. Fully convinced, in my own
mind, of Mrs. Lecount's indifference to me, I had spent
years endeavoring to nourish a corresponding feeling
for her in my heart. The labor had cost me dear, the
struggle had been long and bitter. Still I had conquered. I prided myself on the success of my efforts.
Now I found myself surrounded by the ruins of my
work that I had thought so strong; my barriers of
pride and coolness undermined, overthrown, and swept
away, by a few words in a woman's soft voice; and a
torrent of passionate love and hope mastering me as
of old.

As I reflected calmly on all that had passed, I saw
how I had cast away the heart that I might have won;
and, when I realized all that had since taken place, my
hopes gave way to anxious fears. What if I had lost
forever the power of inspiring the love which I coveted

so much? It was possible. In spite, however, of these gloomy doubts, which would at times intrude themselves upon me, I was very happy, and every thing about me was a subject of interest and pleasure. I longed for the day to come on which I should be able to start for home, and yet I clung to the narrow hospital-room which had been the scene of such intense misery, such intoxicating joy. I should carry away with me, and retain always, the memories connected with it and its inmates. I should see again the rows of little beds with their white coverlids; the quiet figures stretched upon them, some sleeping, others reading; a few amusing themselves with musical instruments and curious puzzles, while here and there two earnest thinkers, with bent brows, supported on thin hands that told of fever, studied the pieces on a chess-board, and made the moves with cautious gravity. I would look in fancy through the open windows at the blue sky, the green trees, the busy crowd coming and going in the street below, and enjoy again the exquisite coloring that foretold the dawn, and the glorious beauty of the clouds at sunset. How far lovelier they appeared now to the longing eyes of the sick men than they had ever done in the days of health, when the mind was too much occupied with the things of earth to concern itself with the wonders of the heavens!

In those weeks of convalescence I saw but little of Miss Pauline Lecount; she was occupied with those who were still in danger; and we, who were no longer sub-

jects of anxiety, were left to entertain each other. On
the day of my departure she came to me where I was
standing in the hall of the building, muffled up in
shawls, leaning on my stick, and waiting for the driver
to put my trunk on the carriage. She had previously
packed my things, arranged some little comforts for
me to use on the journey home, and taken leave of
me. I was therefore surprised when she came hurriedly down the stairs and approached me with visible
agitation.

"Are you sure that you are warm enough, and do
you feel quite comfortable?" she said, nervously.

I assured her that I felt quite well, and would soon
be able to dispense with my heavy cane. "It makes
me think myself very old," I added, laughingly.

"Please do not imagine such nonsense," she said,
looking rather sad, and then going on after a little hesi-
tation. "Will you give Belle a message for me?"

"Certainly, any thing you wish."

She colored painfully. "Tell her that I have cleared
my conscience of the question that troubled it for so
long. Remember, you have promised."

She was gone before I had time to raise an objection
to her singular request, and, penetrating the motive that
prompted her, I understood the cause of her strange
manner. I was still thinking over the subject when I
reached the depot, and took my seat in the cars on my
way home.

On arriving in New York I found that I had overrated my strength. I was completely exhausted, and therefore was obliged to put up for two days at a hotel. I had written to my sister, telling her when I should start from Washington, and declining any escort on the score of feebleness. This unintentional exaggeration of my state of health deceived them so much, that my non-appearance at the appointed time gave them no uneasiness; and when at last I alighted at the station in my own village, a bitter, desolate feeling came over me on seeing that no friendly face awaited me. I had to remain there for some time, as the house was not within walking distance for me, and there was no vehicle to be had at the moment. However, once seated in a comfortable wagon on my way home, the beauty of the weather and the scenery overcame the dreary sensation; and, when I lifted the latch of the gate, my weakness was forgotten in the rush of joyful, thankful emotions that overwhelmed me.

It was a lovely afternoon in September. A gentle breeze was stirring the branches of the trees, causing that peculiar rustling sound only heard in the quiet country. With it came the perfume of new-mown hay, and the busy hum of insects. The flowers were swaying to and fro, bending their pretty heads together, and, as I leaned on the gate, the mingled scent of the heliotropes and petunias was wafted toward me. The sun was already setting in the west, and the front of the house, the porch, and the veranda, were bathed in the flood of its golden light. As I went wearily up the path, a shout of childish merriment broke the stillness, and, looking toward the direction from which it came, a charming picture met my sight. In the shadow of an old chestnut-tree nurse Flo was sitting with baby Jack in her arms, Arthur and Harry were pitching ball, while Dash watched their movements with eager eyes, and made vain efforts to catch it in his mouth as it bounded over the grass. At each fresh attempt, little Edith, who stood by, would laugh aloud and clap her hands with glee. I stopped almost involuntarily to enjoy the bright scene, and the next moment the huge dog came rushing toward me, barking with delight. As it sprang fawning upon me, the children looked frightened, but, suddenly guessing who I was, the two boys started for the house, with the news of my arrival. A minute after, my sister was flying down the walk with outstretched hands to welcome me, and my mother was pressing forward with feeble steps, leaning, as I supposed, on Mrs. Weston's arm. When I raised my head, after embracing her, I found myself face to face with Mrs. Lecount. In my surprise I could not utter a word, but her easy, unembarrassed manner quickly reassured me. She did not know what I had heard.

"Thank Heaven, you are home safe at last!" she said, taking my hand in hers, and smiling kindly. "We were all beginning to feel anxious about you, and Mr. Masters had made up his mind to go in search of you to-morrow."

"Now that we have you, John," my sister said,

'we shall keep you with us; you have done your share of the work, and we want you here."

"I am afraid that it will be a long time before I shall be able to attend to any thing in the way of duty. I shall give you trouble enough nursing me for many weeks to come."

"Say rather, pleasure. And now, to begin with," went on my sister, "do you resign yourself entirely into our hands?"

"Yes, I came home to be petted."

"Well, then, lie down on the sofa in the sitting-room, and Belle will bring you some pillows, while I get your supper ready. Mother will sit beside you, and tell you every thing that is going on in the village."

"Where is Mrs. Weston?" I asked, as I obeyed orders, and took possession of the soft, easy lounge.

"Gone to visit one of her pupils, who is sick. Dear Edith, how delighted she will be to see you."

"Florida has taken all the children off to Mr. Masters', to tell him the news," said my mother.

While she talked cheerfully, on topics interesting and new to me, I lay comfortably ensconced in my corner of the room, feeling intensely happy, in spite of my utter helplessness. It seemed as if, once at home, my strength had all failed me, but, as it turned out, it was only the exhaustion consequent on my day's travel.

My sister went about from room to room, throwing me bright smiles whenever she passed my sofa; mother smoothed my hair, and tenderly arranged the pillows under my head with gentle hands and caressing words. In spite of my years, the soft touch upon my forehead, and the loving expression of her eyes as they met mine, exerted over me the same soothing influence that they had ever done in my childish days. Mrs. Lecount had resumed her seat in the window, and was busy knitting a stocking, now and then taking part in the conversation.

Notwithstanding the gayety of manner which they had all assumed, and the light, would-be-careless tones of their voices, I penetrated the mask, and understood the heavy, grief-struck hearts beneath it. My appearance had shocked them all, and I did not wonder at the fact. What my wounds had spared, the ravages of the fever had taken away. I was worn to a skeleton, I was haggard and pale, my eyes were dim and sunken, with dark circles under them, and the streaks of gray were quite visible in my hair. In the hospital, where I was only one among many, the alteration in my looks had not seemed so fearful nor so noticeable. When I left that, and went among men in perfect health, the change partly struck me, but I never fully realized it until I found myself lying on the sofa in my mother's room, with Mrs. Lecount sitting opposite to me. When I recalled my face as I had seen it that morning reflected in one of the hotel mirrors, and then looked at hers, I felt every hope that I had been feeding upon for weeks die out of my heart, and a feeling of bitter, wild despair take possession of me. It seemed to me that the last remnant of my youth was gone, that the two months of pain and

fever had added ten years to my age. And she—I could
have fancied that the past years, so full of events, were
but a dream, and that she was still the innocent, thoughtless child, yet seeking refuge from danger at my mother's
hearth.

The return of rest and peace had restored the color
to her cheeks and the roundness to her form. The unnatural restraint that she had imposed upon herself for
so long, had all disappeared. Her manner had regained
the softness which had been one of her greatest charms.
As I lay musing thus, only half conscious of what they
were saying for my entertainment, and watching the
pretty features partly turned toward me, I saw a tear fall
from the long dark eyelash, and glisten on the coarse
gray wool in her hands.

She rose hastily, and stood looking out of the window, without trusting herself to speak, while she tried
to overcome her emotion. How well I knew the cause
of her grief! My broken health, my altered features,
might have excited her pity, even had she not held the
secret of my life. Perhaps the conviction that the distance between us had increased, and not diminished, was
coming home to her, as it had to me.

"Don't grow anxious about Arthur, Belle," said my
mother, mistaking her reason for leaving her seat.

"Belle, will you cut some flowers for the table?"
called out my sister, a moment after.

"Oh, yes, do! It is more than two years since John
saw a blossom out of our garden, or smelt the lemon-

verbena, his old-favorite," added my mother. "There is a pair of scissors on the bench," she continued, without taking her eyes off my face.

Mrs. Lecount opened the glass door without answering, and went out noiselessly.

My mother patted my hands and stroked my hair, murmuring, as she did so, her thanks to the kind Providence that had restored her son to her in safety.

Master Arthur Lecount interrupted the quiet by darting into the room, and breathlessly confronting us.

"Where is little mamma?" he asked, as he took off his straw hat politely, and glanced around the place. He was a picture of childish beauty standing thus, with his flushed cheeks, his golden curls hanging about his neck in becoming disorder, and shading the great, deep, luminous brown eyes out of which the innocent soul seemed to look.

"What is the matter, Arthur?" asked my mother.

"Why, they are all coming, Mr. Masters, and Mrs. Masters, and Mrs. Weston, and I ran home to tell you."

Catching my eyes, he hesitated and blushed.

"Come and speak to me," I said, holding out my hand.

He took it in his, and looked attentively at my straps.

"Are you a soldier, like Uncle Victor? He was home, and I played soldier with his sword; but he is gone away again."

"Is he?"

"Yes. Do you know what he went to do?" he

whispered mysteriously, his eyes brightening with wonder.

I shook my head.

"To kill rebs. That is what he said; but little mamma won't let me say it out loud, nor tell Harry." .

He ran away the next moment, having caught a glimpse of his mother's white dress in the garden.

"Where did he hear that name for his mother?" I asked.

"Oh! that is original. It is his way of distinguishing her from his grandmother. He calls old Mrs. Lecount his great mamma, and Belle his little mamma. We think it quite amusing."

Mrs. Weston coming in with her children, followed by Mr. and Mrs. Masters, ended our *tête-à-tête*. For the rest of the evening I played listener, while the others discussed my affairs, and planned endless schemes for my benefit. They wanted me to send in my resignation the ensuing day, and I promised to consider the subject at leisure, not wishing to give too hasty an answer.

Young Mrs. Lecount heard the noisy argument without making any remark on the matter; she only bent closer over the little heads near her, and helped the childish hands to build the block-houses. Mr. and Mrs. Masters had regained their old spirits, and were as happy and good-natured as ever. Mrs. Weston looked stronger than I had expected to find her, and appeared cheerful and contented. Baby Jack laughed and crowed, and was danced up and down by every one in turn until his bright eyes closed with sleep, and Florida carried him off to his cradle. The circle was enlarged after supper by the arrival of a number of our neighbors, and it was quite late when the party broke up.

Mr. and Mrs. Masters went home last, taking Mrs. Lecount and her son with them. For a week my mother and sister were busy entertaining the friends and acquaintances that called on me, and then the house settled into the usual quiet routine of daily life. My mother was still feeble, and seldom left her room until afternoon. I regained strength very slowly, and spent the greater part of each day on the lounge in the sitting-room, where the prattle of the children amused me, and where I could read and write as the fancy seized me. Mrs. Weston went every morning, with cheerful looks and energetic steps, to the little schoolhouse, where she taught with gentle firmness the unruly spirits that filled it. She was winning hearts on all sides, and was so much occupied by her duties that her mind had hardly time to dwell on past sorrows. The encouragement that she had received had set her pride at rest. Independence, and the means of rearing her children as their father would have done, seemed possible. Several influential gentlemen in the neighborhood, admiring her talents and method of teaching, had proposed that she should open a private school, and had guaranteed a number of pupils. My sister warmly approved of the plan, and offered her assistance in establishing the seminary.

The idea was, to have both boarding and day scholars, and to engage other teachers as the number increased. There were several houses suitable for the purpose to let in the village, and, at the time I reached home, the arrangements were being discussed at every possible opportunity. I was at once taken into the council, and my opinions canvassed in turn. Meanwhile, the little ones, for whose welfare all these questions were debated, ran in blissful ignorance from garret to cellar in the old house, and made the garden echo with their merry voices.

Mrs. Lecount flitted about from place to place; at one time, sitting in my mother's room, conversing brightly, as her busy fingers plied the needles; and at another down at Mr. Lecount's, helping Miss Marie and the others with their work. I saw but little of her, owing to my invalid habits and the many calls that she had on her time and purse. The past seemed to be buried in oblivion by all, and I shrank with morbid dread from making the least allusion to it, either in her presence or during her absence. She was, to all appearances, very happy and contented in the quiet sphere of life that she had chosen for herself. Her ambition and pleasures centred in her child. His welfare was her principal care, yet it did not engross her so entirely as to make her blind or indifferent to the wants of others. I learned that she was always ready to help those in distress, ever the first to hasten to the homes visited by trouble. She was a welcome guest among poor and

18

rich, and the pet of all the children in the neighborhood. She would listen with a serious face and thoughtful mind to the many lectures and debates on the education of the little ones, given oracularly by the matrons of the village; and an hour afterward would be out in the garden, entering with all the gayety of youth into the merry games planned by Arthur and Harry. To please them she could be a child again, and her arrival among them as a playmate, in a low-crowned, wide-leafed hat, and looped-up dress, was always hailed with a shout of delight.

Hardly a day passed that I did not see her, or meet her on the road, walking lightly along the grassy footpaths, carrying a basket filled with little luxuries for the sick, with Arthur springing beside her, talking gayly, and Dash, who always joined her at our gate, bounding away in advance. Her manner, when we thus met, was easy and unrestrained. We took up the conversation at the point where we had broken off at our last meeting, with all the quiet confidence of old friendship. A stranger meeting us would have taken us for uncle and niece—she so bright with youth and health, chatting earnestly and suiting her quick steps to my slow, invalid pace, for I had not yet relinquished my cane.

I had partly resumed my practice. People came to see me in my house, and consulted me, so that my time did not hang heavily on my hands. I had sent in my resignation, finding that I could not rely upon returning to the army at any stated time, and knowing that I could rejoin it at pleasure.

I had been home for three weeks. One pleasant afternoon I left the office, where I had been occupied for some hours, and strolled into the sitting-room, intending to .lie down there for a short rest, as I felt rather tired. I was about taking possession of the lounge, when my sister put her head into the room.

"John, I have fixed your pillows on the parlor sofa. Jane is coming in here to sweep and dust; that is, if you will not mind the change."

"I believe I shall enjoy it," I said. "The parlor ought to be cooler at this hour."

"I think it is," she answered, following me across the hall, into the large, quiet room.

She saw that I was comfortably settled for a sleep, darkened the window nearest to me, and opened the blinds of one at some distance, that I might see the sunlight, and feel the fresh breeze that was stirring the flowers beneath. It was a wide, old-fashioned apartment, with windows on two sides of it, out of which one might step on the broad piazza, covered with vines, that extended around the house. From my place in the shaded corner, where I was almost concealed by a stand of flowers, I could enjoy their sweet perfumes, and watch the sunbeams darting into the room, softly playing over the carpet, producing curious effects of light and shade in the pictures, and causing fantastic shapes to dance upon the walls.

I was sinking into a doze, when a sound of steps, approaching along the piazza, roused me, and the next moment a shadow fell on the floor, and Mrs. Lecount, coming in, advanced to the table without perceiving me. She had a basket of flowers in her hand which she placed on it, and then stood arranging them, at the same time humming a favorite air. I lay motionless, drinking in the intoxication of her presence, while every drop of blood in my body seemed to rush to my heart.

She was dressed in her favorite style, that I remembered so well—soft white muslin, with violet ribbons ornamenting it, and a narrow band of the same color holding the drooping curls in their place, and drawing them away from the white forehead. Her appearance, so youthful, so lovely, so free from all care, recalled a host of memories—some sweet, some very bitter. As she went singing out of the room, looking for my sister, I buried my face in the pillows with a heavy sob, and pressed back the hot, blinding tears that filled my eyes. With a passionate impulse, I rose and hurried to the long mirror. While I stood gazing sadly at my own reflection, with its sunken cheeks, dimmed eyes, and gray hair, brushed carelessly back from the temples, voices in the hall arrested my attention.

"Why, indeed, Belle, he is in the parlor," my sister said, in surprised tones.

"Well, I shall look again," was the answer, in Mrs. Lecount's clear accents.

She turned the handle of the door as she spoke, and met my eyes as I turned away from the glass.

"Why, you are here, after all!" she exclaimed. "I must have disturbed you. I stopped in with some flowers for Edith, it is her birthday; and besides, I wanted to see you."

"What is the matter?" I asked, expecting to hear that Arthur had cut his finger.

"I had a letter this morning from Pauline. She says you have a message for me."

I drew back confounded. She raised her bright, unsuspicious eyes to my face.

"What is it? Please tell me."

"She told me to say to you that her conscience was cleared of the question that had so troubled it for many years."

I spoke slowly, unprepared for the effect of my words.

Mrs. Lecount blushed painfully, and then became deadly pale.

"Then you have forgiven me, now that you know all, for the misery I made you suffer."

She looked at me sadly, imploringly, and trembled with agitation as she spoke; then turning away, she covered her face with her hands. I caught them in mine violently; the long-suppressed love overpowered me. It burst forth in mad, wild words, for I was desperate and despairing; only conscious that passion had swept away all scruples, and that I was speaking from my heart, giving words to the hopes and doubts that had tortured me for years.

As I ceased, and gazed in her face, expecting only sympathy, perhaps indifference, I was surprised to find her eyes cast down, and a timid blush of pleasure stealing over her cheeks.

"Is it possible," I exclaimed, "that you can care for me; that you may yet love me?"

Her answer was, to throw her arms around my neck, and nestle her head against my breast.

"Do nothing rashly," I said, afraid to believe in my great happiness, and clasping her tightly, lest it should be indeed a dream. "Think, my child, think of my age, and of your youth. See! my hair is gray now. I love you, but I may not be able to make you happy."

She smoothed the hair from my face, and raising herself suddenly, succeeded in reaching it, and pressing her lips upon it softly. Her eyes sought mine with the old confiding, childlike light in them, as she whispered—

"To be near you is to be happy."

When we went into the sitting-room together some hours afterward, my sister, who was putting preserves into a dish, looked up from her employment with a quick, searching glance.

"So you two understand each other at last," she said abruptly, her voice trembling with joy. "Well, I should think it was about time."

My mother dropped her knitting, in her utter astonishment.

"My little daughter," she exclaimed, as Belle threw her arms around her, and laid her face, so bright and loving, against the wrinkled cheek, "now we shall keep John at home."

We were married in the following spring, and I took my wife, at her own request, to revisit the many scenes associated in our minds with such curious memories and conflicting emotions. We went over the old ground at Niagara, and I was surprised at her vivid recollection of the most trifling circumstances that had occurred there—little things that I had long since forgotten. Returning, we spent some time with her friends in New York; and one day, while walking up Fifth Avenue, we came face to face with Mr. Hammond, looking as elegant, as well dressed, and as well to do as ever. From the fact that he was leaning on the arm of a delicate young man, of rather weak-minded appearance, although clad in the latest and most costly style, we concluded that he had found another victim for his artifices. My wife hastily drew down her veil, and tightened her grasp on my arm. Mr. Hammond, fortunately, did not recognize us, or pretended not to, as I am inclined to believe. He was talking fluently, in his easy manner, and I could not suppress a sigh of pity for him when I thought of his talents, which, if well directed, would have made him a blessing to his fellow-beings, and remembered the unworthy object on which he employed them. We also ascertained that Mrs. Parker was in Europe. Unable to resist the strong feeling of disgust and horror which her own conduct had raised against her, she had gone abroad in search of the society that was denied her at home.

Soon after our return, Mrs. Weston moved to a pleasant house in the village, where she opened her school with the most encouraging success. The deep contentment that independence brings is visible in her appearance. Often, as I sit writing in my office, I pause to listen to her light step coming up the garden-path, and her soft voice addressing gay speeches to a certain very happy old lady, who is generally to be found seated near the window of the room, knitting small white socks for baby-feet. Quietness does not always reign: a stout young gentleman, who is called Harry Weston Wilmer, monopolizes a large portion of his mother's time, and requires a great deal of amusement. Nothing makes him laugh so loud as the sight of Arthur and the little Westons at play; thus, every day, merry games are instituted for his entertainment, and childish feet dance over the floors, while childish voices echo through the house.

Now, when I ride home in the twilight, sometimes sorrowful and perplexed, often tired, both bodily and mentally, the old dreams of impossible happiness come true. A slight, graceful form hastens to meet me, soft arms are clasped around my neck, a loved face is lifted to mine, and I read my welcome in the happy light shining in the deep, truthful eyes.

THE END.

HISTORICAL NOVELS.

A few Words by the Author in justification of the Historical Romance.

The Historical Romance has its great task and its great justification, which is disputed by only those who either have not understood or will not understand its nature.

The Historical Romance has, if I may be allowed so to speak, four several objects for which to strive.

Its *first* object is, to throw light upon the dark places of history, necessarily left unclear by the historian. Poetry has the right and duty of setting facts in a clear light, and of illuminating the darkness by its sunny beams. The poetry of the Romance writer seeks to deduce historical characteristics from historical facts, and to draw from the spirit of history an elucidation of historical characters, so that the writer may be able to detect their inmost thoughts and feelings, and in just and sharp traits to communicate them to others.

The *second* task of the Historical Romance is, to group historical characters according to their internal natures, and thus to elucidate and *illustrate* history. The illustration then leads to the *third* task, which is the discovery and exposition of the motives which impel individual historical personages to the performance of great historical acts, and from outwardly, apparently insignificant events in their lives to deduce their inmost thoughts and natures, and represent them clearly to others.

Thence follows the *fourth* task : the illustration of historical facts by a romance constructed in the spirit of the history. This fourth and principal task is the presentation of history in a dramatic form with animated descriptions ; upon the foundation of history to erect the temple of poesy, which must nevertheless be pervaded and illuminated by historic truth. From this it naturally follows that it is of very little consequence whether the personages of the Historical Romance actually spoke the words or performed the acts attributed to them; it is only necessary that those words and deeds should be in accordance with the spirit and character of such historical personages, and that the writer should not attribute to them what they could not have spoken or done. In Historical Romance, when circumstances or events are presented in accordance with historical tradition ; when the characters are naturally described, they bear with them their own justification, and Historical Romance has need of no further defence.

Historical Romance should be nothing but an *illustration of history.* If the drawing, grouping, coloring, and style of such an illustration of any given historical epoch is admitted to be true, then the illustration rises to the elevation of work of art, worthy of a place beside the historical picture, and as equally useful.

JOSEPH II. AND HIS COURT.

AN HISTORICAL NOVEL.

BY LOUISA MUHLBACH,

Author of "Frederick the Great and His Court" "Berlin and Sans-Souci," "Merchant of Berlin," &c., &c.

TRANSLATED FROM THE GERMAN,

BY ADELAIDE DE V. CHAUDRON.

1 vol., 8vo. With Illustrations. Paper Cover, $1.50; Cloth, $2.00.

———— ◆ ————

"In 'Joseph II.' she transcends her previous efforts, not only in the story wrought out in a masterly manner, but the real characters that figure in it have been carefully studied from the detailed chronicles of the time."—*Philadelphia Inquirer.*

"The series of Historical Novels by Miss Mühlbach are winning for their author a high distinction among a class of writers, of which Sir Walter Scott has stood at the head. The events of history which are interwoven in the romances she has written, are not distorted and falsified for the purpose of making a sensation, but are presented with a truthfulness which gives a solid value to the series. The volume before us is literally one of thrilling interest."—*Fulton County Republican.*

"We regard these books as among the best and most entertaining novels of the day."—*Springfield Republican.*

"The novel is divided into six books, and includes the very large number of one hundred and seventy-six chapters; yet the interest is so well kept up that the reader never tires or notices with regret its unusual length.—*Georgetown Courier.*

"This is an historical novel of intense and thrilling power. The reader is at once fascinated and held spell-bound until the volume is completed. Miss Mühlbach's novels have risen into favor very rapidly, and this fact alone gives a good indication of their real merit. The book is not of the false sensational kind, but the interest of the reader is chained from the first chapter."—*Galesburg Free Press.*

THE MERCHANT OF BERLIN.

AN HISTORICAL NOVEL.

By L. MUHLBACH,

Author of "Joseph II. and His Court," "Frederick the Great and His Court," "Berlin and Sans-Souci," &c., &c.

TRANSLATED FROM THE GERMAN,

By AMORY COFFIN, M. D.

1 vol, 12mo. Cloth, $2 00.

"There is not a dull chapter in it. The interest of the reader is well maintained from the beginning to the close, and we know of no book of similar character which would while away an afternoon more pleasantly."—*Utica Herald.*

"We have rarely read a more fascinating work, or one in which the interest, from the opening chapter to the close, was more thoroughly sustained."—*Jersey City Daily Times.*

"We like this story better than either of Mühlbach's works which previously had fallen in our way. They are meritorious productions, but this excels them in interest of matter as well as in vivacity of style."—*Boston Traveller.*

"This is one of the captivating series of historical novels, or really of novel histories by Mühlbach, and one of the most readable books of the season."—*Baltimore Gazette.*

"The story is exceedingly interesting and possesses points which will render it highly popular among all classes. We look forward with genuine pleasure to the publication of more volumes by the same author, being convinced that they will undoubtedly become the most popular of historical novels."—*Georgetown Courier.*

www.ingramcontent.com/pod-product-compliance
Lightning Source LLC
Chambersburg PA
CBHW021338110726
47900CB00005B/1528